THE SHACKLETON
SIGNAL

JOSHUA T. CALVERT

PART I

THE SIGNAL

CHAPTER 1

"*Artemis II* isn't everything, you know."

Charlie just snorted and shook his head, but Sarah didn't back off. She carefully folded the newspaper she had pretended to be reading and placed it beside the plate holding her half-eaten croissant.

"Think of it as perfect preparation for your first trip into space when the time comes. Dealing with setbacks is part of astronaut training, isn't it?"

"I was a shaky candidate from the start," Charlie replied softly, staring out onto the streets of downtown Houston. The corner café on 146th always had a calming effect on him, ever since he'd begun his astronaut training six years ago. But not today. Whereas the stream of vehicles had usually reminded him that there were other lives out here and not everything revolved around space, now everything seemed pale and colorless. "Harry promised me a seat, but I just learned I've slipped to number five."

Sarah stoically tried to cheer him up. "But that's good, isn't it? You're the first to be moved up." She was a good friend, but right now he would have liked to wring her neck for her optimism. The whole thing was made worse by the fact that she was right. He was usually the one to cheer her up this way.

"I guess I am." He sighed and sipped his coffee. It had grown cold and tasted awful. He put it back with a disgusted expression. Today, even his favorite dish would probably upset his stomach.

"How did it go?" Sarah asked, leaning forward slightly with her elbows on the table and her chin resting on her clasped hands. She looked at him with a mixture of sympathy and curiosity. "The conversation with the head of the Astronaut Office, I mean. With Harry?"

"Harry called me to his office," he explained with a sour expression. "I thought he was going to tell me the final assignment in person. Instead, he told me how important the backups are, and that Director Miller doesn't want any former military personnel on the first *Artemis* mission."

"Why is that? Half the astronaut corps has a background in the armed forces."

"I have no idea. I think it's because of the tensions with China. The dispute over their last Tiangong mission has probably made both sides a bit more cautious now."

"You mean the brief crisis because our intelligence services thought the Chinese had tried to launch missiles from their space station? That was all just nonsense."

"Yes, but it revealed how nervous both sides are, and the White House apparently wants to be a little less brash now that the CIA and the government have embarrassed themselves internationally." Charlie shrugged his shoulders. "For *Artemis II*, it'll only be scientists with civilian background. No fighter pilots, and certainly no former grunts."

"You're being too hard on yourself." Sarah took his hand and looked him sternly in the eyes. "You may be an exotic because, as a former major in the Marines, you're not a combat pilot or a test pilot, but you deserve your place as much as

4

anyone else there. More, in fact. You had to swim against the tide even harder than anyone else. My goodness, you trained as an electrician before sinking your inheritance into a physics degree. That's what I call dedication. When did our country stop rewarding that kind of courage and will to progress?"

"Politics." Charlie shrugged again. "It's all politics. In the end, I can't even be mad at Harry. The decision most assuredly came down from the director and he is just the guy who got stuck with breaking the bad news."

"At least it wasn't your fault. And you're still part of the astronaut corps, *and* there are elections next year." Sarah waved a hand and then pushed a strand of blond hair from her face. "Things could look very different by then."

"But *Artemis*..."

"Yes, I know, I know. The first time an Oreo capsule will orbit the moon."

"*Orion*," he corrected her with a scowl.

She just grinned.

"That was a really bad one."

"My goodness, Charlie!" She leaned forward and smacked his shoulder.

"Ouch!"

"I don't recognize you today," Sarah snapped at him. "Man up and get on with it! How many setbacks have you had so far?"

"Many, but ..."

"How many times have you been told that someone like you will never even reach the astronaut program?"

"Often, but ..."

"How many times have you been at a point where you just wanted to run away because everything seemed to be conspiring against you?" She tapped him on the chest with an outstretched index finger. "You're *Charlie*. You're a *Marine*. 'I never give up. No matter what happens.' Those are your words. You were in the Navy Seals for three fucking years. Two hell weeks because you got hurt during the first one. That's almost David Goggins level. You may not be one of the first astronauts to orbit the moon in this era, but that's a good thing."

"Good?"

"Then at least you'll have the chance to be on the second mission. It's supposed to land at the south pole, isn't it? Do you just want to fly around that dead thing up there as a shooting star, or would you rather put your boots on the dust?" she asked rhetorically.

"Regolith," he corrected her. "It's called regolith."

"I don't care what it's called, as long as you get yourself sorted out. Don't let the fucking politics get you down."

Charlie nodded and even found a smile. "Thank you, Sarah. I needed that."

"Always happy to help." She stood up, straightened her pantsuit, and looked at her wristwatch. "I have to go. The prosecutor's office is about to open."

He also stood up and they embraced for a long time.

"Thank you," he repeated into her ear.

"Show them, Charlie. Just like you always do."

Charlie went to pay the bill, only to realize that Sarah had beaten him to it. He drove back to the Johnson Space Center. The JSC was on the city's southeastern edge, right on Clear Lake, which wasn't a lake at all, but a lagoon in the Gulf of Mexico. The complex was huge, almost a city within a city, with numerous buildings from the 1960s and 70s, and so many parking lots that you'd think there were more cars than people.

Just as he was approaching the barrier of the northern employee entrance, his phone rang. 'Harry Johnson' was on the display.

Charlie sighed and accepted the call.

"Hello Harry."

"Charlie, I need you in the office. The crew is here, and the rest of the backups are on their way," said the head of the Astronaut Office. The former ISS commander sounded more tense than usual, his Boston accent even more pronounced.

"What happened?"

"*Sentinel I* just crashed. Everything else when you get here." Harry hung up.

Charlie accelerated his car. This was the second piece of bad news in one day and he didn't know which was worse.

CHAPTER 2

Harry Johnson's office consisted of nothing more than a long desk, a mattress underneath on which he often spent the nights – a fact that was at least as legendary as the head of the Astronaut Office himself – and filing cabinets on the left wall that were overflowing with old paper files and colorful notes that he had probably never read.

"Ah, Charlie!" Harry called out and beckoned him closer. The bear-like astronaut with the mighty gray moustache pointed vaguely to the area in front of his desk, where Leo, Anne, Walter, and Karen were sitting on the floor in a less than astronaut-like manner next to Louis, Miles, and Anne from the backup crew, to which he himself now belonged. Apart from him, all were wearing their blue overalls, which gave him a brief twinge.

Once again, the odd one out, he thought.

He nodded to the group and sat down beside his colleagues. Ironically, the only free seat was right between the two groups. He wasn't allowed to belong to the one and he didn't want to belong to the other. What an irony of fate.

"The shit's hitting the fan, guys," Harry opened the conversation and went to the slats on the window to close them. It immediately became a lot darker in the small room. "*Sentinel I* has crashed. Mission Control has already confirmed the loss and the Pentagon is breathing down Jessica's neck."

"Do we know what happened yet?" asked Leo Cummings, commander of *Artemis II,* in a calm voice.

"Nothing is confirmed. Possibly a malfunction with the secondary engines, but no errors were displayed, all the valves were working perfectly, and the pressure conditions in the fuel tanks and lines were in perfect condition according to the log files. It simply disappeared from one moment to the next."

"Disappeared?" Charlie echoed with a furrowed brow. "Do you mean crashed?"

"No. *Disappeared*," Harry insisted, shaking his head. "Our observation stations cannot even make out reflections over the south pole. It's as if it just plain disappeared."

"But it could have crashed," intervened Walter, the *Artemis II's* flight engineer. Charlie liked him a lot because he had shown less of the egocentric mentality than their other colleagues. Even so, it hurt that he was the one who had replaced him. "Charlie is right. A malfunction in the secondary engines could mathematically have released enough power to cause a crash."

"The Pentagon has firmly denied it."

"What if they weren't being entirely honest with the specifications? Don't forget, this is a spy satellite, and there are varying degrees of secrecy with every Department of Defense mission," suggested Anne – the one from the backup crew.

"But that only ever refers to the payload and not to the specifications of the satellite in terms of its propulsion and control modules. Then we might as well quit our jobs." Harry let out a low growl and shook his head. "The fact of the matter is, *Sentinel I* is gone. No longer to be found."

"Satellites don't just disappear like that. Especially without anyone seeing anything," said Leo.

"I know that myself. But the data is clear. *Sentinel I* is gone, gone, gone."

"Says Space Command," Charlie interjected and all eyes turned to him. He pushed aside the unpleasant feeling caused by the sudden attention. After the bad news this morning, he would have liked to hide away. Although he knew better, there was this quiet voice in the back of his head warning him that he might look like a failure in their eyes.

"There are over twenty-five thousand objects in Earth orbit, all of which are tracked and recorded by the Space Surveillance Network. That includes anything bigger than ten centimeters. All the satellite sensors, radar stations, and telescopes involved in the recording are under some form of Pentagon control. *Sentinel I* is – *was* – one of their satellites. How much have we ever heard from them, other than the bare essentials? We're just the truck drivers for the Department of Defense."

"What are you implying? That they're lying to us?"

Charlie tensed up. Finally, he jutted his chin out and nodded. "Yes. The thing is, nothing just *disappears* into space. Especially not on a mission as closely monitored as this one.

Remember that *Sentinel I was* intended to initiate the construction of the moon station and support it with permanent sensor data. Its loss is a major setback, one that will cost Congress a lot of money. This means that everyone in the higher chain of command now fears for their position and is digging as deep a trench as possible to avoid ending up on the scaffold. Apart from that, there's nothing in space that could disappear."

"*Once again,*" Harry said with tension clearly audible in his voice. "What are you implying?"

"I'm *saying,*" Charlie replied, meeting his boss's eyes, "that the Pentagon is not telling us the truth, and they are only showing us what they want us to see because someone of standing doesn't want to lose their job. Delay is a common political tactic. I'm willing to bet the phone lines are running hot in Virginia right now."

"He's right," Miles jumped in, having served as a Navy fighter pilot himself and knowing a thing or two about the political tradeoffs that underpinned every Pentagon operation. He looked at the crew of the *Artemis II*. "You have to think of the Department of Defense as a cocoon with tiny antennae. The ones on one side run to anything and everything that's going on in the U.S. – and around the world. The others are a little thicker, and they all lead across the Potomac River to Washington. Ideally, the DOD would like to control everything and everyone without interference but, given this is impossible without the White House and Congress poking their fingers into the pie, the top management always has to weigh up secrecy, the distribution of their own funds, and the stability of their own chair legs. If something *seems* odd about the mission, then it is odd."

"All right, but even assuming Space Command is probably lying to us, how does that help us?" Harry demanded. The stress was clear to see. His cheeks were flushed and the wrinkles of concentration on his forehead had formed deep canyons. "*Artemis II* leaves in three days. How am I supposed to send you up there if I can't even rely on the blasted data from the SSN?"

An embarrassed silence fell over them.

We should postpone, Charlie thought, but if he spoke his thought, it would be interpreted as a pitiful attempt to undo his assignment to the backup crew by buying time. So he kept his mouth shut.

In the end, it was Leo who spoke first.

"It was clear from the start that not everything would go

according to plan. We could recalibrate some of the satellites in higher Earth orbit and use them as relay stations for the moon orbit," suggested the geophysicist. "That increases the duration of the time-out on the other side of the moon by about ... an hour, give or take."

"That shouldn't be something that jeopardizes our take-off," agreed Anne, who was sitting right next to Leo. "Just getting new take-off permits from the FAA will cost us weeks, if not months, if we miss the backup take-off window in two days."

"I know you want to go up there, I can understand that. But Jessica is insecure. I can see what I can do, but at this point I'm not sure if she's willing to go through with it in the current chaos."

Charlie searched within himself for spite or relief. At this point, it looked as if those who had been chosen over him, after his years of preparation during which he'd had no private life, would not get to fly off. But on the contrary, he sympathized with them. They were no different; they too had sacrificed years of their lives to make it aboard the *Orion* capsule. His dream had been shattered prematurely this morning, while theirs now hung in the balance with the same fate on their horizon.

CHAPTER 3

Major Rebecca Hinrichs nodded to the young sergeant who held the door open for her and stepped out onto the tarmac of Peterson Space Force Base. The drive from the airport on the other side of the runway that Peterson shared with the civilian facility had taken less than ten minutes. The sun was at its zenith and, once more, it seemed to her that it shone stronger here in Colorado than anywhere else.

The sergeant came to attention and saluted, which she politely returned before marching toward the Hartinger Building with her aide, Peter Rogers. It was a nondescript 70s building with large concrete surfaces and narrow windows all around, giving it the appearance of a colorless sandwich.

"Has the general contacted you with any more details?" she asked, waiting patiently while the lieutenant hastily scrolled through his tablet. This mission had come at the worst possible time for her. After months of working with the FBI, she was happy about her newfound contacts among the Feds, but she still had an annoying chip implanted in her body that she would like to get rid of sooner rather than later. Obviously, that would have to wait.

"No, ma'am," he eventually replied. "Just that we should keep an eye on the matter for him."

"Nothing about the signal or its nature?"

"Negative."

Rebecca let out a growl. She was used to flying from facility to facility as the eyes and ears for the general, but she usually received detailed memos.

This time it was different. The conversation at the Pentagon had lasted less than five minutes. *Fly to Peterson and make sure they stay calm there.*

However, she highly doubted that her presence had ever caused the base commanders involved to be even remotely calm. Everyone knew that she was Eversman's all-purpose weapon, and that he might just as well have been there himself. At worst, she was seen as a potential executioner, as her will was usually no more than a phone call away, even if she was the lower rank.

"Well, let's familiarize ourselves with the situation first. What do we know apart from the fact that *Sentinel I* has entered its repositioning phase?" she asked, walking past the entrance to the Hartinger Building, which only irritated Lieutenant Rogers for a moment.

"That NASA knows nothing about it and is currently very upset because they believe there may have been a total loss," he replied. "Houston has been requesting records from the SSN almost every minute for the last hour."

"But they didn't get any, I take it?"

"Correct – apparently they were given the wrong data."

"Why?"

"I don't know, ma'am."

"Then find out before we get to the back entrance."

"May I ask why we ...?"

"You may. I don't want to be greeted by the welcome squad and given the rainbow tour, I want to see how things are done here, and how Colonel Smith reacts when things don't go according to plan. That will help me to assess him better," she explained, continuing to walk toward the back of the building with Rogers, who was now on the phone. She slowed her pace a little to give him some more time.

She liked the young man. He was smart, hardworking, and fearless, just like she had been when she was his age and rank. It hadn't even been that long ago, but it felt like an eternity. He was supposed to be trained and molded with the same toughness and fairness as she had been, and that meant she gave him some slack, so long as he didn't notice. She pretended to reorganize her documents – printed out in a black binder with the Space Force insignia, of course – and walked a little slower.

When they arrived at the back entrance, she let Rogers open the door for her and, as expected, was greeted by two young sergeants who looked a little irritated but saluted her properly.

"Excuse me, Major. We didn't know you were going to use this entrance – they were expecting you up front," one of them said.

Rebecca just nodded. "I know. Take us to the control room."

"Excuse me, ma'am?"

"Did you not hear me, Sergeant?"

"Excuse me, please, Major. We just thought you'd like to speak to the colonel."

"You can tell him that I'm in the control room. Unless, of course, he's there already," she replied, and headed for the downward-leading stairs.

The two soldiers were initially confused by the dilemma that had arisen. Not only was she a major, but she also came directly from the Pentagon. However, their base commander was a colonel and had given them clear instructions. Normally she would have had to obey them, not only according to custom, but also according to the rules for visitors from outside. On a military base, the commander's word was law.

Before they could decide which death they wanted to die, she was on the first flight of stairs and heading down with Rogers.

"Ma'am, this is a restricted area!" one of them called after them. Loud footsteps announced that they were hot on their heels.

"I'm aware of that. Don't worry about it. We'd like to take the elevator for the rest," she said when they arrived on the first underground level in a corridor that seemed deserted.

The two soldiers hesitated again, then conceded and led them to an elevator at the end of the corridor, getting in with them.

"You know, Lieutenant," Rebecca said to her aide, seemingly casually. "The colonel would have kept us waiting in his office to show us that he's in charge here. Five minutes is normal and still within the bounds of politeness. Ten minutes or more sends the message that he doesn't want us here, and fifteen or more sends the message that he has no intention of anything more than fobbing us off with a flood of documents to keep us busy long enough to give him legroom."

Again, the two NCOs exchanged uncertain glances, confirming what she had suspected.

"We'll just save ourselves that part," she continued, and they left the elevator after a short ride to sublevel five. It was not difficult to see where the control room was, as there was only one door on the left-hand side. She waited until one of the base soldiers, after a short hesitation – the first beads of sweat now forming on his forehead – gave her access with his key card.

She had not yet seen any photos of the Space Surveillance Network (SSN) control room, but she had certainly imagined more than this relatively small room with many screens on one side and just four desks in front of them. The lights were dimmed, and her comrades seemed absorbed in their work, incessantly talking into their headset microphones in muffled voices.

Rebecca only glanced briefly at the many complex data sequences on the dozens of monitors before looking for Colonel Smith, whom she found in a corner on the far right, where he seemed to be engaged in a quiet conversation with two officers. Apparently he hadn't noticed her yet.

Good.

She dismissed the two soldiers behind her with a quick wave and then headed straight for Smith.

"Colonel," she said when he saw her approaching, and for a moment a mixture of surprise and disapproval flitted across his features. "Major Rebecca Hinrichs. General Eversman sends you his regards."

Smith was a portly man in his mid-50s who must have crossed the line between discipline and old-age softness a few too many times. His chin wobbled slightly when he moved his head, and his gray temples were carelessly shaved. But his gaze was that of a hawk, and she had no intention of underestimating him on the basis of his appearance – a trap into which many less astute officers had certainly fallen.

Her counterpart returned the salute with deliberate carelessness and had long since regained control of his features.

"I would have made you comfortable in my office, Major, because we have a lot to do here at the moment."

"That's why I'm here," she said lightly. "To be supportive."

They both knew that was only half true, but Smith merely nodded. "So what can I do for an intelligence officer from Fort Fumble?"

Rebecca overlooked the informal term for the Pentagon,

which was often used pejoratively among soldiers to refer to the bureaucratic structures of the Department of Defense. If it helped him to come to grips with the situation, he should feel free to add as many slurs as he liked. It didn't matter to her. All that mattered were the results.

"Feel free to tell me about the signal, sir," she suggested. Of course it wasn't a request, but she was below him in rank and had to at least maintain courtesy, even though her rank was irrelevant in this conversation. "The general wants us to get to the bottom of it as quickly as possible."

That was a guess. And a risk, as she had no idea what kind of signal it was.

Smith seemed to wrestle with himself awhile before nodding to his two aides and dismissing them with brief orders and giving them a wave, sending them to one of the desks.

"Corporal, show us," he ordered the seated soldier.

"In what format, sir?"

"I want us to be friends, Major Hinrichs," the colonel said to her without answering his subordinate. "To be honest, I could do with some help, and a bit of back-up, if you know what I mean."

Protection against the general and the possibility of holding me responsible if something doesn't work out, she transliterated mentally, but nodded with a neutral expression. "Of course, Colonel."

"Good." He turned back to the corporal. "In all formats. Brief the major as you have briefed me."

"Of course, sir."

The corporal began typing on his keyboard and called up a different display on each of his three monitors, which surrounded him in a glowing semicircle. On the left was a blue glow against a black background, in the middle a curve that looked like a sine wave, and on the right a hertz curve that Rebecca quickly recognized as a radio wave recording.

"The one on the right is a recording from NASA's Deep Space Network antennas, PSK-modulated in the eight gigahertz frequency range. It's stable and subject to the Earth's atmospheric fluctuations."

"What does that have to do with *Sentinel I?*" asked Rebecca.

"Uhh, the signal comes from the moon, ma'am. From the Shackleton Crater," the corporal explained without turning around.

Smith gave her a quizzical look. No doubt he was wondering how much she in fact *knew*, and whether she had just tricked him into revealing more than he should have. In any case, he would not underestimate her from now on. However, it had also been stupid of him to do it in the first place.

"We picked it up for the first time an hour ago when *Sentinel I* went online," explained the colonel.

Apparently he has accepted his fate. Good. That will save us both time.

"That's why you blindfolded NASA for the time being."

"Yes."

"What is it?"

"We don't know." Smith pulled his face into an unhappy grimace. As the senior figure in Space Command, he was most uncomfortable with anything going on in space that he didn't understand. "It's not one of ours and we suspect it's been there for a while. We just didn't see it because we weren't looking and didn't have anything out there to notice it."

"Could it be from the Russians or the Chinese?" she asked.

"The Russians fly with cobbled-together Soviet technology

and can't even make it to the moon. The Chinese would certainly have the capabilities, but we would have noticed if they had placed something in the Shackleton at some point. After all, that's the location of their planned moon base."

"And ours," she reminded him.

"Yes, but so far we are ahead of them when it comes to space technology, especially when it comes to observing the sky and the moon," Smith replied, unable to hide the hint of pride.

"So then what?"

"We don't know," the colonel repeated. "I had the EXA radio telescope switched on to take a closer look at the recorded radio waves. The signal consists of three repeating frequency patterns at 1420 megahertz and phase jumps between zero degrees and one hundred and eighty degrees. There is a constant amplitude modulation between the patterns. My best soldiers and the eggheads from DARPA have been racking their brains over this for the last hour. One of them, a physicist from the Air Force Procurement Office, encoded the values in quantum numbers, energy levels and spin states, and lo and behold, represented like this, the signal corresponds precisely to the 1S ground state of a single proton with its electron."

"Hydrogen," Rebecca said, enjoying the colonel's surprised blink. He might have enjoyed being able to pepper her with physics terms so that she had to ask schoolgirlish questions, but even though she didn't understand much of his spiel, she did know that a hydrogen atom was at the top of the periodic table. It didn't matter how much you knew, it mattered when you could reveal specific knowledge to make it look like you knew more.

"Right," Smith said, nodding. "We have received the radio image of a hydrogen atom."

"From the south pole of our moon," Rogers remarked. "If it wasn't anyone from here, then ..."

"Let's not jump to any conclusions for now," Rebecca interrupted her aide. "Before we jump straight to E.T., we should first get in touch with counterintelligence and make sure that no one is playing tricks on our sensors."

"That's very unlikely." This time it was the corporal who replied. "*Sentinel I* was transmitting with a triple-coded, three hundred and sixty degree encrypted military signal. I'm sure no one has hacked it, but if they have, we have a problem so big that the security of the United States is at acute risk."

Rebecca thought about it. "Then we should assume the worst. Even if you're right, it won't hurt to alert our counter-intelligence and run tests and heuristics checks on our crypto systems." She turned to the base commander. "If you agree, Colonel, I will forward the appropriate proposal to the general and to the relevant specialist department of the Pentagon."

Smith nodded curtly. "Go ahead. But we should also talk about the alternative."

"Aliens," she uttered, surprising him again. "That is what you're inferring, isn't it?"

"Well ..."

"This is the United States *Space* Command. If you don't consider the possibility, no one will. Even though we should first consider all other causes for this signal, that doesn't mean we can afford to turn a blind eye."

"That's right," he admitted with obvious reluctance. It was clear he had thought about it a lot but felt uncomfortable with the idea. "What's more, we've got *this!*"

He pointed an outstretched finger at the left-hand image of the blue dot. The four decorative buttons on the cuff of his uniform sleeve shimmered in the light of the monitors.

"The optical component," the corporal explained as if on

cue. "It's the test run of the *Sentinel I's* optical scanning laser for recording the surface topography inside the crater. There was an unforeseen reflection. The expected optical echoes from regolith and water ice look something like this." He switched on false colors and what was previously black became red and yellow. "We filtered that out, and what was left was this blue dot. A reflection from a metallic object about the size of a small house."

Rebecca frowned. "How sure are we that these records aren't a measurement error?"

"As sure as we can be with triple redundant systems and multiple evaluations by four offices in Space Command," the corporal replied, and quickly followed up with, "Major."

"To be one hundred percent certain, we'd have to look on site, I suppose," Colonel Smith remarked.

"And that's what we're planning to do with *Artemis III*."

"Next year."

"Yes. If there truly is a house-sized metal structure hidden at the moon's south pole, I would assume it won't disappear any time soon," she replied. "Shouldn't we release this data to NASA so that their eggheads can spend their nights working on the problem? They're experts in this sort of thing and have enough SETI fans in their own ranks to take the whole thing apart."

"I can't release that. It would have to go through General Eversman's desk." She could see in Smith's eyes that he was secretly hoping it would.

"I'll suggest it to him."

"Well, I thought that had already happened because the colonel was already here and ..."

"Colonel?" she interrupted him. "What colonel?"

Smith stiffened. He'd believed she'd known about it, and he waved it off. "Not that important. The only important thing is that the general signs off on it. Otherwise my hands are tied here."

"As I said, I'll suggest it to him." She decided not to press him about the previous visit, as his nervousness was showing. That was enough of a clue for her that it had been someone outside the normal chain of command. As was she. "One more question, sir. Who detected the signal?"

"One of our specialists during the sensor test run. Why do you ask?"

"Well, the signal needs a temporary name. I'm not particularly creative when it comes to that sort of thing, and I'm sure you don't want me to put it down as a *Smith signal* at this stage, do you?"

"No. It was Specialist Walker. His shift was over when the activation process ended, so he's no longer here," he explained.

"Thank you. I should be on the phone now."

Smith nodded. "I'll have someone take you upstairs. You can use my office."

"That's all right, I'll find my own way, if you don't mind."

He hesitated, but then repeated the nod. "Get in touch if you need anything."

"Thank you, Colonel."

Rebecca told Rogers to stay put. Let him keep an eye out for her. As soon as she was upstairs, she went outside and pulled out her secure cellphone, which she used to call Eversman on his work cellphone.

"Major, what have you got for me?" the army general said in his typical gruff tone.

"The colonel also believes in an extraterrestrial signal source. However, I don't think his soldiers will be able to decode it and make sense of it any time soon," she said without beating around the bush. She and her superior officer were very much in agreement about their preferred method of communication. That was probably why they got on so well.

"I'll be damned. Give it all to the guys and gals at NASA. But we're to be involved in every little thought process. Make sure of that, all right?" he ordered. In the background, she heard the roar of aircraft turbines outside.

"If we're going to do this, we should draw a tight security circle before it goes public," she suggested, lowering her voice as a group of young officers came out of the building and walked past her, talking loudly.

"Do that. Give it directly to Jessica Miller. Tell her to keep only her most important staff on it and give each necessary department only the information they need. Maximum compartmentalization. Anyone who leaks anything will lose their job. Make that clear to them."

"Understood, sir."

"Major? *You* do that. I want Jessica to get her ass kicked."

Rebecca nodded. "I can do that."

"I know."

CHAPTER 4

C harlie always took the stairs two at a time. The NASA
administrator's office was on the third floor of the
Christopher C. Kraft Jr. Mission Control Center building,
which had the rather boring name 'Building 30' affixed beside
this tongue twister title.

In his haste, he almost bumped into a group of interns
who came toward him from upstairs, chattering excitedly.

"Sorry!" he called out apologetically, as a young woman
was so startled that she dropped a pile of documents that
floated through the air in a rain of paper.

When he arrived at the door with the simple, eye-level
brass plate that read 'Jessica Miller, Director,' he paused,
straightened his freshly starched overalls and calmed his
breathing before finally knocking.

Shortly afterward, the door unlocked and opened a small
crack, and Jorge Garcia – a giant of a man whom he only knew
briefly from the development department – scrutinized him
before clearing the way and waving him in hurriedly. Before
Charlie could wonder at his strange behavior, Garcia pushed
the door shut and relocked it, and leaned guardedly with his
back against the door.

In addition to Director Miller, who sat behind her desk, were her deputy Nelson Melroy, Associate Administrator Margaret Cabana, CFO Martin Vo Schaus, Chief Legal Advisor Sumara Sheehy, Chief Scientist Jeffrey Thompson-King, and Harry Johnson – Charlie's own supervisor and the head of the Astronaut Office – along with Harry's boss, Director of Flight Operations Lutrell Williams.

"Mr. Reid," Miller said, waving him impatiently in the direction of Harry and Williams. "There you are." The director turned to Harry. "I hope you know what you're doing, or you'll be getting the axe."

"Our current flight crew consists of only civilians. We need someone who is familiar with military procedures," Harry replied calmly, nodding curtly as Charlie came to stand beside him.

"You weren't even in the Air Force, is that right?" Miller addressed him directly.

"No, ma'am, I was a Marine Corps medic."

"Well, at least I can count on your loyalty then, eh?"

"Semper Fi, ma'am," he replied without a trace of irony, and without blinking under her scrutiny.

"In any case, we are now complete. Garcia, you're not letting anyone else in, just so that's clear."

The person addressed nodded eagerly but grew unsettled when she continued to stare at him. "From *outside* the door!"

"Uhh, sure. Ma'am." Garcia slipped out with a red face.

"All right, then."

Miller motioned to everyone present to remain standing until NASA's senior leadership had taken their seats in the few available chairs according to their hierarchy.

"Now, the rest of you can remain standing. This is going to be quick – it *must* be quick. We've received data from SSN, and Space Command has finally stopped stonewalling. It looks like *Sentinel I* is still online. There was just a problem with the data transfer and decoding. Some military bullshit."

Charlie observed the looks exchanged by the others. No one believed this explanation, that much was certain.

"Never mind," the director continued, tugging on her thick brown braid, as she was known to do when stressed. There were amazingly elaborate cartoon drawings of the sight circulating among the staff. "We have the data now and it's highly interesting."

The tension was physically palpable. Charlie saw Chief Financial Officer Martin Vo Schaus and legal advisor Sumara Sheehy exchange anxious glances. No doubt they feared that they would have a lot of work to do if the mission failed and she found out why. But she had said *Sentinel I* was still online. So what was the problem that this small circle of NASA's management team had been brought together – and to include *himself*, of all people?

"The satellite is in its planned position. The problem with the data transmission has been solved," explained Miller, "but there was an anomaly in the sensor recordings that turned out not to be an anomaly. It's an optical reflection at the bottom of the Shackleton Crater, apparently from a metallic object six meters in diameter."

Now it was getting loud in the cramped office. At first it was just whispering, then murmuring, which got louder and louder.

"Quiet," the director interrupted. "That's not all. *Sentinel I* has also picked up a radio signal that is apparently a representation of a hydrogen atom encoded in radio waves – at least that's what a clever person in the Air Force claims to have found out. We are now supposed to examine the data and make sense of it. Yes, you heard right. Sounds crazy, but it's true. I've seen the data myself. The important thing is that this stays between us. The Pentagon has been exquisitely ... *clear* ...

that they will not tolerate a leak. If this gets out, not only am I screwed, but you're all screwed, too. We're supposed to put together teams to deal with parts of the data. Nobody gets everything. What they find out comes to us and we put the pieces of the puzzle together before we share it with the Pentagon. Does everyone understand that?"

She looked around with a serious expression and waited until everyone had nodded unambiguously.

"Good. Any questions?" She pointed at the deputy director. "Yes, Nelson?"

"What's the time frame?" asked the tall bureaucrat, who had only been appointed to the position two months earlier after his predecessor's death.

"Daily briefings, starting tomorrow evening at eighteen hundred hours."

"Every day? That means we should have something in our hands by tomorrow evening?" asked Nelson Melroy incredulously. "They can't be serious."

"They are and so am I. Any other questions?" She pointed to the corpulent chief scientist, who looked as if he had just come from a computer games convention in his checked shirt and unkempt head of hair. "Jeffrey."

"The various specialist areas work with fairly low efficiency if they can only analyze a small piece of the puzzle," declared the astrophysicist. "Interdisciplinary work ensures notably faster results, because each expert contributes their view and a big picture emerges."

"Well, to put it simply, that's *not* going to happen. We have to be as quick as possible while our hands are tied behind our backs by the secrecy. That's just the way it is." Miller showed that she wasn't at all happy about this herself. She jabbed her index finger at one of the three telephones on her desk. "The President's damn Chief of Staff already phoned me and explained quite graphically what happens if anything gets out."

Charlie raised his hand carefully. All eyes turned to him as Miller scrutinized him with a quirked eyebrow. Apparently, he was not supposed to open his mouth.

"Yes, Mr. Reid?"

"Has a reason been given for this extreme secrecy?" he asked. When she frowned, he added, "I think everyone here would be extra motivated to keep the chain of secrecy tight if they knew why. A potentially extraterrestrial signal from the Shackleton Crater – and that is what we're talking about, isn't it? – is a sensation. Why the secrecy?"

The others in the room now nodded and looked questioningly at their superior.

"Space Command is supposedly looking into whether China is somehow involved. Complete bullshit, if you ask me." She hesitated. "The Chief of Staff gave the impression that he was worried that Congress might see the whole thing as a ruse because the budget increase is on the table and will be voted on in two weeks."

"They think we're staging a stunt to influence the vote in our favor," Harry summarized. "Okay, I could understand that."

"Yes. So, everyone motivated enough to shut up?" Miller asked the group, nodding as she looked at the faces in front of her. After another nod in Charlie's direction, she pointed to Sumara Sheehy. "Yes?"

"Aliens?" the chief legal officer asked. "Sorry to pose such a stupid question, but this isn't a sick joke at our expense, is it?"

"Am I known for sick jokes?" the administrator returned humorlessly. "Next question. I've got the White House and Pentagon's hands so far up my ass they can play thumb wrestling in my guts, so get it out or get to work."

"What does the information structure look like?" asked

Charlie. "Everyone here should know who they are providing what information to, where it comes together, and when it is discussed in order to get an overall picture. You've given us the time."

"Good point." Miller nodded. "Eighteen hundred hours, meet in my office and collate all the results. You'll bring all the information here in person." She tapped her temple. "In here. I don't want anything on disks."

Protest flared up.

"Uh-uh-uh," she said with a finger wag, "We're known here for clever minds, not for maximum data security. I have no desire to give that *auntie* from Space Command one hint of a reason to take control of everything, just so that point is clear. No more questions? All right. Let's get out of here and get to work. I'll see you tomorrow at eighteen hundred."

CHAPTER 5

C harlie was sitting in Harry's office, poring over the data from Walter and Karen. They were working on the signal and its decoding as members of the flight crew for *Artemis II.* They were doing all this after their preparations for the upcoming mission launch, so their reports were correspondingly erratic in places. But there was no alternative, which must have been the reason why Administrator Miller had invited Harry – and ultimately Charlie – to the secret leadership meeting.

Walter was a cryptologist and Karen a radio wave physicist, so it made sense to appoint them to analyze the strange Shackleton signal.

Charlie was reading Walter's short report for the third time now and kept pulling his hair back when the door opened and he jumped in shock. It was Harry who stomped in and dropped onto one of the chairs in front of his own desk, panting as Charlie resumed his place.

"That's crazy," said the head of the Astronaut Office, shaking his head. "Simply crazy!"

"Not as crazy as this." Charlie waved the piece of paper on

which Walter's barely legible handwriting rambled in uneven lines.

Harry rubbed his hands over his face and massaged the heavy bags under his eyes. The analyses by the various departments had been going on for three days now and the daily evening briefings in Miller's office were becoming ever more tense. It was no secret that every important person in Washington was breathing down her neck. The Pentagon appeared mostly worried that China might somehow get wind of it before the U.S. had found a strategy for dealing with the data, while the White House apparently only wanted one thing: no aliens.

In view of the many current crises on Earth with the Ukraine war, the war in the Middle East, and the ever-growing tensions in the Taiwan Strait, it ultimately made sense not to open up a new crisis area. And extraterrestrial signals from the moon undoubtedly had the potential to overshadow the other concerns.

"All right," Harry finally said, waving both hands like a boxer challenging his opponent to come closer. "I'm not going to be any more ready."

Upon close analysis of the fictitious radio signal using highly specialized equipment such as quantum digital signal processors, Hilbert-Huang transformation and cognitive algorithms for pattern recognition, several salient features are immediately apparent: An exact 1420 MHz carrier frequency combined with 180-degree phase modulation indicates a connection to the 1S ground state of the simplest hydrogen atom. This corresponds to the magic spin-flip frequency. Furthermore, the three main amplitude pulses themselves most likely encode the three classical principal quantum numbers 1-0-0 of such a simplest hydrogen orbital. The evidence from the signal analyses is therefore quite clear: this hypothetical radio signal is a representation of the quantum states of a single hydrogen atom with its electron in the ground state. From a quantum mechanical point of view, the similarity between the carefully analyzed radio wave pattern and the properties of a hydrogen atom is too high to assume a coincidence. A really exciting thought experiment. I've never thought about radio wave encodings of atoms before, but I could write a paper on this sometime. Until then, however, I have better things to do. You know, flying to the moon and all that.

When Charlie had finished reading, he turned the paper over so that Harry could see how the last sentence had been scribbled down furiously. "Walter is pissed off and I can understand it."

"That's crazy. Did Karen proofread this?" Harry snatched the sheet of paper from his hand and skimmed over its contents again.

"Yes, she did." Charlie nodded. "Either Space Command is playing a pretty crazy trick on us or ..."

"Hydrogen," his superior muttered, shaking his head. "If you were sending a signal to an intelligent civilization, how would you find out if it was intelligent?"

"Hydrogen." He knew what Harry was getting at. After all, he'd had the last hour to think about these very questions. "The first atom in the periodic table. A proton. The simplest, lightest, and most common element in the universe. Without the fusion of hydrogen into helium in stars, there would be no heavier elements such as carbon or oxygen. It is the basic building block of everything. Knowledge of radio waves is an important step toward high technology and understanding the cosmos. A radio signal therefore makes sense for establishing contact. And encoding a hydrogen atom by representing quantum states also directly challenges the higher levels of physics and logical thinking."

Charlie took a deep breath. "If I had to make contact with aliens, I'd probably do the same thing."

"I can't believe we're actually seriously discussing this possibility." Harry puffed out his cheeks, slapped the paper on the table, and leaned back. "Aliens? How are we going to sell this to Jessica?"

"You're the boss," replied Charlie, smiling mischievously.

"Thank you, too."

"If I were the boss, I wouldn't have demoted myself to the replacement crew. Then I would have been happy to state the obvious to my boss." He picked up Walter's paper and held it out to Harry demonstratively.

"I didn't demote you."

"Yes, you did, but I don't take it personally."

"They don't want anyone with a military background. The aim is to reduce tensions with China. It's a sign of good will. They're too nervous about the whole satellite thing. Now that they know we suspected them of putting weapons into orbit, they naturally think that's exactly what *we* are going to do."

"I just wish it could be like it used to be – competence and aptitude coming first. Now even our missions have been politicized." Charlie shook his head. "I actually wanted to get away from all that stuff, to get back to a place where people are judged purely on ability."

"You'll get your chance when this all dies down," Harry assured him, glancing at his wristwatch. "Oh, shit, we've got to get to the briefing." The head of the Astronaut Office scowled and snatched the note from Charlie's hands. "Come on."

They left the office and made their way to the third floor of Building 30. The corridors were bustling with activity. Charlie looked at the many colleagues as they passed by. They were visibly focused, and there was that typical tension in the air that preceded every manned mission launch. None of them knew what was really going on and that *Sentinel I* had possibly detected an alien transmitter in the Shackleton Crater. He could hardly imagine what would happen here if this news were to make the rounds.

Discovering extraterrestrial life had always been NASA's ultimate goal, even if it wasn't written down anywhere. The space missions, the scientific work, the planetary observations – including of Earth – were the bread and butter, of course. But secretly, every employee of the agency hoped that at some point they would be able to answer the question that every human being carried within them in one way or another: Are we alone in the universe?

Had Walter just found the answer for them?

Arriving at the door to Miller's office, Harry squared his shoulders briefly, which was very unlike him, then knocked, and they entered after Garcia nodded to them. The powerful engineer from the development department had by now resigned himself to his boring existence as an unofficial security guard and leaned against the opposite corridor wall.

The office was nearly full. The administrator was sitting behind her desk and most of the others – apart from Associate Administrator Cabana – had also seated themselves on the many chairs that Miller had ordered to be brought in yesterday.

Everyone present looked tired, worn out. They were all working twice as much overtime as usual before the start of a mission and the fact that they were all 'secret bearers' under the threat of dismissal did nothing to help them to relax.

"All right, let's get straight into *medias res*," Miller said after Margaret Cabana had come in and closed the door behind her. "Jeffrey."

The chief scientist cleared his throat and proceeded. "We

were able to reproduce the optical reflections from *Sentinel I's* laser module. The location, position, and size of the suspected object at the bottom of the Shackleton Crater have been confirmed. About six meters in diameter, irregular shape, most likely a metallic surface."

"Any chance this is one of ours? Nelson?" Miller looked at her deputy with an expression indicating she didn't think so. No wonder, since she herself was well aware of which missions had been launched currently and in recent years. NASA might depend on Space Command to monitor the Earth's orbit, but she kept track of what was going on up there, even if it was just a pin that had gone off course as space debris.

It was simply impossible that a foreign power had sunk something unseen into the Shackleton Crater and was now playing tricks on them in the form of strange signals. She knew it and so did everyone else in the room.

"No – nothing of ours," Nelson replied as expected. "The Pentagon has nothing either."

"Then we have to assume for the moment that it's a non-human object," Miller said with a matter-of-factness that didn't quite match the content of her words. She fixed her gaze on Harry. "What about Walter and Karen? Have they moved on yet?"

"Walter came up with the quantum state thing on his own, which led him to the same conclusion as his Air Force colleague. It's the representation of a hydrogen atom in the form of radio waves. I think someone is trying to contact us. No, *we,*" he looked at Charlie, "are *sure* that it's an extraterrestrial communication attempt."

The fact that this statement provoked neither murmuring nor whispering proved beyond doubt what they had already suspected: everyone here had by now solidified their own thoughts about this possibility and knew that there was only one possible explanation, as no local or foreign actors could be responsible.

"Well, I'll pass that on to Space Command for now. So far, we were able to confirm their suspicions with the radio signal and also reproduce the reflections." Miller let out a deep sigh. It was evident she had hoped for more – or better yet, much *less*, a realization that would have made it all disappear into thin air. It wasn't as if she didn't have stress aplenty with all the pressure she was under with *Artemis II.* It was the most ambitious and difficult manned mission since the early days of the Apollo program, and the eyes of the entire world were on her.

The uncomfortable silence was abruptly interrupted by the ringing of one of the telephones lined up on her desk.

"What?" she asked gruffly into the receiver, blowing at an unruly strand of hair that had managed to break free from her tight braid and fall into her face. Charlie's gaze was fixed on her face, just as everyone else's was at that moment, trying to read what it was all about. First the wrinkles on her forehead deepened into deep canyons, after which the concentration lines narrowed above the bridge of her nose, and then the corners of her mouth began to twitch. Everyone in the room had witnessed this expression before, and the atmosphere became correspondingly tense.

"Call the ambulance already."

Miller slammed the receiver back onto the telephone base with a crack. Cabana and Sheehy flinched.

Instead of explaining what it was all about, the administrator reached for the remote control on her laptop, pointed it at the large flat-screen TV on the right-hand wall, and pressed the power button. All heads turned in silent suspense. A still image with the NASA logo appeared before Miller switched to NewsNation. A female reporter in a tight-fitting pantsuit stood with a professorial-looking older man in an equally ill-fitting single-breasted suit in front of a display wall showing a picture of the Shackleton Crater with a blue patch of light in it and a graphically prepared radio wave recording underneath. Charlie had no doubt that it was their own exact data. Even the reflection corresponded to the precise data they had received from Space Command.

An overlay at the bottom of the screen read, 'Alien contact? China claims to have picked up extraterrestrial signal.'

The silence in the administrator's office seemed to suddenly turn into invisible concrete, suffocating every molecule of air and holding them all in their places. No one dared to say anything or even move. The 'sword of Damocles' of Miller's wrath hovered over them. The fact that she just stood there staring at the screen in disbelief did not make it any better.

Then the phone rang – Charlie thought it was a different one this time – Miller flinched. She took a deep breath and then lifted the receiver.

"Miller." This time her expression didn't change, but she grew paler with every passing second. At some point, she hung up without another word.

Charlie gulped and looked at Harry, who licked his lips and stared into space.

"That was a certain Major Rebecca Hinrichs," Miller said coolly. "Space Command is taking control of all current NASA operations effective immediately."

"WHAT?" Sheehy gasped.

"They can't do that!" shouted Jeffrey Thompson-King. By now, the chief scientist's face had taken on a color reminiscent of overripe tomatoes.

"There is only one way this data could have gotten to China: through us or through Space Command," Miller summarized. "Obviously the military thinks it wasn't them.

I'm willing to bet *that* phone is about to ring." She pointed to the one in the middle. "And the chief of staff will be yelling in my ear that the President just signed an executive order putting us under the temporary control of the Department of Defense."

She looked at legal advisor Sheehy and the others followed her example. When Sheehy lowered her eyes, the administrator nodded with a bitter expression.

The phone rang.

"I'll tell you what happens next," Miller explained in a surprisingly calm voice, looking at her wristwatch. "In half an hour, this place will be swarming with men and women in uniform. Your people will be shooed away from their desks and lined up against the wall. They will be frisked and interrogated individually to find the mole. Every computer system will be infiltrated with NSA spy software and turned upside down."

The phone kept ringing insistently and seemed to have gotten louder.

"You will want to put yourselves before your people, but the best way to do that is to follow. When you leave here, you will not talk to anyone about what is to come. We *must not* – we *cannot* afford to appear suspicious. I trust you, but if anyone here has tipped off the Chinese, we must protect ourselves. So, anyone from your teams could be playing foul. That is a fact. You are in leadership positions. Now your leadership is needed, and that means keeping your tails down and putting on a good face. We will cooperate and not be guilty of anything. We will fight in the background. I'm going to Washington, Nelson you hold the fort here. Sumara, you come with me. We're going to pull every lever we know in Congress to undo this. We're a civilian agency and we're damn well going to stay that way!"

If she had expected an approving reaction, she was disappointed. Everyone remained silent, staring in disbelief at the administrator, who decisively interrupted the annoying ringing of the phone by picking it up.

"Miller." She nodded. "I've already been informed. Yes, I understand. No sir, yes sir, of course sir, yes. Of course." When she'd hung up, she pursed her lips and then said, "That was not the Chief of Staff. That was the President. Sumara, get your jacket, we're taking the jet. Everyone else, back to your offices. Remember, full cooperation."

With that, she rushed out of the office, leaving them stunned.

"NASA under military control?" asked Martin Vo Schaus incredulously. "That can only be a joke."

Charlie shook his head silently, while loud discussions broke out as if on cue, as frustration and horror sought an outlet.

"What's on your mind?" asked Harry, who had been watching him in silence.

"They're worried about their jobs, and angry that a civilian agency based on science has to submit to the military. But they don't understand what that really means," explained Charlie. A dense knot had formed in his stomach, making it difficult for him to swallow. Harry seemed to be very aware of what the bad news was doing to him.

"And what does it really mean?"

"The Air Force – and for all practical purposes Space Command *is* the Air Force, even though it has been a separate branch of the armed forces for some years now – is a broadsword. It will drive through every one of our facilities like they are unprotected flesh. Blood, lots of blood will flow, bones will break and tendons will tear. But that's only half the truth. The other is that many of the uniform wearers we are about to see are from military counterintelligence along with covert and overt agents of the CIA and NSA. They are like scalpels with x-ray vision. Every skeleton in the closet will be dissected and a lot of people will lose their jobs over little things after enduring traumatic conversations beforehand," said Charlie, observing the management team of his agency chattering away at each other mindlessly.

They were all seasoned managers and scientists with great academic and political achievements to their credit. But now they looked like children who had done something wrong and were waiting for their parents to come back and give them a spanking. They had no idea.

"That's grim. Really grim, Charlie," Harry observed.

"I know. What about the planned launch of *Artemis II* now?"

"I don't know. But if half the personnel are stuck in improvised interrogation rooms, and the entire organizational structure is no longer functioning, we can't launch an SLS, let alone orbit the moon." His superior shook his head. "I guess that means *Artemis II* is officially dead. At least for the time being."

Charlie knew Harry was right but didn't want to admit it. First he trained for years for this mission, then he was kicked out of the crew at the last possible moment for political reasons and now the entire project was on the brink because someone had let the Chinese line their pockets. It was hilarious.

"I have to prepare myself now," Harry announced quietly.

"But the administrator said ..."

"I couldn't care less. I'll stand in front of my astronauts, come what may. None of you are spies for the damn Chinese!" The head of the Astronaut Office turned to leave, but stopped once more and looked him in the eye. "That thing you said about blood flowing and stuff, that was just a metaphor, wasn't it?"

CHAPTER 6

Rebecca held the handle above her head with one hand, just above the armored window of the rear seat where she sat with Colonel T.C. Feinman. The black SUV drove in the middle of the long column of military and civilian vehicles traveling bumper to bumper at high speed through Houston, heading west.

"Didn't think I'd be going to JSC with one of the general's intelligence officers to take control," Feinman said. He was a stocky, 50-year-old powerhouse who, according to his file, had worked on the founding of the Space Force back in 2017. Back then, he'd already held the rank of colonel in the Air Force, which struck her as rather odd – by now he should have the first or even second star on his shoulders.

Since that wasn't the case, Rebecca would have speculated that he had fallen out of favor with some bigwig like Eversman and had been sidelined. But then she would have found a paper trail – transfer papers to some pointless desk job in an unimportant institution where he could vegetate until early retirement. But she hadn't been able to find anything like that. He was like a ghost, popping up here and there, mostly in interview transcripts as an assessor or on the guest lists of various Space Force facilities.

And *he* was the one who had requested her presence. That didn't make her anxious, but it did make her uncomfortable, as there was a knowledge gap between them. Somehow he knew her well enough to have asked the general for her support in this politically sensitive matter.

Which led her to a well-founded suspicion: Feinman worked for military intelligence, just like she did. For the Air Force, with other areas of responsibility, but also for Eversman. The fact that the general had assigned them both to this task at the colonel's request – she in the junior position – could only mean that they were supposed to keep an eye on each other and that Feinman accepted the fact.

This should be interesting.

"Not very talkative, are you?" the colonel asked with a grunt.

"The situation is indeed very unusual," she replied in a neutral tone. He gave her a sideways glance and smiled. There was the look of a hawk in his eyes – an extremely clever hawk. She would not underestimate him. He had undoubtedly understood her allusion perfectly.

"Surely you realize that we have to do this strictly according to the rules?"

She nodded.

"Good. The President's executive order gives us a lot of maneuvering space. Everything possible within the framework of a parliamentary democracy, that's what we will impose on the eggheads in the JSC. Our colleagues in Washington and Florida see it the same way. The general has been very clear on this, so we can assume that the Secretary of Defense has been equally clear," Feinman continued.

"That's the best way to get a result," she replied nonchalantly. She had to be careful. Someone like the colonel was a fox, but he liked the seemingly open banter of irrelevant words, playing with information and emotions within a conversation to see if he was the big or little spoon. If she acted too glibly, he would trip her up here and there until she stumbled. "I expect we can circumvent some of the negative fallout if we do one-on-one interrogations from the start."

Feinman raised an eyebrow and looked at her with a mixture of interest and astonishment. "That's unusual, to say the least. First the group interviews, then the separation to soften up the interviewees. Isolation from the group is a very good door opener."

"I know, sir, but we don't have much time. The NSA already has access, and we have enough contacts at Fort Meade to take advantage of that."

"So what did you have in mind, Major?"

"We could electronically scatter hints about what people at NASA are facing. A few emails or something like that. Then word gets around that we're about to show up and they get nervous," Rebecca explained calmly. "Then they do what all people do in stressful situations."

"The herd pulls itself close together." Colonel Feinman smiled his vulpine smile. "And by the time we start the individual interrogations, we'll have virtually isolated them from the group without having wasted time on group interrogations. I like the way you think, Major. Determined, pragmatic, ruthless."

Rebecca ignored the criticism disguised as a compliment with a noncommittal smile. "Would you like me to arrange that, sir?"

Feinman scrutinized her from the corner of his eye. Another person might have missed it. She would not. He was probably trying to discern how well connected she was at the National Security Agency compared to himself. As intelligence officers, everything they knew and did was ultimately political, and contacts and knowledge equated to political capital.

"No, that's all right. I'll take care of it," he said after a pause, pulling out one of his work cellphones and placing a call. He then talked for a few minutes while they sped along roads to which access had been cut off by the police at short notice and the traffic lights stayed green for them.

During his subsequent phone calls, she put earbuds in her ears as a matter of common courtesy and looked out of the window. She scrutinized the passers-by who looked curiously after their column. Sometimes she wished she was one of them and not a secret keeper. As a government official in her position, you didn't get rich. The only currency that counted was knowledge. Many of her colleagues enjoyed being part of a small circle of confidants. Just the fact that they were aware of something that perhaps as few as one or two dozen people knew was motivation enough for them to keep doing this tough job and forgo the riches of the private sector.

It was different for her. She wanted to understand what was going on around her. It wasn't enough for her to just live like these passersby, staring in amazement at a military convoy and then telling family and friends what crazy things she had seen. She would want to know the convoy's origin and its destination, why roads had been cleared for it, and what chain of command had led to its appearance. It had always been that way, ever since she had dissected frogs as a girl in high school biology and pursued her inner urge to logically fathom everything that could be fathomed in math and chess clubs. Not that it had helped her personal life much, but friends had always been secondary to her if she could decipher her surroundings.

Colonel Feinman cleared his throat beside her and she turned away from the Houston houses rushing past. After she took out her earbuds, he smiled at her. "The hook is set."

"Good." Rebecca nodded. "That will speed up our work."

He glanced at his wristwatch. "We should be there in ten minutes. When the time comes, take a close look at the Astronaut Office. They're the superstars in the JSC, and pretty much everything revolves around them. Go through there with a flamethrower if you have to. If anyone knows anything and is well connected, it's the astronauts."

Rebecca wasn't so sure. She knew they were put through the most rigorous background checks and were usually ardent patriots who didn't particularly care about money. But, to her, orders were orders and one place was as good as another to do her job. She had her orders from the general, and he certainly had his own. At least that way they wouldn't get in each other's way.

"That's a good idea. You'll be setting up camp in the administrator's office, I presume?" she asked.

"That's right. I'll roll the whole thing down from the top and you work up from the bottom. I have lots of experience with careerists from the civilian sector. When we meet in the middle, hopefully we'll have a good overall picture."

"And the mole," Rebecca remarked. She wasn't interested in his little dig about his sphere of influence.

"And the mole. Of course."

They reached the main access gate to the Johnson Space Center a short time later. From the outside, the area appeared much larger than she would have thought, a huge complex of buildings and parking lots spread out in front of expansive lawns. She had done as much research as she could beforehand, but of course it hadn't been enough. It never was.

The Johnson Space Center was where astronauts were educated and trained, spacecraft were developed, and space missions were managed once they took over from launch control. There was also the equally famous Kennedy Space Center in Florida, which had just received a similar 'visit' and handled most of the rocket launches, as well as the Space Propulsion Laboratory in California, where the Deep Space Network was developed and monitored, and where most of the research and development was based. Similar convoys would soon be on their doorstep, as would the administrative headquarters in Washington.

She and Feinman were not in one of the front cars so it was difficult for her to see what was going on at the barrier. However, the discussions must have been brief as the convoy soon proceeded, making it clear Feinman had instructed his men not to let the JSC security crew waste any time and to apply pressure as needed. As they rode past the guardhouse, she saw that the four uniformed guards had been joined by four heavily armed soldiers, who from then on would take control of who was allowed to come and go.

Rebecca felt as though she were the protagonist of a coup d'état. But how she felt didn't matter. She had to find one or more moles who had betrayed her country to – of all countries – their greatest current adversary.

CHAPTER 7

Charlie stood at the window of Harry's office and watched as Humvees and large civilian SUVs with tinted windows streamed into the parking lot from all directions. It didn't take long for soldiers to swarm across the asphalt and between the cars toward the buildings around them. Occasionally, he saw colleagues freeze in place and watch in disbelief as their workplace was taken over by the military.

Some had just been on their way home from work, while others had come in for a shift change and still had coffee cups from the city in their hands or a cellphone to their ear. It wasn't long before each of them was escorted inside by a soldier.

"I feel like I'm in a dystopian thriller," said Charlie, without taking his eyes off the surreal scenery outside the window.

Harry, who had just been shouting into the phone, hung up and stepped to his side.

"It's a disaster."

Charlie nodded silently.

"After this, nothing at NASA will ever be the same, that's

for sure. Either it will cost President Hernandez his job, or this will become the new normal," Harry continued. His face was reflected in the glass of the window and became more somber. "In that case, this will be remembered as the day the United States changed forever."

"Hernandez won't survive this politically," replied Charlie. "I bet we'll see the first mass protests on the streets tomorrow."

"Unless they really do find a mole," the head of the Astronaut Office pointed out. "Then Hernandez and the Space Force will be celebrated and NASA will be subordinated to Space Command faster than Hernandez can call for *executive orders.*"

"I just can't believe that someone would have leaked something to the Chinese."

"Do you think it's more likely that it was someone in uniform?"

Charlie hesitated a little before he shook his head. "No."

"Well, then, God have mercy on us."

There was a knock at the door and before they had even turned around, in walked a woman with long black tightly braided hair. She was wearing the female-version uniform of an Air Force major – dark blue skirt, a light blue blazer, and a cap on her head. She might have been beautiful if it weren't for her stern mien and the tension around her lips, which made her otherwise pretty nose look like the menacing beak of a raptor. Her presence seemed to suddenly turn the room a few degrees cooler. Charlie didn't doubt for a second that she was an officer of the intelligence service, although there was no insignia to indicate this. Of course.

"Dr. Henry Johnson?" she asked and Harry nodded. "Major Rebecca Hinrichs. Please take a seat."

When the head of the Astronaut Office went to sit down in his chair, she shook her head and pointed to one of the two visitor chairs in front of the desk. He looked at Charlie and gritted his teeth before complying with her request.

"And you are Charles James Reid, I presume?" Hinrichs scrutinized him closely.

"That's correct, ma'am."

"At the age of thirty-five, you were a master sergeant in the medical service of the Marine Corps, completed a bachelor's degree in physics during your career and, after you retired, started astronaut training at NASA as the first former non-commissioned officer," she said in such a neutral voice that Charlie had no idea what the background to her statement might be.

"That's correct, ma'am." He realized that he had involuntarily come to attention because he was talking to a major. Some things just didn't change, and that included the respect he had been trained to show for officers and superiors. And she was a lot younger than himself.

"Graduated from high school in Chicago at eighteen, after basic training at Recruit Depot Parris Island in South Carolina, promoted to E-3, fire team leader, after four years promoted to E-6 as one of the youngest staff sergeants. Three tours in Afghanistan, leaving with the rank of Master Sergeant after seventeen years of service." From her mouth, his career sounded like she was reading from a piece of paper, all the while looking him straight in the eye. "Bronze Star, Purple Heart twice, Navy and Marine Corps Commendation with Gold Star, Navy Achievement Medal, Combat Action Ribbon, Good Conduct Medal, Expert Rifle Marksmanship Medal, and the Navy Cross. That's an impressive list, Sergeant."

"Thank you, ma'am. I was just doing my duty and was lucky enough to survive," he replied automatically.

Hinrichs nodded and motioned for him to step away from the window. He took a few steps to the side and linked his hands behind himself. It went against his instincts to leave his superior alone. The major didn't seem to mind.

She sat down at Harry's desk and spread out a bunch of documents and a tablet that she had been carrying under her arm. She took her time and seemed to arrange everything according to a certain system before she finally raised her eyes.

"There will be some measures to identify possible breaches of duty," she said, fixing her gaze on the head of the Astronaut Office. "It's clear you already know that."

Harry didn't say anything back and she reached for a pen in her breast pocket to make a note. "Who informed you of our arrival?"

"I was looking out the window," he replied without a trace of sarcasm.

"So you were not informed of our arrival beforehand?" she asked. Harry looked at Charlie. "I asked *you* the question. So, look at me."

Charlie nodded to Harry, barely noticeably, before breaking eye contact.

"That came from Administrator Miller," the veteran astronaut finally said truthfully. "She prepared the management team for the changes and instructed us to comply and not to inform any of our employees."

"Did you obey orders?" Hinrichs asked sternly. She looked up from her notes when he hesitated yet again. Finally, she repeated: "Did you obey orders?"

"No, I did not." The corners of Harry's mouth began to twitch.

The major didn't let on what she thought about his reply, she simply made another note. Charlie knew that his boss was starting to boil inside.

"With whom did you speak and when, and where are these employees now?" she continued shortly afterward.

"I've spoken to everyone and how would I know ...?"

"Well, Dr. Johnson, it would certainly be better for you to precisely remember that. Otherwise we'll have to call in our units and local police authorities to look for them, which could certainly lead to unpleasant situations. You wouldn't want that, would you?"

"You're damn right I wouldn't."

She slid a piece of paper across the table and placed a second pen on it. "The list. Now!"

"You might as well ask me politely," he replied and let out a growl. "This is *my* fucking office."

"*Please* make a list of all the staff you informed in advance of our arrival, including their probable current whereabouts," Hinrichs said with no display of emotion and a neutral expression as she looked across the table at Harry. If his tone of voice had provoked any inner reaction, she didn't let it show.

"I don't think I know that. They could be anywhere – they're goddamn astronauts. They're not sitting in the office all day. They're running from training to training because we're trying to get a fucking moon mission off the ground," Harry blurted out. "Now you come along with your flat heads and ruin years of preparation. You're screwing with me, *ma'am.*"

There was a knock at the door and the major straightened up a little so her back was no longer touching the back of the chair. In came a young lieutenant with neatly styled hair and the ascetic look of a careerist. Charlie was familiar with this type of promotion addict, who usually sought an adjutant's position as quickly as possible and then voluntarily kissed ass in order to climb the Pentagon ladder faster and avoid real combat missions.

"Lieutenant, please escort Dr. Johnson to an interview room and assign him Sergeant Decker," Hinrichs ordered.

The lieutenant nodded.

"And tell Tech to send someone up."

Harry bared his teeth and stood up. As he was about to turn around, the major cleared her throat.

"Please put all the items you are carrying on the table," she asked him. He turned around, his jaw visibly grinding. "If you'd like, Lieutenant Rogers can help you with that."

Harry reluctantly emptied his pants and jacket pockets and seemed to expect that he would still be frisked, but the major seemed satisfied. She took his cellphone and threw it to the lieutenant, who just managed to catch it. "Give it to tech and create a full image."

As Harry was led out with a final glance at Charlie, the door closed and Hinrichs pointed to the vacant chair.

"Sit down, Sergeant."

"Ma'am?"

"Just a quick chat." She again indicated the seat in front of her without looking and quickly made a few notes on her piece of paper. Silence spread until he began to hear the first sounds from the corridor. Shouts of protest, discussions, footsteps here and there.

But overall, the chaos he had feared had apparently failed to materialize.

CHAPTER 8

"I have great respect for the Marine Corps," Rebecca said, folding her hands on the table in front of her. She pulled her shoulders back slightly to keep her upper back straight. "And for NCOs like you, Sergeant."

"Ma'am," her next victim replied with an impeccably unrevealing expression. If he had still been on active duty, she would have considered recruiting him for the internal intelligence service, given his controlled manner. Space Command recruited its intelligence officers from all branches of the armed forces. The master sergeant was tall and strong. His long-sleeved utilitarian shirt stretched over defined muscles and his posture was that of a man who had seen war and emerged from it steeled. But there was a haze over his deep blue eyes, possibly from some trauma he had overcome. She hadn't gone that deep into his file.

"I going to be frank with you, Sergeant," she said, leaning in for the first time. "I don't like this situation. If I could have chosen, it never would have come to this. The military is the backbone of our nation, but it's not a precision tool. What we're doing here is melting butter with a flamethrower and hoping to find the breadcrumb in it before it all burns up."

He looked surprised, but nodded.

"Do you think it was one of your colleagues?" she asked bluntly, and his hesitation told her a lot. He didn't know, but he couldn't rule it out.

"That's hard to say, Major. I have little contact with the normal NASA staff, as I spend most of my time in training and simulations. Even my meals and exercise sessions are with colleagues from the astronaut corps."

"Do you think there might be a mole inside the Space Force or the Pentagon?"

The astronaut was visibly squirming. His controlled façade began to crumble a little. He looked as if he suddenly itched all over.

"I think that's less likely, ma'am."

"Thank you for your honesty, Sergeant," she said, making a note before pushing the paper aside and switching off her tablet. Again, she folded her hands purposefully on the table in front of her. "Another topic. What can you tell me about *Artemis III*?"

"Well, I'm sure you already have the documents ..."

"It's not about the documents. What can *you* tell me about it?" she interrupted him and tapped on her tablet. "Documents and plans are one thing, but you're a budding astronaut and as close to the program as anyone can be. I want you to tell me exactly what the plan is."

He seemed to be internally puzzling out what to make of this question and she could see him weighing up his words carefully before he began to speak.

"*Artemis I* tested the SLS rocket for the first time in 2022 and launched an *Orion* capsule into orbit. It then flew around the moon unmanned, returned and landed in the Pacific. Following this successful test, *Artemis II* was scheduled to embark on the same route, but with a human crew aboard, in two weeks' time. And stay in orbit around the moon for a total of ten days. The mission is intended to test *Orion* under real conditions. *Artemis III* is scheduled for next year and will be the first moon landing since Apollo. A colleague will land on the surface with the Lunar Lander and spend a week there," explained Reid.

Hinrichs tried to imagine it all.

The astronaut was now in his element and he began to speak more calmly and quickly.

"The first missions to build the Lunar Gateway space station in orbit around the moon will also start next year. It will be much smaller than the ISS. It can be inhabited by a small team between missions from Earth to the moon or Mars. A stopover, so to speak. And then, from 2026, we will begin the first attempts to establish a permanent presence on the moon, although this has not yet been approved by Congress and it's still in the planning and study phase."

"This is also the point at which private space companies should be more involved in order to build a kind of space economy, correct?"

"That's right, yes."

"Who are the leading players at the moment?"

"SpaceX."

"*And?*"

"After that there is nobody close in terms of capacity, technology, and know-how, but the important companies are still Northrop Grumman, Boeing, Blue Origin, Lockheed Martin, and some less important international companies, some of which are semi-state-owned," explained Reid.

"And what would such a lunar economy look like? What exactly is up there besides dust?"

"Regolith," he corrected her. "There may be water in the form of ice between the regolith. That would provide the foundation for a permanently manned moon base. Hydrogen and oxygen can be separated from water, so astronauts would have drinking water and breathing air."

"But we don't need to fly up there for things that we already have in abundance here," replied Rebecca.

"True. Helium-3 is the big thing. If we make a breakthrough in fusion research, helium-3 would be the new fuel of choice. There's not much of it on Earth and it's difficult to produce, but the moon rocks are probably full of it, and it would probably be quite easy to extract because of the low gravity. A suitably equipped company could produce fusion pellets directly on the moon and shoot them to Earth with unmanned drones to supply us with energy."

"Then we would no longer need oil."

"At least less of it."

"I see. It sounds like the moon is the future of our energy supply – assuming that nuclear fusion works. The latest breakthroughs give some cause for optimism, as far as I understand it?" she asked and he nodded. "So it's quite reasonable that China has a great interest in getting to the moon before we do."

Now the astronaut frowned. "Ma'am?"

"If the Chinese Communist Party goes public and pretends to have found something on the moon, they will have a reason. They'll send their own mission and try to get there before us. Otherwise they would never have alerted their own people," Rebecca explained. "They want the helium-3."

"I don't know, ma'am. Politics is not my area. But it can be assumed that the People's Republic is also interested."

"Helium-3 and potentially alien technology." She nodded to affirm what she already knew. "The signal we picked up came from the Shackleton Crater, the region where a first moon base was to be established according to current plans, is that correct?"

"Yes."

"Why there?" It was exhausting to ask him things she knew and had dissected in detail, but it told her a lot about him and the astronauts' thoughts on the region.

"The south pole region is the most likely to have significant amounts of water ice," explained Reid. "The sun never shines in the Shackleton. At the crater rim, yes, but not inside. It's very deep and quite well protected from meteorites, dozens of which fall every day. Future astronauts would therefore have access to sunlight, meaning energy, and to water ice for drinking water and oxygen. It's the ideal place."

"Could that be the reason why we detected a signal there? That an alien intelligence has built something there because it needs all this too?"

"Well, it would also be a logical place to leave something for a civilization that lives on Earth. The moon is in a bound rotation around the Earth and the south pole is facing us at all times."

"So if an alien power has set up, say, an observation post, then the inside of the Shackleton Crater would be perfect for it." Rebecca unfolded her hands. "It would always be in shadow and not easily recognizable, but it would have a clear view of Earth – of us."

"That's partly true."

"Only *partly* true?" She leaned back and made a prompting gesture. "Please, enlighten me."

"No energy source can be hidden in space. With the simplest infrared telescope, we would see everything that radiates more heat inside the Shackleton than a grain of dust. The moon has no atmosphere and so the temperature there is the same, apart from direct solar radiation on objects such as an astronaut. In the Shackleton, any heat source would glow like a candle. But we've never seen anything there."

"And what conclusion do you draw from this?"

"None, Major." Reid shook his head, looking tired all at

once. "Either it's just a piece of metal, remnants of what aliens may have once placed there, or it is technology so superior that it far exceeds our understanding of physics. To be honest, I don't know which possibility would worry me more."

Rebecca thought about it and inwardly agreed with him. Finding remnants of aliens and then not being able to communicate with them – or at least learn about them or disassemble their technology – would be a huge disappointment. Extremely superior technology that still worked, on the other hand, would be an undeniable danger.

Once more she leaned forward.

"Let's talk about you now. You were recently removed from the crew for *Artemis II* and replaced by Walter Growlings, correct?"

Reid clenched his teeth. "That's correct, Major."

"Please tell me about the crew and the replacement team. In detail."

CHAPTER 9

C harlie was spared further 'interrogations' for the next three days. A strange atmosphere between tension and normality prevailed at the JSC. Surprisingly, the work of the various departments continued as before. The only difference was that soldiers were always to be seen standing around in groups, seemingly at random, or appearing, also randomly, in the various canteens for food or drink. Contrary to his fears, infantrymen weren't standing guard at every door or patrolling the corridors – but they were patrolling at the fences around the grounds. If he hadn't known what was going on, and if colleagues weren't constantly being pulled aside for questioning by strangers, some in civilian clothes and others in assorted uniforms, he might not have noticed that anything was different than usual.

The crew of the *Artemis II* mission continued to train on various mock-ups in the large water basin, and in the replicas of the *Orion* capsule. Launch Control spent most of its time in one of the conference rooms meticulously planning the launch and finalizing the safety protocols, while the Mission Control Center continued to look after the crew and the day-to-day work on the ISS, which could not be forgotten amidst all the hustle and bustle.

While Charlie had initially feared that they wouldn't be allowed to go home, that didn't happen either. Every employee finished their shift as normal and went home. Of course, it was clear to everyone that he or she was bugged or being monitored in some other way. And it made sense from an intelligence point of view. As long as NASA was in lockdown, a possible spy would not make contact with the Chinese, but in the apparent safety of freedom, it was more likely. The question was, of course, how cunning the mole was. A professional would have broken off all contacts long ago and would never use them again. But you never knew. Perhaps payments or collateral were outstanding.

Although he at first found it difficult to concentrate and do his work, Charlie trained diligently with Louis, Miles, and Anne in the *Orion* simulator, supported Leo, Anne, Walter, and Karen in their exercises, and did his share of the little office work that needed to be done. Whether it was due to the stress of the circumstances, he didn't know, but the crew of the *Artemis II* showed surprisingly little of the egocentric behavior of the alpha animals that was usual: orders for errands, picking up laundry from the grandmother or bringing the groceries to the wife or husband.

He used to think these stories were nonsense, that astronauts were virtually infallible people with strong behavioral and moral compasses. And that was the case, but some human quirks were also inherent in them and those that were traditional in the astronaut corps were the most unpleasant: among other things, that the replacement crew were treated like servants.

Now there was hardly a trace of that. As always, the conversation was professional during the exercises and noticeably sparse in between.

On the evening of the third day, he was sitting in the changing room of the large diving pool, peeling out of his wetsuit, when Anne let out a deep sigh.

"This is so frustrating, guys," she said, finger-combing her wet blond hair so she could pull it into the tie she had pulled off her wrist.

"What, Uncle Sam breathing down our necks, or us having to play second fiddle under the eyes of our own former comrades?" asked Louis. The burly former Air Force pilot pulled his wetsuit up to below his navel and stretched his taut muscles.

"Both," Anne replied and finished undressing. She walked to the passageway to the shower rooms and then turned back, despite being fully naked. "This whole mess feels like a bad movie. But the worst thing is that I'm getting more nervous every day."

"Why?" Charlie asked sincerely.

"Because I haven't been interrogated yet. Nothing. Not a word."

Louis and Miles nodded – apparently the cup had also bypassed them so far. When he didn't nod or speak, they all looked at him.

"A major – I'm sure she's from the intelligence service – questioned me on the very first day," he explained with a shrug.

"So, what did she want to know?" asked Miles, leaning forward as he took off his neoprene shoes. They made an ugly smacking sound.

"She grilled me about the *Artemis* plans and wanted to know why the moon is so interesting for space travel." Charlie waved dismissively. "I don't know why. I don't think that's going to help you in your future discussions. In principle, she did not ask anything about possible moles."

"*In principle?*" Anne echoed with a raised eyebrow.

"Honestly, she wanted to find out who I trust more, my former military comrades or my new NASA colleagues. I think."

The others nodded understandingly. They didn't ask him to expand on it because they knew the answer and he was sure that they thought just like he did. 'You could get the soldier out of the military, but you couldn't get the military out of the soldier.'

Anne gave a wave and left for the showers and Miles followed her a short time later, leaving Charlie alone with Louis. The replacement-crew commander for *Artemis II* moved closer to him on the wooden bench.

"There's a rumor going around that the whole program is on hiatus until further notice," he said in a lowered voice. "I haven't told Miles and Anne yet, but I thought you should know."

"Why?"

"Because of your particular situation." Louis shrugged his shoulders. "You know."

Because I was kicked out of the crew and put with you, Charlie thought, and would have liked to sigh in surrender. "It's all right. I feel comfortable with you and don't need any special treatment."

"All Marine, huh?"

"Semper Fi."

Louis nodded and patted him on the shoulder. "Look on the bright side. It's much worse for our chosen ones out there in the basin. Uncertainty is unbearable, I tell you."

"You're right about that. If I could choose, I'd rather none of this had happened and the mission had gone ahead as planned." Charlie lowered his head and finally let out the long sigh that had been weighing on his chest for so long. "But after the signal's discovery, nothing will be the same, for the time being anyway. Even without the whole China problem."

"Aliens, huh?" Louis leaned back until the back of his head sank against one of the lockers. "I just plain cannot believe this. It's like this is all a bad dream. All the stress with the Space Force is distracting, sure, but oh, my God. An alien artifact on the moon? I have no idea what that means for our future."

"Maybe nothing, if we humans are too *human* to do anything with it," said Charlie. "It should get us all excited, create international cooperation. A joint effort to launch an expedition and find out for the whole species whether we are alone in the universe. It's one of the oldest questions, one we've been asking ourselves since we first looked up at the stars."

"Instead, we argue with our own people because we're afraid a political opponent might beat us to it. Seems like we haven't learned much. That's exactly what could have happened during the Cold War," Louis agreed and seemed about to say something else, but was interrupted when the door opened and Montgomery, the head of EVA training, stuck his head in. If he thought it was strange that Charlie and Louis were sitting naked next to each other on the bench, he didn't let on. He seemed upset.

"You should see this!" said the engineer breathlessly.

"See what?"

"The Chinese. They're going to the moon!" With that, Montgomery disappeared. Charlie and Louis quickly glanced at each other and hurried to put on their clothes without bothering to dry themselves first.

Louis hurried out shortly afterward, but Charlie forced himself to go to the shower room first. "Hey, you two, there's some big news from the Chinese. We're over in conf-two."

"We'll be right behind you," said Anne as she turned off the water.

Only then did Charlie give in to his urge not to waste a

second and ran across the corridor to the second door on the right, which had 'Training Conference Room 2' posted on it. When he entered, it was full of colleagues from the training team. They sat and stood around the large table, staring at the big TV monitor on the far side.

NewsNation was on. Reporter Virginia Edgerton was standing in front of the Chinese embassy building in Washington.

" ... has not yet commented on the reports from the Xinhua news agency. However, the ambassador will appear before the press within the next hour. So back to you, Lucy," sounded from the speakers. The image switched back to the studio and Lucy Ingram. In the background, a Chinese flag flew on the display, along with the President and the words, 'Chinese lunar mission to recover an alien artifact?'

"Thank you, Virginia," Ingram said, turning to the cameras. "According to the Chinese news agency Xinhua, President Xi Jinping has confirmed that China plans to launch a manned mission to the south pole of the moon later this year to investigate the origin of the signal that the space agency CNSA claims to have received three days ago.

"Amid growing tensions following statements by President Hernandez that the data was in fact stolen from NASA, this is a further step toward a confrontation between the United States and China. In view of the developments at NASA, voices are becoming louder demanding clarification of what is going on behind the scenes.

"The White House has yet to respond to the Chinese announcement. However, our reporters in Washington agree that it may only be a matter of hours before we can expect an official press release. So the big question remains: How will the U.S. react? Is this the start of a new race to the moon?"

CHAPTER 10

" ... An hour in which we as a nation are being asked to rise to the greatest of challenges, once again. China has announced that it will send taikonauts to the moon, and intends to do so before the end of this year. I come before you today to say this: We will be there first. We did it once, in the darkest hours of the Cold War, when communism challenged us. Now we face the same crossroads in history and I assure you that we will succeed this time too.

"Values such as freedom, the absolute will to progress and cooperation have made us the strongest nation in history. Once more, we will show the world what that means. The next men on the moon will be Americans – this year. But we are not setting out to simply repeat what we have done before. This time we are making plans to stay.

"Reaching for the stars is in our American DNA. Neil Armstrong, Buzz Aldrin, and Michael Collins were heroes, not because they were different from us, but because they were the unconditional expression of what defines us as Americans: we push the boundaries of what is possible. All of that is in you, too.

"Just as our ancestors faced difficulties and countless

hurdles on their great westward journey, so will we. And I tell you: We will overcome them.

"Here and now, I promise you – I promise the *world* – that, before the year is out, American astronauts will be standing on the moon, because we are the country that has always made impossible dreams come true and we will continue to do so in the future.

"We are the country of pioneers. We are the country that will move forward in the name of freedom, justice, and equal opportunity, and today we will show the world how we want to celebrate tomorrow. Only as a united people will we be able to look out into space and say: 'It is not emptiness that awaits us there, but the future.'

"God bless America and all those brave Americans who will be on the front lines of this next challenge to our great nation. God bless all of you, my fellow Americans. What we set out to do will be achieved by each of you."

Charlie switched off the TV and rubbed his tired eyes. He knew President Hernandez's speech by heart by now. Nevertheless, he had been listening to it repeatedly for two days, just to reassure himself that he hadn't imagined it all.

"Pretty patriotic, huh?"

Charlie flinched. He hadn't even noticed Harry in the doorway of the astronauts' lounge. His superior approached the sofa and shook his head. "That speech could have come straight out of the sixties."

"Impossible," Charlie replied, shaking his head.

"You think? Well, if that wasn't a Cold War speech, I don't know what it was."

"No, that's not what I mean. The mission is impossible. Just a few months to land a crew at the south pole of the moon? It's simply not possible," he expressed, puffing out his cheeks to exhale forcefully and release some of the tension that had kept him awake all night.

"I wouldn't say that. SpaceX was awarded the contract for the lander and is already working on it. They're getting virtually unlimited funding from Congress. They're pretty fast, as you know."

"If they can blow enough things up."

"Rapid prototyping. It's worked out quite well." Harry shrugged his shoulders. "Once the FAA is aligned, they'll approve two to three launches a week, then your Starship will be orbiting the moon and able to land there within the next few months. Don't forget, *Artemis III* was planned to use SpaceX's Human Landing System, not an *Orion*. They'll just have to be a year faster now."

Charlie thought about his boss's words and sighed. "Maybe they'll manage. But what about the Chinese?"

"They have no experience with the moon and ..."

"They landed a robot on the back of the moon," Charlie reminded the head of the Astronaut Office. "That was no easy task."

"Admittedly. But they simply don't have the staff and technology required."

"Russia will help them, and lots of money and industrial capacity will do the rest."

"Possibly," Harry admitted. "But we still have the advantage. One way or another."

"I hope you're right. Who do you think they'll send up?" asked Charlie.

"Now that Space Command is calling the shots? I don't want to get your hopes up too high, but I can't imagine them opting for an all-civilian crew to go to the moon in a race with the Chinese. They don't trust us. They've made that abundantly clear."

Charlie thought about it. Secretly, he agreed with Harry, but he didn't quite dare to admit the thought that he might be reassigned to the first crew for the *Artemis III,* which had now been brought forward.

"The question is more whether *you* want to go."

He looked at Harry and raised a brow. "What are you talking about?"

"Surely you realize that the mission is going to be put together with chewing gum and duct tape," the astronaut explained. "Less than a year to prepare for something that is currently the most difficult thing humans can do?"

"We've done it before, and we can fall back on the old knowledge."

"You know how long it took to design and build the SLS, and it's basically just a replica of the ancient Saturn V. There was a lot more improvisation back then and the safety margins were much greater." Harry shook his head. "Then there's the avionics. For Apollo, it was all at the most minimal level – navigation computers and control systems, to name just two. Today they're a hundred or more times as complex. We have to rethink the entire sensor system for landing because the systems and devices available are based on completely different technology and complexity."

"We've become too advanced." Charlie snorted. But he knew Harry was right. As he always was.

"In principle, yes. Our technology is so advanced that its complexity makes it more difficult to unite all the systems and combine them into a flawless whole. And high tech is even more susceptible to the nasty moon dust than the old stuff from back then." Harry's cellphone chirped and he glanced down at the small display on his belt. "Oh, Miller's back."

"From Washington?"

"It looks like it. She wants to see us in her office."

"In Colonel Feinman's office," Charlie corrected him.

"Yes. Come with me."

"I don't think I ..."

"Until we hear more, I'm going to assume that the same people who were at the last meeting are supposed to come," Harry said and held out a hand. Charlie took it and let himself be assisted up from the sofa. "Who knows, maybe you'll get some good news right away."

They left the lounge and made their way up to the third floor to the administrator's former office, which had been occupied by the hulking colonel from Space Command for two weeks. Charlie was glad he'd had hardly any contact with the guy who came across to him like a butcher who'd found a uniform somewhere, donned it, and convinced everyone that he was a real officer. But he had resolved not to underestimate the man. If Feinman was a secret service agent, only he knew what role to play to achieve his goals.

When they got to the office, Louis, Miles, and Anne were waiting there and Charlie's heart skipped a beat. Was it possible that Miller had broken the news to them that they were now the new crew for *Artemis III* because the military favored former soldiers?

The administrator stood behind her desk and motioned for them to sit down. She looked tired and worn out, with deep circles and heavy bags under her eyes. Even her make-up and neatly coiffed hair couldn't hide the fact that she'd had a terrible two weeks.

"Nice to have you back," Harry said and she just nodded absently.

"Sit down, we'll wait for the others before we start," she replied.

"Where's the colonel?" Charlie asked in surprise.

"Not here." Miller bared her teeth like a predator. She seemed about to add something else when the door opened and Leo, the other Anne, Walter and Karen came in. They were wearing their blue overalls. Walter had the tablet from the simulator still stuck to the Velcro on his thigh. "Ah, there you are. Have a seat. There's some news."

"It's good to have you back," Leo said curtly, giving Charlie and his comrades from the replacement crew a cursory nod.

"I spent several hours with the President yesterday," the administrator began without preamble. "And I have good news. He's ready to hand control back to NASA. No mole was found and I was able to make it clear to him that we can't operate at full efficiency with the military breathing down our necks all the time."

Approval spread among the astronauts. Walter even raised a fist triumphantly in the air. Charlie's hopes sank and he felt a little ashamed because he wasn't as happy as he maybe should have been about civilian control returning.

"I wanted you to hear it from me personally. Your training was not in vain." Miller looked to the primary crew and gave them a thumbs-up. "You're still in the game, with the difference that we're skipping your original plan and taking you straight to the moon. And you," she turned to Charlie and the backup crew, "continue as backup. If we pull together and don't allow ourselves any major mistakes, we can do it."

"What about the uniform wearers?" asked Harry. Charlie noticed he was deliberately avoiding his gaze.

"The secret service agents will probably stay here and continue to monitor everything. And the NSA is now officially given access to all systems to prevent China from sticking its nose into our program in any way. We are now at the forefront of the biggest project since the first moon landing. This means that things are going to change and ..."

Charlie stopped listening. The disappointment was too strong. He had hoped to have another chance. At the same time, he was ashamed of his selfish thoughts. Nevertheless, he acknowledged them, accepting the frustration and anger that welled up inside him before he let it all go. He hadn't joined NASA to enrich himself – not with money, not with grand experiences. He wanted to make a difference, to push the boundaries of humanity into space, to be part of something big. He still had that chance, but only if he was a good team player and did his bit, as was his duty.

So he squared his shoulders and pushed out his chest.

CHAPTER 11

For Charlie, the following months passed like a dream that was constantly on the verge of a nightmare. He slept no more than six hours a night and never returned to his apartment in the city center. Instead, he lived full-time at the JSC and trained tirelessly for a mission he would never be a part of. Leo and Walter showed no weaknesses, were as healthy as ever and performed brilliantly in the simulations. The same applied to Anne and Karen, for whom he, as a man, was not an option as a replacement.

So day after day passed with endless shifts, after which they often had to do errands and personal favors for the primary crew because they had even less time, plus tradition demanded it. Nobody said anything against it because it was clear that nobody was allowed to step out of line. Not now, not during a new race to the moon, in which much more was at stake than simply showing which nation, which ideology was the better one.

It was about the alien signal that was hardly ever talked about in everyday life at the Johnson Space Center, but which hung over them like a particularly bright full moon – not glaring, but bright enough to illuminate everything they did. No one mentioned it, but everyone had it in the back of their minds, working extra hard because it wasn't just about beating China, but possibly making contact with aliens.

Sometimes he talked to Harry about it over dinner, in the few minutes a day when he didn't have his hands full. Harry thought it was some kind of signal buoy, perhaps with an AI on board that would make first contact with humanity once it had reached a level of development that would allow it to reach the moon and find them. Charlie wasn't so sure. Of course he didn't know, but he believed – or hoped – that it was a relic, perhaps a crashed spaceship, whose technology they could use to usher in a new age of progress and the colonization of space.

All of it was pure speculation, but he was sure that everyone at NASA, SpaceX, Boeing, and Lockheed, everyone in Washington and in the general population, was thinking about little else. In this respect, it did him good to immerse himself deeply in work all these months so that he didn't go crazy. He didn't even have time to watch the many TV programs that picked the signal apart from front to back and put forward the wildest theories, or to report on the progress made by NASA and the Chinese, of which hardly anything was heard.

In the summer, the time had come. Together with SpaceX, they launched three Starships using the Super Heavy Booster. First into orbit, which was successful except for the re-entry, during which the booster and spaceship were lost.

The second time it worked, the prototype orbited the Earth three times and then landed safely at Cape Canaveral, to everyone's astonishment. On re-entry, the booster began to tumble and was destroyed in a controlled manner over the Pacific. But that didn't matter, because the only thing that mattered was getting the Starship operational. The original plans to dock an *Orion* capsule to the SpaceX spacecraft and thus have a hybrid lander for the moon were quickly scrapped because it would have taken too long to develop and build the appropriate adapters.

In the third test, they sent a Starship around the moon and back to Earth, which caused a real storm of enthusiasm among all of them and throughout the country. The whole nation now seemed to fully believe that they could do it, until two weeks later the Chinese followed suit. The communist regime took the whole world by surprise when it launched a Long March 10 rocket into orbit on the very first attempt and undocked a space capsule, which orbited the Earth for a while and then docked with the Tiangong. Although the system was significantly smaller than the Starship and Super Heavy, it was evidently much more sophisticated technology than originally assumed.

Whereas previously there had been a 'they don't stand a chance' mentality, now even the last China doubters were waking up. The Asians had not slept in the meantime, and the silence with which they surrounded their own program was not due to problems, but to absolute secrecy and a completely different approach than the Americans.

The mood then changed drastically. Everyone seemed to work even harder and be driven in a way that was more tense, more hardened. In addition, there were more frequent attempts by the Chinese to obtain information about NASA's program. Hacker attacks on NASA and government facilities became a weekly occurrence. One of them set them back two weeks because they lost important data that was destroyed by an advanced computer worm that kept the intelligence agencies on their toes for several days.

Charlie was sure that their own people were doing the same with the CNSA, but he had no definite proof. However, no one had any doubt that the conflict was coming to a head and was going far beyond a normal race to the moon. Neither side wanted to lose face, and the rewards were so high that the risks were correspondingly high.

For them, this meant even stricter controls by the military, less networking and more varied data carriers and backup systems, costing them valuable time that would have been better spent on the lander systems and the integration of NASA and SpaceX technologies and processes.

The first attempt by a Starship to land on the lunar surface took place at the end of September. A site near the Shackleton Crater was chosen for this, which was significantly flatter than the areas closer to the crater rim. The sensor technology of *Sentinel I* was particularly helpful, as it provided precise measurement data from orbit and served as a relay station to Houston and Hawthorne. The attempt failed when *Starship 4* fell over shortly after landing. However, due to the limited fuel on board – a return was not planned at this stage of the testing phase – it did not explode and had been lying there like an overturned trashcan ever since. The engineers were sure that they had underestimated how soft the regolith at the landing site was. The landing nozzles had sunk in too far on one side, and future landing systems had since been undergoing a fundamental overhaul.

The biggest moment came two weeks later when the third attempt was successful. After *Starship 5* exploded and crashed on approach due to a faulty valve, *Starship 6*, also unmanned, managed to land and had been standing there ever since. Fortunately, Administrator Miller had prevailed and instead of a test payload – which was usually rocks, believe it or not – she had ordered supplies and tools be loaded on board equivalent in terms of tonnage to the expected weight of the upcoming manned mission. So, they now had an outpost with supplies on the moon, which caused a storm of enthusiasm in Washington and throughout the western world. After the first attempt by the Chinese had failed two weeks earlier because their 'Long March' had missed the orbital injection around the moon and disappeared into the vastness of space, many thought the race was already won.

Charlie did his best not to participate in such optimism, worried that it might prove premature. But more often he found himself believing that they would make it.

Miller then announced that they had chosen an official launch date: December 1st. At that point, it had been no more than three weeks away. One successful landing attempt had been enough to convince their country's leadership that they were ready. This fact drove home to him just how frayed the nerves were in Washington, and how much was at stake. The aggressive rhetoric between East and West had continued to increase, including threats from Moscow to destroy the signal source if it was not made accessible to all nations, and if Russia was not explicitly involved. In response, Washington threatened the Kremlin, Beijing threatened Washington, and so it went.

It was frustrating and without the pressure of the preparations, Charlie would almost have died of worry. They were about to make history, to accomplish a technological masterpiece, to bring a national *tour de force* to its crowning conclusion through hard work and the cooperation of a wide variety of people in different locations. And the world could think of nothing better than to shower each other with threats.

As a result, Space Command became increasingly present and took the protection of NASA facilities and computer systems ever more seriously. They were now also stationed in Boca Chica and Hawthorne at SpaceX and appeared much more frequently. In Florida and Texas, they kept taking over new NASA rooms and forbidding access to unauthorized personnel. Charlie realized that they were setting up their own command centers, intelligence hubs in the middle of the civilian space industry.

The stakes were as high as they could possibly be. In addition, President Hernandez and Xi Jinping declared that the outcome of the race would set the course for the future of humanity. A directional decision between two systems and possible supremacy for an indefinite period of time. And there was technology potentially up for grabs that would put everything that had gone before in the shade.

In preparation, they were flown to Florida together with the primary crew, where they had to spend two weeks in quarantine. The legendary Astronaut crew quarters in the Neil Armstrong Operations and Checkout Building at the Kennedy Space Center were used for this purpose. Although they had been renovated, they still exuded the 60s and 70s charm of the legendary Apollo heroes. This made the long isolation a little easier to bear.

And then the time came.

Launch day had arrived.

PART II

THE MOON

CHAPTER 12

Launch day is the biggest thing in the life of a directly involved NASA employee – and of course every astronaut. Everything comes down to this one day. Tens of thousands of components and systems that have been tested and assembled into a complex puzzle must prove themselves here and now. The stakes are enormous, with human lives on board and the risk of failure hanging over them, which in this case would mean not only the loss of human lives and unimaginable sums of money, but also handing over the future to a communist regime.

Leo, Anne, Walter, and Karen were correspondingly tense the whole time. Despite their professionalism, you could tell that this time was different. When they were picked up seven hours before the launch, they said goodbye to each other briefly and exchanged little more than the usual friendly words. Over the last two weeks Charlie had planned so much that he wanted to say to them, but it was all forgotten when the doorbell rang and the cars pulled up outside.

He gave them all big hugs and wished them the absolute best. He deliberately ignored his own ambitions and aspirations, without which he would never have made it from a simple high school graduate and non-commissioned officer to a physics degree and into the astronaut corps. Now his only job was to support the first guard and stand by, especially in mission support. Once the launch was successful and his comrades were in orbit, it would be up to him and his backup crewmates to support the communication between Mission Control and the four most important astronauts in history. Nobody knew the mindset and needs of astronauts as well as other astronauts. In addition, there were no other major experts in handling the Starship HLS – Human Landing System. No one else had spent more time in the simulators and knew every move inside out.

When the door closed behind the crew and the four of them were left alone, they retired to the large living room and drank some water. No one touched coffee, as it was too diuretic. If someone did have to step in, they had to be well hydrated, but not *too* hydrated. Peeing excessively into the spacesuit's mandatory diaper was not what space travelers wanted.

"I imagined this moment would be worse," Louis said with a sigh. The beefy commander of the backup crew shrugged his shoulders. "It feels like the moment before the final exams in college, and it must be a lot worse for those guys and gals."

"Nah," said Anne, who had been braiding, undoing, and re-braiding her hair for hours. "At least those four have the distraction of being busy all the time. We're stuck sitting here, alone with our thoughts. That's the worst thing."

"Yo," Miles agreed with her. He stared unhappily at the TV monitor on the wall, which showed images from the Launch Control Room and the launch pad, where the Super Heavy was standing with the Starship mounted on it. It was only the second time that the behemoth would fly from Cape Canaveral, as it had previously always taken off from SpaceX's

Starbase in Boca Chica. But for this launch, there was only one place that came into play, and that was right here, where history had already been made. The Air Force avionics engineer held out a hand. "There's the baby. How I wish I could have ridden it."

"We're all wishing that," said Louis, waving his hand. "But it is what it is."

"Right now we should be thinking about the others and keep our fingers crossed for them," Charlie added. "Good teammates do that. And there's a lot more at stake than our personal wishes. Our time will come."

Miles searched his gaze and nodded after they had looked into each other's eyes for some time.

"You're right." Miles took a sip of water and sat up a little straighter. "They must be rocking it now. To think their boots will touch moon soil this week and they might make contact with an alien artifact ... Good God! That seems way too crazy to be true."

"Things will change soon, that's for sure," Charlie agreed. "No matter what things you might mention. Just the fact that aliens were here at some point and that we'll soon have proof in our hands that we're not the only ones in the universe. That will change us as a species."

"I hope for the better," grumbled Anne.

"It will."

"What makes you so sure?" she asked with interest, giving him a look that expressed an eagerness to hear something positive.

"Because this race to the moon will either destroy us or make us better. I am convinced of that."

"We can do this," Louis said in his normal determined way. The former Navy fighter pilot had that typical pilot's disposition, bursting with flaunted optimism. Charlie had always wondered whether a certain type of person became a fighter pilot, or whether every person who became a fighter pilot took on this disposition because they emulated the superstars of the Navy and subconsciously morphed into their role models. "The Chinese are good at copying, but they are not innovative. Good ideas need freedom of thought, which is why we are ahead, and why they have become so quiet. I'm telling you, we'll kick their asses and make sure we continue to set the tone. A hundred dollars on it!"

"I'm not betting against America." Miles pulled his face into a grin.

When the countdown reached 'T -4,' the refueling process for the liquid methane and liquid oxygen began. The gigantic rocket began to freeze on the outside from bottom to top, starting with the super heavy booster. The white layer of condensation was clearly visible even in the long-distance camera shot.

"I wonder how many thousands of people are sitting in the stands now," mused Anne. Her braiding project had almost reached the end. Again.

"I don't know, but supposedly over two hundred million people will have switched on their televisions in this country alone, five billion worldwide. That's more than twice as many as watched the World Cup," said Louis.

Charlie tuned out the small talk and watched the images on the TV monitor. You could see the silence in the Launch Control Center. Tense, focused faces, occasionally someone talking into their headset. In addition, the rocket stood erect on the launch pad, with thick steam rising from the coolant. The Mission Control Center in Houston, which he was so familiar with, looked just as quiet. Until the two rocket stages were separated, his colleagues there would just watch, and then they'd take over from Cape Canaveral after the orbital injection – which didn't mean that the concentration levels there were even a shade lower. The entirety of mission control was the responsibility of Houston.

Two hours later – in the meantime they had eaten something and the others had spoken to their families on the phone – Leo, the other Anne, Walter, and Karen were driven to the launch pad in a large convoy with flashing blue lights after saying goodbye to their loved ones in a media-effective manner – without being allowed to touch them due to quarantine regulations. When they got off at the launch pad and waved for the cameras, the dimensions of the Starship on its booster became clear. In front of the 120-meter-tall monster, his comrades looked almost tiny in their white spacesuits.

Leo spoke into the camera, probably saying something historic, but they had turned the sound off because they wanted to concentrate fully on being ready in case of necessity. There was zero chance of that at this point, but their professionalism dictated it.

"He's probably making a joke about our similar names," Miles said, chuckling. "Louis and Leo, Anne, and the other Anne."

"When I was born, people still had taste," replied Anne, who had since unbraided her hair and was starting over.

"Here we go, for real." Louis leaned forward and folded his hands in front of his mouth. On the screen, their comrades were striding toward the large tower of steel struts in which the elevator to the top was located. SpaceX groundcrew members wearing black suits with caps and face masks swarmed around them like ants as they walked.

"You can do it," whispered Anne, letting go of her braid and leaning forward. Charlie could hear the wall clock ticking in the background, as if someone had turned up its volume. "*We* can do it."

The cameras captured the elevator as it ascended the steel frame, while a second image showed a distance shot of the entire structure with the rocket and the bridge leading to the cockpit of the Starship.

"A cable has come loose," Louis remarked. Charlie tried to figure out what he meant. Then he saw it too. At the upper part of the tower, a cable was wriggling back and forth like a snake.

"It must be a thick hose when you look at the steel beams in comparison," he said.

"Is there fluid coming out?" Miles asked tensely. "Shit, it *is* leaking. I hope they don't abort the launch."

As if on cue, the countdown froze.

"Turn on the sound!" shouted Anne.

Charlie, who was sitting closest to the remote control, followed her request.

" ... it looks like there's a problem with one of the coolant valves. Launch safety has stopped the countdown for the time being until we get to the bottom of the problem. It is not yet clear whether there will be a delay, or whether we will be able to launch today," explained the spokesman from the Launch Control Center.

Just then, accompanied by complete silence, a fireball appeared on the screen. First the lower section of the booster exploded, then the huge detonation continued upward – in such a short time that everything seemed to happen at the same time.

Charlie watched in horror as the rocket and tower went up in flames, and with them their comrades and their shared dream of the moon.

CHAPTER 13

"Shit!" Louis was the first to break the silence. Anne began to cry silently and Charlie went to her to give her a hug. He felt sick. "What shit!"

"I don't believe it," Miles said in a strained voice, stepping closer to the TV monitor as if the reduction in distance might reveal a great hoax. A mirage. "It can't be."

"But it is." The commander of the backup crew clenched his hands into fists, went to the screen, and switched it off. "What the hell was that?"

"There was a torn tube that was leaking fluid," said Charlie, continuing to hold Anne. If he had a little more inner strength, he would let himself cry with her to lessen the horrible feeling of loss and powerlessness. But he was still a former Marine who had been trained with the bullshit idea that a soldier doesn't show emotion. It was only years later, after his last tour in Afghanistan, when he had been forced to see a psychologist, that he had been told how important the body's natural mechanisms were for regulating stress and maintaining resilience.

"Yes, I saw that!" Miles exclaimed. "That's what I said. Could have been the liquid methane. Or the liquid oxygen.

These are highly insulated hoses because both liquids are highly reactive in the ambient air."

"And today is a sunny day." Charlie nodded weakly. "If the steel of the tower had heated up enough, contact with one of the liquids could theoretically have caused ignition. A fire starts and continues because the cooling circuit is interrupted. And the booster was half full of fuel by then."

"What a disaster," Louis muttered as he continued to pace back and forth.

Anne gently pushed away from Charlie and gratefully squeezed his arms for a moment. She wiped the tears from her cheeks and shook her head. "We can't change what's happened, so let's pull ourselves together. There are contingency plans in place."

"Yes, *Starship 8*," Miles groused. "It's taking forever. They have to gather all the components, rebuild them, install them – we only had this one chance."

"He's damn right. It was all thrown together under pressure so we'd get there ahead of the Chinks." Louis clenched his right hand into a fist and looked like he was going to punch the TV at any moment, which was now as dark as a black hole that had opened up in the room and sunk all their hopes.

"*Chinks?*" asked Charlie. "Really, now?"

"There is no 'Plan B,'" Louis continued, as if Charlie hadn't said a word. "Only this one, and it's just gone up in flames. We're lucky we're only the backup or we'd be volatile gas clouds out by the pad."

"There are always solutions," Anne insisted with a brave face. Not for the first time, Charlie wondered whether the former Air Force maintenance engineer wouldn't have been the better commander. She was free of pseudo-harsh demeanor, had not been ashamed to show her tears, and had put the shock behind her. Now she was composed and pulled together, faster than all the rest of them put together.

"Let's hear them," Louis grumbled. Frustration was written all over his face.

"I can't say this instant. Anything we discuss here and now will have nothing to do with the real possibilities and will only serve as a useless outlet," she countered. "We have thousands of colleagues who are racking their brains right now, and most of them are smarter than we are, and they know the procedures and systems inside out. They'll think of something."

"So we're just supposed to twiddle our thumbs and rely on others to glue the pieces back together?" Their commander snorted and made a dismissive gesture with his hand. "That's not how I work."

"She's right," Charlie affirmed their crewmate's message. "The best thing we can do now is pull ourselves together, be professional, and get over the shock. What happened can't be changed now, but we should make sure that everyone involved can rely on us. We are the backup crew. We are needed right now."

Louis scrutinized him and ground his teeth. Finally, he nodded with a grim expression.

"You're right, Sarge." The former fighter pilot straightened his shoulders. "You're right."

"*She's* right," Charlie corrected him and pointed at Anne, who gave him a fleeting smile.

"There will be a thorough investigation," she said when the silence seemed to be growing uncomfortable. "Administrator Miller and the leadership team are probably in her office discussing alternative solutions by now."

"I'm sure of it," replied Miles, who had pulled out his cellphone in the meantime and was now demonstratively holding it out to them with the display lit. He had obviously opened a news page, but Charlie couldn't make out any details. The text was far too small to read. "I hope they're fast."

"Why is that? What's that?" Louis asked gruffly.

"China has just sent their official condolences on the disaster. It's all over the news. They are, of course, terribly affected," explained Miles, his voice dripping with irony. "That's why their President announced the launch date of their own mission in the same breath."

Charlie held his breath and could see that Louis and Anne were doing the same.

"Sunday."

"What?" they all blurted out at the same time. "That's in six days!"

Miles nodded silently.

"There's no chance we'll make it," Anne was sure. "In a month, if we were quick. But like this? I don't even know if there's a launch window for a moon transfer at such short notice."

The planned moon transfer was the most efficient way to reach the other celestial body. Basically, the physics behind it was quite simple: the rocket is first brought into a near-Earth orbit and then ignites the spacecraft's engines again to build up the necessary speed to escape the Earth's gravitational funnel. The goal is a lunar transfer orbit that passes the perigee – the point in the Earth's orbit that is closest to the Earth – and then reaches the moon on its orbit at apogee, the furthest point on an elliptical orbit around the Earth. This 'transfer' orbit makes optimum use of the gravitational conditions between the two celestial bodies to enable the most efficient change between orbits.

"No such luck," said Charlie. "Saturday or Sunday, the alternative dates for today, in case today's launch had to be canceled."

"So we're fucked," Louis said. "The damn Chinese will get there before us."

No one said anything in response. They all knew that was the truth. No matter what magic their colleagues in

Houston worked, there was no way they were going to assemble a replacement rocket and get it from Boca Chica to Cape Canaveral within a few days. The journey alone would have been far too long. They had lost, at least as far as the first step was concerned. The Chinese would be the first to reach the moon, and with it, the alien artifact. What a disaster.

Charlie felt disillusionment and a devastating sense of defeat spreading through him, draining all the strength from his limbs.

"Nothing is lost yet," he said, gritting his teeth so hard it hurt. "This battle, maybe, but not the war. A lot can happen between here and the moon."

"I respect your optimism, Charlie, but ..." Louis began, but the sergeant didn't let his commander finish.

"Their rocket may also have a malfunction. It's even less sophisticated than ours. They could miss the lunar orbital injection like they did on their first test flight. Something could go wrong with their lander – you know it as well as I do. The list of potential problems and points of failure is virtually endless."

"They've landed before," Miles objected.

"Yes, once. Once can be luck, twice a sign, three times a pattern," Charlie reminded him.

"In any case, defeatism won't get us anywhere. He's right," said Anne. "The Chinese have the ball now, but they haven't scored a goal yet."

Louis seemed to think about her words and took several deep breaths before his gaze cleared a little. "It would be nice if someone would get in touch here soon."

"I think we're the last people who are the priority right now," said Miles. "They've got enough other things on their minds."

"We are currently the most valuable four people in the

western hemisphere. If something happens to us, we're not just behind on points, we're *completely* out of the game."

"That's true." Charlie had to agree with him on this point. There simply hadn't been time for a third and fourth crew, nor had there been any capacity. "But in here, we're in one of the safest places in the United States. We're in military lockdown, in quarantine, shielded from the public. They'll keep us in here for as long as they can."

"Until they have a plan." Anne nodded. "And they will have it soon, believe me."

If Louis was annoyed by her optimism, he didn't let it show. Instead, he reached for the remote control and was just about to switch the TV monitor back on when there was a knock. For a moment, they looked at each other in irritation. Charlie hadn't heard where the knock had come from, as there were several doors leading into their area.

Then they heard a voice. "This is Major Hinrichs. Come with me immediately."

CHAPTER 14

Major Rebecca Hinrichs ran through the narrow corridor into the lounge and found the four astronauts from the backup crew standing like deer dazed by headlights. Their eyes were wide and they appeared frozen with shock. If she had always imagined astronauts to be superhumans with unshakeable nerves, she was now proven wrong. Presumably, everything that was attributed to them applied above all to extremely controlled environments – in fact, there were hardly any environments more controlled than in rockets and spaceships. But now, control was a beautiful dream that had just gone up in flames before their eyes.

"I told you, come with me immediately!" she stated with enough sternness in her voice that each of them involuntarily came to attention indicating their old soldier reflexes had taken over.

"What's going on, Major?" asked Louis Delamain, a former Navy colonel, if she remembered his file correctly.

"Vehicles are waiting for us outside and you must get into them now. *Immediately!*" she emphasized in a cold voice. Now was not the time to get involved in a discussion.

Delamain understood and nodded after a brief hesitation,

whereupon he walked past her into the corridor with the other three. Only Charles Reid paused, and she almost bumped into him because he was the last of the group.

"My phone ..."

"Does *not* matter. Go!"

"Ma'am," he mumbled and continued walking toward the side exit. Outside, ironically, it had started to rain. The predicted storm had come earlier than the forecasters had believed. So, the launch would have been delayed anyway.

Two black SUVs with tinted windows were parked right in front of the door with their engines running. The droplets on the glass reflected the many lights of the NASA complex and sirens echoed.

Rebecca shooed the astronauts inside, two in each vehicle, and took a front passenger seat.

"Let's go!" she ordered the driver, a young corporal who accelerated shortly afterward. They sped through the darkness of the Kennedy Space Center, the streets eerily empty apart from the rain that drifted in thick veils through the beams of their headlights. From the window, she could see the massive clusters of blue lights from the rescue and fire-fighting vehicles at the back of Launchpad 39A. Spotlights illuminated the skeleton of the destroyed steel tower and the clouds of dark smoke still rising from the wreckage. There was no sign of *Starship 7* or the Super Heavy Booster.

It was an apocalyptic sight, even at this distance.

"My goodness," breathed Charles Reid from behind her. He was sitting in the back seat with Anne Mosby, both staring out of her side window. "It's over now. Really over. It will take months just to rebuild the tower. What am I talking about? To build a *new* tower."

"No new tower is being built," said Rebecca.

"What, we're just giving up?" Mosby asked, dumbfounded.

"NASA is giving up, yes," she confirmed. "They won't admit it, and they'll pretend to the public that they're trying their damnedest. But there are growing factions in Congress who are going to the barricades over the exorbitant spending and instead inventing a conspiracy narrative that there's nothing up there. No signal, no mission."

"Politicians." Mosby practically spat out the word.

"Yes."

"Then it is truly over," Reid murmured disappointedly. "I thought we had a Plan B."

"We do."

"Didn't you just say NASA is giving up?"

"NASA, yes. But not Space Command," Rebecca replied, pointing to the right as she saw a soldier with glow sticks in his hand directing them to turn at the designated gate. The driver turned off at so high a speed that she feared they would overturn due to aquaplaning.

"What?" asked Reid and Mosby simultaneously. They sounded perplexed, which was good news. So at least one secret had managed to stay just that: a secret.

"You didn't believe the Pentagon would just accept that we couldn't find the mole within two weeks, did you? Those in Arlington no longer trust NASA. So we pursued our own Plan B."

"A Plan B?" Reid leaned forward so far that she could feel his breath on her cheek. He smelled of mint gum.

"What Plan B?" Mosby inquired, no less eagerly.

"I'll tell you as soon as we've left the Air Force Base," Rebecca replied. "After all, we're kidnapping you right now."

"With the help of the base commander, I imagine," said Charles Reid, not sounding like he was objecting to his abduction.

"Yes. He works for the Pentagon, remember?"

"Why don't you just fly us out?"

"All airspace is closed within a twenty-mile radius. We'll divert to Patrick Space Force Base and fly you out from there." Rebecca didn't like giving so much away to the two of them. It was true that hardly anything could go wrong now, because base commander Jenkins held all the reins and they had already left the first security perimeter. The way south via Port Canaveral to the other side was clear and would remain clear. Since they were theoretically still on military property, it was also unlikely that the civilian police could get in their way. Unless the NASA bureaucrats got wind of the action sooner than expected, or the astronauts rebelled and informed their colleagues.

What Colonel Feinman had tasked her with was nothing less than a tightrope act. She had to convince the backup crew to play along without *forcing* them to do anything. The plan could only work if they were fully on board and behind the mission. So she had to feed them enough breadcrumbs to turn them into allies, and at the same time be careful not to give them so many details that, in the worst-case scenario, they would choose to bail out.

Fortunately, the two did not dig for any further information until they'd crossed the bridge between the northern part of the lagoon and the southern part. Two fighter jets, Lockheed Martin F-22 Raptors by the sound of their engines, flew over them at low level, witness to the great nervousness of all the institutions after the disaster at Launchpad 39A.

"Boca Chica," Charles Reid said all at once as they sped south along the two-lane road, passing several Humvees from the oncoming direction. A few kilometers away, they could see the lights of the tarmac and the lined-up fighter jets being refueled.

Rebecca didn't say anything, but her lips compressed.

"SpaceX has Starships and boosters in stock. Their rapid production is legendary," the astronaut continued. "The problem is the interior and the electronics. I'm sure Musk didn't have to ask for long to prepare and equip a replacement spaceship with the appropriate funds from the Pentagon. But the sums involved are too high."

"It can't be that much," disagreed Anne Mosby. "Not considering the total cost of the booster and spaceship."

"It's not that," said Rebecca, her eyeroll unseen by them. Career officers were often naïve. Isolated from the reality of the bureaucratic and political processes within the military.

"Then what?"

"The secrecy," Charles Reid replied in Rebecca's place. "*That's* what's exceedingly expensive. Compartmentalization requires separations within existing protocols and processes. The responsibilities and the knowledge pool are set up like an onion and a project like this requires complete reorganization of units and infrastructure. What's more, it must not appear on any official channels. Is that about right?"

"Roughly," Rebecca confirmed. A clever fellow, this one. Of course, he wasn't aware of all the intricacies, the reshuffling of black budgets in the Pentagon and the many agencies that had to be activated and operated for this, the dense network of private contractors who were involved without knowing just what they were involved in. But she recalled, he was 'only' a Marine staff sergeant.

"You're saying we have a second rocket? Just like that?" asked Anne Mosby incredulously. "I can't believe that."

"You better believe it, because you'll be on board."

The young corporal sped them straight onto the tarmac and stopped next to the Marine Corps McDonnell Douglas F-18 Hornet, which was still being refueled. Soldiers in uniform with yellow high-visibility vests buzzed around the red electric sleds, checking the fit of the hoses or chatting with the pilots in the heavy rain. Others pushed the rolling ladders up to the two-seater cockpits. "So, are you ready?"

"Wait a minute, you're flying us to Texas in Hornets?" Charlie asked. "Are you serious?"

Rebecca turned and looked at the two of them, who didn't look at all like astronauts, but like excited children who had just been told that they would be celebrating two birthdays in a row. "It's 1,500 kilometers from here to the Starbase in Boca Chica. At Mach 1.8, that's 45 minutes. Also, no radar records. You'll land at Brownsville South Padre Island International Airport, where the authorities will be visited by Air Force controllers in ..." she glanced down at her wristwatch, "twenty minutes."

"I never thought I'd say this," Mosby said, looking her in the eye. "But at the moment, I'm finding it hard to get angry about your interference. Maybe it should have been a military venture from the start."

Rebecca just nodded. "Come on now. They're expecting you."

CHAPTER 15

"Master Sergeant, eh?" asked Lieutenant Commander Malcolm Falconer via on-board radio. They had just taken off and the g-forces had almost elicited a whoop from Charlie. Falconer had launched the aircraft at a very steep angle, presumably to impress the astronaut a little and because he knew that Charlie had undergone intensive g-training.

"I earned my money with honest work," he replied in a tone of voice that made it clear he was joking. He had to consciously remind himself not to put an automatic 'sir' behind it.

"I always liked you guys."

"Thank you. You were our superstars. Even though we never wanted to admit it, of course, and preferred to make jokes."

"Chairborne Rangers? Jet jockeys? Zoomies?" asked Falconer with a laugh. He led them into a steep left-hand bend and accelerated to maximum speed within half a minute. Charlie wondered how often he had done something like this. A 45-minute flight at maximum speed would probably significantly shorten the machine's maintenance cycle.

"Among other things. I guess we were just jealous that you

guys were flying those crazy planes and bringing death from above while we were down there digging in the dirt," Charlie replied, instinctively holding on tight as they chased through the cloud cover of the storm front. The turbulence wasn't as strong as they'd feared, probably because the aircraft was moving so fast. Everything shook and jolted for a few seconds and then it became still, almost as if they were motionless. The world below them turned into a sea of darkness, which became silvery with the light of the rising moon and seemed to take on a complex structure.

Charlie looked at the pale disk. "A real tragedy," he said, freely expressing his thoughts.

"What do you mean?"

"The mission. *Artemis*." Charlie shook his head. What would he have given a day ago to be allowed to fly in an F-18? For a Marine, that was a virtually unattainable dream. But now he could hardly enjoy it. He wouldn't have called anyone from the primary crew his *friend* because they had spent too long as rivals in astronaut training. After a few missions together they might have become friends, like most astronauts. Training was divisive because of the competition, while time together in space bonded them. Nevertheless, the loss of Leo, Anne, Walter, and Karen hit him hard, perhaps because there was so much more to their deaths. Possibly the end of American supremacy in space and then around the globe. What would a world led by China and its ideology look like?

"Tragedy?" the lieutenant commander interrupted his musings. "That was an attack, if you ask me."

"An attack?"

"Of course. If that wasn't an act of sabotage by the Chinese, then I don't know what is. A methane hose accidentally tearing off its flow valve? Right where a piece of metal in the elevator cables got too hot? Never, ever."

"I don't think the Chinese planted a spy in Cape

Canaveral. The security screenings were even more detailed than usual," Charlie replied.

"Just as impossible as stealing our signal?" The pilot snorted, which sounded like a cat sneezing into the radio. "When it comes to espionage, the Bamboo Benders know exactly how to do it."

"My mother came from Indonesia... I was called names like that as a child," Charlie replied. Even though he knew that most of the racist slurs were the result of unenlightened habit, he found them insulting toward his mother, who had been the most warmhearted person he had ever met.

"Sorry, I didn't know."

Doesn't make it any better, he thought, but remained silent. He wasn't in the mood to argue about something that didn't matter right here and now.

"Do you honestly believe it was an accident? I'm just hearing what I'm hearing and thinking my own thoughts," continued the Lieutenant Commander. "But you were there, you probably know all the technology."

"The technology is complicated. There are tens of thousands of parts that can fail, tens of thousands of processes a problem can creep its way into, and tens of thousands of employees who can make mistakes," Charlie replied. His voice sounded muffled through the mouthpiece in front of his face. It matched his depressed mood, ever since the adrenaline had started to wear off. "But all the parts are checked umpteen times, there are redundancies for just about everything, the processes are rehearsed ad nauseam before the launch, and the staff are the best of the best with years of training."

"So what do you think?"

"I don't know," Charlie admitted honestly. "I simply don't know. But the idea that the Chinese somehow managed to infiltrate our best-secured space facility on a military site honestly scares the shit out of me."

They remained silent for the rest of the flight. Charlie stared out of the window at the peaceful landscape of south Texas with the lights of the coastal towns lined up like a string of pearls. In the moonlight, the Gulf of Mexico far below them looked like black velvet sprinkled with silvery glitter.

Less than 15 minutes later, they were descending and he could see the runway of Brownsville South Padre Island International Airport. It seemed mind-bendingly absurd to him that they had flown from East Florida to the east coast of Texas in such a short time.

After landing, he said a friendly goodbye to the lieutenant commander, who wished him, "Good luck, whatever you do."

Charlie was met by a young Space Force lieutenant in civilian clothes and ushered to a large SUV. The car looked like a clone of the ones that had driven him and his crewmates from the quarantine quarters to Patrick Space Force Base. Louis, Miles, and Anne, sitting up front and in the back, greeted him curtly. If he hadn't known better, he would have thought they were simply overtired. It was more likely, however, that the initial adrenaline flood had worn off and they were increasingly pondering what the hell they were doing here.

Presumably a large-scale search operation had been ordered – or it would be as soon as the Kennedy Space Center had completed the acute response to the disaster at the launchpad and was able to take care of the secondary crew. Had they called in the police? How long would it take before there was an open dispute with the Space Force? Every secret could only be kept for so long. No wonder Hinrichs had flown them to their destination in fighter jets. Creating facts before anything else could be changed.

The drive to SpaceX's Starbase in Boca Chica took less than 20 minutes, which was due in part to the lieutenant's lead foot. They drove through Boca Chica State Park for a long time, with its large lagoons and grasslands beside the lonely, unlit road that seemed to lead to nowhere. Charlie was surprised that there was no escort. Feinman, or someone higher up in the Pentagon, must have decided to make as little fuss as possible – ironic, considering that they had landed in fighter jets at a civilian airport.

Starbase soon emerged as an island of lights in the darkness. Several Starships, illuminated by construction spotlights, loomed from the complex like spaceship drawings from the 1950s. Far in the distance, 'Mechazilla' could be seen, the huge steel frame with its gripper arms that would catch landing spaceships in the future and 'plant' them on fresh boosters in the shortest possible time.

However, they turned into the main complex, in front of which 'Starbase' was written in bright white letters. Charlie saw the factory tents, the large hangars for the Starships they produced, a trailer park and residential buildings, and an inconspicuous factory building on the right, in front of which stood two palm trees.

"The colonel is waiting for you inside," the lieutenant said after stopping the car right between the palms. Two soldiers were standing outside the door and seemed to be waiting for them.

"Well, let's see," said Louis.

They got out and walked through the gentle breeze coming from the sea toward the single-story white building. Inside was a small reception desk with the word 'Receiving' written above it, a white wall behind it and lots of boxes to the right and left. On one side, an employee was driving a forklift truck to pick up a pallet, which he then took away through a side entrance.

"Nice," Anne commented on the scene.

"Ah, the crew," said a young woman in jeans and a black T-shirt who appeared from behind the counter and came around to shake their hands one by one. She smiled broadly and introduced herself. "I'm Jackie, normally responsible for receiving goods from suppliers."

Charlie felt strange, as if they had been flown out on a school trip for a sightseeing tour, and not in a smoke-and-mirrors operation by the Navy to take part in a secret space project.

"Hi Jackie, nice to meet you," Louis replied. "No offense, but we'd like to speak to Colonel Feinman."

"Sure, come with me. His meeting with Elon should be wrapping up." She motioned for them to follow her and led them around the white wall into the middle of the warehouse, to an office with a window. They could see the colonel behind a desk through the glass pane. He was on the phone and looked very upset. The few times Charlie had met Feinman during the investigations at the JSC, it had been no different.

"Ah, there you are," the Space Force officer rumbled and waved them in. Four uncomfortable-looking aluminum chairs were lined up in front of his desk. "Have a seat."

Feinman picked up the phone again and said gruffly, "Just do it and move your ass!"

Then he hung up and casually settled back into his chair. "I'm glad you came so quickly. I wanted to call the major crazy at first, but I guess I made the right decision with the jets. How much do you know so far?"

"That there's a Plan B," Louis replied, "and we're supposed to be part of it."

Charlie mentally paid respect to his commander. It was wise not to interfere in the politics between intelligence officers, to which Feinman undoubtedly belonged. Remaining vague was the perfect decision.

"That's right." The colonel nodded and gestured behind him to the wall. "We have a finished clone of *Starship 7* on the launch pad. Everything is laid out as you know it from your simulations."

So you stole the plans and simulation protocols from the JSC and copied them, Charlie thought. But he wasn't surprised. The Pentagon had probably always known about every detail of NASA.

"We'd launch first thing tomorrow if we had our way, since we don't have to wait for FAA approval," Feinman continued, clicking his tongue. "But this damn tropical storm is throwing a monkey wrench in the works. So we'll have to wait until the weekend, when it's supposed to clear up."

"The Chinese are also launching on the weekend," noted Miles.

"Yeah, what a fucking joke of fate, eh?" The colonel laughed harshly, almost an unhealthy-sounding cough.

CHAPTER 16

Rebecca told her aide to stay close to the FBI emergency vehicles as they sped along Interstate 4. The rain continued to fall in thick veils a day after the disaster. The windshield wipers struggled to keep up with the masses of water, making nasty juddering noises. Rogers sat leaning forward in the driver's seat, doing his best to stay close enough to the SUV in front of them, which was heading for the downtown Orlando exit. Rebecca couldn't see the three cars in line ahead of that one.

Fortunately, there was hardly any traffic in the middle of the night and they got through relatively quickly. The tip-off from the NSA had only reached them half an hour ago. The fact that the FBI had greeted them less than ten minutes later on the operations center's rooftop helipad spoke volumes about how nervous they were in Washington. When cooperation between the military and the Feds was arranged within minutes, it was clear to everyone involved that something was wrong.

This was also clear to the agents she had briefed regarding the individual they were dealing with. No one asked any questions, even though their target seemed harmless and insignificant on paper.

They turned twice, skidding through deep puddles with squealing tires, and then pulled up next to the three emergency vehicles that stopped in front of the Hilton Garden Inn, blocking the entire driveway in front of the main entrance. Agents in the typical blue jackets with yellow 'FBI' lettering on the back came swarming out of the doors, followed by heavily armored SWAT members with submachine guns.

Rebecca got out and turned briefly to Rogers. "You stay behind the wheel. Do not take any calls."

"Understood."

She then ran to Special Agent Nichols, a broad-shouldered man in his mid-50s with the hard face of a boxer, and went with him past the concierge, who was standing dumbfounded beside a potted plant flanking the entrance. Nichols put a hand to his ear and looked at Rebecca.

"Fourth floor, Room 404," he told her.

She looked at the reception desk, where a stunned and pale-faced receptionist was talking to two agents and holding out key cards.

Rebecca overtook them with Nichols on the way to the elevators.

"SWAT covers the two stairwells," said the special agent, waving his heavily armed colleagues in the direction of the relevant doors. The few guests who were in the lobby at the time seemed to be in a state of shock. A young couple wanted to leave the hotel through the front door, but they were prevented from doing so by a young female agent who was directing all guests to a group of seats in the breakfast area.

Rebecca got into the left elevator with Nichols and two other agents, and four others got into the right elevator.

"May I ask what our target is accused of?" asked the head of operations as they rode upward with soft elevator music.

"Espionage, treason, sabotage of a military facility," she replied curtly.

"Should we have taken more of the SWAT guys with us?"

"Ideally, this will be a surprise and we'll catch him right at the beginning of his flight to China."

"Are you saying the target has something to do with the explosion of the *Artemis* missile?"

"Yes." There was a *bing* and the elevator doors opened. The first SWAT officers came out of the stairwell at the same time. Rebecca was amazed they had made it up here so quickly. She looked at the directional signs for the various rooms and right. Once outside Room 404, she stepped back at Nichols' signal and waited while SWAT personnel and agents positioned themselves to the right and left of the frame. One came down the hallway with a battering ram, waiting for a nod from his supervisor, who in turn looked to Nichols.

Nichols spoke into his headset. "Shut down, now."

The lights on the entire floor went out, along with the electricity. Flashlights were switched on, then the officer with the battering ram was given the order and drove the steel monster forward. There was a loud crash as wood splintered and metal screeched.

The door flew inward and the heavily armed men stormed in.

"FBI! GET ON THE FLOOR!"

"FBI!"

"DOWN! GO, GO!"

Rebecca noticed how her fingers tingled and the hairs on the back of her neck stood up. She wasn't usually involved in operations like this. Normally she researched within the various branches of the military. Ninety-nine percent of the time it was Air Force or Space Force. Adrenaline seemed to be in the air, the taste and smell of violence.

She waited with Nichols and the other agents until they

heard "CLEAR!" shouted from inside and the special agent was reassured by radio that there was no danger.

Then she followed him inside the premises, a suite with a living room, two bedrooms, and a bathroom, all connected by a shared hallway. There were at least two SWAT officers in every room and three in each bedroom. On the far left, a woman sat on the bed holding her arms protectively around two small loudly crying children. Rebecca wasn't interested in them and went to the other bedroom, where their target was standing against the wall in boxer shorts, his arms stretched upward, trembling. Two policemen were pointing their submachine guns at him. A torn nightshirt on the floor indicated that they had not been squeamish when they searched him.

"Dr. Lee Taylor?" Nichols asked sternly.

"Y-Y-Yes?" stammered the NASA technician.

"He's clean," said one of the officers.

"You can stand down. I need to question the suspect," Rebecca said into the room, whereupon Nichols pulled his lips into a frown and met her stare with his own for a few seconds before he nodded reluctantly and gave his men a wave.

When they left the room, Lee Taylor was still standing against the wall, trembling, his hands raised as if his life depended on it, not a sight she would have expected from a shrewd spy. However, it was certainly what a shrewd spy would have her believe.

"You can turn around," she said sternly, which he did. "Sit down."

She pointed to the bed. He sat down and looked at the rumpled bedspread. He had obviously been torn from sleep by the officers. After she nodded briefly, he covered his upper body with the quilted cotton.

"M-may I ask what's going on?" Taylor asked, his voice quavery.

"You were responsible for the final connection check of the outlet valves between the methane tanks and the booster. Is that correct?"

"W-What?"

"Answer *yes* or *no*," she admonished him. "So, were you responsible for the final connection check of the outlet valves?"

"Yes." The engineer sounded like he was going to start crying at any moment. She sincerely hoped he wouldn't. She'd had enough stress already.

"That's remarkable, because you requested a shift change while the booster was being refueled. Why?"

"I ... I ..."

"And why aren't you at home? What are you doing in this hotel room?" Rebecca asked, putting all the coldness into her voice that she had reserved for a traitor of his caliber.

"M-My sister and my nieces were in town for the launch," moaned Lee Taylor. "There's not enough room in my apartment, so she took a suite here in the hotel. When I came back from my shift, I just ... I didn't want to be alone. I was so scared."

"Because of what you did," she speculated.

The engineer hesitated, gulped visibly, and then nodded like a shy dog. She was beginning to find it difficult to imagine him as a hardened spy who had knowingly sent dozens of employees to their deaths.

She continued to press him. "Where were you going from here, huh? To the airport?"

"To the airport? To what? No! What do you think I ...?" His eyes widened. "Do you think I sabotaged the mission?" Now he looked at the door and ruffled his hair. "Oh God! You think I'm a Chinese spy!"

"Yes," she said bluntly. "And believe me, I'm going to find out."

"But I'm not a spy! I may be guilty of ... oh God."

"Guilty of what?" She almost hissed the words and took half a step toward him.

"I ..." Lee Taylor began to cry quietly. His upper body rocked back and forth. "I let Sarah take over, but she just wasn't ready to handle the pressure yet. I think she missed a porous ring on the second visual inspection."

"You left your post and handed it over to Sarah Westerman, even though that was strictly forbidden." Rebecca gave him an even sterner look. "I already know that. Everyone knows."

Taylor buried his face in his hands. "I couldn't stay at my post any longer and had to find a solution." His voice sounded muffled through his fingers.

"You *couldn't* do your job? What do you mean?"

"I can't tell you that."

"Oh, no? That's enough for me now. I'll have you taken to a black site and then my colleagues from interrogation will take care of you." She turned to leave and pulled out her cellphone.

"W-What? Wait!"

Rebecca paused impatiently. She hadn't been bluffing. *"What?"*

"If I tell you, they'll fire me!" the engineer howled. His eyes were moist, the corners of his mouth twitched back and forth.

"If you *don't* tell me, they won't be able to fire you because you'll live in an assisted living facility – at best," she replied.

"I had a panic attack," he finally admitted. "I've been undergoing treatment for it for months and I shouldn't have reported for duty that day."

"Why didn't you inform your managers?"

"I spoke to my psychologist, but it's all covered by patient confidentiality. *I* killed them, it's all my fault." He now began to cry unrestrainedly and was shaken by increasingly violent sobs.

Rebecca dialed Roger's number and instructed her aide to order a search of Taylor's psychologist's office. Half an hour later, spent in the kitchen with Nichols, she got a response. Units of the local police had seen the patient's file thanks to a court order, and Rogers himself had been granted access. Apparently Taylor hadn't been lying.

"Do you still need us here?" the special agent asked as she stared at the kitchen floor and thought.

"Huh?"

"Do you need anything else from the FBI? Otherwise I will pull my people."

"Perhaps. Please wait a moment."

She dialed the number for General Eversman.

"Major. Tell me you have something."

"Negative, sir," she replied. "Dr. Lee Taylor is certainly partly to blame for the disaster, but I don't think he's a spy."

"Are you sure?"

"Well, I can't be one hundred percent positive. However, almost all the evidence speaks against it."

"What do you mean, *almost all?*" the general retorted.

"He could be the best spy I've ever met and have managed to pull the wool over my eyes without even one of my inner alarm bells going off," she explained.

"Bring him in for a full interrogation."

"But sir ..."

"Major," Eversman interrupted her. "The nation is in shock. We need to show that we are active, and we can only do that by *being* active. At worst, we'll have distracted the press a bit and can take our time to find the real suspects."

"That will ruin his career."

"It is already ruined, and the sick bastard has no one but himself to blame." The general hung up.

She stared at her cellphone and thought feverishly before returning to Nichols. "There is something more that you could do for me. You could monitor Taylor's psychologist."

"For what reason?"

"I don't know yet."

Nichols looked at her closely. She expected him to come up with rules and regulations, which she would have understood, but he just looked at the bedroom, at her cellphone, and then back to her eyes. "I'll assign one of my people to this, for twenty-four hours. Unfortunately, that's as much as I can do."

"That's longer than I'll need. Thank you."

The special agent shrugged his shoulders. "I want to find out who betrayed us as much as you do."

Rebecca nodded and then followed her orders. She had the distraught Taylor led away in handcuffs. He no longer seemed to understand where he was or what was going on. And a horde of cameras was waiting for them outside the door.

CHAPTER 17

They spent the first day and night in a four-bedroom house provided by SpaceX. Charlie didn't get much sleep, waking often and pondering as the hours passed, wondering what might be going on at JSC and Kennedy in Florida. He deliberately didn't switch on the news so as not to add to his headache.

On the morning of the third day, they were picked up for the first time. A young Space Command lieutenant took them to a factory space where dozens of Raptor engines were stored. Colonel Feinman was waiting for them in a separate area, visibly protected by uniformed guards. He was standing in front of military transport crates with a handful of soldiers, signing some lists and only noticing them when Louis cleared his throat.

"Ah, there you are." Feinman beckoned them over and, with a flick of his finger, instructed one of his soldiers to open one of the crates.

Charlie stood next to his comrades and clasped his hands behind his back. When the lid came off, he frowned. The unmistakable silhouettes of M16 assault rifles lay in dense polymer mounts, only these specimens were gleaming white.

"Sir?" Louis asked, sounding just as confused as Charlie felt. "Why are you showing us this?"

"These are new specimens from DARPA, developed for use in low-gravity environments," explained Feinman. "Painted white with a particularly heat-resistant paint. All openings and valves are specially sealed against micro-dust, and the shock pads for the shoulder have been provided with special damping."

"Wait a minute," Charlie intervened. "You want us to take *weapons* to the moon? Are you *insane*?"

He didn't even realize he'd made a mistake as he stared at the assault rifles in disbelief. The colonel's lips narrowed. If Charlie had still been on active duty, he would probably have had to listen to a very special lecture and endure an informal disciplinary session.

"You may not be in the Corps anymore, Sergeant," Feinman said, giving him a withering look, "but I'm still the one sending you up there."

"It doesn't look to me like you have a choice, with all due respect," Charlie replied. "And no, I'm no longer in the Corps, and I certainly won't be taking a weapon into space with me."

"He's right," Anne agreed. "We would be setting a precedent that should never be set. The Outer Space Treaty of 1967 prohibits military activities in space – including the moon and other celestial bodies."

"I know the old document. In the section dealing with weapons, there is explicit mention only of nuclear weapons and that no military bases may be set up or exercises held," the colonel insisted.

"It's clear that an armed mission is a military mission!" Charlie roared. "The Chinese aren't stupid! If they get wind of this, we'll have a whole new set of problems."

"You think Beijing won't follow suit if we take this step?" Anne said angrily. She shook her head vigorously.

"There's no way I'm taking a damned weapon to the moon."

"Amen." Charlie crossed his arms in front of his chest and looked at the mission commander. Louis had remained conspicuously quiet and was staring thoughtfully at the rifles. Feinman was grinding his jaws and seemed on the verge of an angry discourse. But instead he also looked at the former Navy pilot.

"Louis," Anne said, trying to rouse him from his trance-like state. "Tell him that this is a totally stupid idea."

"Is it?" Louis turned to them and tilted his head.

"You can't be serious!" said Charlie and Anne at the same time.

"We don't have to use them. But it's better to at least have them with us. We can set maximally strict rules for their use. For example, if we are attacked. Then it wouldn't be bad if we could defend ourselves, would it?"

"But we would have brought them in and broken the treaty. *We* would be the ones not abiding by international treaties and taking the first step toward a dangerous escalation," Anne reminded their commander. She sounded desperate.

"No. The precedent would be to show the weapons. The next would be to use them," Louis insisted. "They remain locked and secured. Only if there's an absolute emergency will we use them. Look what the Chinese are doing: The constant hacking attacks on NASA and the Pentagon, the sabotage of our launch ..."

"We don't know that for sure yet."

"The news is full of it. Every expert agrees that it would be far too much of a coincidence for a crappy flow valve to fail. These things are constantly being checked and replaced. Don't tell me you don't trust the Chinese to do that."

"Of course we wouldn't put it past them," Charlie replied

angrily. "But I wouldn't put it past *us* either. And so far, it's just an accusation made in an extreme situation. We can't use something like that as the basis for a momentous decision like *this*." He pointed at the guns as if they were poisonous snakes.

"I'm not contradicting you. And I don't disagree with you either, Anne. But I haven't heard any argument against having them on board as insurance and not using them unless absolutely necessary."

Feinman nodded with satisfaction while Louis said this, and neither Charlie nor Anne offered an immediate disagreement.

Charlie would have liked to scream in frustration. The joy and relief that they had a chance of eliciting the alien object's secrets and that he himself was suddenly back in the front row threatened to bubble over. But the thought that they could unleash a war on the moon, which at worst would lead to a nuclear missile exchange on Earth, was terrifying. At the same time, Louis was not wrong, and he was not an irrational man.

"It would be naïve to think that our Chinese counterparts aren't thinking along the same line," Louis continued in a conciliatory tone. "I'd bet big bucks that they'll be taking weapons themselves."

"We can't know that," Anne protested, but she no longer sounded so resolute.

"But would you bet your life – and the success of the mission – on them making the sensible decision and playing their cards straight? After all the political foreplay and hardball involved in this race to the moon?" asked Louis. "Would you bet *our* lives on it just so we don't break the contract, even though in the most likely scenario no one would ever find out?"

"No," she admitted quietly after hearing his points.

"I still don't like it," Charlie insisted. "Space should be

explored peacefully. We mustn't spoil the moon with our weapons and violence."

"And we won't. Unless they force us to," Louis assured him.

"You will not be authorized to initiate armed force against any taikonauts you may encounter," Feinman echoed. He sounded calm and level-headed now, which was strange coming from him. Charlie didn't buy the secret agent's façade for a second, no matter how convincingly it was played.

"Tight rules," Charlie demanded. "And *we* formulate them."

Feinman hesitated, looked at Louis, who was already nodding, and then sighed. "You have until tomorrow morning. We've been given a launch date and time. Friday, O six hundred hours."

"That's the day after tomorrow!" blurted Miles, who had been conspicuously silent this whole time.

"That's why you only have until tomorrow morning," said the colonel, pointing to the box. "We need time to install it and record the rules for its use in the standard on-board protocols."

Colonel Feinman gave the soldier at the crate a wave, whereupon he resealed it.

"Does SpaceX even know about this?" Anne inquired.

"No. Our conversation with Musk was not particularly ... purposeful."

"He refused," Charlie translated. "And that's the right thing to do."

"I'm not reopening the discussion. We agreed that we weren't going to agree. But that shouldn't concern you." With that, the colonel left the tent, followed by some of his soldiers. The others began to load the crates onto electric sleds.

"I don't like it," grumbled Charlie. "Not one bit."

"The company that's sending us up there doesn't know

every detail about the cargo?" asked Anne, snorting. "What could possibly go wrong?"

"You're right," said Miles, making a worried face. "That's not a good idea. Not at all. I can't think of a time when even the tiniest detail of a space mission wasn't recorded and accounted for."

"The Space Force is not stupid." Louis shook his head. "They'll give them the correct data on mass and anchoring and make sure that nothing can shift around. And it won't be the only secret component on board. They launch missiles with payloads from the Pentagon every week that are so secret that nobody here knows about them."

Charlie wanted to disagree, but Louis was right. Apart from that, contraband also made it onto the ISS now and again. Mission parameters were always tight, but not so tight that they missed their orbit because there was a bottle of vodka on board.

"The decision has been made. So we need to start formulating the rules of engagement," Louis continued, "and preparing for the launch."

CHAPTER 18

Rebecca sat in her office on the 3rd floor of Mission Control in Houston and went through the mission report for the third time. She was doing what she did best. Her specialty was finding mistakes, inconsistencies, something that anyone else would have overlooked, but she never did. But today, she just couldn't focus on it, which was a clear indicator that something was wrong.

Her eyes were exhausted as she punched holes in the printed papers, one stack after the next, and clipped them into the dark brown military binder with the Space Force seal. Then she stood up and paced back and forth along the windowless wall.

Lee Taylor was not a spy. Of that much she was certain. Nevertheless, the circumstances under which he had left his job were suspicious. But that didn't change the fact that his alibis were watertight, and she had come face to face with him. This man was a lot of things, but no way was he a spy, because that required strong nerves.

There was a knock on the door.

"Come in."

Lieutenant Rogers poked his head in and looked for her. "Uhh, Major, the colonel wants to see you."

"Feinman?" she asked in surprise. "Shouldn't he be in Boca Chica or Hawthorne overseeing the launch?"

Rogers just shrugged helplessly, so she nodded, "Thank you."

Her adjutant withdrew.

Feinman was like a ghost, constantly popping up everywhere when you least expected him. She did not like him, precisely because he was a slippery-fish sort of guy. Someone high up in the Pentagon had to have his hand on him, probably even including access to black budgets. That was something even she was denied, despite her contacts, including General Eversman. But Feinman had been in the game longer and had a head start. She wouldn't be surprised if he called her in just to show her that he seemed to be everywhere at once.

She took the file containing her and Special Agent Nichols' mission report from the desk and tucked it under her arm before leaving the office and walking toward the other end of the hallway.

Lieutenant Colonel Collins, Feinman's 'aide-de-camp' in Houston, had set up an office for him in Jessica Miller's office as a show of force. The administrator had been banished to Washington – or moved to NASA headquarters for *administrative duties*, as the official press release had announced. Of course, the truth lay elsewhere.

After the loss of the crew and the rocket, it was clear in Washington that heads had to roll, and the ongoing concern about an act of sabotage by the Chinese was so great that NASA was no longer trusted by those in the White House to protect itself adequately and make the right decisions. Since then, the Space Force had been back in charge.

Operationally, not much changed, except that Lieutenant

Colonel Collins chaired the leadership meetings and all communications were monitored. Private cellphones were not allowed on the premises, and security precautions had been redoubled.

Rebecca reached the door, which still read 'Jessica Miller, Administrator,' and knocked.

She heard Feinman's gruff voice. "Come in!"

"Colonel," she said as she entered, saluted, and closed the door behind her.

He raised his hand carelessly to his forehead and waved a mere hint of a salute. The colonel sat behind the desk, on which there was a whole jumble of different colored printouts, some of which were marked with colored Post-it notes. There were piles of daily newspapers on the phones to the right.

Feinman motioned her closer, but not for her to sit down. So she stood in front of the table and assumed an at-ease stance with her hands linked behind her back and her chin jutted forward.

First, he lifted the top newspaper from the pile.

"FBI looking for spies in Houston. What's the Space Force got to do with it?" He read out the headline and tossed the paper in front of her on the small desk area that was free. It was the New York Times. She could clearly see the snapshot on the front page showing her leaving the hotel with Nichols and Taylor.

"FBI and Space Force arrest NASA engineer. A Chinese spy?" he continued, tossing the Wall Street Journal on top of the Times. A similar picture adorned the front page, showing a lost- and helpless-looking Lee Taylor.

"Here, this is the best one," Feinman said, lifting the next paper from the stack and reading aloud: "Is the Pentagon using the FBI for a new J. Edgar Hoover-style purge?"

"I strictly followed the rules of engagement, sir," Rebecca replied, ignoring the latest frontpage photo. She didn't appreciate it when someone made a mockery of reprimanding her.

"Oh, did you? Then how come the press found out about it? And so quickly that they were *all* there before you even left the damn hotel?"

"I don't know, sir. But I'm sure there's an explanation."

"Yes, there is. You should have had the area cordoned off."

"Sir?"

"The damn driveway to the hotel. No journalist should have been on it. Now the press is starting to dig. We're constantly getting requests for commentary, but we need as little attention as possible so as not to scare off potential spies and give them clues through television."

"With respect, Colonel, I'm a trained Air Force intelligence officer, not a federal police officer. I made a request to the FBI, which was coordinated with you ..."

"With my *office*," he corrected her, and she immediately grasped the nature of the conversation. Someone in Washington or Arlington was angry about the journalistic fallout, and Feinman had no interest in getting hit by the spit-spray from his superiors. Meaning she was to become his shield.

"You were not available."

"But the general was." The colonel glared at her with his little piggy eyes, in which there was much more intelligence than it seemed. "You called him directly."

Rebecca's expression remained impassive, even though it took great effort not to grimace. He felt ignored. But that wasn't something that would move him to a reprimand like this. Not as a seasoned secret agent whose games were never based on emotion, but always on calculation.

He wanted to get rid of her, and she was sure that he had long since spun the perfect web.

"I informed the general that I had no hands-on responsibility whatsoever because you didn't involve me," he explained unsurprisingly. "But the general knew that, because you spoke to him directly from the hotel room."

Rebecca growled inwardly. She had made a mistake. Only a small one, but it was enough to let him make a fool out of her. The only question was why Feinman so badly wanted to get rid of her.

"I can see that you understand. Good," the colonel concluded smugly, leaning back in Miller's office chair. He planted his elbows on the armrests and folded his hands in front of his face like a coach contemplating what to do with a player who was late for training.

"I'm the best tool you have at your disposal to find potential spies," she said. "If you feel you need to shut me down for any reason, you should keep that in mind."

"I've just given you the reason."

"Of course." She made no effort to hide the irony in her voice.

He leaned forward. "I'm sending you back to the Pentagon. From there you can follow our efforts and prepare them for the general."

"I'm supposed to push papers."

"You're supposed to help from your desk. Then you can't make any mistakes in the field. You are not trained for that anyway, as you just said, right?" asked Feinman.

He had outmaneuvered her again. Something like anger rose up in her. It was an unusual emotion for her, one she was not used to. Rebecca bit her lower lip and nodded. "Of course, Colonel. Anything else?"

"No, you may go. There's a car waiting for you downstairs to take you to the airport." Feinman pretended to have lost interest in the conversation and waved her off with his right hand, while already opening one of the many files with his left and beginning to read.

Rebecca saluted and clicked her heels together before executing a military about-face and leaving the office.

Rogers was waiting for her in the hallway and knew her

well enough to keep quiet. He walked silently beside her as she returned to her small office to pack her things. As soon as she closed the door, she put her laptop and work phone in her Tempest bag. It looked like a simple leather bag, but the fabric was interwoven with metal and carbon fibers that blocked NATO-standard signals. She also asked Rogers to put his phones inside. Then she zipped it up and stepped close to her aide.

"Go to the airport and get some burner phones. Four of them, and eight SIM cards," she told him. "Then wait for me in the entrance area."

The lieutenant knew when not to ask questions and just nodded without asking for either of his phones back. After he left the office, she waited another ten minutes, then took her personal phone out of her pocket and adjusted the fit of her uniform before going downstairs.

CHAPTER 19

"Hawthorne, *Liberty*," Louis said, checking the pressure gauge readings for the tank valves. "All values nominal."

The refueling of the *Liberty* was almost complete. Charlie thought the name of their spaceship was terribly cheesy, but he was aware that they had several overlapping missions to accomplish: to investigate, perhaps even recover, an alien artifact from the Chinese; and to show the world that America still had a well-founded claim to leadership in geopolitics and cultural policy. And, whether they wanted it or not, the whole circus was a PR show for the big political world stage.

"Got it. Looks good, *Liberty*," replied the muffled voice of the launch director from the speakers.

"It's really time," said Anne, who was strapped in on the far right next to Charlie. The row of seats where they had been secured had been moved into the take-off position so that they were now lying on their backs and looking at the displays above them. Everything was the same, of course, as in the mock-ups and simulators.

"Oh, yes," Miles rejoiced. "And the Chinese don't fly out until the day after tomorrow."

"God bless the weather." You could tell from Anne's voice that she was grinning. Charlie couldn't help but feel a certain sense of triumph as well. The tropical storm had passed more quickly than expected because it had turned south off the Texas coast – unlike the meteorological forecasts had predicted. As they had been driven to the launch pad, they had been able to see the dark mountains of cloud in the distance as a reminder of what might have been.

"Now the pressure is on. This time it will work," Miles said with certainty. However, his enthusiasm – whether genuine or not – could not hide the fact that each of them had their own worries about possibly ending up in a scorching fireball like their comrades on the primary crew. The possibility of another mistake or act of sabotage loomed over them and the mission, and there was nothing they could do about it.

Charlie's palms had become damp in the semi-flexible gloves of his white spacesuit, and he was much hotter than he had been in even the most stressful simulations.

Once we're in orbit, I'll be able to relax, he told himself. And if something did happen, he probably wouldn't even notice it and, unlike his comrades, he wouldn't leave behind a spouse or children. His sister, Molly, would miss him, but it wouldn't break her. They had drifted too far apart in recent years for that. His dream of joining the astronaut corps had demanded everything from him, including any social life.

"*Liberty*, refueling complete," announced the launch director from Hawthorne, interrupting Charlie's musings.

"Confirmed, Hawthorne," Louis said with the same calm professionalism. "Everything looks good from our side. Pressure in the tanks stable and within the norm, valve closures on contact, temperature green in all areas."

"Thank you, *Liberty*. We'll stay on the starting line."

The countdown was now at T minus ten minutes. Charlie began to knead his hands. Now the cameras were switched on as planned. There had been long discussions about whether or not to broadcast the take-off and flight on television and the Internet. The danger was that if it failed again, the whole of America would be even more embarrassed and a new national trauma could arise. But that was already the case since the Cape Canaveral disaster, and this was their best and possibly only chance to heal it. If they succeeded, it would restore optimism to the nation and the entire West and create a wave of euphoria in place of dejection.

At least that was the idea. Bet it all on one card, bet it all on victory. In ten minutes they would find out whether the President had made the right decision.

"Hello out there," Anne said into the camera above her console area. She had been chosen to make this speech after a long debate as to whether she, as the female crew member and a popular former Youtuber, should take this role, or Louis as commander. In the end, however, the crew had agreed that Anne was the right choice and so she had prevailed.

"Surprise, I hope. We are here on the launch pad in Boca Chica and are ready for the final countdown. We are setting off for the moon. For humanity. The loss of our friends has hit us hard. Whatever you have felt, we have felt. Whatever worries you have had have been on our minds and in our hearts. I apologize to you on behalf of everyone involved that we had to keep this replacement mission a secret from you and hope that you can understand our motivations.

"Today is a special day. We are going to the moon for the first time in fifty-one years, when Gene Cernan was the last man to leave the moon on Apollo 17. I want to tell you what his last radio message from the lunar surface was then: *Bob, this is Gene, and I'm on the surface. As I take man's last step from the surface back home for some time to come — but we believe not too long into the future — I'd like to just [say] what I believe history will record: that America's challenge of today has forged man's destiny of tomorrow. And, as we leave the moon at [the valley] Taurus-Littrow, we leave as we came and, God willing, as we shall return, with peace and hope for all mankind. Godspeed, the crew of Apollo 17."*

Anne made a rhetorical pause so that Cernan's words could take effect. Charlie had to admit that he hadn't remembered this quote.

"'Peace and hope for all mankind.' That's what Cernan wanted and that's what we're looking for," Anne continued. "Perhaps the greatest mystery in history awaits us and we are determined to unravel it for the peaceful future of us all. Without you out there, however, none of this would be possible.

"We have the privilege of carrying out your mission, but you have financed it with your tax dollars. We may be shot to the moon by an explosive fuel mixture, but we are carried by you. For this we thank you and take you with us on our journey. God bless this mission, God bless you and all those who have given their sweat and blood to get us back to the moon."

Charlie turned his head to Anne as best he could and nodded approvingly at her. That was a good speech. Above all, it had been free of any military rhetoric, which he particularly liked – probably also because the opposite might be the case with Feinman. Who knew what was going on inside the colonel's mind?

"The last minute is fast approaching," Louis said as he held out his right hand. Miles took it with his left and held out his right to Charlie, who took it and reached over to Anne so all four of them were linked. As there was now nothing more to do on their part except read the rather tidy data from their flight displays, he was glad of the contact. Knowing he was between comrades and friends – the preceding week had at last made them into such – felt right.

"T-minus one minute," said the launch director calmly. "Starship in start-up."

Charlie took a deep breath.

Hawthorne announced, "Flight computer has control."

Charlie let out a long exhale. Adrenaline shot through his veins. Now the flight computer had taken over and that meant there were only 30 seconds left.

"Ignition!" Louis shouted at the same time as the launch director.

The 33 Raptor engines 120 meters below them roared to life. Turbopumps shot liquid methane into a fuel-enriched antechamber, while liquid oxygen was simultaneously pumped into its antechamber and the two fuels met in the main combustion chamber via a network of turbines and control valves. In the combustion chamber, they reacted to form a hot plasma mixture, which was ejected from the nacelles in the heat exchanger and generated 230 tons of thrust in each of the Raptors.

Everything began to wobble and shake. A little at first, then more and more. Charlie was pressed firmly into his seat, then the almost 7,600 tons of thrust became more and more palpable, as if a giant had settled onto his chest. He held his companions' hands tightly and concentrated on the displays – all nominal – so as not to imagine the unprecedented elemental force they were riding toward the vacuum.

"Breaking the sound barrier," said the launch director in his typically soporific voice.

So fast, thought Charlie.

"Max q reached."

The maximum dynamic pressure was the point at which the speed of their starship and its booster in combination with air resistance generated the highest aerodynamic pressure. Due to the highest resistance from the air molecules, the structural load on their vehicle was never stronger than at that point.

This was a critical part of the journey, but they were still alive and the air resistance had begun dropping as they reached altitudes where the molecular density was significantly lower and continuing to decrease.

A few minutes later, the second welcomed message came from Hawthorne just as an only slightly perceptible jolt went through the cockpit: "Main engine separation complete."

The Super Heavy Booster had broken away from them and lurched back toward the Pacific.

"Second stage ignition successful."

Their own Raptor engines had ignited and accelerated them further toward their first target orbit, which they would gradually increase according to the Hohmann transfer protocol.

The speed display read 28,311 kilometers per hour – their orbital speed around the center of the Earth – they had arrived in orbit.

It had happened so quickly.

"*Liberty*, Hawthorne. Congratulations on achieving orbit!" Now the launch director sounded almost exuberant by his standards.

Charlie allowed himself a loud cheer and the others immediately joined in.

"Hawthorne, *Liberty*," Louis said with a relieved laugh. "We're on Go!"

CHAPTER 20

C harlie hovered in front of one of the large windows in the huge cockpit of the *Liberty,* which was – even without its gigantic Super Heavy Booster – a real monster.

They had retracted their row of reclinable seats and folded them against the wall, giving themselves as much room as possible. It was easy to see that this spaceship had been designed for future Mars missions with as many as 100 astronauts per flight. Although the cockpit was only in one half of the top, there was enough space to float around next to the emergency equipment and the many devices attached to the wall with nets.

They had been circling Earth and increasing their orbit for several hours. Ten minutes ago, as pilot of the *Liberty,* it had officially been Louis's job to initiate the Hohmann transfer to the moon, even though he had basically just confirmed with the on-board computer the right point at which he should initiate the appropriate thrust. He had done so, and accelerated them parallel to the orbit at perigee, so that their orbit had since stretched into an ellipse that would almost reach the moon at the calculated end point, the apogee, which currently continuing to move toward this point – just like them. Once they were there, they would have to turn around and apply thrust again to slow down and transfer into their orbit around the moon. But that time was four days in the future.

It was now Charlie's job to explain all of that, as it was his PR time for the livestream.

"Hello out there," he said with a broad smile in Anne's direction. She pointed the small camera at him and gave him a thumbs-up. "We're currently flying eight hundred kilometers above you at a speed of twenty-eight thousand kilometers per hour. That probably sounds pretty crazy to you, but since we don't have to fight any air molecules out here, there's nothing that could slow us down or be dangerous. Apart from space debris, but that's a problem Miles will talk to you about later."

Charlie pointed behind him through the window. "Today I want to explain to you, simply and clearly, how we get from here to the moon and why it takes four days. Some people have said it's surprisingly slow. Well, we could actually do it faster, but it would be more fuel-intensive and every rocket – that's the *Liberty* in principle – is in a dilemma: it burns something and shoots the plasma out the back to *push* us forward.

"Basically, you don't even have to burn anything. Think of a garden hose that shoots water out with a lot of pressure. The hose will move in the opposite direction. But let's stick to burning for now. We work with methane and oxygen here on the *Liberty*. The faster we want to fly, the more of it we have to burn and the amount of fuel required increases with the mass. But more fuel means more mass, which means more fuel is needed – you can see the dilemma. Our Starship therefore travels to the moon as energy-efficiently as possible with the help of translunar injection, according to the Hohmann transfer principle.

"And it works like this: Imagine throwing a ball up into the air. First it goes fast, then slower, and as it nears its apex, where it will begin to come back down, it is at its slowest – until gravity pulls it back down. Then it speeds up as it drops. In our case, the fastest point – we are the ball in this analogy – is on this side of the Earth. We are now, at perigee, as close to it as we will ever get and we have accelerated our flight to increase our orbit. We have simply turned a circular orbit into an elongated ellipse, toward the end point of which both we and the moon are now moving in a circular orbit around the Earth. This is the apogee of our journey, the furthest point from Earth. Like the ball, we have let gravity help us, saving us valuable fuel. To begin to orbit the moon, we have to 'catch' it, so to speak, which means that we adjust our speed at the end with a braking thrust so that we fly around the Earth at the same speed as the moon. That way, we are in the same orbit and can then begin to circle our target destination."

Charlie, with his feet hooked onto a handhold, clapped his hands and then spread them out. "That's the physics behind our transfer to the moon. It may take a while, but we'll have plenty of time up here to get used to the weightlessness and prepare everything for landing. I would also like to tell you that we are happy to have you with us virtually on this journey, because we are always aware that we are not here for ourselves, but for all of you. Whatever we discover belongs to all of humanity and our common future."

Anne grimaced slightly but nodded. She knew that some people in Washington and in the Space Force would not be at all happy about his choice of words, but she agreed with him. Charlie didn't care. He was a patriot, otherwise he wouldn't have served in the Marine Corps, but first and foremost, he was human. That would never change.

When Anne had said a few more things to the camera and then handed it over to Miles, who explained something about the cockpit – of course only things that the Chinese were allowed to know or already knew anyway – she hovered very close to him.

"You really have balls," she said appreciatively and grinned.

"What are they supposed to do? Shut me up because they don't like my opinion?" Charlie snorted. "That sounds to me like something the regime in Beijing would do and what we, the democratic West, supposedly stand against. We're here in the name of freedom and democracy."

"So we can exemplify both." Anne nodded. "Have you heard yet? The Chinese launch date has been set. And the name of their spaceship, too."

"No, I was preparing for my little speech."

"*Celestial Dragon*. In twenty-eight hours."

"*Celestial Dragon*," he repeated. "Doesn't sound very peaceful."

"There are many opinions on this, from what I've heard. The dragon has always stood for imperial power in China and power in general. But a *celestial* dragon could also be a connection between the divine and the earthly. In Chinese, contextuality is always decisive. Even more so than in our language."

"So only the leadership in Beijing knows what is meant by it." Charlie sighed and looked out at their beautiful planet. It looked delicate and fragile with its thin layer of air. It seemed like a miracle that, due to gravity alone, those volatile gas molecules did not simply escape into the endless darkness of the vacuum. Instead, they formed a tiny dome of oxygen and nitrogen around this blue ball of stone, water, and soil. It was nothing short of a miracle, and a single glance from up here was enough to make anyone realize that. "It's amazing."

"What do you mean?" Anne hovered very close to him and looked through the window. Their cheeks were almost touching.

"The Earth's crust consists almost entirely of silicate rock, iron, aluminum, and other metals and elements. The core is made of iron and nickel. Above that is a tiny layer of rock, iron, magnesium, and nickel – the mantle. And only above that is what we see. Soil and dust that is so thin that a breeze could carry it all away. What we see, what the plants grow on, makes up only 0.005 percent of the Earth's crust and only one half to one percent of the total mass of our planet."

"Right. It's only a ball of stone in the void with some dust sprinkled on top, held together by a layer of light gas molecules," Anne said, nodding. "It's so fragile."

"And we can't think of anything better than threatening each other, elevating our ideas to ideologies, and trying to impose them on those who think differently. We're a strange species," said Charlie, suppressing a sigh. He didn't want to sound fatalistic, but it was difficult not to be annoyed by human narrow-mindedness when you saw this fragile beauty in front of you. All that life, the rich colors amidst the sheer endless darkness.

"I'm sure we'll get our act together."

Charlie turned his head and looked at Anne. Only a few centimeters separated them. The blue glow of Earth shimmered on her pale skin in a pleasant aquamarine hue and gave her an extraterrestrial quality.

"What makes you so sure?"

"In the end, the good in us always wins." She returned his gaze and put on a broad smile. "Cuban Missile Crisis – almost a nuclear war. Cooler heads prevailed. In the end, we're all in the same boat and have no interest in leaving our children a smoking wasteland."

"I hope it will be the same this time. The stakes are pretty high. Bloc thinking is stronger than it's been since the Cold War, and now it's about alien technology... It sounds so totally unreal when I say that."

"Speaking of which," said Anne, "we should be able to see the moon soon."

CHAPTER 21

They spent the next couple of days doing more livestreams to keep the public on board in more ways than one. They explained many procedures that did not reveal sensitive information, taught viewers simple orbital mechanics and space facts, played a little with fluids and objects in zero gravity, and answered questions from viewers.

In between, during the timeouts, they had time for themselves and some personal privacy. They ate together and talked a lot, but not about what might await them. Charlie was aware that each of his companions had their own thoughts about what might happen as soon as their boots touched the moon's surface.

But no one knew, so they didn't drive themselves crazy with speculation. Instead, they laughed about their experiences during training and talked about their childhood heroes, especially Armstrong, Aldrin, and Collins. It even got humorous at times when they told each other stories from their time in the armed forces and the three former officers teased him for 'only' being a master sergeant.

It was an amazingly 'normal' time, Charlie thought, as if they were on an exciting journey together. But none of it was normal, and the further away from Earth they got, the more they realized that. The conversations became shorter, the laughter quieter, the somber expressions more frequent.

They could no longer see their home from the second day onward due to the orientation of the *Liberty,* but by then Earth had shrunk to the size of an apple while the moon had continued to grow. It was now glowing white in the darkness in front of the cockpit, as large as an orange and similarly uneven. The craters stood out clearly like dark oceans. A dark crescent marked the terminator, where shadow and sunlight formed a sharp boundary. Somewhere at the south pole, very close to the Shackleton Crater, was their landing zone.

The only time when nothing was normal came in the middle of the second day with the launch of the *Celestial Dragon.* Charlie had mixed feelings as he sat in front of the screen with the others to watch the television images that Beijing was broadcasting on state television.

The huge 'Long March' rocket stood in the middle of the green forest that surrounded the Wenchang Space Launch Site with its tiny space capsule and attached landing module compared to its starship. On the one hand, he hoped that the taikonauts would succeed with the launch, because the stakes were just as high for them as they were for him and his comrades. On the other hand, there was a little voice inside him that wished for failure so that there would be no potential conflict.

But he did not allow himself to think these unkind thoughts. Whether Chinese or American, people were people, and he didn't wish death on anyone. Besides, he had no way of knowing what would happen if the *Celestial Dragon* exploded. It was possible that the mutual accusations of espionage and sabotage between the power blocs would boil over and escalate even further. Perhaps the regime in Beijing would see itself with its back to the wall and decided to flee forward in order to save face and not lose ground.

So much of this was all-but-literally written in the stars.

The launch was successful, without incident, and the Chinese rocket made it into orbit. According to Chinese television and the speculation of Western experts, the *Celestial Dragon was* now also on course for the moon, two and a half days behind *Liberty*. The knowledge that the taikonauts were now hot on their heels changed something in him. He felt hunted, under pressure, and he could sense that the others felt the same way.

When they crawled out of their sleeping bags on the fourth day, the moon filled most of the cockpit windows and sent so much reflected light into the cockpit that they all looked pale as corpses.

"Soon it will be time for our braking maneuver," Louis announced with unmistakable anticipation in his voice. Charlie felt the same way. The four days had been bearable, but the excitement had been steadily building, and it was time they got closer to their answers.

So, they washed themselves with wet wipes, brushed their teeth, combed their hair if necessary, and ate something. Then they moved the row of seats back to the launch configuration and resumed their places with seatbelts fastened so that they wouldn't float away.

"Houston, *Liberty*," Louis said. "We're online."

"Good morning, *Liberty*. How are things with you? Everything ready for the final approach?" Harry's voice rang in their ears. Mission Control in Houston had taken over from Launch Control in Hawthorne once they had reached Earth orbit, so Harry's presence, at least audibly, had been very familiar over the last few days.

"Hi, Harry. Nice to hear from you! We slept well and are

ready for the finale. The vector data looks good. All systems *go.*"

"Perfect. That's what I wanted to hear. Hang tight, you're almost there."

"Fuel lines are open," Miles said, taking a cue from Louis. "Valve controls active, on-board computer reports no errors."

"Temperature in the combustion chambers constant, Draco maneuvering thrusters online and ready," Anne added.

Charlie once again felt a little useless because he had no direct function on this part of the journey. Of course he was involved in simple maintenance and control tasks – there was no waste of manpower – but most of the technical tasks fell to the three former pilots and engineers. If all went well, his main role as a medic specializing in space missions would not be needed.

"Very nice," Louis said. "Mission control, we are ready for the braking maneuver. Whenever you give the *Go,* we'll initiate the turn and braking thrust." Due to the delay of a little less than a second that the radio signal took from the ship to Houston and then the same time back, there was always a small gap. It had grown gradually longer during the journey and made them realize just how far they had flown.

"Good. Then have all the trajectory data spit out one last time and check it manually," ordered the flight director, Miguel Cortez, in a calm voice.

Charlie thought Louis was going to sigh, but he just nodded and called up the relevant displays, which showed their speed data, their relative position in relation to the Earth and moon, the distance they had traveled, the distance remaining to the apogee of their journey, and the calculated gravitational influence on their trajectory through the Earth and the moon. The columns of numbers seemed almost endless and the graphic representations no less overwhelming, but Charlie understood every single one of them; no question he had trained long enough for this!

"All right, you've heard Flight Control. Everything is being checked manually. We have forty minutes until the last possible point for initiating the braking maneuver," Louis said. "So take your time. We want to get this right."

They all knew at that moment that the on-board computer, with its highly developed artificial intelligence, could calculate much more efficiently than they could, but the guidelines were clear. Every step had to be checked by the astronauts.

So they began to evaluate the relevant data, put it into relation, and make calculations to be able to draw conclusions as to whether everything that was shown to them with green lights was correct.

"There's a mistake," Miles said suddenly. Charlie thought it was a bad joke at first, but when he turned his head to the left and looked his comrade in the face, he noticed the deep furrows on his forehead.

"A mistake?" Louis asked incredulously.

"Yes. I've gone through it three times now. The navigation parameter data is incorrect. Here." Miles pointed to a long sequence of numbers. These were the delta-V calculations, the velocity changes required to successfully complete the Hohmann transfer and enter lunar orbit. "My delta-V calculations differ from what is written here. If I use our distance traveled and velocity, something is wrong. It's just a small deviation from where my calculations say we should be and where the on-board computer thinks we are."

"Hmm," Louis said.

"He's right," said Anne, running her fingers through the menus on the touch display in front of her face. "There are small discrepancies in the sensor data. Slight fluctuations in the gyroscopes and accelerometers."

"An unintentional twist?" Charlie asked.

She nodded. "It's possible that one of the Draco jets fired for too long when we adjusted our position after initiating the transfer trajectory. Half a second too much would have been enough to send us into a spin – just slightly enough for us not to notice when looking through the window."

"No, that would be negligible," Miles countered, shaking his head. "Even a subtle rotation wouldn't explain the deviation in our orbit. Not with the differences in distance."

"Then what?"

"The solar and infrared sensors." Louis let out a low growl and called up the corresponding sensor data on all the displays. Charlie didn't see it until his third glance. The solar radiation was too strong for their current position. It should have been steadily decreasing. In absolute terms, it was minute fractions of a percentile, but measurable for the very finely calibrated sensors.

"If they detected too much radiation, then the on-board computer thought we were further away from the moon than we in fact were," said Miles. "So it increased the acceleration slightly to compensate for the incorrectly assumed discrepancy and catch up so that we could return to the transfer orbit."

"Shit," Louis said. "That would mean we're too far."

"Yes," confirmed the former pilot.

"Uhh, Houston, did you get that? We have a problem here."

"Yes," said the flight director after a two-second delay. "Our teams are already on it. Give us a few minutes."

"All right, Houston, we'll recheck everything, just to be on the safe side." Louis looked at them and wiped a drop of sweat from his forehead. "All right, then. Let's do it again. We need to be sure."

They began to recalculate, but ten minutes later it was clear that they had flown too fast and therefore too far. Their elliptical orbit was so elongated that they would shoot past the moon if they didn't act quickly enough – if it wasn't already too late. In that case, they would hurtle into the endless nothingness of space until they ran out of oxygen or water and the *Liberty* would fly on for millions of years until it was attracted and captured by the gravity of a distant sun or gas giant. But given the emptiness of space, even that was unlikely.

A scary idea.

"*Liberty*, this is Flight Control. We've been able to isolate the problem. It is probably an unforeseen reflection from the *Liberty's* hull, which has led to a tiny deviation in the infrared sensors. We have calculated a solution, but you will have to use up a large part of your remaining fuel supply and initiate braking within the next four minutes and change the angle to precisely match our specifications. We are currently sending the data to the on-board computer."

Louis waited to make sure Flight Control was finished with the announcement. Then he replied: "Shall we check everything again?"

A few moments of silence, followed by, "Negative, *Liberty*. There is not enough time. We have accounted for the underestimated reflection rate of your hull and adjusted the data of the infrared and solar sensors accordingly. As soon as we have time, we'll send you an update for the sensor software. Right now, we all have to trust our team to have calculated correctly. The computers have confirmed it."

"All right, then." Louis took a deep breath and looked at the new trajectory data. A white dashed line showed their originally planned route, which should have taken them directly to the moon. A dashed red line marked the direction they were currently heading – out of the Earth's gravitational funnel and the moon's sphere of influence, into the void.

Looking at the trajectory, Charlie realized another problem: they would get much too close to the moon if they didn't counter-steer. Ideally, they would have reached it at the target point in its orbital path, but now they were faster, which meant that they would reach its position before it did. If you thought of the moon as a moving truck, then they were a small scooter trying to catch up with the truck at a certain place by adjusting their speed and driving parallel to it, ultimately to grab hold of it. Now they were going too fast and would soon pass the area the truck was speeding toward: directly in front of it on its path.

"Risky," Miles remarked after a few minutes. "But doable. We change the angle by 1.2 degrees and accelerate for eight seconds, then we turn around and start the braking thrust in twenty minutes. We're using lunar gravity to help with the braking. That's pretty daring."

"It's our only chance. Otherwise we won't have enough fuel for the landing," Anne informed them, pointing to the predicted fuel quantities once the maneuver was complete.

Louis looked at his watch. "We still have thirty seconds until the designated starting point of the maneuver. Any objections?"

Miles and Anne shook their heads. Louis looked at him too, and Charlie responded likewise.

"All right, then." Their commander pressed a button to order the on-board computer to initiate the maneuver. The control software waited a few seconds until the correct moment was reached and then ignited the engines, which the crew heard as background noise, and then they felt a small jerk to the left, then another, and twice more. The noise continued for several more seconds. Then it was silent again, except for the hum of life support.

"Thrust phase completed. Trajectory correction completed."

"Looks good," Miles said, sighing with relief.

"Houston, are you getting the data in? Everything looks

on schedule from our end. It would be nice if you could confirm that."

This time it took more seconds than the increasing signal delay required for Flight Control to respond.

"Yes, it looks good for us, too," Cortez finally confirmed. "It looks like we're off the hook for now."

Charlie breathed in deeply and blew out while the others also released some of their tension. Anne smiled with relief when their eyes met.

"Good work, Miles," Louis said approvingly, gripping his comrade's shoulder. "Exceptionally well done."

Miles merely nodded and puffed out his cheeks. "I scared myself."

"Reflection rate of the shell," said Charlie. "Such a tiny detail."

"The reflection rate is not so easy to calculate," Anne replied. "The material can only be tested on Earth, with simulations and calculations made for space. They were clearly incorrect. That happens."

"And almost cost us our asses," said Louis.

"But it didn't. So, let's look at it this way," Charlie suggested. "We've mastered the first challenge. Now, after four days, we're awake and ready for what's to come."

Twenty minutes later, during which they constantly monitored the instruments and data columns from the sensors, Louis initiated the braking maneuver. The Draco maneuvering jets ignited in their pre-programmed pattern and turned the colossus – which weighed 400 tons with the remaining fuel – around within a few moments. Outside the windows, a sliver of which Charlie could see below the edge of the displays, the moon disappeared, replaced by star-speckled blackness, until Earth could be seen at last, the 'blue marble' in the darkness. Their engines faced toward the moon.

"Initiate braking thrust," Louis announced, whereupon

they began to hear the roar again. As with their previous acceleration phases, gravity kicked in, pushing them toward the engines. It wasn't much compared to the take-off in Boca Chica, but it was a welcome feeling after four days of weightlessness.

The maneuver lasted less than five minutes. Then the quiet returned.

"*Liberty*, Houston," Cortez's voice rang out from the speakers.

"We hear you."

"That was good. Everything here in Mission Control looks just as we imagined it would. Can you confirm that?"

"Give us a moment," Louis replied. They set about checking everything again. First Anne gave a thumbs-up, then Charlie, and then Miles. They had managed to shorten their vector considerably and bring it back to an ellipse. This would take them behind the moon, where they would reach its orbital speed around the Earth. "Exactly according to your calculations, Houston. Thanks everyone. Great work!"

"Glad to hear it, *Liberty*."

Despite the good news, the mood remained tense and Charlie knew why. The perilune of their flight, the closest point to the lunar surface, would bring them within 150 kilometers of the moon's rugged topography before they reached a stable, slightly elliptical orbit.

"We suggest you put on your pressure suits now," Cortez informed them. "Just to be on the safe side."

"Roger that, Houston." Louis activated the electric suspension of their row of seats, whereupon they moved backward and the displays retracted. "So, you heard the boss. We're getting dressed. It can't hurt."

It took almost half an hour to get them all into their pressure suits, the sleek white and gray version developed by SpaceX. The much bulkier EVA and moon suits were down in the airlocks. Since they were no longer in zero gravity due to the braking thrust, it was both easier and more difficult to put them on. The individual pieces were heavier than expected, and this time they didn't have whole teams to help them dress as they'd had before departure. But nothing floated, and they didn't have to keep looking for a foothold to avoid drifting off.

After checking that all the connections and valves were in place, they got back into their seats, 'buckled up,' and let the electronics drive them into position and pull the displays close to their helmets.

"Anne, have you looked at the fuel supplies yet?" asked Louis as they waited for the braking thrust to subside and take them into target orbit, where the engines could shut down and let their speed, Earth, and the moon do the necessary work to keep them in place.

"There's not enough for the return," she replied straight-forwardly. "We have enough to land on the moon and return to orbit. Just one trip. But then we can't go any further."

Louis just nodded. "Houston, *Liberty*. Did you hear that?"

There was the usual two seconds of silence.

"Yes, we are coming to the same conclusion. We have several teams – including SpaceX – working on the plans for a propellant mission. We will do everything we can to send you either a tank or *Starship 9* without a crew. We just need to find a solution for the necessary docking procedure," explained Flight Control.

"Thank you, Houston."

Charlie found comfort in the message that they wanted to look after them like this, but time was short. Their stay was planned for a maximum of one week before they had to return. Oxygen and water supplies had been planned accordingly. Even with the supplies from *Starship 5*, which was near the landing zone and had its storage space full, it wouldn't be sufficient for more than two weeks.

How were the engineers on Earth going to find a solution that was tested and reliable enough? They would either have to convert a Starship into a tanker or send an unmanned *Starship 9* equipped with a docking adapter. This adapter would have to work in such a way that *Liberty* didn't need one, because it hadn't been designed for such maneuvers. They did not have an airlock with an adapter ring. Accordingly, the best they would be able to do was use an EVA to get from the *Liberty* to the other vehicle, which was very risky.

But no one raised this obvious point. Nor did it matter. All they could do was deal with one problem at a time and try to survive to reach their destination. The possibility that they wouldn't make it back had always been there. The priority was to recover the alien object.

"You know what's important," Louis said.

As if they had all been reading his mind, they nodded resolutely.

"Good, because in twenty minutes we'll have reached our orbit, and then we'll start planning the landing sequence."

CHAPTER 22

Rebecca had Feinman's people drive her to the airport where she met Rogers in the departures area. He wanted to give her the phones he had bought, but she only took one plus a single SIM card. No one had followed her out of the car, but she was sure the colonel was keeping a close eye on what she was doing and to whom she was talking. He might not be allowed – or able – to tap her work cellphone, but that didn't mean he wouldn't exhaust every avenue to make sure she was out of the way.

And that would only be the case once she had disappeared from his sphere of influence.

She handed Rogers her bag and gave him his ticket. "Go ahead and wait for me behind security. I need to use the restroom."

The lieutenant took the handle of her rolling bag and proceeded without further inquiry toward security check-in.

Rebecca avoided looking around for possible tails and went to the nearest women's room. As it was quite crowded at the airport, she stood in line for a few minutes, enough time to wonder if she was becoming too paranoid. But being paranoid was something of a life insurance policy in her job, and there was something wrong with the way the colonel had handled her so effortlessly. It almost seemed as if he had cast his net with great precision and accuracy to catch and mothball her.

But for what reason? They were not enemies and, according to the general, it was Feinman of all people who had wanted her to be involved in the whole thing. Inarguably, that had now changed.

When it was her turn, she cleaned the toilet seat and sat down to pee. Since she was here, she might as well use the time.

I didn't do anything objectively wrong, she thought. *Except that I should have tried harder to reach the colonel before I went hunting for a potential spy with Special Agent Nichols.*

She tore off some toilet paper and wiped herself, her mind continuing to churn.

But he wants to get rid of me. That makes no sense. I'm most useful right now. She wiped herself a second time, stood, pulled up her underpants and straightened her uniform. *Unless he didn't want me* there *in the first place.*

She chewed on this thought for a moment. Then inspiration struck. What if she was looking at the question the wrong way round? What if he had brought her onto his team so that, by being there, she couldn't be anywhere else? Maybe he didn't want her to be ... *somewhere else.*

She thought feverishly about whether the puzzle could be reassembled in this way to form a coherent overall picture. Then she remembered the conversation with Colonel Smith, the base commander of Peterson Space Force Base, the man she had visited at Eversman's behest after discovering the signal. Smith had spoken of a colonel who had been there before her and who had given him the feeling that he had long since set the necessary levers in motion. But that couldn't have happened, as the general had only released the signal to NASA after her call – and presumably made countless inquiries with the White House.

Feinman, she thought. *He was at Peterson before me. But why? Did the general send him? But that doesn't make sense. Eversman doesn't waste time and resources on duplicate work. Not for a simple intel job like this.*

That could only mean that Feinman had been there on his own initiative. And when the matter of the NASA takeover by the Space Force came up, he had requested *her* of all people.

When she opened her stall door, a waiting lady stood facing her with a stern expression, giving her a piqued look.

"Got a few things off my mind," Rebecca said, and went to wash her hands before going out and looking for the TSA offices. The Transportation Security Administration had used bug-proof offices at every airport since 9/11, and that's where she was headed. Secret service agents like her knew the network of shielded offices all too well, as they often used them for phone calls – just like colleagues from the NSA and CIA who monitored local terrorist threats and didn't carry their own equipment. She couldn't allow herself to be on the official visitor list or Feinman would quickly find out. But she didn't even need the shielding, just the absence of prying ears.

"Can I help you, Major?" asked one of the officers standing in front of the access door to the offices. He spoke respectfully, having looked at her uniform, and seemed friendly.

"Yes, I think so. I've just been to the toilet and my bag is no longer there," she lied.

"You've lost your bag?"

"That's right."

The officer nodded and cleared the way. "Come along. We'll find it for you."

She entered the office, a simple, elongated room with six desks, only two of which were occupied. Further ahead, a door led into another, smaller room, presumably belonging to the supervisor.

"I'm on my way to the Pentagon," she said, "and I need to get the bag back. It shouldn't fall into someone else's hands, if you know what I mean."

The officer – Wilkins, according to his name tag – scrutinized her and then nodded. "Of course. Come with me."

"Jenkins?"

"Hmm?" A uniformed woman behind the last desk looked up.

"We've got an Air Force major here who's missing her bag. Can you help her?"

"Sure. Hello, Major. What does your bag look like? Then I'll make an announcement to our staff."

"It's black, made of fabric, with four wheels and an extendable handle. It's about the same size as a typical carry-on bag," said Rebecca. "It has the Air Force logo on it."

"Ah." Jenkins laughed. "I thought, 'Aha, just like every other suitcase.' But with the Air Force logo? We can manage that. Just wait. You can sit up front."

"Thank you very much. Do you mind if I make a quick phone call?"

"No, of course not. Just don't go too close to the boss's office. You won't get any radio reception in there," explained Jenkins, and picked up her radio to announce the supposedly missing bag.

Rogers felt a little sorry for Rebecca, but he'd have to bite the bullet for a few minutes.

She went to the other end of the office, inserted the SIM card into the simple flip phone, and dialed General Eversman's direct cellphone line.

"Yes?"

"General, this is Rebecca Hinrichs."

"Major? What kind of number is that?"

"My other phone isn't accessible right now," she said. "Feinman is sending me back to Arlington."

"I know. I signed off on it. You made mistakes, Rebecca," Eversman replied in a reprimanding tone. "Mistakes I'm not used to you making,"

"Yes, sir, I apologize. However, I would like to suggest a better use of my resources than twiddling my thumbs at the Pentagon," she explained. Now it was time to see if he was working with Feinman against her, or if the colonel had spun his web alone.

"I'm all ears."

That was a good sign. "Send me to Peterson, sir."

"To Peterson?"

"Yes. Congress will be hoofing it and requesting all protocols and data evaluations from the signal and the *Sentinel I* mission. I can carefully prepare the documents so that we can quickly fulfill our accountability to the institutions in case of doubt and nothing is overlooked or misinterpreted, if you understand."

Eversman was silent for a while. "Good thinking, Major."

Rebecca felt a wave of relief go through her body.

"Where are you right now?"

"At the airport in Houston."

"All right, get on the next flight to Colorado Springs and get to work."

"Thank you, sir, I will ..." Eversman severed the connection. In a whisper, she concluded, "I will get to the bottom of the matter with Feinman."

She removed the SIM card and dropped the cellphone into a handy wastebasket. Then she returned to Jenkins, letting the SIM slip from her hand into another wastebasket along the way.

"Uhh, ma'am? We have a Lieutenant Rogers here who claims to be your adjutant and says he was instructed to carry your bag," the TSA officer explained, holding the radio to her chest.

"Oh, Rogers, of course." Rebecca shook her head. "I forgot I gave him the bag before I went to the bathroom. I'm so sorry for the inconvenience. I guess I've been under too much stress."

"So this is yours?" Jenkins pointed to her monitor. A camera image showed Rogers with her bag. He was standing slightly away from security, accompanied by two officers.

"Yes, that's definitely mine," she confirmed. "Again, sorry."

"No problem, I'm just glad we were able to find it. Have a good flight, Major, and thank you for your service."

"You, too." Rebecca left the office and went to Rogers, who had not yet passed through the security queue. She waved him over to a quiet spot.

"Is everything all right, Major?" asked the lieutenant.

"Yes. There's been a change of plans. I spoke to the general on the phone and we're flying to Colorado Springs." She looked at the departures board. "There's a plane leaving in an hour. We'll take it."

"Do you think we can still get tickets ..."

"Yes, we'll get them. We'd best go straight to check-in."

"May I ask what we'll be doing there, ma'am? I'm guessing it pertains to Peterson?"

"Quite right." She nodded. "I want to unravel a web in which I've become entangled. And maybe I can catch the spider while I'm at it."

CHAPTER 23

Planning their landing near the lunar south pole was a challenge that required even more calculations and simulations than for the correct translunar injection that had brought them this far.

Miles and Anne therefore took lots of time to recalculate the procedure using the fresh radar data they had obtained from orbit. The preparations had been exceptional, and they had managed to land the unmanned Starship HLS at the south pole, but they only had this one attempt, which made them particularly cautious.

Especially as they were still two and a half days ahead of the Chinese, and there was no reason to rush things.

As Miles was the pilot who would monitor the landing and intervene in an emergency, this time it was up to Louis to handle the last live stream from orbit. Charlie was grasping one of the holding nets above him with one hand while the commander positioned himself in front of one of the windows, behind which it was completely dark.

"Are you ready?" Charlie asked and Louis grimaced.

"I hate this shit. I'm not a TV presenter, I'm a pilot and an astronaut."

"And a superhero."

"A what?"

"For most people, you are a superhero. Astronauts are the pinnacle of human performance for many. Children want to be like you when they grow up. The others envy you at the same time they pity you, but all of them look up to you," explained Charlie. "*That's* who you're talking to."

Louis sighed, but nodded. "All right, let's get this over with."

Charlie pressed the record button and gave a thumbs up.

"Hello out there," Louis said a little awkwardly, putting on a smile that made his face look a little less set in stone. "We're checking in here one last time before our landing. Miles and Anne are in the middle of final preparations for our landing, so I have a little time to explain what's going on."

He turned slightly to look out of the large window and pointed a thumb out into the starless blackness. "We're just past the periselenium, the lowest point of our orbit around the moon. But it's in shadow, which is why you can't see anything, even though we're only fifteen kilometers above the surface. We are flying at seventeen hundred meters per second. This is the fastest point of our orbit. At the furthest orbital point, the aposelenium, we are going slower and we're at a distance of one hundred and twenty kilometers from the moon.

"My crewmate Charlie has shown this to you using a ball. So, the orbit is elliptical. You can imagine it like an egg. That's because we can save fuel and because the moon's gravitational pull is significantly less than that of the Earth. And there is no atmosphere. So whether we're speeding along at a height of fifteen kilometers above the surface or a hundred and twenty makes no difference in terms of friction or anything like that.

"There is a vacuum here. The only thing that matters is gravity, which both accelerates us and decelerates us a little when we're in an elliptical orbit so that we consume less fuel. What else ...?"

Louis scratched his head. But just as Charlie was about to save him with a question, he began to speak again: "Oh yes, our orbital period is currently about two hours."

Now he looked satisfied and seemed to be waiting for Charlie to switch off. He had forgotten that they were supposed to answer questions from the public. At least two.

"Louis, the people at home have put questions on the ballot, and the one with the most votes is:" – Charlie read from his tablet – "Why is it so difficult to land on the moon now, when the Apollo program was able to do so in the 1960s and 1970s?"

"Ah, sure." The commander nodded and his face became a little more serious for a moment.

"There are several reasons for that. For one thing, the Apollo program was incredibly expensive. Adjusted for inflation, one hundred and twenty billion dollars. NASA doesn't get that kind of money for a project these days. Not a chance. It was a feat of strength for an entire nation and at times accounted for a significant part of the national budget.

"The next problem is technological regression. Back then, there were entire industries that specialized in supplying NASA. The best engineers of an entire generation were involved in designing the space shuttles, rockets and landers, and the finished products were really complicated. They consisted of hundreds of thousands of components that nobody makes anymore. All of those people have long since retired or died and their companies no longer exist or have shut down those production lines fifty years ago.

"What's more, today's technology is much more complex and therefore consists of even more parts and systems to be integrated, all of which have to be tested. The need for safety is much higher today, while the willingness to take risks has decreased. Then there is the political aspect."

As Louis was catching his breath for his next sentence, Charlie decided to interrupt him. A rant about Congress and the capriciousness of politicians would probably not be the best idea right now.

"The second and final question is: Why is our planned landing zone such a special challenge for us?"

"Ah, the south pole." Louis frowned and nodded. Behind him, the terminator line of the moon moved along as if in fast motion and the moon filled the window like gray glowing wallpaper.

"First of all, the terrain there is very uneven. There are countless craters that are permanently in the shade. At these so-called cold spots, it's as cold as minus two hundred and forty degrees Celsius. This is due to the axial tilt of the moon, which means that part of the south pole is located exactly on the terminator, that is, the transition zone between the day and night sides. All around it there are mountains that are permanently in sunlight – at least on one side. It can be over one hundred degrees there, quite hot.

"As if that wasn't enough, there are constant changes between day and night – every few hours to be precise. This means that the temperature is always changing between two extremes, which makes work challenging for the sensors and all of the materials.

"Imagine you want to land somewhere, but it is constantly getting light and dark, hot and cold, and the ground is extremely uneven and crisscrossed by deep, eternally dark craters. That's what we're dealing with here, and that's why Miles and Anne are working their heads off right now."

Charlie gave a thumbs-up and nodded.

"Okay, that's it from us. We'll take care of the touchdown next, and get back to you when we've done it. *Liberty* out."

Louis raised a hand, and sighed with relief as Charlie switched off the camera.

"Well done."

"We got it behind us, anyway," the ex-pilot grumbled. "All right then, Miles? Anne? How's it looking?"

"Everything looks fine so far. We've gone through everything again with the update for the infrared and sun sensors and also calculated everything from scratch, without the basis of the on-board computer," stated Anne. She looked exhausted from all the mental gymnastics. But she was by far the best of the four of them at calculating. "Miles should check it himself, though."

Louis thought about it and then nodded. "Sure – how much time?"

"Three or four hours," Miles replied, "at least. I'd like to compare and discuss our results with Houston."

"Sure, we should take our time. Okay, let's get started. I'll check the suits and the quarters section with Charlie." Louis gave him a wave, whereupon they floated through the hatch into the lower sections.

The HLS version of their starship was huge and had a correspondingly large amount of space, even when the drive section with the engines and tanks was taken into account. With a diameter of nine meters, there was plenty of room for pretty much everything.

Roughly speaking, the lower 60 percent of the *Liberty* belonged to the raptors at the end, the main tank for the liquid oxygen, the fuel pipes and the methane tank above, which filled the entire middle section. Then came the true cargo section, which in *Liberty's* case consisted of a corridor with multiple hatches.

Behind them were two airlocks, two storage areas, a quarters section and an exercise area. One of the airlocks was intended for moonwalks and showed the floor, ceiling and corresponding markings relative to the direction of the drive section, which would be 'below' after landing. It contained lockers with their lunar-surface suits, the control system for an external elevator, and an integrated air system to free them from the stubborn moon dust. The other airlock was for emergencies, in case they needed to perform an EVA to repair something, for one example. It held four of the new NASA bulky spacesuits secured on transport hooks.

They hadn't used the quarters yet, nor the exercise room, because both were designed for a gravity environment and difficult to use in zero gravity. One of the storerooms contained their equipment and supplies. The other was empty except for magnetically attached weights that kept the *Liberty* balanced for landing operations. Ideally, they would remove them, stow the captured alien technology in their place, and bring it back to Earth.

Louis led Charlie to the exit airlock on the starboard side and opened the door. He unlocked the manual wheel and then turned it until they heard a soft hiss. As much electronics as possible had been omitted on the *Liberty* in order *to* minimize the number of potential sources of error.

"Let's have a look at those babies, then," Louis said, pointing to the cupboards where the moon suits were stored. Each door had been engraved with one of their names.

Charlie opened the first one and began to check the fasteners and seams one by one. The suit, made by Axiom Space, was mostly charcoal gray with orange sections over the knees, boots, shoulders, and hands, as well as dark and light blue stripes in places. The helmet was smaller than those used on the Apollo missions, looking like an upside-down goldfish bowl and topped with a semi-circle of lights and sensors.

"I can't wait to get out there with these things," Louis said, fiddling with the next suit. "It's been fifty years. Only twelve people have ever set foot on the moon. Twelve."

"Hard to believe, isn't it?" Charlie opened the valve ring of the helmet and ran his finger along it to check for any irregularities. "I'm curious to see how it really feels."

"What do you mean?"

"The one-sixth g down there. Flying a thirty-second parabola every few minutes in the vomit bomber is not enough to convey the real feeling of what it's like to walk around on the moon for a long time."

"More like 'hop around,' you mean."

"Well, yeah."

Louis was silent for a while, during which Charlie set to work on the electronic interfaces between the helmet and the life support system, which was carried much like a large soldier's backpack, but those were stowed on the other side of the exit airlock. He checked that there was no contamination anywhere.

"What do you think we'll find, Charlie?" Louis asked several minutes later in an unusually pensive voice.

"I don't know," he answered honestly.

"I realize that. But what do you *think*? What are you imagining?"

He could sense from Louis's words that it was somehow important to him, so he thought about it. Not that he hadn't already mulled it over extensively, especially in the last four days, but he needed to organize his thoughts.

"I think," he said slowly, "that whatever we find ... it will change our world forever. A discovery like this is beyond anything we ever dreamed possible."

"But what if it's nothing?"

"Nothing?"

"I mean a simple transmitter, or a telescope that hasn't been active for a long time," explained his crewmate. "That wouldn't be very impressive."

"Then at least we'd know that someone else had built it

and put it there. At some point. And it would be proof that we are not alone."

"Or *were*. They could have died out in the meantime. Or a predecessor civilization from Earth, long before us, could have built it."

"What are you trying to say?" asked Charlie, opening and closing the arm fasteners.

"Perhaps nothing will change, and we will only provoke a conflict between us and the Chinese with this race. That's my biggest worry."

"Mm-hmm." Charlie nodded. "But the thing is sending a signal, don't forget. So maybe it's active and wants to make contact."

"And then what? What do we do then?"

Charlie was about to answer, but then held back. He now understood what was bothering Louis so much. It was the impossibility of all the potential decisions he had to make as commander from here on. If it was an alien artifact, should they remove it from its place and take it with them? How would the Chinese react? Science in space was open to any nation under the Outer Space Treaty. If they couldn't take it, for whatever reason, but the Chinese tried, should they stop them? Should they claim the object for themselves? What if both teams were on site? These were all questions he didn't know the answers to, and Louis couldn't know, either.

"We can only play it as we see it, I guess," he said. "I have a feeling that this artifact will be very different from what we're imagining now."

"What you said about the weapons," Louis suddenly changed the subject, "was important and right, by the way."

Charlie paused for a moment. "Thank you."

"I just hope you understand me. I was a fighter pilot and you were in the Marines. We both know, as does every soldier who has ever been in combat, that everything must always be done to avoid war, to avoid killing. I have never forgotten that. At the same time, the question of war and peace is, unfortunately and forever, one that only politicians can answer. Up here, that's me, even if I wish it weren't so. I'm not concerned about what's happening on Earth, with things we can't control, but about my crew."

"About us?"

"Yes. I will not allow anyone to put you in danger or attack you. If in doubt, I will make sure that we can defend ourselves, even though I will do everything in my power to prevent such a situation. You can count on that," said Louis, and pulled Charlie's cupboard door back so that they could look each other in the face. His expression showed how serious he was.

"I know," Charlie replied and nodded. "I know, Louis. Let's make sure it doesn't come to that, shall we? On Earth they each have an agenda. Up here we should be scientists first. I'm sure we'll find out more by working together with the Chinese than on our own."

"Scientists," Louis repeated. "Exactly."

CHAPTER 24

They began their approach to the moon seven hours and four minutes later. The calculations had taken longer than Miles estimated and the checks by Houston had resulted in a few more sensor tests. After all of that was completed, the on-board computer was confirmed ready for the tricky maneuver. The crew put on their pressure suits, locked their helmets, and sat down on their bench with the four separate seats, their visors close to the touch displays with their amazingly tidy readouts.

From now on, all they had to do was check the displayed values in real time, which were used by the control software as a basis for navigation and control.

The flight downward began at the periselenium – when their orbit reached the closest point to the lunar surface – at an altitude of just over 15 kilometers. They came from the night side and sped toward the day side at 1,700 meters per second. Then the main engines fired to reduce their orbit. In accordance with orbital mechanics, this was not done by steering in one direction as on Earth, but simply by slowing down.

The *Liberty's* elliptical orbit around the moon gradually

shortened as a result. The first 60-second braking maneuver of the Raptor engines generated a thrust of 30 kilonewtons, which reduced their speed to 300 meters per second and reduced their orbit to an ellipse of 100 kilometers altitude at the aposelenium and 10 kilometers at the lowest point. Three quarters of an hour later, they reached the next periselenium and the Raptors ignited again, this time for 30 seconds with their 30 kilonewtons of thrust, which reduced their horizontal speed to zero and the vertical speed toward the ground to 3 meters per second.

"Vertical descent phase initiated," Miles announced. Although he was sitting right next to Charlie, the radio made him sound far away.

"Pressure, temperature, and hull integrity on target," said Anne.

"The moon's pulling hard on us." Miles stretched out a finger and pressed the button for the precise breakdown of the acceleration values. His hand shook because the whole ship was vibrating, as if the moon was resisting their arrival. "We're picking up speed, 1.62 meters per second squared."

This corresponded to the acceleration of mass due to the moon's gravity. This meant that they were accelerating by 1.62 meters per second – exactly the expected value.

"Confirmed. Descent rate nominal," said Anne. Louis remained conspicuously silent.

Charlie looked at the altimeter. They were below two kilometers. Glancing sideways through one of the windows, he could make out the silhouettes of rough mountain slopes that looked almost white in the sunlight, as if they were covered in snow. It was like being surrounded by a screen on which a black-and-white movie was being played.

"Seven hundred and fifty meters!" declared Anne. Now the ship jerked and wobbled a little more, as the Draco jets took over attitude control with their nitrogen bursts and kept *Liberty* vertical in a stable, spin- and tumble-free trajectory. Each cold gas blast was audible as a muffled, short-lived hiss.

"Extend landing gear!" It sounded as though Miles was doing it himself, but it was the on-board computer that triggered the appropriate technology at the 750-meter point. There was a loud *poof!* as the four massive props extended from the tail section using pyrotechnics.

"Five hundred meters!"

"Final engine ignition!"

A gentle jolt went through *Liberty*. Charlie was pressed lightly into his seat as the Raptors ignited and slowed them sharply. Now the smaller nitrogen jets all over the hull were firing frequently, as often as needed to keep the ship precisely upright.

At 250 meters, the hydraulic shock absorbers in the stilt legs activated to cushion the impact.

Charlie said a silent prayer and closed his eyes. A few moments later, the engine noise died out and shortly afterward they touched down on the moon with a heavy jolt at a vertical speed of less than five kilometers per hour.

"Houston," came Louis's exuberant voice, "*Liberty* has landed!"

"YES!" shouted Charlie triumphantly.

It wasn't long before the others joined in.

"WOOHOO!"

"We've landed, baby!"

"Amazing!"

They slapped hands with each other and raised their fists, which was so easy in the barely noticeable lunar gravity it led to Miles almost punching one of the displays.

They quickly calmed themselves so they could hear Houston, but all they could hear from there was unrestrained cheering from everyone in the Control Center. So, with their regained professionalism, they checked the displays to verify that all was in order.

"Everything is green, all parameters within their normal ranges," said Anne. "Picture perfect landing, Miles! Picture perfect."

"I didn't do anything." He raised his hands. "Thank the on-board computer and the best damn nerds in the world back home in Houston."

"You bet your ass." Louis grinned. He unbuckled his seatbelt to go to one of the windows, falling as he did so. Charlie thought it looked as though his brain was set on slow motion.

"As soon as the microphones are off, he lets out everything he's been holding back for the last few days." Anne laughed.

"They are not off, *Liberty*," Cortez reminded her from the Mission Control Center. "And in the next stream, he's welcome to speak more appropriately."

"Understood, Flight Control. We are now preparing for the exit."

"All right. We'll stay online. Good work, *Liberty!*"

Charlie unbuckled his seatbelt, too, and carefully and purposefully made his way to Louis. His hours of training during the parabolic flights had prepared him for lunar gravity, but the short intervals had been different from now. His body felt light, as if someone had inflated it with gas that wanted to lift him up.

As he stepped up to the window, followed by Anne and Miles, Charlie stared in fascination at the lunar landscape. They were situated in a small depression in front of a sunlit ridge that was several hundred meters high. The reflected light shimmered almost imperceptibly on the regolith surrounding the landing zone. Myriads of tiny dust particles sparkled in the air, having been stirred up by their engines as they landed. Due to the low gravity, it would take quite a while for the particles to resettle.

Through this veil of extraterrestrial glitter, he saw a large crater about 500 meters away, which on Earth he would have thought was a lake with a mirror-smooth surface. Because of their elevated position in the *Liberty's* cockpit, he could make out the round shape and had no doubt that it was the Shackleton Crater.

"Do you see *Starship 5*?" asked Charlie, letting his gaze roam over the barren landscape. The ridge on the right along with one half of the crater rim were in the sun, the other half in the shadow of a higher mountain on the left. The source of the signal was now within their grasp without them being able to see it.

"No, it would be eight hundred meters further west, over there in the shadow of the mountain," Louis replied, pointing to the left.

A landing zone in the sunlit area had been deliberately chosen for *Liberty* after the bad experience with *Starship 4*, which had crashed in the shade because its sensors had received too little light. It had worked out well with *Starship 5,* after a few improvements, but the danger from the extreme heat had seemed less risky to the engineers in Houston than the risk that they had only gotten lucky with the successful landing of *Starship 5* in the dark.

"Okay. We've landed." Louis clenched one hand into a fist. "We may not get out of here, but we'll get to the Shackleton Crater first, where the greatest mystery in space exploration is waiting for us, folks."

"In *human* history, more likely," Miles corrected the commander. He was pressing his nose against one of the other windows with Anne.

"I somehow imagined it would look more impressive," Anne said abruptly. "Sure, I knew the moon was a regolith wasteland with no atmosphere, but this looks like I'm trapped in a black-and-white movie."

"That's the fascinating thing, to me," Miles remarked.

"Just remember that no living creature has ever set foot here before," Charlie said. "Everything you do here is being done for the first time."

"Unless the aliens brought this thing here to the Shackleton themselves," Anne replied.

"Then at least we are the first humans."

"True."

"All right," Louis said, "let's take a few more moments to enjoy the view, then we'll get to work on the plan. You all know what it looks like. We'll go out, walk around a bit, and take a few photos with the flag. Then we'll set up the Rover and the solar installation."

"Can't we at least look into the crater for a moment?" Miles asked, sounding almost like a disappointed child.

"Negative. We stick to the protocol. Half a kilometer doesn't look like much, but we're not wasting time under unnecessary cosmic ray exposure. First the basics, in effect, the set-up. Then we check everything and if it goes well, we rest, eat something, and then make our way to the crater – two of us, while the other two hold down the fort here."

"All right." Miles sighed and walked carefully to the hatch into the corridor, where two ladders on the wall, vertical since landing, had become their way up and down.

"Well then, moon, here we come. And we've come to stay," said Louis, turning away from the window.

The euphoria in the cockpit was palpable and Charlie could feel his growing excitement. What had been a longtime dream would soon become a reality.

CHAPTER 25

They spent over an hour in the exit airlock before disembarking. Although the moon's low gravity made it easier to lift and put on the relatively heavy suit components, it was a different story when it came to operating the dozens of fasteners. One-sixth of the Earth's gravity also meant one-sixth of their motor skills, at least until they got used to it.

Straps repeatedly slipped out of Charlie's hands. He pulled too hard on the zippers and then too softly on the levers of the fastening rings. So, Louis and Miles helped until he and Anne had put on everything except their helmets. Like two anthracite-orange marshmallows, they filled most of the airlock. Louis and Miles in their overalls looked like little worms by comparison.

A special moment came when they put on their backpacks. They had been so heavy during the training exercises that Charlie's legs and shoulders had been sore for the first few days. Here he hardly noticed the weight. It was a fairly simple procedure that they had practiced hundreds of times during their Houston sessions. Every move was performed correctly, and yet they needed much more time – not only because of the change in gravity, but also because there was much more at stake this time. Making a mistake now meant more than embarrassing themselves in front of the others, or repeating the exercise, or having to work overtime. Potentially, it could mean death.

Any leak, no matter how small, would force blood through their skin due to the pressure gradient, while they would either freeze to death or boil in their own sweat, depending on their position. A short circuit in the helmet system – in the headphones, for example – could ignite the pure oxygen that filled their suits. The dangers were manifold, and Charlie was relieved that they had such a big head start on the Chinese. Because of that fact, they didn't have to rush anything.

The final check was carried out via direct-connection ports on their tablets. Using cables, the small devices were linked to the maintenance access points on their helmet rings and back-pack-like survival units so they could read out the data.

"Everything is as it should be," Miles said to Charlie, then showed him the tablet so he could see for himself. Louis had not finished checking Anne's data and was connected to the neck of her suit by her tablet's cable. It looked strange, as if he had inserted an umbilical cord into a Michelin man.

"It's good here, too," the commander said to Anne after he had read out the diagnostic program. All the markers were green. "Oxygen quantity at target, all valves without errors, contact connections report no errors, and the communication and monitoring systems are online."

Anne nodded and looked toward the outer hatch behind Louis. After all their years of training together, Charlie knew her well enough to sense that she was excited and anxious in equal measure. In such cases, she became taciturn and Intro-verted. Unlike him, she had spent time in space before, at least two months on the ISS. It was his first time.

Charlie watched Louis take his helmet out of the locker to attach it onto his neck ring. "Louis," he said.

"Yes?" His commander paused and met his eyes.

"Thank you."

"For what?"

"You could have gone out first yourself."

"Oh." Louis shook his head, and a smile began to split his face as if it were hewn from rock. "When you eventually have your own command, you'll see that your main job is to get the best out of your people and enjoy watching them perform at their best and get better and better. That doesn't work very well when you're a selfish asshole." His smile widened into a grin. "Besides, I'm a shitty speechmaker, and your first words will eventually be heard and dissected by the whole world. Not my cup of tea, buddy."

"Thank you," Charlie repeated, looking him seriously in the eye.

Louis nodded and lowered the helmet over his face. With a focused mien, he took care of the ring fasteners and read off his tablet. Charlie looked over at Anne and Miles. She seemed quiet, but noticed his gaze and smiled a little tensely before giving him a thumbs up.

"How's your radio?" asked Louis, whose voice now sounded slightly metallic and seemed to be speaking directly into Charlie's ears.

"Loud and clear," he replied.

"Head-up display?"

"HUD is working perfectly." Charlie saw the life support display projected onto his visor, making it look as if it were running like a hologram in his field of vision. In addition, there was data from the rangefinder, infrared sensors, and his distance to *Liberty,* which was displaying '0' with an arrow that couldn't decide which way to point.

"Wonderful. Then you're ready." Louis ticked off the EVA

protocol and pressed his finger on the confirmation field before waiting for Miles to finish the same process for Anne. Then the commander and Miles withdrew.

Miles remained at the inner hatch of the airlock, watching them through the porthole so that he could intervene in the event of an emergency. Louis, meanwhile, returned to the cockpit per protocol to monitor everything and maintain contact with Houston.

"Right then," Charlie said to Anne, and joined her in front of the outer hatch. "Ready?"

"You can bet on it. Okay, Louis, we're ready to exit."

"Understood. Radio signal stable. I'm unlocking."

The small LED above the lever on the left-hand side jumped from red to green and Charlie pulled it down with one hand, causing the warning light above them to light up. Then came the intrusive whine of the pressure alarm. Its red light had something ominous about it and made the white walls around it look dull. There was a tiny porthole through which they could see out, but they would have had to lean their helmets right up against the glass. So they simply waited until the pressure equalization was complete, which he first noticed because he could no longer hear the alarm. So all the gas molecules had escaped, and with them the atmosphere.

It became eerily silent. He had to concentrate to hear even the background hum of the life support system, which pumped water into the cooling hoses of his multi-functional undergarment and distributed the oxygen in his suit via small fans.

Then the hatch opened, folding outward like the platform of a balcony, and revealing the monochromatic yet impressive landscape of the lunar south pole. Above them, the darkness stretched into a glittering canopy of stars that dwarfed anything he had ever seen on Earth. Even in places without light pollution, such as Australia's Outback or

Antarctica, he had never seen this abundance of twinkling lights. Lights from distant stars, many of which no longer existed, but whose photons would travel through the universe forever.

It was overwhelming in beauty and intensity.

Charlie pressed the button for the railing, whereupon the floor of the platform swung open and metal runners extended on the outward-facing sides, so that it now looked even more like a balcony, or a very crude elevator cage from a coal mine.

"We're stepping out onto the platform now," Anne announced, whereupon they cautiously stepped forward together and stood on the steel of the former outer hatch. Through the porthole, which was now part of the floor, they could see the ground almost 40 meters below them.

"The Earth is in the new moon phase," Charlie remarked, pointing upward. "Or new Earth phase?"

Anne followed his gesture and he saw her head nod inside her helmet. "Wow."

Seen from the south pole of the moon, the Earth went through phases similar to those of the moon as seen from Earth, from the new moon to a growing crescent to the full moon and the waning crescent.

"Earth and sun are in exact conjunction," Charlie said with a dry mouth. Their home planet was like a circular black hole in the sky with shimmering edges, almost like the accretion zone of a wormhole. It looked as if God himself had cut a piece out of the firmament with a pair of glowing scissors.

"Do you see that, *Liberty*?" asked Anne, audibly moved.

"Yes, we can see it through the window. That's amazing!"

They took a few minutes to silently observe the spectacle and let it sink in. It was incredible that they had landed precisely in the short conjunction phase, which occurs every 27.3 days, and looked up at the sky. At some point, one side of the glow would become stronger, reminiscent of the narrow crescent of a waxing moon, even though the Earth above them was about four times the size of the moon from Earth.

"Extending the crane now," Louis announced from the cockpit above them. Shortly afterward, an arm made of steel struts extended from the airlock like a telescope. As the mechanism was optimized for absolute safety, it took a long time for it to attain its full length and reach the front edge of their 'balcony.'

Charlie and Anne untied the four steel cables hanging from the winch and attached them to the four anchor points provided on the railing before checking the fit of the hooks and eyelets once again.

"Hooks attached securely. We're ready," he radioed as he went back into the airlock to remove the control panel from its cargo hatch and attach it to the contact port on the side railing.

"Then you have the *Go*," Louis replied. "Miles will move your equipment into the airlock now. Give him a moment and use the time to get your bearings."

"Understood." Charlie had no problem with this order. Although it was hard not to look up at the imposing sparkling sky, whose stars seemed as numerous as the dust beneath them, the landscape of the moon was also breathtaking.

The region around the south pole was one of the most extreme and inhospitable areas of the Earth's satellite, with the McGuire and Leibniz mountain ranges, up to 2,500 meters high, rising north of them like dark walls from the white-gray monotony. To the east, the edges of the rugged Faustini Plateau and Amundsen Crater stood like shining giants in the merciless sunlight.

The northern canyons between the mountains lay in full darkness beyond the 40-kilometer-diameter Shoemaker Crater. In front of them, the Shackleton, which was half the size, seemed small where it lay in the plain like a gigantic lake of darkness. At its northwesternmost edge was the south pole, which had been meticulously calculated a long time ago.

The shadowy transitions between the higher ridges and peaks and the eternally dark crater floors were rugged and bizarre, reminding Charlie of grimacing demons. This impression was reinforced by the many dark areas between the areas of light-colored regolith, which seemed to move like liquid obsidian through the wild surroundings. He knew that these were solidified lava flows from the early history of the moon, when volcanoes erupted regularly. They were called *lunar maria*, 'lunar seas.' They covered large parts of the surface and had taken different shapes at the south pole due to the special topology.

To the west stretched the vast Aitken Basin with its countless, varying sized impact craters. Charlie thought he saw a silvery sheen there, as if something was reflecting.

"The view from up here is *fascinating*," said Anne.

"Yes." He nodded and looked down. He wasn't afraid of heights, but 40 meters was no short distance. He looked back across the surface and stretched out a hand. "See those flashes of light out there? West of the crater?"

"That should be *Starship 5*," Anne replied, narrowing her eyes. "According to the rangefinder, eight hundred and thirty-three meters away from us."

"That would be about right." He hadn't even thought to make use of his rangefinder. The laser-based device worked even more smoothly outside an atmosphere of interfering gas particles. It was 478 meters to the edge of the crater at Site 404, where a permanent lunar station was to be built in the future as part of the *Artemis* program.

"Okay guys, I'm ready," they heard Miles say. "You can open up now. Pressure equalization has been completed."

They turned around and saw that the secondary airlock door was closed and sealed airtight to *Liberty's* hull. It was a built-in replacement hatch cover for the one that had now been converted into the elevator platform. Through a small inspection window, Charlie could see the many crates that were stowed inside, and Miles's face looking through the porthole of the inner hatch. They waved to each other.

He checked his forearm display to make sure the airlock was indeed empty of air and then opened it. They couldn't be too careful, because one explosive decompression and they would be hurled into the depths – to injury or death, which in their situation was likely to be the same thing.

Six large crates the size of small coffins were stacked three high in the airlock. From the training sessions, Charlie knew that each one weighed approximately 100 kilograms, which was a little more than 16 kilograms in lunar gravity.

Despite the low weight, they proceeded methodically, lifting each crate together by their respective handles and placing them on the elevator platform. In doing so, they had to take tiny steps that turned into little hops because it was impossible to perform the correct movements after decades of habit from Earth.

At one point, Charlie stumbled and hit his knee against the edge of the airlock. After an instant of shock, however, it was clear that his suit was intact and he could tell he hadn't seriously injured himself. Ten minutes later, all the transport crates were stacked on the platform and Anne and he were standing between them.

"We're ready," she said.

"Then go get the moon back," Louis replied from the cockpit. "*Liberty* out."

That was their agreed catchphrase to indicate that he would maintain radio silence from now on, until they stepped on the surface. Then they could find their own words, which would go down in the history books one way or another. Charlie had thought it through and discussed it with Anne during the journey, about the logistics and what they wanted to say. And now the moment was close.

He operated the winch mechanism via its control display, which was clamped onto the railing like an ancient military computer, clunky and with a black and white screen. A brief shudder went through the platform and they slowly descended. The winch above them looked far too fragile, and the fact that such a small cable was carrying the entire load at just one suspension point made him uneasy. But that was just his cerebellum. He *knew* that the low gravity and the lack of any wind would minimize the load on the system. With the six crates and their body weight plus the suits, they didn't even total 150 kilograms of payload.

The 40 meters to the lunar surface seemed to take an eternity. In silence, they looked out over the relatively flat landing zone, which rose slightly toward the edge of the crater but otherwise remained flat. Then the platform lowered onto the soft regolith and they felt another shudder.

Charlie turned to Anne, who licked her lips and nodded. He unlatched the gate in front of them and pushed his side forward, whereupon it swung open. Anne did the same on her side and the way was clear. They remained standing on bare steel, but just one step and they would be the 13th and 14th humans in history to walk on the moon, and for the first time in 50 years. Charlie had insisted that Anne should have the honor. She was more senior and experienced than he was, in addition to becoming the first female in history. And she had agreed.

Now she hesitated, looking at the white-gray moon dust and then at him. He was about to say something, to encourage her to take the plunge, when he noticed that she was holding out her left hand to him. He looked at the empty glove in confusion before he understood.

"We are now going to step onto the moon together," she

said and smiled. Warmth spread through him as he grasped her gloved hand with his own and nodded.

"Together."

So together they each lifted their right foot and stepped onto the moon.

The surface felt soft and gave way slightly.

"Once again, we are venturing here, beyond our habitat," Anne said. She emphasized the words normally, as if it were a simple statement, knowing that her words would soon be broadcast to the world after NASA's review. "Beyond what nature has given us ..."

" ... so that our children may one day inherit the stars," Charlie concluded in accordance with their previous agreement. Their eyes met and they smiled at each other before releasing their hands.

Charlie turned around and opened the first box, from which he pulled out two flags. He handed one to Anne and unfolded the other with its slightly stiffer edge facing upward. When both were ready, they stuck them into the ground about two steps away from the platform. One was the United States Star-Spangled Banner and the other was the flag of the United Nations. The latter had been a NASA decision that Washington had accepted after lengthy discussion. It was important to show that this was a U.S. achievement, yes, but they wanted the moon to be subject to and abide by international law and treaties. It was a sign that they were here for all of humanity, and perhaps also a sign of détente with China. At least that was what Charlie had hoped when he had suggested it.

After a brief moment to pause and take in the unfamiliar surroundings, the real work began, almost as if nothing had happened. They turned to the *Liberty,* which loomed before them like a giant, sharpened candle, and began to unload the crates and arrange them in two rows.

Then they opened them one by one and began to unload their contents.

First they lifted out the folded solar modules, which they spread out on the ground right next to the *Liberty*, and connected their finger-thick cables. They plugged the other ends into a transformer box the size of a computer and routed its cable to the connection on the edge of the engine section, which Louis opened for them from the cockpit.

When they finished an hour later, there was a small field – 10 x 10 meters – of solar panels on the regolith and they received confirmation that the electricity was flowing.

Charlie raised a hand and Anne followed suit.

"Now for the Rover," she said. "It's a good thing I loved Lego technology as a child."

"It's a good thing I learned to follow inane orders in the Marines," he joked, gesturing for her to go first.

CHAPTER 26

The Delta Airlines plane landed in Colorado Springs ten minutes before its scheduled arrival time.

Rebecca called Colonel Smith's office and had his secretary send a car to the airport. While she waited with the lieutenant, they got coffee. They didn't go outside until after her work phone rang. She didn't answer it.

A young specialist with a Texan accent drove them to the base, where two even younger specialists were waiting for them and led them straight to Smith's office. He had obviously learned from her little stunt at their first meeting and had no interest in being duped again.

The impression Smith must have gained of her – she had subtly flexed her muscles, which no commander liked, especially not a higher-ranking one – was something she should take care of as quickly as possible.

"Wait here," she instructed her aide in the anteroom, where the secretary got up from her desk and greeted her.

Rogers took her bag and sat down on one of the free chairs.

"The colonel is expecting you, Major," said the tall staff sergeant. She was a pretty woman with a predatory smile and a piercing gaze, exactly the kind of filter that every commander liked to install outside his door to keep out unwanted conversations and unloved guests.

"Thank you, Sergeant," Rebecca replied and entered Smith's office.

The colonel was standing at a small coffee machine, sipping an espresso cup. When he heard her, he turned and nodded to her. "Ah, Major. I didn't expect to see you again so soon."

"Colonel," she said, squaring her posture and saluting. A little respect would certainly help to prepare the ground for renewed cooperation.

"At ease. Would you like a coffee?" He looked at her invitingly, but there was something more in his gaze: calculation and caution. The man was tense.

"Gladly, sir. Black, no sugar."

Smith nodded and took a mug from the small cabinet next to the coffee machine. He pressed a few buttons and then it hissed and crunched before a roar sounded and the black liquid ran into her mug. He held it out to her and she thanked him politely.

"Sit down." He pointed to the free chairs in front of his desk and returned to his chair. "So, Major, what can I do for you this time? You weren't even announced to me."

"I generally do things that way, sir," she replied, sipping her coffee. She nodded approvingly. "It's good."

An expression of pride flitted across his features. It was like a vacation for Rebecca to sit across from a normal career officer rather than other intelligence officers, with whom every conversation was a dance on eggshells with sharp thumbtacks hidden inside. The colonel was easy to read, even though he was probably convinced that he was in thorough control of his face and mannerisms.

"Thank you. My wife gave it to me for our twentieth

anniversary. So, Major, what can I do for you? I would have expected you to be in the middle of a search for the Chinese spies." Smith waved a hand in front of his face. "That should keep all the intelligence officers of the branches of the armed forces busy, shouldn't it?"

So, his unspoken question was whether she had come to Peterson because of that search. Now she understood his tension. He feared she might turn his base upside down, something every commander, whether of a land-based facility or a ship, hated more than anything else. No matter how meticulous and protocol-driven you were in running your house, there were always lapses, especially within a highly bureaucratic system like the Department of Defense and its armed forces. It was like searching for groundwater: you just had to dig deep enough and you would *always* find water. The only question was how deep you had to go.

"That's not why I'm here." She shook her head and sipped her coffee calmly to let the words sink in. And indeed, his shoulders visibly relaxed. All that was lacking was for him to let out a sigh. "On the contrary. I came here because I want to help you."

"You want to *help* me?" asked Smith, suddenly back to looking worried.

Good.

"Congress is currently busy saving our moon mission and the face of our nation," Rebecca explained, shifting the cup to her left hand. "Both chambers are distracted, and the White House is in crisis mode. But how long will that last?"

"Until we can't go any further and the roof burns because we've failed, or after the victory, when it's time to pick up all the pieces. It's always like that." Smith waved it off, but he looked no less tense. He was waiting for the reason she wanted to help him. The mere hint of a problem made him sit up and take notice. And that was what she wanted.

"Exactly. Then Congress will start digging. That usually starts with backtracking all the paper trails."

The colonel stiffened a little. He knew she was right. After every crisis, whether mastered or not, heads had to roll so that others could stand on their shoulders. That was politics.

She let the penny fall. "You were the first to report the signal that set everything in motion."

"Yes, but I only reported data that ..."

"It's perfectly all right." She placed the coffee cup on the desk and raised both hands soothingly. "You have not made any mistakes, and the general very much appreciates your work. That's why I'm here. I'll sort everything out and get it put into proper order for you."

Smith seemed to think about what she meant before nodding cautiously. "All right ... now, what does that mean?"

"It means that we will fulfill our accountability to Congress when the time comes and not waste time gathering the ... the *right* documents."

"Oh. Well, that seems like a good idea." He waved his hand again. "Saves time, and besides, I need every soldier at his post right now. *Artemis* demands everything from us here. We can't have a bureaucratic sideshow."

"That's right. I've got your back." Rebecca tried to smile. It felt ... unusual.

"I'm glad to hear it. What do you need?"

"Access to the intranet and all the files from the past nine months," she said without hesitation. "The entire period since the start of the *Sentinel I* mission."

"You've got it. I'm not guilty of anything. If the general agrees, I'd be happy if you could compile the relevant evidence for the Pentagon and Congress." He reinforced his not-partic-ularly-subtle hint with a wink. He would not have made it through basic training in the secret service, that much was certain.

"That's what I'm here for," she replied lightly, and followed his example as he stood up.

"Make yourself at home here. Sergeant Myers will help you."

"Your secretary?"

"Yes." Smith nodded and came around the desk. "She knows this base and every one of my soldiers better than I do."

"Thank you very much, sir."

"Thank you, Major." He looked her in the eye and held out his hand. "I have a good memory. You can tell the general that, too."

"I will at the first opportunity."

Smith nodded again and left his office. He left the door open. Rebecca wasted no time before calling the sergeant and Rogers inside.

"Ma'am?" asked Sergeant Myers. If she was surprised to be working for Rebecca now, she certainly didn't let on.

"I need files, lots of them. And I need access with full privileges to the base intranet," she ordered, turning to Rogers. "Get me a desk in here. We've got a lot of work to do."

CHAPTER 27

The stacks of files became mountains in front of the window and the cupboards. Rebecca hoped that Smith was serious about letting her set up camp here, because the sheer flood of documents made the prospect of a quick wrap-up exceptionally unrealistic. She didn't shy away from paperwork. She never had. On the contrary, there was something markedly satisfying about chasing down traces that eluded the fleeting and – above all – unwilling glances by others. Ink on paper did not lie, did not argue, did not pretend, did not try to be something it was not.

She liked that.

She liked the composition of a bureaucratic mosaic even better when she knew what she was looking for: Colonel Feinman. She knew – well, she had a very strong suspicion – that he had been here ahead of her. Not on this visit, but her first one, right after *Sentinel I* had discovered the signal, when the general had sent her here to check the validity of it and make sure this potentially sensitive information was handled properly.

"The colonel won't make it easy for us," Rogers remarked. He was going through the visitor lists from one week before to one week after the protocol date for the signal detection note. He was sitting on a chair at a small folding table in front of the coffee machine.

"No, he won't," she confirmed. In front of her were the daily orders for the base, which were issued by the commander every morning at 0400 hours. The time period corresponded to the one her adjutant was currently searching through. Everything around the signal detection seemed to her to be the most logical starting point. "But it couldn't have been long before me."

"Are you sure he registered at the gate under his real name?"

"No. Normally he has to, but it's not entirely uncommon for intelligence officers to operate under alternate identities when it comes to sensitive issues or undercover investigations within the military ."

"Maybe we should just ask Colonel Smith if Feinman was here," her aide suggested. "We could show him a photo. Or describe him if we can't find one."

"That could be found in the Pentagon's database. He may be able to change his identity, but not his personnel file at the Department of Defense," Rebecca said, thinking about it before shaking her head. "No, I don't want Smith involved in any way. Maybe it all turns out to be just paranoia on my part, and I don't want him to get hurt. He has nothing to do with this."

Rogers nodded, but looked disappointed.

"But we could ask at the gate. Someone there must have recognized him, because not even a four-star general can get in here without a security check. Apart from that, base commanders are kind of like God on their base, no matter what rank they hold." She savored her own words in her mind and thought back to her first encounter with Smith. "Oddly enough, Smith was pretty submissive when I was here back then."

"You think Feinman might have intimidated him?"

"I would not rule it out. It would also fit that he didn't tell Smith his name. Why would he do that?"

"Shall I get you Feinman's file from the Pentagon database?"

"No," she said bluntly, and shook her head. " I don't want him to know, and someone in HR or IT might red-flag it because of your request. We should do this as best we can under the radar."

"Of course, ma'am."

"I'm going to the gate," she declared and left the office. Sergeant Myers jumped up from her chair like it was spring loaded.

"Major? Do you need anything?"

"No, thanks, I'm just going to stretch my legs." Rebecca gestured to the woman who towered half a head over her that she could sit back down and left the building toward the main gate. The Colorado winter sun was weak, but it reflected off the many piles of snow along the cleared runway used by both Colorado Springs Airport and the Space Force Base.

Two soldiers were standing guard at the barrier, and a third soldier – a corporal – was sitting in the small guard shack next to it cleaning his rifle. She approached the latter, giving a curt salute to the ensigns, who quickly came to attention and returned her salute.

"I have a question," she said without beating around the bush, which seemed to startle the man. He dropped his gun and jumped up from his chair. Only then did she notice that he was watching a porn video on his cellphone, which was propped up at an angle against a water bottle on the desk.

"Of course, Major, excuse me, Major, ma'am," he stammered and saluted, trying to knock the phone over with his hip. He succeeded, but by some mishap it apparently landed on the volume button and the groans grew louder, drowned out by the sneering comments of a man's voice.

The corporal closed his eyes and pressed his lips together. He was probably dissolving inside with shame, but Rebecca simply didn't care – or rather, she found it useful.

"You're welcome to switch it off at your leisure," she said, and waited until he had complied with her request.

"Excuse me, Major. That was just a stupid video from 9gag that a friend sent me. I'm in one of those WhatsApp groups and ..."

"Aren't you supposed to be on guard duty?"

"Of course, ma'am."

"Is the exchange via WhatsApp also part of the guard duty, Corporal?"

"No, Major, of course not." He gulped and looked out at the two ensigns, who were trying their hardest to pretend they were unaware of all this.

"Don't worry, I won't report it, but you should work on your attention to duty. I'm not stationed here, but the colonel talks to me a lot. I'd like to tell him next time about how attentive Corporal ... Cunningham is." She read his name from the patch on his chest.

"Of course, ma'am, that would be very kind, ma'am."

She turned to go.

"Major?"

"Yes?" She turned around. In his eyes she could see the restlessness and the unconditional will to please her and to get rid of some of the shame and the impending trouble, or at best to minimize it.

"Is there anything I can do for you? You've just come here ..."

"Yes, you could indeed." The breach had been made, and now she had to widen it a little. Given that she didn't particularly like human emotions, it was easy for her to use them to her advantage. "At the beginning of the year, a colonel came as a guest. His name was Feinman, but he may have had a different ID. Space Force Intelligence."

The corporal's eyes widened.

"He's about my height, has a square face, is a bit stocky but muscular, looks a bit like a butcher. His voice sounds like sandpaper being rubbed together. Did he pass through here? You'd remember."

Cunningham thought, but she could see right away that it hadn't *clicked,* and he was just looking for a way out, a way to please her, even though he couldn't tell her what she wanted to hear. "No, ma'am," he said. "But we have another access gate for logistics. I could ask about that. Visitors don't usually come through there, but ..."

"You do that, thank you very much. But please don't make a fuss. I have to go through all the files and I don't want anyone messing them up for me, if you understand," Rebecca said, and the corporal nodded eagerly before reaching for the receiver of the landline phone on the desk and pressing a button.

"Hi Joey, Wayne here from the gate. Tell me, earlier this year ..."

"Around signal day," Rebecca mouthed to him.

" ... around the day *Sentinel I* went online, did you have a car come through with a colonel? Maybe an intelligence officer from Arlington. He looks ..."

"Yo, I remember him well," she heard Joey say. Cunningham had pressed the speaker button. "I won't forget him either. A real asshole."

The corporal grimaced apologetically, but Rebecca ignored it.

"But that's not the only reason. Specialist Walker, the tall red-haired guy who was with us at the Christmas binge, remember?"

"Sure, rumor has it that *he* detected the signal," Cunningham replied.

"Well, he was in the car, too. I don't know why."

Dozens of thoughts came to life in Rebecca's head at the same time: The colonel had Walker with him? Why? How did they know each other? Was it before or after the signal was discovered? What was their relationship?

"When?" she asked, barely audible.

"Do you remember when that was?"

"I don't know, man. Sometime around the date when the Chinese held this press conference and we were told that we were the first. Nobody tells us poor saps anything. Why do you ask?"

Rebecca shook her head and mimed slicing her hand across her throat. "Oh, nothing. He came by our place, too, and was a real asshole."

"Told you."

"Thanks, I'll see you Wednesday." The corporal hung up.

"That's helpful," she said. "I'm an intelligence officer myself. If you keep this confidential, I'll speak to the colonel in confidence and commend you."

Hope glowed in the eyes of her counterpart. "Thank you, ma'am, and please forgive me."

Rebecca left the guard shack and went back to the Harting Building and the office.

PART III

THE DISCOVERY

CHAPTER 28

"I found it!" Rogers crowed triumphantly, two hours after they had gone back to searching for the right rosters. The base's counting and dating method was a nightmare and followed a system that wasn't up to Pentagon standards. Rebecca guessed it was because the formalities within the Space Force had yet to be sorted out, the branch having only been established less than ten years ago. In addition, many of the base commanders were careerists who had been promoted out of the Air Force and brought their own people whom they trusted with them, but who were not necessarily the best choices when it came to handling the formalities.

"What's wrong?" she asked, looking up from the January 18 time sheet.

"Specialist David Walker starting work on January 17 at 7:30 am. No wonder we didn't find him earlier: He either didn't clock out or was on base for three days straight."

"Are there even barracks here?"

"No, I don't think so. There are a few accommodations for the late shift and the guards, but the personnel pretty much all live in Colorado Springs and the surrounding area," her aide explained, standing up to hand her the printout, but she raised a hand and motioned for him to sit back down.

"I saw the occupancy plans here somewhere," she mumbled, leafing through one of the many piles piled up in front of her. She kept moistening her index finger by licking it because the air was so dry that the pages kept slipping away from her. "Ah! I've found it." She went through the color-coded lines. "Specialist David Walker, registered for Room 8, Block 2, January 17th through the 20th."

"*Sentinel I* went online early in the morning on the 20th. He was probably working overtime in direct preparation. The satellite was already in lunar orbit, wasn't it?"

"Yes." She nodded. "It took several days for to maneuver it into the correct orbit and get it into position over the south pole."

"Then it's probably nothing special."

"Well, we now know that Feinman was here already on the 17th. Three days before the discovery of the signal and the recording of the reflection in the Shackleton. Why would a highly decorated intelligence officer like him be interested in this project?"

"Well, it was and is one of the Space Force's most important projects this year," Rogers said. "Maybe he just wanted to make sure everything went according to plan?"

"It's not impossible that he was involved in the project and got pressure from the Pentagon to make sure there wasn't another loss like Zuma." The loss of the stealth satellite in 2018 had been a major setback for the Space Force in particular, and the Pentagon in general, as Zuma had been a multi-billion-dollar project that would have catapulted U.S. observation and space capabilities into a new era. "But something else is really weird."

Her adjutant listened.

"On the evening of the 20th, Walker went off duty. We knew that from Colonel Smith."

"No wonder, after three days of continuous shift work."

"True. But he's never shown up here since." Rebecca had leafed through the time sheets but couldn't find his name anywhere. That was part of the reason why it had taken so long.

"How is that possible?"

"I'm not sure." She pressed a button on the desk. "Sergeant, how far along are you with digitizing the timekeeping systems?"

"Uhh, somewhere in April, Major," she heard the metallic, distorted voice from the built-in speaker.

"Please see if a Specialist David Walker shows up after January 20."

"Of course, ma'am." The clatter of a keyboard could be heard. Then Sergeant Myers spoke again, "Negative, Major. No Specialist David Walker. Last mention is January 20th. He's the one who detected the signal, isn't he?"

"That's right. Do you know anything about his whereabouts?"

"Yes, ma'am. He was transferred, if I remember correctly."

"Do you remember where?"

"No, but the transfer papers should be in folder 24-01-CCB. Would you like me to find them for you?"

"No need, thank you very much." Rebecca pressed the disconnect button and stood up. The relevant folders were on one of the roll-top tables in front of the window. She ran her finger along the numbers and then fished out 24-01-CCB. She began to leaf through it until she found the transfer paper. "This is *strange*."

The lieutenant stood up and came to stand by her. She handed him the relevant paper and he began to skim through it. His forehead creases deepened as his brows rose closer to his hairline.

"Vance?" he eventually asked, confused. "Why would he be transferred to Oklahoma? He's supposed to be famous. The operator who discovered the alien signal."

Rebecca nodded and thought about it. Vance Air Force Base, an hour and a half north of Oklahoma City, was a fairly small base that was used to train pilots and didn't have its own fighter jet squadron.

"Someone like David Walker, who is trained in satellite control and orbital mechanics, would *not* be transferred to Vance," Rogers continued.

"Not unless you want to get rid of him." Their eyes met. "But it could also be," Rebecca continued, "that they simply wanted to take him out of the line of fire. As the discoverer of the signal, he's certainly one of the Space Force's most wanted."

"Hmm."

"I think we should fly to Oklahoma City."

"That won't go unnoticed. If Feinman or the general wanted to get rid of him and hide him, they won't like it if we seek him out."

"I'm not here to please anyone, I'm here to get answers. The colonel is playing some game I don't understand, and I don't like being yanked around. Besides, I'm convinced General Eversman doesn't know about this or he wouldn't have let me come here and snoop."

"Are you sure, ma'am?"

"Yes. It would have been easy for him to just order me back to Arlington and sideline me for the time being. He didn't even think about it – he had to pull me out of Houston because his hands were tied. But the fact that he granted my request shows that he still has use for me and that I'm an important asset." She shook her head. "Whatever Feinman is playing at, the general doesn't know about it, I'm sure of it."

"Or, that's what he wants you to believe," Rogers objected, wincing when he noticed her facial reaction.

"You're getting better and better at this, Lieutenant," she praised him. "In our job, you can't be paranoid enough, you can't make assumptions, and you have to be committed to finding evidence."

"Thank you, ma'am." He'd misread her face.

She stood up and lifted her jacket from the chair. "We are flying to Oklahoma City."

Rebecca was aware that she was taking a big risk. On the one hand, she had told the general that she would clean up the paper trail at Peterson, and put it all in order; on the other hand, she was digging around in Feinman's affairs. It wasn't that she was driven by vengeance because he'd double-crossed her. She respected players from whom she could learn something. But she didn't accept defeat, always seeking the improvement of her skills. He may have spun her into his web, but she intended to cut the web and eat the spider.

Her instincts told her that the colonel wasn't playing by the rules, and that was even more motivation, because without rules they were all just cavemen bashing each other's heads in.

CHAPTER 29

The debriefing of the first part of the mission lasted two hours, during which – after their showers – they logged everything, went through the recorded data, and compared the results with the simulations and expectations. During his training, Charlie had been fascinated by how much NASA knew about the moon.

The Apollo program had been a bit like the Wild West, with the most swashbuckling cowboys of the generation accomplishing incredible things thanks to some of the best engineers of all time – Wernher von Braun, for one – and brilliant mathematicians. But despite this improvised and technically limited set of circumstances, the men and women of Apollo had collected an incredible amount of data. They had accomplished everything that had been possible in their time. When he thought about everything that had been unknown to Armstrong, Aldrin, Collins and company, he shivered. They had set off for a celestial body about which virtually nothing was known, apart from observations, calculations, and physics-based deductions.

On Apollo 11, Neil Armstrong had steered the lander manually because there had been no autopilot. The chosen landing zone had been full of rocks, which had not been known during planning. So he had used two small 'joysticks,' the few sensors the ship had, and his eyes, to find a reasonably safe zone and land the ship. Instead of touching down in a flatter highland, he had to take them down in a rocky area that had been anything but ideal due to a shortage of fuel – the braking thrusts of the cold gas jets had also been miscalculated. And the moon dust had different properties than anticipated. It turned out to be much finer, settled into the suit systems, and would have destroyed them if the astronauts had stayed longer. Armstrong was almost unable to open the upper hatch because it had become clogged with the regolith, which he would later describe as 'concrete.'

Today, NASA, he and Louis, Miles and Anne could draw upon all that knowledge – firsthand knowledge. Nevertheless, they found themselves in a most hostile and highly dangerous environment. Every step was therefore carefully planned and coordinated with Houston.

" ... the amount of dust is significantly less than expected. So, Axiom has done a good job," Miles was saying into his headset. "And the extractors in the airlock seem to be coping just fine with the tiny grains."

"Very good. We should now start planning the construction of the winch," continued Mission Director Ramaswami. "I'll hand things over to the Shackleton team for that."

"Understood, Mission Control."

Charlie stretched. They were in the cockpit, the seats of which they had tilted so that they were aligned vertically with the moon's gravity. The windows looked out at the stunning starry sky, in which Earth had become a blue crescent – very thin, but clearly visible. Because of the glowing terminator, it looked like the moon from Earth, only zoomed in about four times.

"Hey, *Liberty*, it's Marty," came the voice of the potbellied engineer from the Shackleton team, with whom they had spent a lot of time working on the hoist simulations in Houston. He was a gentle nerd with nickel-framed glasses and a cheerful face, one of those employees that everyone liked.

"Good to hear from you, Marty," replied Anne, who, as the ship's engineer, took the helm for this part of the conversation. Although Charlie only listened, he knew the plans inside out and the few points of discussion where they mulled over small changes were so specific that he had nothing useful to contribute.

That changed two hours later, after they had gone through the entire external mission, including two changes to the angle of attack of the crank. There was no longer a true 'problem,' except for one: sleep.

They had been awake for 18 hours, so according to the mission specifications, they were two hours overdue for sleep. Tired astronauts made mistakes and mistakes meant death out here. But the Chinese were only 16 hours away, leaving them less than eight to set up the winch and platform – which was tight for two people in low gravity. And, they wanted to take possession of the artifact before the taikonauts could.

"A fucking dilemma," Louis said, letting out a low grumble.

"If we don't sleep, the danger is too great," Anne said, shaking her head. "Race or no race, we can't risk rushing into something that could cost one or all of us our lives. After all, that wouldn't help anyone, would it?"

"Arriving first and then returning empty-handed is not an option, either."

"Anne's right," Charlie intervened. "It's not just sleeping and setting up. First we have to find a suitable location. The latest images from *Sentinel I* indicate that there is a cliff face very close to 404 ..."

" ... which is eligible for elevator construction!"

"Yes, but we have to find the right anchoring point for the winches, measure the depth, and even then, after we've gone down, we have plenty of kilometers to cover. That's a matter of many days – at least."

Louis gritted his teeth, knowing Charlie was right but finding it difficult to accept the facts. Understandably. The responsibility of the mission was on his shoulders.

"Mind you," Miles spoke up, rubbing his chin, which was showing the signs of a three-day beard, "we've still got our head start. We'll finish our elevator and get down below, and that's a project they'll have yet to complete."

Louis nodded. "Besides the landing, the Rover setup, the power supply, and everything else."

"That speaks even more in favor of not rushing things," Anne stated with certainty. "The head start won't be lost. The Chinese have to sleep, too. If no accidents happen, we should get to the artifact before they do."

"Accidents," said Charlie. "They're the only factor that can cost us the lead. And accidents happen when you're overtired."

"And acting rashly," Anne added, whereupon they nodded to each other and looked at Louis.

"You're right," Miles said with a sigh. "This is typical choking."

"Choking?" they all asked at the same time.

"Yo, I think it's a term from sports psychology. The athlete or an entire team that has a lead and thinks they've got the game won, but fails just before the end. They feel even more pressure because they are on the verge of achieving everything. The thought of not losing any ground distracts them. Or they tense up, or become too cautious, or individuals lose concentration because they are constantly checking on their pursuers. There can also be a turn of events that they didn't see coming, and although it would be enough, they are too rattled by it. That must *not* happen to us."

"Yeah, you're right," said Louis. "We'll just do our thing and not take any risks. If we're systematic and deliberate, we'll bring this thing home – whatever it is."

"If the artifact is transportable. Maybe it's just the periscope of an entire underground facility," Anne replied with a shrug.

"We'll see. Now let's go to sleep." Their commander held his tablet in their direction so they could all see the latest data from NASA, which showed the Chinese spacecraft, the *Celestial Dragon*, on its approach vector into an elliptical lunar orbit, much like their own. "They are expected to be down here in sixteen hours. They have to decelerate, stabilize the orbit, take their measurements and compare them with the expected value, undock the lander, and fly down. That may take even longer than we think. So let's go to bed, get a good night's sleep and then get back to work."

After eating something – a paste that was supposed to be chicken fricassee and didn't taste too bad – they washed it all down with their obligatory cocktail of vitamins, minerals and trace elements, brushed their teeth, and lay down in their beds for the first time. Although they had also slept in them during the journey, they had been tied into their anchored sleeping bags so that they would not drift off in microgravity due to involuntary body movements. This time there was a direction of gravity, so they could lie down unrestricted, and turn over as desired, and the brain knew up and down. Charlie had been looking forward to this since the beginning of the journey.

His bunk was above Anne's, while Louis and Miles's were on the other side of their living quarters. There were no portholes, but there was a display with camera images from outside so that they could see the surface of the moon and the starry sky.

Lying in bed was strange, as he felt like he was going to lift off or at least fall out with the slightest movement, so after a few moments he took the tightening straps and put them around his legs, hips, and upper body just to be on the safe side. However, he left them loose instead of tightening them. Shortly afterward, he fell asleep and dreamt of a deep hole into which he was lowered as a ball of light.

He was rudely awakened by a tinny voice: "*Liberty,* come in, please."

After a few moments of absolute disorientation, Charlie remembered where he was and realized that the voice had come from the speaker in the living quarters. Below him, he heard the rustling of Anne's sleeping bag, and Louis and Miles were just getting up and rubbing the sleep out of their eyes.

"Mission Control?" he asked. "What's going on? Is there a problem?"

"Yes. The Chinese have reached their target orbit and it looks like they will land much earlier than expected," Ramaswami explained. He sounded as tense as Charlie suddenly felt.

CHAPTER 30

On the approach to Oklahoma City's airport, Rebecca looked at the city of 700,000 inhabitants through the small window of her business class seat. The small financial district with its handful of skyscrapers – or buildings hoping to become skyscrapers when they grew up – was the only landmark in the area. Because the city was largely sprawling, with many single-family homes and low-rise commercial areas, it stretched out like a gray carpet. All around were the green and brown checkerboard patterns of endless fields that were so typical of Oklahoma. Here, one farm led to the next.

After landing, she sent Rogers out to get a rental car and gave him her personal credit card. If necessary, she could request it later as an expense. For now, however, she wanted to play it safe and leave as few traces as possible for her employer. The general trusted her and she had no intention of undermining that trust by leaving a paper trail in his direction in case this all turned out to be a wild goose chase. Even though her instincts told her something was up, the ease with which Feinman had cold cocked her had made her doubt the reliability of her intuition.

This didn't mean that she would give up her habit of

poking her finger where it hurt. After all, that was what she had been trained for.

While Rogers took care of the car, she sat down in a small café and pretended to read a newspaper. Instead, she was observing her surroundings attentively, taking frequent sips of the awful airport coffee she had been served and using those moments for seemingly random glances around.

As far as she could see, however, no one was following her. Either that, or the pursuers were so good that they could fool even a trained intelligence officer. If that were the case she would probably have bigger problems than her paranoia covered.

After half an hour, her new cellphone rang.

"Yes?"

"I'm outside Exit 2 with the car," said Rogers and hung up. The shorter the phone call, the better.

Rebecca got up and went outside. Outside the door, she was greeted by cold air and crowds of people hailing cabs or streaming to the rental car lots with their collars turned up and noisy rolling suitcases in tow. It took her a few moments to spot Rogers in a Ford sedan that looked so plain and boring it would be easy for observers to forget.

"Good choice," she said after putting her bag on the back seat and getting in the front next to him.

"Thank you, ma'am." The lieutenant even managed not to smile contentedly, but to drive past the many cars of families picking up their loved ones with an impassive expression. He was a quick learner, and she had a feeling that would be necessary.

As he drove them from the airport, she entered the address of Vance Air Force Base into the GPS system. With the current traffic situation – it was midafternoon – it would take them just under two hours to reach Enid.

They barely spoke during the ride because Rogers was

focused on driving and she was trying to find out as much as she could about David Walker. He had transferred from the Air Force to the Space Force as a data analyst in pay grade E-3 and after a year – last year – had been promoted to Specialist E-4. That was not unusual. What was strange, however, was that someone with his skills had started out in the enlisted ranks. He had completed training as a data analyst in Washington. His criminal record may have played a role: multiple drunk driving charges, assault, attempted robbery, a total of two months in jail in New York. As he had been born in Boston, she guessed that he had been a member of one of the many gangs there – poor parents, perhaps addicted to drugs, the wrong friends. The usual.

The military was good at straightening out difficult personalities. The fact that he had become a data analyst was proof that someone had recognized his potential. However, she was surprised that he had joined the Air Force two years ago and wanted to start from the bottom. Unless the job interviews hadn't gone as hoped after the training. People with criminal records had a harder time. Even in the armed forces, a real career was difficult when background data like this was noted in a file.

All in all, she didn't find anything particularly noteworthy. Stories like his were a dime a dozen in every branch of the U.S. military. A second chance in uniform.

When they reached Vance Air Force Base, south of the small town of Enid, Oklahoma, population 50,000, the sun had just disappeared below the horizon, making the sky glow as if God had poured out red liquid.

To get to the base, they left the interstate and navigated a large traffic circle, beyond the last exit of which were two large, covered gates with integrated guard houses, reminiscent of somewhat outdated toll stations. To the right and left, the huge area was cordoned off with tall, barbed wire fences.

"Good evening," a uniformed sergeant greeted them and peered into their car. Rogers handed him their badges.

"Major, Lieutenant," said the non-commissioned officer after a brief inspection. He came to attention and saluted. "Excuse me. You weren't mentioned on any guest list. Are you expected?"

"No, we're just passing through. I'd like to have a chat with the base personnel officer," Rebecca replied.

"The BPO? Excuse me, Major, but I'm afraid you'll have to speak to the commander first." The sergeant looked at her apologetically. It was standard protocol. Unannounced visits by officers from other bases was not something that happened every day, and she had no appointment and therefore no official reason to be here. She could wave her credentials as an intelligence officer, but she preferred to save that for an emergency.

"I understand that, Sergeant. Then please announce me."

"The colonel is currently off duty, ma'am."

"That's unfortunate," she replied, although she had expected to hear it. "Do you have quarters for us for the night?"

"Of course, Major. Specialist Hobbs here will assign you guest rooms." The sergeant waved one of his comrades over and spoke to him briefly. Then he turned back to them. "May he ride with you? He'll direct you there and get you squared away."

"Of course."

Hobbs, a young specialist with a baby face, sat down somewhat embarrassedly in the back and guided them along the road through the base proper, which was as big as a small town. They took the first turn to the guest accommodations, which looked like a colonial motel. Hobbs got out of the car and disappeared briefly into a small office, returning with two keys.

"You'll have the two rooms right here." Hobbs pointed to the doors on their right and left.

"Thank you, Specialist. That will be all." Rebecca saw that the young man hesitated. "You can pick us up tomorrow morning at eight o'clock, unless you want to watch us sleep."

"Uhh, no, ma'am. I mean, of course, ma'am." He turned on his heel and seemed for a moment not to know what to do before heading off at a trot, presumably toward the gate. That would certainly cost him some time.

"I don't suppose we're going to sleep?" asked Rogers as they looked after the Specialist.

"No. We're going to the BPO," she replied. "Before Hobbs arrives for his scolding at the gate, we'll probably have fifteen minutes. At least."

"That will stir up trouble."

"We're not here to make friends. As intelligence officers, we never have that option, so best you get used to it. Go in the little building there and ask for directions to the BPO's office."

"Of course, Major."

Rogers hurried off and returned a short time later to guide them through the maze of the base. They passed a refueling station for small aircraft and a 24-hour general store before heading toward a long office building. The fourth door led them into a wing of open offices, only a few of which were occupied this late in the day. The lights were dimmed and the few NCOs on duty were either on the phone or talking into their headsets. Behind them was an office with a closed door.

"That should be it," she said and went inside. The four soldiers present didn't give them more than quick glances and didn't pause in their work. Arriving at the door, she knocked briefly and then entered.

A fairly young captain was sitting on a chair behind a wide aluminum desk, going through a few stacks of files. He looked a little taken aback when he saw her come in with Rogers, but he stood and saluted, albeit not as crisply as the sergeant at the gate.

"Major," said Captain Breidenbach, as the name badge on his uniform identified him. "Excuse me, I wasn't expecting any more visitors."

"That doesn't matter. My adjutant, Lieutenant Rogers, and I are here on an investigation."

"*Investigation?*" The captain visibly tensed.

"That's right." She waved her hand. "It'll be quick. There's a Specialist E-4 named David Walker working on your base. He'd have been transferred here a few months ago. He was in the Space Force for a year, but he's come back into the fold of the Air Force, it looks like."

"That's quite possible, ma'am. We have almost fifteen hundred active soldiers and reservists stationed here, plus the same number of civilian staff," the captain replied hesitantly.

"I don't suppose you get very many returnees from the Space Force. Especially as he only changed branches of the armed forces for a year, and he's a data analyst. He has absolutely nothing to do with flight training, or even aircraft." She pointed to his computer. "Take a quick look at your personnel program."

Breidenbach looked at her with a pained expression. She could see his mind working behind his eyes, how he was trying to assess the situation and what kind of trouble he could get into.

"Do you have a specific order for this?" he asked cautiously.

"No."

"Major, I'd love to help you, but Colonel Withers won't be too happy if I hand over the personal data of one of his soldiers to an officer from outside the base. Perhaps I should give him a quick call." He picked up the phone, but then hesitated and licked his lips.

"As I said, I'm here as part of an investigation." She handed him her badge. She held her finger covering the place where her current stationing was indicated: the Pentagon.

Breidenbach's eyes widened as he apparently assessed benefits versus risks.

"We won't be staying long, and from what we can see, hardly anyone here has noticed us," Rogers interjected, and Rebecca gave him a barely perceptible nod. His improvisation was getting better, too.

The captain took a deep breath and then started typing on his keyboard.

"What do you need regarding Specialist Walker?"

"His place of residence. I don't suppose he's quartered here at the base?"

"No ma'am. He lives in Enid, 401 N Adams Street."

"Was he on duty today?"

"Negative, ma'am. He's on leave. At his own request, it seems. He hasn't been on duty for weeks. I don't know how he got six weeks, but apparently I agreed to it." Breidenbach frowned and rubbed his broad chin.

"Thank you, Captain." Rebecca stood up, but the BPO didn't seem to notice her as they walked out.

"Now he's got his own puzzle to chew on," she muttered to Rogers.

By the time they were back in their rental car, a total of 14 minutes had passed.

"Should we wait until tomorrow?" asked the lieutenant.

"No. I'd rather not lose any time. Who knows if the query of Walker's name in the program has tripped a red flag somewhere. If so, I'd rather have a head start."

Six weeks leave, she thought. That was indeed strange.

Without further ado, she dialed the cellphone number of Colonel Smith, the base commander at Peterson Space Force Base.

"Major," he answered after the second ring. "I understand you've left us again. I don't suppose you want to leave my office as I left it to you?"

"Yes, sorry, sir. We'll take care of it when we get back. It's just a short trip."

"I see." The colonel didn't sound as if he understood at all.

"May I ask you, sir, if you know anything about the transfer of Specialist David Walker?"

There was silence for so long that she looked at her cellphone to make sure they were still connected.

"Colonel?"

"I'm still here. I'm just thinking about which rope I want to hang myself with," grumbled the base commander. "I can tell you this much: I recently tried to find out why he was taken off Peterson. I was told that he was now back in the Air Force. Can you imagine that?"

"To be honest, yes." She exchanged a glance with Rogers, who blinked in surprise. "Sir, do you happen to remember when that was?"

"What, the transfer? Sometime early this year, after he discovered the signal. The Pentagon probably wanted him out of the line of fire before there even was one. Damage control, in case something went wrong. You know how it is. When the shit hits the fan, all the journalists arrive like blowflies and pounce on the fattest chunks. Then it's one documentary after another."

"Yes, I know how it goes. I'm interested in your research, sir."

"At the beginning I wrote to the Space Force High Command asking for clarification because there was nothing in the handover file. But my inquiry went unacknowledged. Then a few weeks ago I had a phone call with my old pilot instructor at Vance, who asked me if I was doing my job right because the NCOs were supposedly fleeing from me – back into the arms of the Air Force." Smith grunted angrily. "He was just making a stupid joke, but I got really pissed off and made a few more phone calls. I still know a lot of people at Vance."

"I guess nothing substantial came out of that?"

"No, but how do you know that?"

"Just a hunch. It's all part of what I'm trying to find out," she replied.

"Good. If you could pour me some wine, I would be very grateful," said Smith.

"I will, sir. Last question. You said, 'a few weeks ago' Do you remember exactly how many?"

"At the beginning of November, I think. So about six weeks ago."

CHAPTER 31

"They don't have a lander?" asked Anne, mumbling around her toothbrush as she cleaned her teeth.

"That's sure what it looks like." Charlie nodded for emphasis while pulling on his functional underwear. Louis and Miles were up in the cockpit, analyzing the situation with Mission Control as he and Anne prepared for the field mission.

"I don't understand." Anne spat the toothpaste into the sink and rinsed her mouth. "They've got a pretty big capsule, so all the analysts assumed the second stage of the spaceship would be the landing module."

"Now we at least have an explanation as to how they were able to set up a mission so quickly. They have developed a capsule that can land, but probably not return to orbit."

Anne turned to him and slapped her forehead. "Of course! Thanks to *Chang'e*, they learned how to land an unmanned lander on the far side of the moon. That means they could collect this data. All they had to do was make the vehicle bigger and equip it with life support. Coming down and landing is quite different from returning to orbit, docking with the capsule, and flying back to Earth."

"Yes." Charlie stood up to straighten the pants part of his skin-tight functional underwear, smoothing a number of minor wrinkles. "Less fuel, less payload. Half of our space and weight goes on the return journey, which they can't make. They've saved all that – along with half of all potential sources of error."

"And they only needed half the preparation and planning time." She now began to get dressed as well – more skillfully, he noticed. "That means the taikonauts have come here on a one-way ticket."

Charlie took a deep breath and shuddered. "I wonder what kind of personality would agree to do that."

"I don't think there is anything about 'agreeing' in the Chinese astronaut corps. They are all recruited from the military and follow orders. When the leadership says *jump,* they just ask *how high*?"

As soon as they were dressed, they climbed up to prepare their suits in the airlock, where Louis and Miles joined them.

"Hey, is there any further news?" asked Charlie.

"Yes, all four of us are going out."

"What?! Why?"

"Houston thinks that the Chinese will initiate the braking thrust with the lander at the next periselenium and then be down here half an hour later. That would be in three hours at the latest," Louis explained, squeezing past him and Anne to open his locker. "We thought about it for a long time, but the four of us are twice as fast and can keep an eye on each other."

"But according to the mission specifications, at least one of us has to stay in the cockpit at all times and monitor the field operation," Anne protested. "What if there's an emergency?"

"Well, we can only treat it in the *Liberty*," Miles replied. "More of us outside actually makes it safer because we can more easily carry someone with an injury."

"What if communication with Houston breaks down? They don't have a direct view of our radar and windows."

"They see what our on-board computer sees. Don't worry. If there's anything wrong, they'll let us know via the radio relay," Louis stated with certainty. "We're not giving up our damn advantage. Houston also thinks that the risk doesn't outweigh the benefits, so it's a done deal."

From the tone of their commander, it was clear that he considered this discussion to be over.

This change of plan meant that he and Anne had to get outside, and they couldn't help the other two get suited. Those already in their suits were far too dexterity-limited to be of any real use, due in particular to the stiff gloves, so either Louis or Miles had to take the risk of being the last one fully suited. Not a very big risk, as they had thoroughly practiced dressing themselves in their suits, which had been incredibly strenuous and difficult on Earth, but there was still a risk. A visual inspection by a fellow astronaut was no substitute for the real thing done with the tablet links.

But that was the way it would be done, and Charlie didn't question orders after they had been discussed.

Half an hour later, he stood with Anne on the elevator platform and watched through the porthole as Louis and Miles hurriedly squeezed themselves into their Axiom suits with the precise movements of professionals. At some point, Charlie turned around and looked up at the starry sky. One of the shining points was probably the *Celestial Dragon*.

"They'll be here soon," said Anne, who had followed his gaze.

"Do you think we'll be able to set it up before then?"

"Unlikely." She shook her head inside her 'fishbowl' helmet. "Unless everything is going perfectly according to plan and we're being incredibly clever."

Charlie tried to inject a little optimism. "The taikonauts

also have to land successfully first and wait for their sensor data, get dressed, go out – that will all take time."

"I already factored that in."

When Miles and Louis joined them on the platform and they had all checked the radio control of the airlock systems several times via the displays on their forearms, they sealed the airlock and began their agonizingly slow descent.

Miles and Louis got out and prepared the Rover, while Anne and Charlie rode the platform back up to the cargo hatch, which they opened with a command to the on-board computer. Inside were eight transport crates, which they pulled out of their slots and stacked on the platform. This process alone took them half an hour.

They brought everything down to the surface and loaded it onto the Rover's cargo area along with a smaller crate that Miles and Louis had brought down with them on their last moon walk. It contained replacement CO_2 absorbers and oxygen cartridges, as they would have to stay outside for much longer than two and a half hours this time.

Then they drove toward Site 404, which might one day become a lunar colony shared by the international community. This idea now seemed like a dream to him, while he stood at the edge of the cargo area and held on to the Rover's antenna bracket while Louis steered. None of them said anything, and so the perfect silence of the moon enveloped them like a cocoon. This place didn't care about them – it had been the same for millions and millions of years. What they were doing here, and what made them so excited, seemed petty and ridiculous against this monumental backdrop of timelessness.

And yet, he reminded himself, the reality of life on Earth was different. What he and his crewmates were doing here was highly relevant to everyone there. He could not make the mistake of dismissing everything to do with Earth as unimportant, knowing it affected eight billion people, their own families, dreams, and fears.

Charlie felt the burden of this responsibility on his shoulders, and the worry that it was being handled wrongly never left him.

The ride was bumpy, and yet smooth at the same time because every bump and change of direction happened slowly, as if someone had dimmed time like one can dim a light source.

Arriving at the crater rim, Louis and Anne got out of the Rover's seats while he and Miles got down from the sides.

"All right then. According to the plan, there's a steep drop-off somewhere to our right," explained Anne, who was responsible for constructing the elevator. She pointed to the east, where the edge of the crater looked a little more rugged and had a small bulge, as if someone had piled up snow that froze instantly. "We need to find it and then figure out the best place to set up the structure. I suggest we go and have a look on foot and then come back and drive there."

"Let's do it that way," Louis agreed and turned to Miles, reminding Charlie of a Michelin man. "You stay here with the Rover. It has the strongest radio link to *Liberty*. Make sure you don't lose contact with Houston."

"Sure," Miles answered, and the three of them set off with long hops toward the east.

They carefully approached the edge of the crater at one spot first, and then moving to another and yet another, and looking downward at each one. As this part of the crater was out of the sunlight, it was pitch black, but their headlamps enabled them to see that the wall sloped down relatively gently – not so gently that he wasn't afraid of falling off, because he certainly wouldn't have reached the bottom alive, but it was not steep like a cliff. It looked relatively flat-surfaced, but that impression could be deceptive.

Then, after a few hundred meters, during which they fell several times because they had not yet become sufficiently accustomed to the moon's gravity, Anne, who was more agile and 'running' ahead of them, held up a hand.

"I've found the spot," she radioed. The two men caught up with her. Charlie's breath rushed in and out inside his helmet, echoed in his ears, and became a familiar companion in the background, reminding him of scuba diving.

They stepped carefully to Anne's side. She stood at the crater's edge, her right foot touching the rim. The edge was slightly raised to the right, and to the left, but the spot she had discovered was level for several meters. It was the ideal spot.

She bent forward and peered into the depths. "Look."

Charlie slid his right leg forward and made sure he had firm footing before bending his upper body over the edge of the crater and looking down. When the cones of light from their two helmet lamps disappeared into a seemingly endless abyss, he was inwardly terrified. But he did not flinch, remained calm, and tried to lean a little further so that he could see the crater wall.

It consisted of rugged moon rock that looked relatively unspectacular. The gray matter reminded Charlie of granite, interrupted by dusty patches with small areas of debris. It went down, down, down for hundreds of meters, as if a huge drill had been used to make a vertical shaft.

"Shit, it's deep," Louis gasped. "Our lights don't even reach the bottom."

"No, but our rangefinders will." Charlie looked at the display in his HUD. According to the laser, which measured the travel time of the reflection, it was almost 2.5 kilometers to the bottom.

"Two and a half kilometers," said Anne. "That means it's about 1.7 kilometers from there to the crater floor. But the artifact isn't in the middle, it's six kilometers to the southeast, in our direction. If we're lucky, we're only five or six hundred meters away from it at the bottom."

"That means we could do the rest on foot, eh? A thirty degree incline shouldn't be a problem up here, with only a sixth of our terrestrial body weight." Louis sounded triumphant. "That's damn good news. We can set up the mobile module down there and then we'll be at the artifact before the Chinese can say *ni-hao*."

"Possibly. But first we have to build the elevator."

"The dimensions here are simply incredible." Charlie breathed, looking down into the depths. The Shackleton Crater was twice as deep as the Grand Canyon. The kind of asteroid that must have hit here was beyond his imagination. And then, what about this abyss in front of them? He didn't get spooked easily, but the hole in front of him looked like it was lost in the infinity of the universe itself. The perfect darkness seemed to fill it like a liquid with a life of its own, hiding secrets from them and at the same time trying to attract them like a demon snake.

"The initial data from the first lunar orbiter showed that the crater is quite flat right up to its deepest point," Anne explained, as if she had read his mind. "But more recent images from *Sentinel I* have confirmed what many astronomers have suspected for some time. That is, the Shackleton Crater is a relic from the moon's early days. The asteroid, a major chunk, probably hit at an angle, which is why the crater walls are not even and are steeper on this side. Another large visitor from the Oort cloud probably hit the rim here later, relatively vertically, and dug this hole. Later, the walls could have collapsed and led to this steep cliff. We don't know exactly. But we should be prepared for a deep, quite uneven debris field on the crater floor."

"Exciting," Louis said and straightened up. "But let's just get to work now."

After stepping back from the edge of the drop-off, they summoned Miles, who steered the Rover in their direction, accompanied by a cloud of glittering regolith that swirled upward behind the tires, seemingly weightless before it fell back down in slow motion.

When he arrived, they first checked the radio connection with Houston, which was relayed by using *Liberty* as a relay station.

"The delay is a little bit longer," Ramaswami said, "but we hear you. Harry will take over with Marty from now on."

"Got it, Houston," Louis said. "Any news from the Chinese?"

"They will reach the periselenium in eighty minutes."

They got to work. The 'elevator' that Marty's team of engineers and astrophysicists had devised worked very simply, in principle. It was a cable-guided transport gondola with two vertical cables made of carbon-reinforced polymer strands, very lightweight but strong enough to handle the moon's gravity. They ran along the underside of the supporting structure, which protruded slightly over the edge, and served to stabilize the cabin, which could be raised and lowered using two additional cables and pulleys. Their suspension would be located further up at the top of the planned superstructure.

First, they rolled out a carbon composite mat and laid the segments of the base plate on it, in which countless recesses had been prepared for screws and hooks. Miles screwed everything together with his multitool, while Charlie and Louis drove the four rock anchors into the ground at the corners. This was followed by the aluminum scaffolding and the attachment of the pulleys for the Kevlar-coated Dyneema hauling cables. In the middle of this work step, when they had assembled almost half of the pre-assembled components, Marty's voice came in from Houston.

"There's news. I'm handing you over to Mission Control,"

said the engineer, and Charlie leapt to the conclusion that something was wrong.

"The Chinese have started their landing approach," Ramaswami said without preamble. "They are currently in the final braking thrust and should come down somewhere near the Shackleton within the next fifteen minutes."

"Understood, Mission Control." Louis's reply was so formal that Charlie knew how tense he was. They paused in their work and collectively stared up at the night sky. At first, everything looked the same as before, but then he recognized a brighter object among the myriads of others, which moved like a shooting star and seemed to flicker slightly.

"We won't make it before they get here," Anne realized. "We have at least three hours, if not more, to go. And we're into our second life support kits."

"I know," Louis replied with a growl. "But we can't change that now. Charlie, you keep an eye on our new arrivals and we'll get on with it."

Charlie nodded and took a few steps away from the platform before looking up at the sky again.

"Any predictions on where they're coming down, Houston?"

"Negative," Ramaswami replied. "They are still too high to be able to predict the trajectory, and *Sentinel I* offers only limited ability for monitoring their flight. They are likely to be steering manually."

"All right. I'll keep an eye on her." And he did. He followed the growing shooting star with his eyes, soon recognizing the flames of the firing engines, and a few minutes later the gleaming metal cone of the *Celestial Dragon*. Ironically, it looked a bit like the old Apollo modules, and several dimensions smaller than the *Liberty*.

The space vehicle descended toward the rim of the Shackleton Crater and began to drift sideways before braking sharply once more, kicking up regolith. The moon dust shot off in all directions at lightning speed, silently yet violently turning into a gigantic cloud. Due to the absence of any air molecules or wind, the dust spread out evenly in all directions and obscured the Chinese spaceship for many minutes until it slowly subsided and the veil thinned out. But even then, Charlie couldn't make out much more than a small bump in the landscape, so far away was the *Celestial Dragon*.

"Charlie?" asked Louis.

"If I've aligned myself correctly, they came down a kilometer from here, northwest of *Liberty*, much closer to the crater rim," he replied.

"But they didn't crash?" His friend and commander might have sounded a little disappointed.

"Negative. At least it doesn't look like it."

"Then help us. We should hurry."

CHAPTER 32

Rebecca watched the lights of the cars moving along the main roads – yellow and white in one direction, red in the other. A dense band of cloud had gathered over the city, illuminated by the lights of Enid, and seemed to hover over the rooftops like a pathological ulcer.

The place where David Walker lived was in a nondescript block with a mixture of larger apartment buildings and houses that had small front yards begging for a bit of maintenance. Some of the streetlights flickered, adding a ghostly quality to the scene.

"How do you want to proceed, Major?" Rogers asked as he parked diagonally opposite the blue two-story house and switched off the engine. A light shone through the curtained front windows.

"We'll observe and take a closer look at the premises first," she decided, and reached for the door handle. "I'll look around the back. Maybe I can see into the house from there."

"Understood, ma'am."

Rebecca left the car and walked back along the road to the small footpath between two fenced back yards. She had spotted it as Rogers had driven past. It was unlit, but the ambient light reflecting from the glowing red clouds was enough to make the contours of the walkway stand out.

At one point she was startled when a dog suddenly began barking right next to her. The fence between them was made of wooden slats so she couldn't see the beast but it sounded like a large one.

While the adrenaline rush made her scalp tingle and was slow to subside, she reached the next street and walked to the left until she spotted the two-story blue house where Walker lived. From here, it stood behind a single-story, abandoned-looking colonial structure with rotting wooden shingles and moss growing on the roof. Instead of windows, all she could see were yawning dark holes.

After looking around – there was no one else on the street – she entered the yard of overgrown grass and circled an old, rusty motorcycle that must have been there for at least a decade.

Once on the other side, she pressed herself against the wall of the house, which smelled of mold, to blend in with the shadow of the roof, which stood half a meter above. Then she searched Walker's apartment. On the upper floor, all the windows were covered, on the lower floor apparently only those on the other side, the street side, facing Rogers. Through a large pane of glass she could see a family sitting at a long table, apparently eating a late dinner. She counted four children, roughly between the ages of 4 and 16. They were obviously arguing with each other.

Rebecca dialed Roger's number.

"Yes?"

"It looks like Walker lives on the top floor. See if there's a separate entrance to his apartment," she said quietly.

"I went forward a bit. There isn't one. At least not on this side," replied her aide.

"Hmm, then he's probably this family's renter. That complicates things a little."

"Yes. What's on the other side? Is there a back entrance?"

"Just a glass door to the yard. No hatch either, so I don't suppose the house has a basement." She knew that basements were rare in Oklahoma, but smaller bunkers under the houses were accessible via a hatch in the foundation. This was due to the high frequency of tornadoes that hit the state. The hatch in the yard was designed to ensure that if the building collapsed, it would be outside the debris field and thus allow escape for those seeking shelter.

"Do you have a plan?" Rogers didn't use her rank or his obligatory 'ma'am' over the phone. He was being more cautious than even she would typically have thought necessary. It seemed like he was consciously emulating her.

"I'll be back."

She took a photo of the back of the house and then returned to the car via the small footpath and the barking dog. Once she was back in the passenger seat, she pointed ahead. "Drive off. We need civilian clothes before we ring the bell."

"Do you think anything is still open here, Major? It's after 8 pm." The lieutenant started the engine and drove off.

"The town isn't very big, but it's not a village. We'll find something."

So they drove back toward the center, which took less than five minutes. It resembled that of any other Midwestern town, with low houses and large facades along checkerboard streets, storefronts, and billboards reminiscent of the set of an old western movie.

"Over there," she said, pointing to a store where the lights were on and which advertised '24-hour General Merchandise.'

Rogers changed lanes to the left and stopped along the dashed line between the two lanes to let a car through that was coming from the east.

Rebecca didn't know if it was a coincidence, or if her ever-heightened alertness made her react so quickly, but she glanced in the side mirror and saw a pair of headlights behind them turn into their lane at the same moment they had, and the lights quickly grew larger.

"Drive!" she shouted at Rogers, pointing to the left. Without questioning her, the lieutenant reacted immediately and pressed the gas pedal.

The engine howled and they drove far too fast across the oncoming lane onto the sloping parking strips alongside the stores. The vehicle behind them just barely hit them on the bumper, only grazing them, and continued straight ahead as it had built up lots of momentum.

But in the milliseconds it took, Rebecca heard tires squeal as the dark SUV that had rearended their car braked.

Her eyes jerked back to the front and she instinctively thrust her hands forward to support herself on the dashboard as they collided with a car from the oncoming traffic. The driver tried to brake, but their sudden maneuver made it far too late. It caught them on the front bumper and there was such a crazy noise that her ears rang. Windows shattered and metal was crushed. Their rental car went into an uncontrolled skid, collided with a parked car and almost came to a standstill.

"Step on it!" she shouted, pointing to a small alleyway between two stores. Rogers, whose nose was bleeding, blinked and let out a groan, but apparently had enough situational awareness to obey her. However, he didn't seem to be in full control of his motor skills, and he drove the dented front end into the corner of the right-hand store in front of the alley.

Rebecca fumbled for the door handle with trembling fingers and pulled on it, but nothing happened. After glancing over her shoulder, she saw through an unsplintered section of the rear window that the large SUV that had hit them from behind had skidded to a halt a few hundred meters away and was already turning around.

The driver who had rammed into them had just got out of his vehicle – apparently mostly uninjured – and looked confused.

"Rogers!" she said, reaching for her aide. His nose was bleeding so badly that it was soaking his uniform, but he nodded and his eyes looked bleary but showed mental clarity. "Can you get your door open?"

He began to fiddle with the handle and shook his head. She suppressed a curse, pulled her own lever again, and then banged her shoulder against the door several times before it burst open with an ugly squeal.

The energy she had built up sent her tumbling onto the cold blacktop, quickly getting to her hands and knees and then to her feet. However, she remained crouched behind a parked van, which now shielded her from the view of other drivers, some of whom were starting to pull over.

She helped Rogers, pulling roughly as he climbed over the center console and hit his head on the dashboard. He let out a groan and landed on his shoulder, but she straightened him up and pointed into the alley, which was full of garbage containers and assorted bulky trash.

They quickly wove their way through garbage bags and old furniture and hid behind a large dumpster.

"Are you injured, apart from your nose?" she asked, pulling a Kleenex out of her battered uniform jacket.

"My ribs hurt a little, but I can breathe okay," the lieutenant replied, gratefully accepting the two wads she had twisted from her torn tissue. With short movements of his thumbs, he stuffed them into his nostrils and wiped the blood from his face with his uniform sleeve. "What about ..."

"Shhh," she said, putting a finger to her lips. Suddenly voices could be heard.

"Stay back, we're trained in first aid," said a deep male voice. The crunching of broken glass echoed through the alley.

Rebecca peered over the container and between the leaves of a dying indoor palm tree that seemed to be growing out of the garbage. Two burly men in dark jackets and peaked caps approached her rental car from both sides. Not directly, but in wide arcs. She didn't need a second glance to realize that they had military – or at least police – training.

"They're not here, sir," one of them said so quietly that she could just hear. When his gaze went to the alley, she flinched. "No, sir. But I think I know where they fled to. Are you sure, sir?" There was a pause. "Understood."

Rebecca dared to look again and saw that the two were retreating. Sirens sounded in the distance.

"Did you hear something? My ears are still ringing," Rogers murmured.

"Yes. I think we need to hurry."

"With what? What the hell happened?"

"We were being followed and they rammed us," she explained curtly. "Can you walk?"

"Yes. I think so."

"Then come with me. We've got to act quickly."

"Act quickly? To do what?"

"To keep those who intended to kill us from getting to Walker before we do."

CHAPTER 33

C harlie kept peering in the direction of the Chinese space capsule, the little thing on the horizon that stood out against the ever-rough lunar landscape, but nothing appeared to be happening yet. In the meantime, they had set up the aluminum beams, attached the winch and pulley, and bolted everything together. Anne and Miles were in the process of screwing the elevator platform together and attaching the railing, while he and Louis were attaching the cable guide together with the cross pulley to the frighteningly fragile-looking structure that would later be above the 'cabin.'

Even when they had finished – the cabin and elevator base were ready, connected to each other and the cables for the guide system had been lowered into the depths – the Chinese had still done nothing.

"Maybe they did have an accident?" he spoke his thought aloud, feeling a little shamed by the sense of relief he felt. For the most part, however, he hoped that the taikonauts had survived and that their landing maneuver had been a success. He knew both crews were pushing the boundaries of what was humanly possible in such a hostile place. It may sound trite, but up here they were all just people trying to survive.

"The CNSA and the party office in Beijing have already reported the success of the landing," Mission Control replied to his question. "We are still evaluating our own data, but so far we can't see anything on our images that indicates a crash."

"Which doesn't rule out much," Anne said. "A lot could have gone wrong. Maybe a life support failure? Their airlock could be blocked, or an unfavorable short circuit could have paralyzed the outer hatch controls."

"We'll carry on," Louis decided. "Speculation won't help us now."

After replacing their CO_2 filters and oxygen cartridges, it took them another 30 minutes to slide the cabin between the two front pillars, and then they set about anchoring the elevator platform, which now rose three meters into the air. It didn't look particularly impressive with its fragile aluminum frame, but it was practical and it would work. To avoid putting too much strain on the rock anchors when lowering the cabin, the plan was to create counter tension on the other side, facing away from the crater, using several carbon-reinforced cables and tension. They had to pull a total of four of the 100-meter-long cables taut and use the gas hammer to drive one-meter-long bolts with eyelets at their upper ends into the lunar surface, which proved to be surprisingly solid.

However, they had to take their time to find suitable, rocky places that were not just loose regolith.

"I see something!" Louis said suddenly, just when they had reached the next to last bolt. He stood there and peered into the distance. Charlie also straightened up and turned in the direction of the Chinese spaceship. And indeed, a small cloud of dust rose on the horizon and spread out like the wings of a gray butterfly, almost perfectly symmetrical, and with a quiet gravitas that concealed the fact that their opponents were getting closer.

"So much for the question of whether they had an accident," Miles said. "They're going to the 404, aren't they?"

"Or coming to us. The 404 is right on the way."

"Should we go back to the *Liberty?*" Anne asked.

"No," Louis replied, shaking his head. "We'll finish our work. I don't think they're going to come here and push us into the crater."

Miles let out a short laugh, but it sounded neither amused nor happy.

"We'll carry on. I'll keep an eye on the taikonauts." Louis pointed to the third bolt they were about to sink into the rock.

So they went back to work, setting the bolt, using their muscle power to tighten the reinforced cable until they could pull it through the eyelet atop the bolt, and lashing it down. They groaned under the strain, but managed to do it this time, too, and only one anchorage remained when Louis stood up and put his hands on his hips.

His heavy breathing could be heard over their radios.

"They're at the 404," he said, stretching out a hand. Charlie saw it too, three figures in shiny white spacesuits standing 200 meters away by the American flag that Louis had set up there. He watched silently with the others as the Chinese walked around, turned toward them, and stared in their direction for a few moments before walking to the edge of the crater and apparently looking down into the sea of darkness.

"What are they doing?" asked Miles.

"So far, looking around," replied Charlie, whereupon the taikonauts returned to the flag as if on cue and unceremoniously pulled it out of the ground and rolled it up.

"I'll be damned!" Louis roared. "These bastards are going straight for it."

Charlie looked over at him. The former fighter pilot was

visibly angry; his lips had narrowed and his eyes had narrowed to slits.

"What should we do?" Miles had his hands clenched into fists in his gloves.

"Let me think."

"Nothing," said Charlie. "We don't want to directly stage a conflict just because they removed our flag, do we? I'm a patriot just like you, but that is just childish."

"It's symbolic, Charlie," Louis corrected him. "We're up here for many reasons, but letting China show us up isn't one of them."

"But if we react like angry children now, that's exactly what they're hoping for," Anne objected, defending Charlie's position. "Then the whole world will shake its head at us."

"That's why I'm thinking about it. We have to respond, but not react impulsively."

They watched as one of the taikonauts hid the flag behind his backpack and another set up the Chinese flag. Two of them then posed with it – as far as Charlie could tell from a distance – and the other stood in front of it.

"Is he taking a photo right now?" asked Anne.

"It sure looks like it."

"Space propaganda, of course," Louis grumbled.

"It's not as if we didn't do that," Charlie replied, earning himself a scowl from his commander.

"You are determined to defend them, aren't you? We were sent here by a democratic state, if I may remind you."

"I know that. But, of course, each party is going to take pictures for themselves and their people at home and send them back. And also to remind everyone that you are one of the first Chinese to ever set foot on the moon."

"Look," Anne said and stretched out a hand.

Charlie looked back at the taikonauts. They had apparently

finished their photo shoot and the one with the American flag, which he had hidden behind his backpack, brought it back out. At first he feared that the Chinese would destroy it or throw it into the crater, but instead he unfurled it to its full size, extended the telescopic shaft, and stuck it beside the Chinese flag.

"Did he just put it back, right next to *theirs?*" Miles asked incredulously, and Louis gave Charlie a quick sideways glance. He merely raised his palms in reply, the equivalent of a shoulder shrug.

"That doesn't prove anything."

"I think it's a very nice touch," said Anne.

"It would have been a fine move if they hadn't started by removing our flag." Louis pointed to the last bolt in Miles's hand. "And we should finish our work and not use up valuable oxygen."

"Shouldn't we make contact somehow?" asked Charlie. He found it strange for the two groups not to approach each other out here, at a distance so great that the blue planet would fit 30 times between the two celestial bodies.

"Why? What could we discuss with them that would get us anywhere?" asked Miles.

"I have no idea. A wave would be enough, right? Or any sign that we won't be at each other's throats?"

"Are we absolutely sure about that?" Louis continued to look straight ahead in the direction of the taikonauts, while Charlie gave him an incredulous sideways glance.

"I hope that we, at least, do everything we can to keep it that way."

"He's right," Anne said with a little more emphasis in her tone.

"Shit. Yes he is." Louis's answer surprised them. "But I don't have to like it. Miles, Anne, you two stay here and get back to work. I don't want to waste any oxygen. We need to finish up out here. Charlie, you're the peace diplomat here, you're coming with me."

With that, their commander trudged toward the Rover and sat down in the driver's seat. Charlie hopped in after him and paused before carefully taking hold of the metal frame of the passenger seat and sitting down on it in his bulky suit. Shortly afterward, they drove in silence toward the taikonauts, who had noticed their approach by now and simply stood there, motionless, staring in their direction.

The distance became smaller and smaller as they bumped along and eventually slowed down and stopped. One of the taikonauts suddenly turned on his heel and ran back toward the Chinese space capsule with long hops. The other two remained rooted to the spot where they were.

They're sending one back in case we've come with hostile intentions, Charlie thought, and when he looked at Louis and their eyes met, he could see from his commander's expression that the same thought was going through his mind.

"I hope this wasn't a stupid idea."

"I hope so too," said Charlie as he got out of the Rover. The taikonauts were only five paces away and were facing them. Since their sun visors were down, he couldn't see their faces, only the golden color of the protective visors.

It was probably the same for their counterparts, because without protection from the unfiltered light of the central star, they would rapidly go blind. Louis slowly came to stand next to him and then an endless, uncomfortable moment followed. The oppressive silence and the feeling that every movement could be a mistake they would regret turned it into something sinister. Above them was star-studded darkness, to their right the darkness of the crater, and in the background the third taikonaut was running away as if his life depended on it.

"And what now, Charlie?" asked Louis. "Do you have a

brilliant idea? Without the right frequency bands and technical specifications, we can't communicate with them, even if they speak English."

"I know." Charlie took a step forward and raised both hands placatingly. He hoped it was a gesture that was international enough. He was aware that the signs and body language customs of the Chinese differed massively from their own, but he had no idea in what way. His specific knowledge of such matters did not go beyond what he'd seen in a few documentaries or magazine articles in waiting rooms.

"What are you doing?" Louis asked.

"I'll try to show a little relaxation." He walked over to the two flags, whereupon the taikonauts turned toward him in such a way that they always presented their fronts to him. The lack of any body language, or even facial expressions behind their white suits, was eerily intimidating.

Charlie touched both flags one after the other with his hand and made his placating gesture again before stretching a thumb upward.

The Chinese turned to each other briefly, then the one on the right returned the gesture. A name tag was sewn onto his chest, albeit in Chinese characters.

"Good, very good. The flags stay. Next to each other. Everything's cool," said Charlie, licking his dry lips.

"We should try to establish a radio link somehow," Louis blurted out. "That would make a lot of things easier. But we need help from Houston – and the CNSA."

"That's a good idea." He tapped his right ear – or rather his helmet – with one hand and then made a telephone sign with his thumb and little finger. He then pointed to himself and Louis and then to the two taikonauts, bringing the fingers and thumb of his right hand together in quick succession. "Talk, talk, talk."

The taikonauts turned to each other again, then one of

them repeated Charlie's pantomime and stuck his right thumb up.

"I think they get it," said Louis.

"It looks like it." Charlie briefly considered raising a hand to say goodbye, but then decided against it. He didn't want to overdo it. Instead, he nodded, even though no one could see it, and only reopened his sun visor when they were sitting on the Rover and facing away from the sun, just like at their construction site, which was behind a large rock in the shade.

"Houston, this is Louis."

"Hey *Liberty*, this is Harry. Are you all right?" came the radioed reply.

"Yes, we've just made first contact."

"Uhh ...?"

"With the Chinese."

"Ahh." Harry paused. "How did it go?"

"There are two flags up here now. One of them is unsightly, to say the least," Louis replied dryly.

"If it's just that, we're perfectly fine here in Houston. How did the taikonauts behave?"

"Quite passively, I would say. We could only work with hand signals. Charlie did that, and it went pretty well," said Louis, giving him a sideways glance.

"I'm glad to hear that."

"That's why I'm getting in touch. We need a way to communicate with the Chinese, somehow. But our radio frequencies are different and so are the specs. Can you help us with that?"

"Hmm, we'd have to get in touch with the CNSA to achieve that. But we can't do that without the approval of the Space Force and the Pentagon," Harry replied more hesitantly than usual. "And they won't lift a finger unless they get the green light from the White House. Not on this one."

Charlie wondered whether the Space Force contact officers were on site, looking directly over the shoulder of their CAPCOM in the Mission Control Center, or whether they were limited to monitoring every single communication. He was a hundred percent sure of the latter and Harry was probably going crazy. The fact that he was managing to control himself so well could only mean that things were downright serious at home.

"Then you'd better ask. Charlie doesn't want to cause conflict between them and us, and he's damn right. Two competing teams up here who can't even talk to each other is the perfect recipe for disaster," said Louis, parking their Rover next to Anne and Miles, who were in the process of attaching the fourth tension cable. The construction looked solid with the tight cables – fragile, however, when he looked at the rather large structure of the elevator base, but so far all the NASA teams' calculations had been right, so Charlie would trust them.

"I'll see what I can do," Harry replied after the usual two second pause during which the radio signal went to Earth and back.

"Thank you, CAPCOM. Don't take too much time!"

They got out and briefly told their fellow astronauts about the encounter, even though they had heard most of it thanks to radio coms. Then they secured their little lunar construction site by leaving the electric motor packed in its crate and loading it back onto the Rover's cargo area. They also stacked all but one of the empty crates in the Rover and then rechecked the elevator cabin to make sure it was centered precisely on the base and not peeking over the edge. Even without wind, earthquakes, or other environmental influences, it was a natural reflex to verify the result of their work. Finally, they took the last crate and pulled it two by two over the regolith around the construction site so that the dust was resmoothed, added it to the cargo area, and drove back to the *Liberty* with a full Rover.

They returned on the route by which they had gone, past Site 404 where the two flags were. Louis steered them along the same tire tracks they had made when they drove to the work site.

"I want to be able to see if *they* are driving or walking somewhere," he said when Charlie asked him about it. There was no sign of the taikonauts, and they speculated that the Chinese had gone back to their spaceship, as the footprints pointed in that direction.

At the *Liberty*, Charlie and Anne returned to the airlock first and quickly undressed before making room for Louis and Miles.

An hour later, sweaty and exhausted, they gathered in the cockpit and stared out of the window through which the *Celestial Dragon* could be seen in the distance. It was so far away that it was no more than a silver dot of light on the horizon, standing out against the shadowy slopes of the huge canyon on the horizon.

"Do you think the Space Force will get involved?" Anne asked hesitantly. "The thing with the radios, I mean."

"I doubt it," Louis said. "The political situation is so muddled that they haven't even been able to agree on contact officers to coordinate our respective missions in order to prevent incidents."

"I can't imagine them revealing our radio frequencies to the Chinese, of all people," Miles agreed, crossing his arms over his chest.

"What if we try it ourselves?" suggested Charlie, staring into the distance at the silver glow of the Chinese spaceship.

"Excuse me?" Louis responded.

"We are up here, not them. We are the ones who have to prevent a catastrophe. On Earth we may have a political conflict, but up here we are explorers. We're standing on the precipice of a crater that makes the Grand Canyon look like a laughable ditch. There is an alien artifact at its bottom, over four kilometers down," he enumerated and looked at his crewmates. They looked tired, with their sweaty hair and dark circles under their eyes from the many hours of hard work.

"It's plain crazy that we're bringing the divisive politics from Earth here with us," Charlie continued. "I don't care whether they're communists or not, whether our leaderships can't stand each other, whatever. What matters to me is the safety of you – and honestly, the safety of the taikonauts out there. If there's one cast-iron law among space travelers, it's to support each other when there's a problem."

"But there's no problem yet," Miles objected.

"Not *yet*, true. But without a means of communication, you can be sure there will be misunderstandings. Just think of the flag situation. If we hadn't kept calm, we might have done something stupid. We *must* do everything we can to prevent it from getting that far in the first place."

"Of course that's right," Louis said, nodding thoughtfully. "The best solution to a disaster is to prevent it from happening in the first place. To take precautions."

Charlie returned the nod gratefully. He had expected Anne to be relieved, but instead she looked outside with concern.

"What is it?" he asked.

"Even if we override Mission Control's orders and try to do this on our own, it's going to be really difficult."

"If we get arrested when we get back, I don't care." Louis snorted contemptuously. "We're covering our asses here, so we might as well set an example for all the warmongers."

"Besides, we're not going back either way," Miles interjected. When they all stared at him, he raised his hands defensively. "I'm just saying. So it doesn't matter what they think. If we're going to die here, at least we can do it right."

"That's not what I meant," said Anne. "We can't do it *technically*. In order to establish joint radio communication, we would first have to check our respective radio equipment for technical compatibility. This means that we first need to know which frequencies have been set in our VHF devices. They were preset by NASA and the Space Force, and they are mission-specific."

"Yes, but we could change them," Louis replied.

"No, not without a lot of work. To do that, we would have to intervene in the software settings of our radios, and the Chinese would have to do it in theirs. Without the right equipment and firmware access, we don't stand a chance."

"And we'd have to get them from Houston," Charlie said, ruffling his hair before exhaling a long, drawn-out breath.

"True. And even then – the practically impossible step – it would be necessary for us to establish communication protocols." Anne shook her head. "The language would be the easiest, because English is the only option. My Mandarin is virtually non-existent. But what about code words? Who speaks when? That would certainly be manageable, but what I'm saying is: even without the technical difficulties, it would be a challenge."

Louis waved them off. "Not to mention the fact that Beijing will never agree to the taikonauts disclosing their radio frequencies or reprogramming their radios. That would mean they could no longer listen in. Forget that."

"It will go the same for us," said Charlie. "Just wait and see. Harry will reluctantly send us a rejection."

No one disagreed. It was frustrating. That they had the technology to fly to the moon, to survive and work in this inhospitable environment, and to have found a technical solution for the descent into the crater, but then to fail to communicate. He simply couldn't believe that two teams of astronauts were unable to talk to each other despite having radio equipment. But Anne was a brilliant engineer and if she couldn't see a way, there was no way.

"What if we press our helmets together? The vibrations from the voice should theoretically be audible in the other helmet, right?" he suggested, but she was already shaking her head before he had even finished speaking.

"A good idea, but unfortunately not possible. For one thing, our helmets are soundproofed, which is due to the strong insulation from external influences such as cold and radiation. Sound waves would therefore be transmitted nowhere near strongly enough to understand anything. Apart from that, pressing the helmets together is at least a small risk. Would you want a taikonaut to accidentally be a little too impetuous and you end up with a scratch in your visor that might turn into a fracture? Our suits are inflated with pure oxygen and are pressurized. No, that wouldn't work."

"Then we'll write," said Louis. "We have our tablets."

"But they won't last long with the radiation out there. We could only use them in the shade and the moon dust would destroy them in no time," Anne objected. "That's why we have the filter systems in the airlock. The regolith crystals are tiny and fit into even the tiniest of openings."

"Then we weld one together."

"But we couldn't write on them. The touch displays work via infrared heat. The gloves won't work."

"Oh hell!" Louis cursed and let out a long growl. "So it's practically impossible to talk to the damn Chinese?"

"We might come up with something else, but we'll definitely have to get creative, that's for sure."

"We should all take showers and eat something first," their commander suggested in a softer tone. "Then our heads will work better. Anne, Charlie, you go first. I'll hold down the fort here with Miles."

Charlie exchanged a glance with Anne. 'Hold down the fort' obviously meant keeping an eye on the new neighbors, and he couldn't deny that it made him feel better. The idea that they were out there doing something without knowing what ... was *not* reassuring.

So they nodded and retreated to the living area.

"The next time we go out," Anne said as they were climbing down the ladders, "we might take the elevator into the crater."

"Do you think we'll find water?"

"The preliminary data is pretty clear. Do you think we'll find aliens?"

Charlie repeated her words. "The preliminary data is pretty clear."

CHAPTER 34

Rebecca felt bad as she ran out of the alley and toward the man standing somewhat perplexed behind her battered rental car. She recognized him as the one who had collided with them. Her own car – the rental – was no longer roadworthy, with steam billowing from the dented hood, but it wasn't as wrecked as it had seemed during the accident – or else she probably wouldn't have escaped with only a few painful bruises.

"There you are!" said the man. "Are you all right?"

"Yes, everything's okay," she replied.

"What on earth possessed you to move over like that! Didn't you see me?" The portly man in the flannel shirt angled his head.

"I'm sorry, we were being attacked."

"Attacked. What ...?" He looked at her carefully for the first time and only now seemed to notice her uniform.

"I need your vehicle. I'll bring it back."

"Excuse me? Are you ...?"

"Then drive us, please," she interrupted him, seeing the black SUV driving away on the other side of the street. But in the wrong direction. Not that she doubted where they were going, but they obviously didn't want to go in the same direction as the police and ambulance.

"Drive you where? If we drive away now, it's a hit and run and we ..."

"I'm an intelligence officer in the Air Force and I'm on a mission. These people who were just here tried to kill us."

The man's eyes grew wide and almost popped out of their sockets when he saw Rogers limping out of the alley.

"God damn it!"

"Please drive us to the hospital quickly," she said loudly so that the numerous bystanders who had gathered around the accident could hear her and would stop asking if everything was all right.

"Uhh, yeah, um, sure," the driver stammered and went to his car. Rebecca and Rogers followed him and got into the small back seat.

"401 N Adams Street, second turn ..."

"I know my way around here, ma'am. I just hope the police ..."

"Give me your phone," she interrupted him, and fished it from his hand as he handed it to her over the seat back while maneuvering past the onlookers. Rebecca paid no attention to them. There was no longer anything inconspicuous about any of this. She pulled her ID card out of the inside pocket of her uniform jacket and took a photo of it with his cellphone before dropping the phone onto the passenger seat. "Show this to the police when you're questioned. They can then contact me via the Pentagon."

Rogers gave her a sidelong glance.

"I know," she said. "The general will find out for sure, and so will many others. And whoever is after us will redouble their efforts."

"Feinman?"

"Possibly. We have to get to Walker first or we'll never see him alive, that's for sure." She turned to their driver. "Step on it!"

In fact, the man who had just been involved in an accident was now driving at full speed along the main road and, with screeching tires, turned onto the 401, which merged into the residential area after a few minutes. Whatever it was about her that had convinced him to help seemed to have worked very well.

"Stop! Let us out right here." After the car had stopped, she was about to get out, but stopped short. "Do you have a gun?"

"Sure, but ..."

"Give it to me," she urged him. "You have my data, I'll replace it."

"I can't just ..."

"Oklahoma doesn't require firearms to be registered. We don't have time. GO!" she yelled. The man opened the glove compartment, from which he pulled a Glock 21 and handed it back to her. She took it from him, checked the chamber to see that it was loaded, and opened the door. "Get out of this area and then call the police."

With that, she jumped out and ran toward the two-story blue house with Rogers dragging a leg but somehow keeping pace. Rebecca hurried along the small, cobbled path to the front door and had to force herself to ring the bell only once. She took out her ID and held it out as the father of the family, a slightly stocky man in his mid-40s with a kind face, opened the door. When he saw the gun, he widened his eyes and took half a step back.

"Shhh," she said and waved her ID again. She said quietly, "We're here about Specialist Walker. Internal investigation. Take your family and leave the house immediately. Don't pack anything, just go! You are in danger."

The man stared in amazement at her ID, then at the gun, before swallowing and nodding.

"Let's go!"

He ran back into the hallway and toward the living room. Rebecca followed him two steps, waiting until Rogers closed the door. Outside, she could hear the car that had brought them driving away. She turned to the stairs and motioned for Rogers to go ahead. Gun at the ready, she followed him up the steps. Some creaked slightly, but the excited conversations that broke out between family members in the living room masked most of the sounds.

The short flight of stairs ended at a wooden door. Rogers looked questioningly at her and sniffled, which sounded like a low drone with the pieces of tissue in his nose. They were soaked with blood by now.

When she nodded, he knocked. Shortly afterward, they heard footsteps.

"Ralph?"

"Yeah," Rogers replied, whereupon the door was pulled open by a still-chewing David Walker – tall and lanky, with the untoned body of a man in his early 20s who chose to live an unhealthy lifestyle and got little exercise.

"What the …?" Lieutenant Rogers pushed the door wide and went in. Rebecca followed close behind and held the gun on the specialist.

"You have an escape route. Where is it?" she asked bluntly. "I'll only ask once."

Walker swallowed his food, took quick note of her bruises and the cut over her right eye and the rank insignia on her shoulders, and then Rogers, who looked like a zombie. It wasn't long before he decided to take her seriously and pointed to one of the curtained windows.

"There's a slanted roof outside it. The glass can be broken out with a blow to the center of the top frame," Walker explained nervously, raising his hands a little higher as she waved the Glock and closed the door behind her.

"We don't have much time, so don't waste it," Rebecca said grimly. "Who ordered your transfer?"

"It came from the Pentagon, ma'am. Look, you, I don't know ..."

"Save it, or I'll leave you to the men who are about to show up here. I'm pretty sure they'll kill you so you can't talk. So you only have us." Out of the corner of her eye, she saw Rogers walking to one of the windows facing the street and peeking through the curtains at an angle.

"Headlights coming."

Rebecca spoke sharply to the ashen-faced Walker. "We can leave through that window, but don't waste any time."

"They just stood me up. After the colonel gave me all that stuff, everything went straight to hell," the specialist whined. "First they put me on sick leave, then they transferred me. Back to Vance, can you imagine?"

"The colonel? Feinman?" She put her free hand in her pocket and reached for her cellphone.

"He never told me his name."

Rebecca quickly described the colonel.

"Yes, that was him! He offered me money and promised me that I would be well looked after."

The squealing of tires could be heard from outside.

"What did he give you?"

"I had no choice. Honestly!" the Specialist howled, looking toward the window as Rogers turned to them and sliced a hand across his throat.

Rebecca licked her lips. *"WHAT did he GIVE you?!"* she repeated fiercely.

"It's over there. In the desk. I should have destroyed it, but until the payments come in, I wanted some insurance and ..."

"Bring it to me. GO!" she screamed at him and exchanged a look with Rogers.

"They're here!" said the lieutenant in alarm.

"How many?"

"Two."

She nodded and turned back to Walker, who returned with a finger-thick file for her. "I didn't do anything, Major. You have to believe me. I ..."

"Let's just get out of here," she interrupted him and gestured to the window. "You first. I hope your escape route is as good as you say."

The specialist nodded, and ran directly to the window. With his elbow, he hit the frame at the top center, and it rattled loudly as the whole structure broke outside and the pane shattered.

Walker leaned forward into the opening and Rebecca was about to follow, ahead of Rogers, when she stopped abruptly and threw herself to the side. A shot whipped past her ear, a sharp whirring sound.

"Down!" she yelled, whereupon Rogers crouched down. He had only just crossed half of the large room that made up the entire upper floor.

David Walker's feet were still on this side of the window frame, and the rest of his body was outside on the porch roof.

"Shooter. In the yard or across the street," she said in a softer voice as she heard the door being forced open downstairs. A shrill scream rang out.

"They're inside the house," Roger murmured.

"Yes. Find yourself a weapon," she ordered him. "But keep your head down."

The lieutenant nodded. With his swollen face and puffy eyes, he looked pitiful. The pain must be excruciating, but he barely let on.

"I'm going downstairs," she said, stuffing the file into her uniform jacket, which she tucked into the waistband of her underpants so the file couldn't fall through.

"That's too dangerous, Major."

"I'm a good shot and we're trapped up here." Rebecca crawled to the door, which was a hand's breadth open, and grabbed a broom that was standing right next to it. When she heard the first creak of a stairstep, she tapped the handle of the broom against the wood of the door at about head height while she remained lying down. Less than a heartbeat later, she heard the loud 'phfft, phfft, phfft' of three silenced shots punching holes through the pressboard and sending a rain of splinters into the room.

Rebecca had been expecting this. She dropped the broom, pulled the door open further with her free hand, and pushed her other hand through the gap at lightning speed. She only just recognized the outline of one of the two men who had been at the scene of the car accident, and she shot him twice in the chest and once in the face.

His forward motion ceased and he fell backward like a plank. She took advantage of the noise and tore the door wide open to run down the stairs. She took three steps at a time, fell after her second step because her right leg was slightly weak, and turned in her fall so that she fell forward onto the body of her attacker. The impact was painful, but she absorbed most of the energy by rolling forward.

She crashed into the front door and hit her head. Hot blood ran down her forehead and cheek. When she jumped up, she staggered slightly – which saved her life by causing a volley of bullets to narrowly miss her.

Rebeccaa fired blindly in the direction from which she had seen the muzzle flashes, grabbed the dead man's gun, and ran into the hallway. She kept firing until the Glock was empty and then darted into the first door on the right to get out of the line of fire.

Blinking, she tried to wipe away the tears caused by the blow to her head. She was in the kitchen, which was connected to the living and dining room by an archway. Behind the kitchen counter, she could see a woman in the reflection of the stove, crying silently and holding two children close to her.

Through the open window, she heard the wailing of sirens coming closer. A pair of shoes lay beside her, their laces tied together, so she grabbed them with her left hand and threw them into the living room. At the same time, she turned to the right and ran back into the hallway.

Two silenced shots rang out behind her, but she kept running down the hallway and was just turning the corner of the doorframe when a second shooter – she had seen him in the accident, too – wheeled around to face her and realized his mistake. Using the stairway shooter's gun, she shot this guy between the eyes and tried to run to the father of the family, who lay bleeding next to the dining table with his two teenagers on the floor beside him, sobbing and hugging their knees to their chests.

A shadow to her left made her freeze.

"Turn around," she heard a raspy voice. "Drop your weapon."

She gritted her teeth as she felt cold metal on the back of her neck. First she dropped her pistol, then she slowly turned and looked into the hard face of a man who towered over her by a head and was now holding the barrel of a Beretta to her forehead. He was wearing normal civilian clothes – jeans and a shirt with a lined jacket over it.

"Where do you have it?"

"Have I got something?" Rebecca asked with her chin jutting out.

"The file."

"I don't know what you're talking about."

"We're supposed to let you live, if possible, but I'll take it off your dead body if I have to," the stranger replied. His eyes flashed coldly.

"In my jacket," she said. "I can get it out."

"I'm not stupid. Shut up and keep your hands up." He took his free hand and reached for the top button of her uniform jacket.

She only had one chance and she took it. In the brief moment he looked at her buttons, she tried to turn to the side, but his reflexes were far too quick.

He pulled the trigger.

Click.

Nothing happened. They both looked at the pistol in disbelief, then he was the first to break free from the shock and smack the pistol grip against her temple.

Dazed, she staggered to the side. Everything spun and glittering stars whizzed around in front of her eyes. A second blow came from the right, which she only saw as a blur. She raised her left arm and blocked it rather poorly, but the force was so great that she fell to the side.

She saw a blade flash as the attacker lunged after her. One hand gripped her neck and squeezed. Instinctively, she tried to fight it with both hands, but the man's grip was as tight as a vise. She rattled and gasped, but the airway continued to narrow.

Then she felt the cold metal touch her neck and, as he tried to cut her jugular and she could only see a blurring shadow, there was a loud bang. A heavy body crashed down on her. The knife hit the floor.

"Major?" she heard a voice.

"R-R-Rogers," she croaked. Struggling out from under the corpse covering her, she blinked a few times and tried to catch her breath. Rogers was standing in the hallway, a gun outstretched, looking first into the kitchen and then lowering it as he slowly approached her.

"Thank God," he said, breathing heavily, and came to the living room door as a shadow emerged from the kitchen door behind him.

"B-b-be- ...," she tried to warn him, but it was too late. A fourth attacker overcame the two steps at lightning speed, and before Rogers had even turned around, he stabbed Rogers' abdomen again and again with lightning speed.

The lieutenant let out a pitiful whimpering moan and dropped to his knees as the stranger drew the blade upward and across his neck.

Meanwhile, Rebecca searched in panic for the pistol that Rogers had dropped. Her fingers found the handle as the black-clad stranger jumped over the body of her aide and toward her.

Her hand clutched Walker's Glock and jerked it up, two shots ringing out. Both hit the attacker in the neck and sent blood spraying into the room.

I hope there were only four, she thought as she got to her feet. To be on the safe side, she crouched down and ran to the two whimpering teenagers at the dining table. Rebecca almost fell to the side as she was seized by a wave of vertigo.

"Come. Your mother is in the kitchen," she whispered, and looked around with a blurred expression. Outside, the sirens had become deafeningly loud.

With her free hand, she pulled the boy to his feet. His sister had already snapped out of her stupor. With their heads bowed, they scurried together into the kitchen and behind the work area in the middle, where the mother was hiding with the two younger children.

Rebecca put a bloodied finger to her lips as the terrified

woman threatened to have a screaming fit and pointed her gun across the countertop.

Less than five seconds later, the door was forced open.

"POLICE!"

CHAPTER 35

After showering, Charlie removed the lithium hydroxide filters from the life support units in their suits and replaced them with new ones. The CO_2 filtration was at least as important as the oxygen supply. For the latter, he pulled the cable of the compressor unit in the airlock out of its holder and refilled each of the backpacks.

Afterward, they ate together in the recreation room, going over the upcoming mission.

"We're going out today. Before the next sleep phase," Louis declared, and sucked a mouthful from his mashed potatoes and gravy tube. Smacking his lips, he continued, "I've discussed it with Houston. We just have to hook up the cabin and install the engine."

"And lay out the solar panels," Anne added.

"Yes. That, too. It shouldn't take more than an hour, including the ride there. Right?"

She nodded and drank from her water tube.

"There will be three of us this time. Miles, you stay here and watch over the Chinese and keep an *eye* on the *Liberty*."

Miles nodded. If he was disappointed, no one could tell.

"Then Charlie and I will go down into the crater," Louis

continued. It was immediately obvious to Anne that she would have preferred to go down herself, which her commander also noticed. "If something goes wrong with the engine or what-have-you, I want you up there to fix it. Besides, one of us needs to be up there in case our new neighbors come by and do something stupid."

"What could they do?" asked Anne.

"Do you think they have their own elevator with them? In their little spaceship?"

"Hmm... not likely."

"Exactly. So we'll remain peaceful but vigilant, right?"

They nodded in turn. Louis looked satisfied and clapped his hands. "Good. Then let's get ready. Maybe the three of us can make it through the airlock together. That would save us a lot of oxygen. Charlie, is everything ready?"

"Yes, all set to go."

"Good."

After lunch they climbed to the airlock and began to get suited up. Miles kept slipping between them like a fish, helping here and there to pull fasteners, straighten things out, and check the fit of individual components.

Miles stepped back inside when they were done, and secured the hatch. The three closed their helmets and switched to their suits' life support before letting the atmosphere out of the airlock and then stepping out onto the platform, which they slowly rode down.

The view was once more breathtaking, even though it was Charlie's third outdoor mission on the moon. The pure darkness of the crater 'lake' looked like a mirror of the darkness of the sky, only without the myriads of stars. The crater looked like an abyss, the canopy of stars like a window into infinity.

And the ones who left an artifact in the Shackleton were from one of those stars, he pondered, shivering at the thought of descending into the depths today and coming face to face with real alien technology.

Once the elevator platform reached bottom, Louis and Anne climbed into the front seats of the Rover and Charlie stood on the cargo area again, his hands holding onto the large sensor bar. The journey took 15 minutes, during which they used their tracks from a few hours earlier and kept an eye out for others. But if the Chinese had their own lunar vehicle, they either hadn't used it yet or it wasn't working.

When they reached the construction site of their elevator base, they were in for a surprise. Footprints could be seen all around the aluminum structure, and three of the four retaining cables were broken and lay in the regolith like coiled snakes.

Louis got out first while Charlie and Anne quickly followed. For a few moments they stood next to each other, speechless, staring at the silent scene.

"Those damn bastards sabotaged our damn elevator!" their commander said, gritting his teeth audibly. Over the radio, his voice sounded even more rumbly than usual – like stones rolling down a steep rocky slope. Charlie wanted to contradict him, but he didn't know how. They had covered their own tracks to prevent any question about what they were seeing now. Since there were no other humans within a radius of almost 400,000 kilometers, the Chinese were the only candidates. The patterned imprints of the spacesuits also matched this.

Anne was the first to stir and went to the front security cable. She bent one knee to squat next to it and lifted the end.

"Cut." As if to prove it, she held up the frayed end.

"Houston," Louis said. "Come in."

"We're here," Harry replied after a few seconds. "Are you at the elevator yet?"

"Yes, and it obviously had visitors. The retaining cables have been cut and there are boot prints all over the place."

Charlie looked at the prints and then in the direction of the Chinese spaceship on the horizon. The trail led in the direction of the *Celestial Dragon.*

"Are there any taikonauts near you?" asked Harry after the unavoidable signal delay.

"No. None that we can see from here," Louis replied.

"Good. Remain on standby and I'll get back to you in a minute."

"Understood."

"They didn't even try to cover their tracks," Charlie noted thoughtfully.

"Because they wanted us to see what they did."

"But why?"

"To tempt us into an aggressive act, of course!" Louis snorted contemptuously. "First the flag, now the sabotage."

Charlie didn't answer and continued to stare in the direction of the Chinese, as if he could coax their secrets out of the silver space capsule on the horizon. What were they up to?

"It won't work like this," said Anne, pointing to the severed cables. "We can hammer the bolts in again, closer to the platform. We'll probably lose about a meter each because we'll have to make new loops. But that one meter times four could be the icing on the cake. The tolerances in the structural calculations are not particularly large. In the worst-case scenario, the elevator and the base station could collapse."

"Those bastards." Louis pointed to the suspension eyelets on the platform. "At least they were stupid enough not to cut in the middle. Otherwise we'd be completely fucked."

Anne nodded and turned back to them. She pulled down her sun visor and stepped out of the shadow of the large stone that blocked their view of the *Liberty,*

"*Liberty*, CAPCOM here," Harry stated, returning to the

radio. "The leadership team has just had a meeting. They want you to protect American property at all costs."

"What *exactly* does that mean?" Louis asked.

"It means that you may use whatever means you deem necessary to prevent the taikonauts from sabotaging your equipment a second time. The Chinese ambassador has been summoned to the White House. A formal protest will be lodged, and they will make our position clear to the ambassador," Harry explained.

If you knew Harry well, as Charlie did, you could hear from his voice – even distorted by the radio – that he was uncomfortable with his own words. "There must be no further sabotaging of our equipment."

Louis breathed in and out loudly. His golden visor remained motionless, as if he were staring into the distance. "Charlie, you go back to the *Liberty* and get the box from the secure compartment. The access code is 8745."

"You mean ..."

"Yes, that's what I mean!" the commander interrupted him. "Peaceful coexistence is a good thing, but it only works if both sides see it that way. We won't start any revenge campaigns, but we won't let them butter our bread, either. Our mission is to get to that artifact." He stretched out an arm and pointed into the dark crater that filled the entire northern horizon and merged with the dark sea of stars at its end. "And the Chinese won't stop us."

Charlie knew when there was no point arguing with Louis. Besides, the instruction from Houston had been clear and, to be honest, far from unreasonable. So he nodded, even though no one could see it, and went to the Rover.

"Understood. Take care of yourselves."

"We will, but hurry anyway."

Charlie took a seat in the Rover and started the electric motor using the large toggle switch next to the steering wheel.

His gloved hands were soaked with sweat, although life support was doing its best to keep his body cool. He had hoped that common sense would be the foundation for all astronauts – and taikonauts – and that things would be much more peaceful and less petty on the moon than on Earth.

He had been proven wrong. Perhaps he was just too naïve to recognize the true nature of man.

He drove the same route they had taken so he wouldn't have to rely on his sense of direction. As an astronaut, the iron law of simplicity applied: no matter how tiny, any risk that could be avoided was to be avoided. And the risks included, above all, deviations from the standard.

But after the first 100 meters, when he could just make out the flags clearly, despite their relative lack of color on the monochromatic lunar surface, he saw something unusual: figures, between 100 and 200 meters away from Site 404. It had to be the Chinese.

He drove on to the flags, where the tracks described a 90-degree bend, and slowed down considerably. There was no doubt about it. Two taikonauts were standing there on the edge of the crater, working. It looked like one of them was hitting something.

Charlie wanted to drive on, but eventually stopped the Rover. He waited until the two noticed him, which didn't take very long. They turned in his direction and stared motionlessly.

Go back to the Liberty, *Charlie. Carry out your orders,* he admonished himself as one of the taikonauts raised a hand.

Something about it seemed strange to him. Had one of the Chinese just greeted him? And shouldn't they be acting much more nervous? He knew they must have seen him coming from the direction of the building site.

The taikonaut moved again. This time, Charlie was sure he was waving at him.

What should I do? He thought about radioing Louis and asking him for instructions, but then he would probably say that he should go to the *Liberty* quickly because it was definitely a trap. But what if it wasn't? What if he could still prevent weapons from coming into play?

But what if it really is a trap? What if they want to steal the Rover?

Charlie quickly got off and pressed the button for the engine lock, which could then only be unlocked via the PIN entry field, which consisted of a keypad with nine oversized, dust-sealed buttons.

Then, with long hops, he made his way to the two taikonauts who were waiting for him. At least they had stopped working – whatever they had just been doing – and stood facing him.

The closer he got to them, the more he slowed down to lessen the risk of a fall, and to appear as unthreatening as possible. When they were only 25 meters apart, he realized what the Chinese were working on. A bolt as thick as an arm was stuck in the ground between them, with a thread on its head. One of the taikonauts was holding a large winch with a screw cap in his left glove. Next to him was a small box with a plastic socket. Charlie assumed that the winch could be mounted on the screw thread of the bolt and that it had come out of the box.

He instinctively stopped – which almost ended in the fall he'd been trying to avoid – when he saw a large hammer in the other man's hands. Only 15 meters now separated them. They stared at each other silently. Charlie breathed heavily and looked at the hammer.

A tool, or a weapon? He took a step back. Being condemned to slow motion by low gravity made him feel helpless.

The two Chinese turned toward each other. Perhaps they

were talking. The one with the hammer squatted down and placed the tool on the ground next to the bolt. Then he raised both hands and took a step to the side. A large pulley, almost as tall as the taikonaut, appeared behind him.

Charlie was surprised to have not seen it before. Or had he simply been too focused on the hammer?

Then the pantomime began. The one on the right, who was slightly taller, put the winch back in the case and locked it. Then he pointed to the man-sized bolt and wiggled one hand.

"Okay, you probably tried to drop a cable into the crater. Over the winch," he said into his helmet.

"Charlie? Are you all right?" he heard Louis ask.

Fuck!

"Yes, I've just bumped into two taikonauts."

"What? Is there a problem?"

"I don't think so. Wait a minute." Charlie watched as the shorter man pointed to the cable – presumably carbon fiber – and he wiggled his hand as well. "It looks like they tried to rig a winch to rappel down from here, along the gentler slope."

"What's happening?" Louis inquired.

"They've dismantled it."

The shorter one pointed to the cable and then behind Charlie, perhaps in the direction of the Rover.

Or our construction site.

Charlie raised his hands, somewhat perplexed. "What are you trying to tell me?"

The taller one knelt down all at once and picked up a piece of the coiled cable. Then he held it between both gloves and bent it before turning around and wiggling a finger.

"The cable is no good?" asked Charlie.

The taikonaut pointed behind Charlie again, and then made a gesture with two fingers as if he were …

"Run! You want to walk. There?" He turned toward Rover and the construction site far behind.

The taikonauts each raised a thumb in his direction.

"Uhh, Louis, Anne?"

"Would you kindly tell us what's going on now?"

"I think they want to come to you."

"What? Why?"

"I'm not sure, but they've made it clear their plan with the cable and the winch isn't going to work."

Charlie walked toward the taikonauts, holding his hands out so as not to appear threatening. Then he saw that the head of the bolt had melted on one side. No wonder they had packed the winch away. It no longer fit. However, they had managed to melt the metal of the bolt.

"Are they armed?" asked Louis.

"No. Not that I can see," he replied. "And I don't think there's anywhere to hide anything on a spacesuit. What do you want me to do?"

"There are two of them?"

"Yes."

"Then bring them here. But at the slightest sign that something is wrong, you pull the ripcord, all right?"

"Sure," Charlie promised, without knowing what Louis meant by 'ripcord.' He couldn't simply dissolve the taikonauts into thin air with magic.

As he pointed in the direction of the Rover, the two Chinese picked up the huge cable. It had to be long enough to reach down into the crater. Barely thicker than the cords of a parachute, the coil was as big as a man and probably several kilometers long.

He hopped ahead and kept turning around. They were dragging the cable behind them and literally had their hands full. They were certainly no danger to him.

It took quite a while, during which he had to keep reassuring Louis that everything was all right, until they finally arrived at the Rover. At his signal, the Chinese loaded the cable onto the flatbed and then just stood there. Only when Charlie pointed to the cargo area did they climb up and sit down.

He went to the driver's seat himself and unlocked the engine before switching it on and driving off. The back of his neck tingled because the adrenaline in his system kept trying to warn him that the taikonauts were going to attack him from behind. The fear was made worse by the fact that, in his suit, he couldn't look over his shoulder.

But nothing happened, and he drove them to the construction site, where Louis and Anne were waiting for them, standing about ten paces apart. The commander held one of the wrench in his hands and tried in vain to make it look like it was simply because he'd been working.

Charlie got out and the taikonauts got off. They stood there silently for a few moments, staring at each other, before the taller Chinese man raised both hands and walked toward the front of the holding bolts on which the carbon-fiber tensioning cables had been stretched. Louis and Anne turned with him, but otherwise didn't move.

"What's he doing?" Louis asked tensely.

The taikonaut took the end of the cut cable and wiggled it with one finger. He then pointed to the drawbar eye of the bolt and also wiggled a finger before picking up regolith with one hand and rubbing it between his fingers. It trickled toward the ground like weightless dust.

"What is he trying to tell us?" Louis asked.

"I don't know, but it would be pretty strange for a saboteur to come here with a cable and do a pantomime, wouldn't it?"

Anne approached the Chinese man.

"Careful," Louis admonished her.

"Don't worry." She took the cable from the taikonaut's

hand and held it close to her visor. She then went to the bolt and examined the eyelet.

Charlie watched her and noticed that she was standing half in the sun. The last time they had driven away, it had been in the same place, but in the shade. For the most part, the sun always shone on the same part of the moon – but only as seen from Earth. As the satellite rotated in a bound rotation around the blue planet, the 'far side' of the moon was always illuminated by the sun. Here at the south pole, the conditions were special. The sun was always low above the horizon and one day lasted about two weeks, followed by two weeks of darkness. They were currently at the end of a 'day.'

He turned around and looked for the brightly glowing disk in the black sky. It was no longer fully over the western ridge. A considerable section was already missing. Yesterday, the underside had only just disappeared a little behind the summit.

"The sun," he said. "Could it be that the temperature difference has caused the cable to expand? The three bolts were previously in the shade, but they are now all in the sun."

Anne turned toward him. One of the taikonauts seemed to interpret her body language correctly and now pointed to the sun as well, before sticking a thumb up and then down.

"Wait a minute." Anne lifted the cable again. "Maybe he's trying to tell us that the extremely fine, sharp-edged regolith on the narrow eyelet destroyed the cable. That's not so unlikely. The cable is made for use in the sun, at high temperatures, unlike those in the crater. But we tightened it in the shade because of that stone there. We shouldn't have done that. When the material was extremely cold, it expanded a lot with the sunlight, a difference of 200 degrees. The expansion could have led to friction with the sharp regolith."

When she had finished, she paused.

"What?" asked Charlie and Louis at the same time.

"I'm not sure if there was enough tension on it for such a strong material to tear. Carbon fibers are amazingly tear-resistant. The resin mixture between the fibers could have been the problem with the temperature amplitude."

"So are they pulling our leg?" Louis asked.

"I'm not sure. It's possible. So both."

"Great."

"What if they cut it so we don't crash?" suggested Charlie.

"I think it's great how you're standing up for peace, but that's incredibly far-fetched," Louis said and snorted.

"They didn't even cover their footprints. So, they made no secret of their presence."

"Or they wanted to provoke us into a reaction."

"Or save us from falling. None of us thought about the fact that the shade had become the sun," Charlie insisted.

The taller Chinese man went back to the Rover.

"Hey!" Louis exclaimed. But before he could do anything, the two taikonauts lifted their cable from the cargo area and placed it on the ground between their two groups. Then the taller one pointed first to the cable, then to the four bolts and knotted two of his gloved fingers together.

"Do they want to give us their cable?" asked Anne.

The shorter Chinese man got down on his knees when they didn't react and smoothed out a large area of the regolith before starting to draw with the index finger of his right hand. Charlie came closer, Anne followed his example, only Louis kept a greater distance.

"Okay, that's obviously the base station of the elevator," said Anne and, as if he had heard her, the kneeling taikonaut pointed to the base station. "And those are the four retaining bolts."

The taikonaut pointed to the cable and began to draw four lines between the bolt and the station. He then made a grand gesture.

"All of us?"

The stranger pointed unmistakably into the crater.

"Ah, I think I understand," said Charlie.

"What?" Louis demanded.

"I think they want to offer us their cable as a replacement and go down there with us in return," he explained. "They had installed a very simple rappelling device on the crater rim, but one of their threaded anchor bolts is broken, however they managed it. They can't get down there without us. At least not safely."

"Ah, and that's why they cut our cables, so we don't have a choice, eh?" Louis snorted like a bull. "Such bastards."

"Possibly," Anne admitted. "But it's also possible that they've simply seen that neither method is working as planned and they want to combine our efforts."

"Half full or half empty." Charlie shrugged in his suit. "It looks like we don't really have a choice if we want to get down there."

"With saboteurs! Who knows what they'll do?"

"They don't look aggressive to me now. Better cunning but cooperative than stupid and violent, I'd say."

CHAPTER 36

Rebecca was sitting in the small interrogation room of the Enid police station. After the officers had stormed the house, she had been disarmed and then led out with the family. The mother had testified that Rebecca had been the one who had taken care of them, but the police had not been entirely convinced.

So they were separated and taken away, and she was put in this room. Three walls, one of them mirrored, a door, a fixed table, two chairs that were also secured to the floor. The only difference between her and a typical criminal was that she hadn't been led in with handcuffs.

Nothing had happened in the last few hours – she didn't know how many, as her wristwatch had been shattered and both of her cellphones had been taken away. She had just sat in silence. No one had come, which made her angry because they had also taken the file from her.

At some point, however, the door opened and a large policeman entered. He was dressed in jeans and a tight shirt that emphasized his bulky muscles. His angular face was showing a three-day beard, his eyes small but alert. He could have graced a bodybuilder magazine with his looks.

"Major ... Rebecca Hinrichs, thirty-four years old, military intelligence, Air Force, North American 9 millimeter and 7.62 millimeter marksmanship champion two years ago," he read aloud from a file that looked tiny in his hands. He took a seat on the chair opposite her and laid the open folder in front of him before looking at her. "That's why you like handing out headshots, I take it?"

"I like to be effective when I'm defending myself," she replied.

"I see. I'm Detective Lucas Darwi, and I've been assigned to your case."

"*My* case?"

"Well, no one else is alive except a family scared to death," Darwi replied.

"I would like to make use of the Fifth Amendment."

"A lawyer, I see. That sounds suspicious to me. Doesn't it to you?"

"Your standard lines won't work on me," she replied impatiently. "I understand that you're just doing your job here and going through the internal checklist, but I was part of an Air Force investigation into Specialist David Walker, who was the victim of a murder, as was my adjutant, Lieutenant Peter Rogers. That means there will also be a CIC investigation. So, I hope you've given plenty of thought to everything you say and do to me."

Detective Darwi kept his cool, she had to give him that. But his powerful jaw muscles were unmistakably beginning to clench.

"So bring me my phone and let me make the call." She leaned forward slightly. "After all, I have four or five witnesses who I'm sure have told you that I didn't murder the husband, and certainly not my comrades. If not ..."

"Then what?"

"Then the phone call I'm about to make will take a

slightly different direction." Rebecca shook her head. "But I really don't have time for that. Because while I'm stuck here, those who killed my comrades and tried to do the same to me will already be taking the next steps and will be breaking in here to steal the file you took from me."

The detective blinked in surprise and his powerful shoulder muscles twitched. "The file from your jacket."

"Yes." She rolled her eyes. "I know you can delay my phone call, at least a little longer before I can cause you trouble. You have a lot of bodies, and several firearms with my prints on them, at least one of which is also a murder weapon that took the life of the father of the family. You want to know what's going on here and I urgently need to read the file and talk to my superiors. How about we make a deal?"

"I'm listening."

"You bring me the file and my phone. I'll take a look at the file and take photos, then you bring them back to where you keep them and I'll let you in on what's going on here – without cameras or recording devices. We'll keep that to ourselves and I won't say anything to the CIC."

Darwi breathed in and out thoughtfully and pursed his lips. He was probably weighing whether it was worse to be dragged into her investigation or to lose the case because she was making sure the Pentagon pulled some strings in Oklahoma. Blowing cases that made the precinct look bad was the best way for a detective to derail his career.

Without another word, Darwi stood up and left the room like a mountain made flesh. He barely fit through the doorway.

Ten minutes later, he came back with her file and cellphone and placed them on the table.

"There's no signal in here," he stated with a definite don't-even-bother-to-try look.

Instead of answering, she slid the bloodstained file in front of her and opened it. Hastily at first, then with forced patience, she went through the pages, first skimming them and then reading them again more carefully. There were only eight pages, with no letterhead or other identifying features of the author, but they were stunning.

"I have to make a phone call," she mumbled without taking her eyes off the file. She narrowed her eyes in disbelief and read the most important passages again, and yet again. Especially the statement at the bottom and top of each page that this document was to be destroyed – on a specified date: the day before *Sentinel I* went online and the signal was detected.

"Have you searched the premises of Specialist David Walker?" she asked.

"Yes."

"What did you find?"

"Firearms, half of them registered, a vial of poison, lots of ammunition, and a pile of books," the detective replied surprisingly frankly. Was it part of his strategy?

"Books? What kind of books?"

"Scientific books."

She stared at the file cover. "Physics? Radio waves?"

Darwi raised an eyebrow in surprise. "Yes. Several books on hydrogen, one on interference modulation or something, and lots on radio telemetry. A bunch of stuff was marked in them. But only for certain key points ..."

" ... as if he had to recite key words." She nodded.

"We have a deal," Detective Darwi reminded her, making a prompting gesture.

Rebecca looked at him in irritation. "You saw for yourself that ..." She interrupted herself and nodded. "Of course, you didn't take a look because you're not allowed to do that with military documents without clearance from the Pentagon."

Darwi shrugged his shoulders. "It says *Top Secret* in red on the cover – including a bloody handprint and a few blood splatters. I didn't make it to homicide detective because I'm stupid."

"But if you ask me what's in this file, maybe you would be." She looked him in the eye, hoping that he was a good investigator and recognized her honesty.

He grimaced and stood up.

"Follow me. Leave the file here. I'll lock the room."

Rebecca got up and followed him as he left the room and locked the door. He then led her across the corridor, past a few colleagues who greeted him, and toward a room with a telephone in it.

"You have the right to five minutes," Darwi explained. "I'll give you ten. But if I feel like you're setting me up, even the Pentagon can't help you. Clear?"

"Crystal," she replied. Rebecca sat down on an aluminum chair that was identical to the one in the interrogation room. She quickly dialed General Eversman's cellphone as soon as the door snapped shut behind the detective.

"Yes?"

"This is Rebecca Hinrichs, sir."

"Major? Half an hour ago, one of my aides stormed into my office and said you'd been arrested in a murder case. May I ask what the hell you're doing in Oklahoma?" He sounded angry. The fact that he didn't even make a secret of it was an alarm signal.

"Sir, I've come across something I need to tell you."

"Then let's hear it. But I'm warning you, if I don't like it, you and I will have to have a serious heart-to-heart as soon as you get back to Arlington. And that will be sooner rather than later."

"I understand, General. I was sorting through the files in Peterson as promised when I came across something strange.

Specialist David Walker, discoverer of the moon signal, was transferred after his discovery."

"Not unusual. I'm sure Colonel Smith wanted to get him out of harm's way in case it aroused media interest and someone dug too deep. *Sentinel I* is still a secret Space Force project," Eversman said impatiently.

"Yes, but he was transferred back to the Air Force. To Vance," she continued, and the general fell silent. "So I flew to Oklahoma and did some digging because Smith told me that his inquiries were brushed off. Meaning it wasn't Smith who transferred Walker."

"Then who?"

"Colonel Feinman."

"Excuse me?"

"Feinman showed up at Peterson the day before the signal was discovered – together with Specialist Walker. But under a different name," Rebecca explained. "And, Feinman disappeared again with Walker. Here's the thing. When Colonel Smith was investigating six weeks ago, the specialist had been put on indefinite leave at the same time. With pay, sir."

"That's ... unusual. Go on," the general instructed her in a neutral voice.

"Walker handed me a file before he was killed by unknown operatives. Four men, ex-Special Forces, I assume. They also killed his landlord – the father of the family whose upstairs he rented – and Lieutenant Rogers." She faltered briefly and bit her lower lip. She couldn't allow any emotions to surface, and must certainly not show them. Not now.

"What kind of file? What was in it?"

"It was a complete listing of the signal specifics. Wavelengths of the radio signal, the exact pattern, including brief explanations of the individual sections and how the data is arranged in the computers of *Sentinel I.* Plus a note to destroy these documents on the day the signal was detected."

"Are you saying that Walker didn't detect the signal?"

"Literature on the subject of hydrogen and radiometry was also found in his apartment, including marked locations that exactly match the signal that *Sentinel I* claims to have picked up." Rebecca took a deep breath before continuing. "I believe Colonel Feinman gave these documents to Specialist Walker before *Sentinel I* even went online."

"That would mean ..."

" ... that Feinman knew about the extraterrestrial artifact on the moon even before *Sentinel I.*"

CHAPTER 37

Attaching the elevator cabin was easy with five people working together in lunar gravity. The process was designed so that it could be carried out by two astronauts, so it took them less than 15 minutes. Anne then checked all the systems, including the motor control via the signal amplifier on the threaded head, through which they always had to be in contact with the electric motor located at the end of the coil.

One of the two taikonauts drew an 'O2' in the regolith, whereupon they returned to their previous place of work and exchanged their oxygen cartridges. Apparently they had an exchange system similar to NASA's to simplify longer missions.

When they got back, Louis, Anne, and Charlie had done the same and had two and a half hours of fresh oxygen and new CO2 filter cartridges.

"The platform only carries four people," said Louis. "Anne ..."

"I know, you already said that. I'll stay here and take care of radio contact between you and the *Liberty*," she said with a subsequent sigh.

"I'm sorry."

"That's all right. Just take care of yourselves and don't do anything stupid."

Charlie raised a hand and clasped hers. Then, without another word, he climbed out onto the platform. It swayed slightly, and a glance at the bottomless depths below them made him feel dizzy. They were standing in a slender aluminum construction with a thin railing over a two-kilometer-deep abyss in which darkness was so complete it seemed to suck out the light of the stars.

The two taikonauts joined them and it became cramped in the open cabin. Charlie looked at the four carbon fiber cables that led from each corner to a massive carabiner connected to the main cable that ran over the pulley and was connected to the winch above the engine.

For a brief moment, he thought about how easy it would be for the Chinese to simply push them over the railing, which only reached up to their hips, but he immediately chased the thought away as adrenaline shot into his circulation and made his skin tingle.

Don't drive yourself crazy, Charlie!

"Ready?" asked Anne. "Have you got the spare cartridges?"

"Ready, right here," Louis confirmed, tapping the bag in front of his stomach. They looked at the taikonauts, who put their thumbs up.

"Miles? Houston? We're about to start lowering the cabin into the crater," Anne radioed, raising a hand in farewell. Then she activated the motor, which was indicated by a green glow on the small control panel on the front railing. Unlike the control display of their elevator on the *Liberty,* this was a completely analog system that was thoroughly protected from extreme cold, especially as there was no back-up system here. There were three toggle switches: one for lowering, one for raising, and one for the parked position.

Louis flipped the lowering switch and a single shudder went through the cabin, as if they had rolled over a gentle speedbump. Then they began to slowly glide down into the darkness. For the first ten minutes, they traveled at a fraction of the maximum possible speed in order to test the system under real conditions. Ultimately, it had been designed on Earth, with the tensile strength and statics calculated with corresponding calculations from the known lunar conditions. Everything they did up here was comparable to a test flight of a military aircraft, only under more difficult conditions.

Charlie was accordingly nervous, so much so that he didn't even think about the fact that they were sharing the ride with two taikonauts from a competing nation. The ten minutes seemed like an eternity to him, especially after they had left the short stretch of crater wall illuminated by sunlight behind them and had been swallowed up by darkness.

The output from their helmet lamps disappeared into nothingness. Everything around them was pitch black, except when he turned and shone his light between the taikonauts and onto the rock face, which was rough and riddled with long grooves. There were occasional patches of loose-looking regolith on small ledges, but overall it looked relatively smooth, like a cliff in the Grand Canyon – only without any color or shading.

From time to time he thought that something was moving at the edges of the shadows, fleeing from the light, but it was just his senses playing tricks on him because of the shadows cast by the helmet lamps. There was nothing alive here but them.

"Anne, you can set the engine to full power if everything is OK up there," Louis radioed after a long silence.

"Got it!"

If the speed changed as a result, Charlie didn't notice. If he looked up at the edge, it might have been moving away a little faster, but it was impossible to tell because they had essentially nothing as reference points.

Then he noticed that they still had their sun visors down. He turned to look at the others and tapped his visor, then opened the golden sun filter. Shortly afterward, Louis did the same, and after a moment's hesitation, so did the two taikonauts.

In the light of their respective helmet lamps, he scrutinized the two Chinese, just as they were presumably scrutinizing him. The taller one had a stern face with thin lips and small eyes that looked out of narrow slits. His cheekbones were high and his hair disappeared under a padded cap that looked very similar to Charlie's own, but bore the red star emblem of Communist China on his forehead. He estimated that the taikonaut might be in his early 50s. The shorter one had a softer face with narrow cheeks and smooth skin, and an attentive gaze. His full mouth showed the hint of a smile.

Charlie raised a hand in greeting and smiled – it was the best general form of communication he knew. The shorter one returned the gesture and the smile, while the taller one remained serious, but raised his hand and nodded to him and Louis in turn. Perhaps it was intended to indicate a formal bow, as he did it very slowly.

"Okay, Charlie," Louis said and looked at him. "That's probably better than constantly spying on each other. Good work, man."

"Thank you. I took a risk and I'm glad it paid off," he replied, and turned back to the crater, although it made him feel queasy. But the situation was getting weird because they were standing so close together that they would have been staring at each other otherwise.

"Shit," Louis said, holding onto the railing with both hands. When he'd reached out to grab it, it had looked like he was moving through water. "I've always thought a lot of my nerves. Fighter pilot, great, and a test pilot – you need big balls and nerves of steel. Perfect for astronauts, right? But when I look down there, my blood is freezing in my veins."

"I feel the same way," mumbled Charlie. Not even the tiniest floating particles hung in the air in front of him – because they didn't exist here. "Pitch-black vacuum. Minus two hundred degrees Celsius and an alien artifact somewhere. Even a horror movie writer couldn't have made it any creepier."

They descended at just over one meter per second, which resulted in a travel time of around 30 minutes. The cabin floor had several redundant laser-based distance sensors so that the ride would be slowed down accordingly when the time came.

This happened after a seemingly immeasurable period of time during which Charlie stared into the darkness and concentrated on his breathing, as he had been trained to do. Inhale for four seconds, hold for four, exhale for eight. He had always believed himself to be true astronaut material, because hardly anything could rattle him, and even in the most stressful situations he remained calm and rational in order to make clear decisions. That's how it had been in combat, and that's how it had been in astronaut training. But he had to admit to himself that he was reaching his limits.

Charlie suddenly saw something in front of him. Or more precisely, diagonally below him. His first reaction was fright because it looked as if a monster was jumping out of the darkness toward them, but then he realized that it was a monolithic rock sticking out of the darkness, a gray, pointy lump in the void. Shortly afterward, the ground also came into view, an uneven surface of gray-shaded rubble. Smaller stones and larger ones were scattered everywhere, as if the result of a meteor shower.

The cabin was slowing down. Above them, the cable was lost in nothingness. The edge of the crater, bathed in sunlight, seemed infinitely far away, forming a circular sky full of stars and the large crescent of the rim in the middle. Despite being accompanied by three other space adventurers, and Anne and Miles up top, Charlie had never felt so alone in his life.

"Well, here we are," Louis said in his matter-of-fact way, flipping the toggle for 'park' and bringing Charlie back to himself, which was a relief. He opened the simple latch of the railing when they had stopped and touched down. Then the two Americans stepped forward and off the platform at the same time, and cleared the way for the accompanying Chinese, before taking a closer look around.

Behind them was the crater wall, a dark, bare, towering rock face. It had been about two meters away at the beginning, because the cabin was clearly separated from the wall by the pulley, but the wall was touching the rear railing at this point. They had probably been scraping along it for quite some time.

There were individual sections in the rock that were somewhat shinier and others that almost sparkled. All around, the ground sloped slightly and stretched as far as the helmet lamps could reach, forming an endless field of large menhirs and head-sized boulders. Loose regolith covered the areas in between. It looked more or less the same as the surface above, only rougher because there was more loose rock lying around and the shades of gray were different, although that could be because there was only the yellow artificial light of their lamps here instead of sunlight.

Louis reached into his pocket and pulled out four battery-powered glow sticks, which he handed to Charlie while he placed the radio amplifier on a flat rock.

Charlie took the four forearm-sized lamps, switched them on, and placed them about ten meters away from the elevator cabin. The ones at the back were positioned right against the rock face and illuminated it in such a way that they made a visible area of about 100 meters in diameter, so that they now had a visual reference point and a counterweight to the darkness everywhere else. The Chinese, meanwhile, began to look around, but did not run ahead toward the center of the crater, as a pessimistic voice in his head had feared.

Instead, the taller man took a small hammer out of his pocket. Charlie stiffened involuntarily when he saw it. How could he have missed the potential weapon?

The taikonaut then unfolded the handle, which lengthened it. But instead of going after them – *I need to turn off that negative voice!* – he went to one of the menhirs and began to hit it in an attempt to dislodge some chunks. The shorter one stood next to him and pulled a large plastic zipper pouch from the pocket on his right thigh.

Meanwhile, Louis checked the radio link to the top.

"Anne? Can you hear us?"

"Loud and clear. How are things going with you?" their crewmate replied. Charlie breathed a sigh of relief. It was good to hear her familiar voice down here and to know that she was connected to a lifeline up there – even if it only consisted of invisible radio waves.

While Louis was talking to Anne and optimizing the positioning of the radio relay, Charlie looked back at the Chinese, who were working on a piece of rock with their gloves as though they were rubbing a magic lamp.

Then they started gesticulating wildly, as if they were arguing. Charlie tapped Louis on the arm. "Hey, Louis."

"Yes?"

"Look at this. Something's going on with them."

"Are they fighting? Shit, I hope they're not …" Charlie faltered as the Chinese came running toward him with long hops. Their faces were distorted. With rage? The taller one still had the hammer in his hand.

His heart began to pound and he was about to dodge away to avoid them when they stopped just in front of them and he realized that they were not looking angry. They were beaming with joy, laughing. Confused, he exchanged a glance with Louis, who had taken up a defensive stance. Then the shorter man held the plastic bag with the stone in it toward them, while holding a flashlight against it from behind with his other hand.

Charlie's jaw dropped. What had looked like a dirty lump of rock continued to look mostly like stone, but with some changes visible thanks to the focused light. He saw glistening patches, and ones that almost looked like sooty glass.

"Water," he said. "You found water ice in the regolith!"

Even Louis clapped his hands and laughed. They had discovered water on the moon. It looked different than on Earth, but he had no doubt that they would discover H_2O when they analyzed samples of it on the *Liberty*. This was nothing less than a sensation, and minus the alien artifact, this would have been the crowning achievement of the entire *Artemis* missions.

They enjoyed this moment of transnational elation, in which there was no sign of a new Cold War or the worries of a tangible conflict that had plagued them above.

Here and now, they were simply four space travelers holding the future in their hands and sharing the same joy.

CHAPTER 38

Rebecca was back to sitting in the interrogation room and on the verge of biting her nails – a bad habit she had fortunately gotten rid of after her West Point studies. Nervous intelligence officers were neither welcome nor effective.

General Eversman had told her over an hour ago that he had to dig into what was going on at the Pentagon. He was furious that something like this could happen without his knowledge, given his position as the Commander-in-Chief of the Space Force, the newest branch of the U.S. military. The fact that Feinman was operating secretly under his nose, apparently involved in clandestine actions that were hidden from Eversman, was like a slap in the face.

She could picture him summoning his best contacts and throwing a tantrum. He wasn't a secret service agent and was commonly referred to as 'old school,' which meant he usually approached things with a bit of rough-and-tumble mentality.

There was a knock at the door and Detective Darwi entered. The walking mountain of muscle sat down opposite her. His aluminum chair creaked, sounding as if the metal was begging him to stand back up.

"You wanted to see me?" he asked.

"Yes. I have to fill you in," she replied frankly.

"Excuse me? I thought it would be better for me if I didn't know anything?" Darwi frowned. "Why the sudden change of heart?"

"Because I'm pretty sure I need your help."

"You spoke to the Pentagon on the phone, I assume. Did they drop you? Because in that case I can't do much ..."

"No, no," she interrupted him. "That's not it. I have a suspicion that the moon signal is a fake."

"Excuse me?" Darwi leaned forward. Now she had his attention and he knew what she knew, potentially making himself a target. She wasn't proud of the move, but she feared it was necessary.

"Specialist David Walker knew about the nature of the signal and its specifics even before *Sentinel I* went online," she explained, folding her hands in front of her on the tabletop to avoid venting her stress and suppressed emotions by biting her nails or picking at the skin around them. "We don't know why, but it looks like certain elements in the Space Force knew about the alien artifact and its existence in the Shackleton Crater beforehand."

"That is ... that would be ..."

"A scandal? Yes. But the worse scandal would be that the Space Force leadership knew nothing about it."

"Okay, if that's true, that would be a big deal, but what does that have to do with me? I'm a detective in Enid, Oklahoma," Darwi replied, noticeably unsettled.

When she explained, his eyes got so big that she was afraid they would come loose from their sockets and burst. But he didn't say no.

After another hour, during which she revealed her plan to him, there was a knock at the door. Darwi went out and returned shortly afterward. "Telephone call for you."

"Wait a minute," Rebecca said and waved him back. She pointed to his notepad and he handed her a piece of paper with the pen. She wrote down a phone number and a name.

"Who's that?"

"One of my contacts at the FBI. Robert Mueller. He will help you implement all of this."

"I haven't said I'd help you yet," Darwi replied.

"You didn't *say* it, but the decision was made a long time ago."

"How do you know that?"

"If I hadn't recognized it from your body language and your questions, I'd be a pretty poor intelligence officer, now wouldn't I?" she replied, and he said nothing. Instead, he tore off the note and headed for the door. "Come."

He led her back into the shielded room with the landline telephone. It was the general.

"Major," he said. There was a click and a scratchy sound on the line, and a brief dial tone sounded. "This line is now secure."

She nodded to herself. "Were you able to find out anything?"

"Yes. I instructed the Internal Investigations Division to visit the SpaceX premises in Hawthorne. With my personal clearance, they were able to view the mission specifics of the Falcon Heavy vehicle that launched *Sentinel I* to the moon. Musk's people took the security clearances very seriously and even called here to confirm the paperwork before they let my people access the documents," the general explained, audibly tense. "Now brace yourself. According to the mission logs, *two* payloads were launched into lunar orbit."

"Two, sir?" Rebecca frowned. "That means there are two satellites?"

"It looks like it. The size of the objects carried – about which SpaceX has no knowledge because of the secrecy – must have been roughly similar. But the second object had more mass."

"So the Space Force stationed two satellites over the south pole?"

"I'll be damned if they didn't."

"But how is that even possible?" she asked. "I'm not a physicist, but I thought it was impossible to hide anything in space."

"It is true, because of the low ambient temperature, that everything glows like a light bulb in the infrared spectrum if it even emits as little energy as a dead household battery. But," he replied, "it is possible to mask things."

Rebecca thought about it. "So the second satellite is behind *Sentinel I* as seen from our viewpoint?"

"Absolutely right. There is a blind spot for our telescopes. Due to the great distance to the moon it's not particularly large, but with the heat radiation from *Sentinel I,* it's large enough to park a satellite there. As long as they are synchronized, you would never be able to detect it from here."

"But I don't understand, sir. Why would Colonel Feinman go over your head for approval to launch a top-secret satellite and, without your knowledge, put it into position over the moon?" she asked.

"I don't know, but I'll damned well find out, you can bet your career I will."

"Apparently the secret is so important to the conspirators that they kill their own people to keep it."

"All the more reason to put a stop to them. Someone in the Pentagon has diverted black budgets and betrayed me," said Eversman with ill-concealed anger.

"With respect, sir, isn't that only possible with backing from the very top?"

"I realize that someone with access to the Pentagon's

financial information is involved. The only question is, who? We have to find out."

We echoed in her mind. He had already made plans for her. "I assume, sir, that I play a part in this?"

"Yes. I'm sorry, Major, but you're in it up to your neck by now. We need to find out what *Sentinel II* was designed for and why it's so top secret that someone thought to send it up there behind my back," Eversman replied, sounding almost apologetic.

Rebecca suppressed a sigh. "What can I do?"

"I'll extract you personally. You will be picked up from the station in thirty minutes by a Major Hines and a dozen MPs. Hines is one of my trusted men in the Air Force. He will drive you back to Vance where you will board a Chinook. Hines and one of his pilot friends will fly you to an abandoned airfield near Cincinnati where a jet will be waiting for you. I need some time to organize this and make sure there's no paper trail. That's why the Chinook is a good choice. The jet – with a crew I've selected – will then bring you to the Pentagon, where you'll report directly to me."

"With respect, General, don't you think Feinman will notice? He'll know that I'm being taken to Vance."

"Yeah, but he's not going to kill twelve MPs who are prepared for it. They're all freaked out in Vance about the murders of Walker and Rogers. My condolences, by the way."

"Thank you, sir," she murmured.

"My team will do everything they can to make sure you arrive safely. They will monitor everything. I wouldn't be surprised if they even send up a surveillance drone," the general continued unperturbed. "Don't worry about it."

"It's not that. It's more the fact that they could chase the helicopter. A Chinook, especially without a payload, can fly pretty far, but it's not fast. What if he's waiting for me in Cincinnati?"

"I didn't end up at my current post because I'm naïve. You will be accompanied by a Wraith Aggressor. If anything approaches you, I will know and contact the nearest Air Force base. Whoever is following you will then be warned off or shot down."

Rebecca was amazed. The RQ-170 was one of the Air Force's best reconnaissance drones, with excellent stealth capabilities. The fact that Eversman was so well connected within the Air Force that he could make a domestic mission possible at such short notice reassured her somewhat. Perhaps she would live to see the backside of this, after all.

"All right."

"Good. Hines and the MPs will be with you in thirty minutes."

"I need a little more time to sort things out here," she said.

"What ... Okay, just hurry up and take care of yourself. When this is over, you won't just be promoted, Major. I'll bring you straight into my team," said the general, then hung up.

Rebecca let out a long exhale and went to the door. She knocked until Darwi opened it.

"And?"

"Is the doctor here yet?"

CHAPTER 39

L ouis and Charlie only briefly discussed whether they should find their own sample, but then decided against it. They had a limited supply of oxygen, which with luck would last as far as the bottom of the crater, and then spare cartridges for the way back. They had no time to waste, and who knew if they would succeed as quickly as the two taikonauts?

So they put the search for their own sample of water ice on the back burner and set off with their Chinese colleagues toward the center of the crater.

The ground here sloped slightly, so they made even faster progress than on the surface, but also had to be careful not to fall. The many stones lying around were constant reminders of how dangerous such an accident would be. Not only was there a risk of slitting a suit, despite the rein-forced material, or hitting a sharp rock with their visor, even a minor injury wasn't 'minor' because they were literally miles away from what little help they could expect on the moon.

Louis and he were a little more agile than the two taiko-nauts, which was probably due to the extra day they had spent walking around and working in lunar gravity. Their muscle memory had developed relatively quickly.

The big taikonaut fell a few times at the start, but he let himself be helped up and, after a quick check verified there were no holes in his suit, they proceeded to hop a little more slowly over the uneven terrain toward the darkness.

The cones of light from their helmets moved up and down, forming overlapping trails on the gray background that were so erratic the shadows at the edges appeared distorted. Charlie felt as if they were being besieged by demons who were only kept at bay by the photons that their lamps sent into the vacuum.

Unlike the Apollo astronauts, they had been able to prepare for lunar gravity and were well practiced thanks to the extra time. This meant faster progress with their long hops or jumps than would have been the case on Earth. Just 15 minutes into the journey, they had reached a kind of rocky bulge that rose up a few meters with gently angled slopes.

"That must be the edge of the crater within the crater," said Charlie. "Where a second impact took place, which we can thank for the cliff face."

"It looks like it," Louis replied. "Let's check it out."

To be on the safe side, they climbed up on all fours, as the surface was very loose and they didn't want to take any risks. On the other side, the descent was much steeper. The incline of around 30 degrees looked scary and felt even scarier as their jumps became more difficult to control. So they slowed their movements and forced themselves to proceed more cautiously, even though they had used up 50 percent of their oxygen by now. This was more than expected, probably due to the adrenaline and increased heart rate.

"We should fan out slowly," Louis suggested, glancing at his forearm display. "The artifact is in this half of the crater, on the edge between the slope and the crater floor. According to

Houston's trigonometric calculations, each of the slopes is just under 8.4 kilometers long, and the bottom has a diameter of 5.45 kilometers. So we should only be about a kilometer away from the artifact and heading straight for it if we aligned ourselves correctly at the beginning."

"I wouldn't bet on it."

"Nah. One hundred meters distance between us should be enough, then we cover three hundred meters, plus if the guys on the edges look around, maybe another hundred on each side, makes five hundred. That should work."

"Sounds good." Charlie waved to the shorter man as he looked in his direction and they came toward each other. The Chinese man caught him as he tripped over a stone and almost fell. "That was close."

He nodded gratefully to the taikonaut and indicated a bow, while Louis began to explain his plan. He drew four stick figures in the moon dust and drew arrows with a '100' underneath. The Chinese understood immediately and nodded at the same time they heard Anne's voice.

"The Shackleton, surface."

"Acknowledge."

"We've just heard from Houston that we're expecting an impact event in the next thirty minutes. It's a big chunk, but it's going to hit some distance to the east of the crater. So there's no immediate danger," she said. "Harry told me to tell you, even though it might sound worrying. But as I said, the data looks good."

Louis and Charlie exchanged a glance.

"Thanks for the warning, Anne," his companion finally said. "We're approaching the calculated location of the artifact."

"Understood."

"Is everything quiet upstairs?"

"Yes. No development."

"Good, we'll be in touch."

"Good luck."

Charlie stared at the edge of the crater, four kilometers up and almost six kilometers away in a straight line. The shimmering gray rim looked as if it was glowing from within, so strong was the sunlight in contrast with the deep darkness that surrounded them.

"Okay, let's get going," Louis ordered. They swarmed out into a line 100 meters apart, which they measured with the rangefinders in their helmets. Then each raised his right arm to signal he was ready, and they continued their descent.

Charlie had taken the far-right position and regularly scanned to his left, but he was more concerned with searching the area to his right. Like a searchlight, his helmet lamp cut swaths through the darkness and repeatedly revealed the same sloping regolith fields until, suddenly, a reflection flared as he turned his head. He was startled by the sudden change in his otherwise-monotonous field of vision and turned his head to bring the light back across the area. There was indeed something artificial half-buried in the regolith.

Charlie jumped toward it, his mouth suddenly feeling dry. That had to be it. The alien artifact!

The first thing he saw resembled a shovel of sorts, made of silvery material, stuck vertically in the moon dust at the outer edge of a small crater. Beyond it lay debris that looked like a metallic insect had jumped into the hollow and died. Golden booms lay crisscrossed, reflecting so strongly that it blinded him.

"I've found something!" he shouted. He had almost forgotten to open his mouth. His voice sounded hoarse and he had to clear his throat before he could continue. "I ... I found the artifact."

"We're coming!" Louis replied with unmistakable excitement.

Charlie looked over his shoulder and saw the three figures coming toward him. Their glowing helmet lights bounced up and down.

Then he looked back down at the debris in front of him and carefully circled it to the right side, ten meters away. It was not as big as NASA had assumed – much smaller, in fact. And there was no doubt that it was the remains of something that had once looked different. He found a kind of hull that might once have been cube-shaped, about the size of a small car with eight long tubes at the front, several of which had something red in them. The entire structure was badly damaged. Perhaps half of it was buried underneath the crater floor. As the latter was still very sloping, it was difficult to tell.

Then Charlie's gaze fell on something else: a cylindrical structure about a meter and a half long, half hidden in the regolith with a long tip at one end and a thickened section at the other. He staggered back a step and almost fell when the beams of his helmet lights fell on the star-spangled banner of the U.S. printed on the front of the rocket.

"Louis!" he shouted breathlessly. "Don't come here! Don't come here under any circumstances."

"What? Why is that? What's happening?" His companion was breathing heavily, he was in such a hurry. Charlie wheeled around to him and realized that he was not far away and that the Chinese had almost caught up. They could see the outer contours of the crashed satellite themselves, no doubt about it.

"It's not an artifact!" he said in horror. "It's a satellite of *ours,* damn it. And it was *armed*."

Louis said nothing until he had reached his side and gasped for a few breaths of air. Together they stared at the rocket in disbelief.

"Oh shit! No! No, no, no!" Louis turned to him. "If the Chinese see this, then ..."

Charlie turned to the taikonauts, intending to run toward

them but it was too late. They were there, moving slowly and also looking at the crashed satellite, which should not have even existed. A silver plate that reminded him of crumpled aluminum foil hung on its top. Charlie guessed that it was what had reflected in the images from *Sentinel I.*

He licked his chapped lips and watched the taikonauts. They looked at the satellite with wide eyes and mouths open in astonishment and then also spotted the rocket in the regolith. The American flag looked pale in the absence of an atmosphere but was clearly recognizable as such.

Seconds passed, perhaps a minute, during which none of them moved or dared to say anything. Then the taller man reached into his pocket and pulled out a small camera. It flashed as he snapped his photo.

CHAPTER 40

Major Hines, a wiry little man with a humorless expression, picked her up from the station accompanied by two MPs. She said a quick goodbye to Darwi while Hines completed the paperwork and confirmed that the CIC would take over her case if there was sufficient evidence of a felony under Oklahoma law.

Then they walked out toward three Air Force armored personnel carriers. Six MPs with submachine guns flanked the sidewalk, peering into the night. It had started to rain.

Hines climbed into the middle car with her and pointed to a stack of clean clothes – an Air Force utility uniform and a winter jacket with a major's insignia.

"I thought you might want to change."

"Thank you," she replied and began to undress. The major cleared his throat and turned around. Rebecca ignored him and put on her fresh clothes. She put her bloody and partially torn uniform remnants in a pile. Then she took her two cellphones and put them in the jacket's inside pockets. "I'm done."

"Good." By now they were driving south on the main road from Enid, where the large Air Force base was located just outside the city. "The Chinook is being refueled right now. My co-pilot, Captain Ludwig, is a close friend of mine whom I would trust with my life. Don't worry, we'll get you to the rendezvous point safely."

She was tempted to point out to him that the safety factor was more likely thanks to the *Wraith* flying silently behind them, but instead she nodded. "I appreciate that, thank you."

"We have spare tanks with us, so we don't need to stop to refuel. That means we can get to Cincinnati without stopping."

No stops also means less risk of Feinman interfering, she thought, nodding silently.

During the journey, she kept looking out of the tiny, armored window behind her. She scanned the sky for a drone, but couldn't see one. Whether that was a good sign or a bad one, she didn't know. Events had come so thick and fast in the last few hours that her brain couldn't seem to keep up. The loss of Rogers hit her right in the heart – a region she thought she had long since switched off. Because of work. But she had liked the lieutenant. He had been her professional foster son and she had seen how much he had become like her.

There was also anger. Anger at the men who had killed her comrades, but above all anger at Feinman, who was to blame for all this. But she quashed the fiery anger. So far she had kept a cool head and she had to keep going that way if she wanted to have a chance of getting out of this in one piece and bringing him to justice.

Pull yourself together, Rebecca, she admonished herself. *Stay calm, stay rational, and analyze the situation.*

Fifteen minutes later they were rolling up to the gate of a side entrance to Vance Air Force Base, through which they were hastily waved. Eversman's influence went a long way indeed as a four-star Air Force general who had transferred to the Space Force to lead it as part of the Joint Chiefs of Staff.

Their little convoy stopped in front of a barracks where she and Hines got out and entered the front door of 'Block C.' The MPs drove on.

There were no lights on in the building, so Major Hines flipped switches as they entered the hallway and led her to a small room where he found a pilot's uniform and put it on. He then grabbed a helmet and handed her soundproof headphones.

"Joshua is already waiting for us in the helicopter," he said when she looked around questioningly and he motioned for her to follow him.

They left the building on the other side and crossed a lawn. Behind the next barracks, a long 1970s building, she could see and hear the Chinook. The massive twin-rotor helicopter was standing on a helipad and the two three-bladed rotors were idling and making plenty of noise. The cockpit looked like a dented glass snout, behind which a total of six portholes extended to the thickened tail section. There was a metal bulge of sorts around the fuselage where the fuel was located, as she knew from her training.

Although she had never been part of the air service, basic training in the weapons technology used by the Air Force had been part of her education. A small hatch with a stepladder was unfolded. Hines led her straight to it and let her go first. She hunched her shoulders against the rain and took the two steps at a run.

The interior was extremely spare. Two rows of seats along the right and the left, the bare metal floor full of eyelets, and straps for safety belts. That was it.

"Sit down and fasten your seatbelt," the major told her, turning around and pulling the hatch closed. There was a loud crash as the locks clicked into place, then he operated the safety lever and walked through the narrow passageway into the cockpit, where Rebecca could see the shoulder and arm of his co-pilot, Captain Joshua Ludwig.

She fastened herself in the middle of the right-hand bank of seats with one of the simple belts and pulled it tight. Then she put on the soundproof headphones and watched as they took off shortly afterward. The rotor noise – muffled, but plenty loud – increased significantly and became a strong background noise before they lifted off the helipad as if weightless. Rain pelted the metal of the Chinook like tiny bits of shrapnel as Hines pointed them northeast. The lights of Vance Air Force Base grew smaller and smaller below them, the glowing cones on the wet tarmac shrinking to ghostly apparitions and merging, as they rose even higher, with the far-reaching lights of Enid and North Enid.

The Chinook accelerated with its two turbines, which supported the counter-rotating tandem rotors, and built up additional speed. The nose lowered slightly as they reached cruising speed and flew off into the night.

After about half an hour, the co-pilot came to her and handed her a different model of headphones with a microphone. She nodded her thanks and replaced the one she was wearing with the soundproof headphones. The brief moment when her ears were not protected was so loud that her ears rang. The rain was now coming down in sheets, turning every drop into a small projectile that crashed into their flank and made a hell of a racket.

"Can you hear me?" asked Captain Ludwig.

"Loud and clear."

He gave her a thumbs up and returned to the cockpit.

"We're now at cruising altitude," said Hines via their headsets. "Unfortunately, in the middle of a band of clouds, but we should be out of there in half an hour at the latest. Then it will become less bumpy."

"All right."

"There's something else I need to talk to you about."

Rebecca listened up. "What is it?"

"The general asked me not to tell you until the flight," the major continued. His voice was slightly distorted by the radio.

She swallowed. Was Eversman involved in all this too? She had hardly given it a second thought. Because it would mean that she no longer had any influential allies – at least not in the military – and there was no chance for her anyway, unless she went directly to Congress under the Whistleblower Protection Act. That would end her career, but at least she would have some basic protection from those who wanted to kill her. But the idea that the general was a conspirator seemed absurd to her.

He doesn't even have to be a conspirator. If the President had signed off on a secret project that Eversman was handling for him, buried within the official Pentagon budget under the utmost secrecy, it couldn't be ruled out. She gulped again, and this time it almost hurt her throat.

" ... said."

Only now did she realize that Hines had been talking the whole time without her listening to him.

"Excuse me, can you repeat that from the beginning?" she asked with a dry mouth.

"The general said that he had this flight registered at the Pentagon," the major said and she stiffened instantly. "But he did it so that he could immediately see who was accessing the data and when. That's all I know, but I'm guessing you can do something with that information."

"Yes." Her thoughts were already starting to race again.

He doesn't just want to evacuate me and take me to safety, he wants to use me, she thought, grinding her teeth. *Of course he does. He's setting a trap for Feinman because he knows the colonel is keeping a close eye on everything to do with Vance right now. With this action, he may find out who his allies are and, in the best case, he can have Feinman confronted and arrested by his own people in Cincinnati. Then he would have won.*

She chewed on this thought for a long time. She didn't like being used as bait, and felt a little betrayed that the general had used her so freely and limited the information flowing in her direction. It would have been decent of him to tell her directly instead of using her against her knowledge.

But Feinman will never show up. He's far too clever for that. And the general is not an intelligence officer. He shouldn't have done this without consulting – or at least informing – me. But now it was too late. She was flying straight into a trap that, ironically, her ally had set for her.

CHAPTER 41

The flash died away on the metal remains of the satellite. Charlie stood there with Louis at his side, staring at the Chinese man with the camera, who carefully folded it up and stowed it in the breast pocket of his pressure suit. The shorter man looked worried, glancing back and forth between them and the military satellite without moving.

"Charlie," Louis said quietly, as if the taikonauts could otherwise hear them. "We can't let him send that photo home."

"What are you trying to say?" asked Charlie. His mouth felt as if he had eaten a handful of sand. He found it difficult to swallow. He had an idea of what his friend was trying to tell him and he didn't like it.

"If this photo gets to China, what do you think Beijing will do? Arm space, too? Shoot American military satellites out of orbit? Station its own rockets in lunar orbit?" Louis snorted. "Our country would lose credibility for decades and China would be strengthened. Do you want to live in a world like that?"

"But this is *our* fault."

"Yes," Louis admitted. He sounded bitter. "But does that

justify making it worse? We'll send the pictures to NASA and then ..."

" ... the Space Force intercepts them."

"Charlie, you can't want ..."

Charlie looked at the Chinese because he was afraid they had done something while he was looking at his friend. But the two taikonauts were just staring at them, discussing with each other. With somber expressions.

The moment seemed to freeze for what felt like an eternity, time dragged on. Then the taller man turned away from the debris and began to run. He took a long leap. His boots kicked up the gray regolith. It took until the next movement for Charlie to react, he was so surprised. The shorter man followed his companion and Louis also started to move. He crouched a little and made a leap, running after them with skillful moves.

Charlie followed them. His heart began to pound violently as adrenaline shot through his veins and made him feel hot.

Louis was more skillful because he had more practice and slowly caught up with the taller man. In his haste, the taikonaut caught a foot on a stone and stumbled, whereupon Charlie's commander hit the taller Chinese man on the back and brought him down. They began to wrestle while he ran toward them. Apparently Louis was trying to open the taikonaut's breast pocket to take out the camera.

"Stop it," he shouted to Louis. A dozen meters still separated him from them as the two combatants rolled over each other in their scuffle. Their movements seemed strangely slowed under the low gravity, as if they were holding back. But Charlie could hear Louis groan with effort. An object fell out of the taller man's leg pocket. It was the hammer.

"NO!" he shouted as he saw the little taikonaut pick up the tool from the ground, unfold it, and hit the astronaut with it. The curved, pointed side of the hammer smashed into the center of Louis's visor.

The former fighter pilot cried out, but his scream was immediately stifled as the Chinese man pulled out the hammer and hoisted his fellow taikonaut to his feet.

Charlie reached them at that moment and saw that the shorter man had raised his gun, but he didn't shoot.

"Louis!" he shouted, kneeling beside his friend. He pulled at Louis's helmet to check the damage, but it was clearly too late. The pressure inside had blown the small puncture into an uneven hole and all the breathable air had escaped into the vacuum. His suit was sagging in several places by now. The temperature of minus 173 degrees Celsius formed small ice crystals on his face. His eyeballs were swollen and blue underneath and his entire face had turned red and blue. He could see individual marks where the capillaries had burst.

"I'm here," he said. Louis's lips moved slightly. Charlie thought about going after the Chinese to vent his anger, but as hard as it was for him, he wanted to be there for his friend in his final moments. There was no chance of plugging the hole as it was already forming cracks and was too big. The worst part was he *knew* what was happening to his friend. Louis's lungs had ruptured due to the sudden loss of pressure and the loss of oxygen was robbing him of consciousness at that moment.

" ... Charlie? CHARLIE!"

Only now did he notice Anne's voice in his ears. She sounded panicked.

"Yes," he said hoarsely.

"Miles says we're not receiving any more vital signs from Louis. What's going on?"

"He's dying," replied Charlie and slowly let go of his unconscious friend who fell limply into the moon dust. The taikonauts were already 100 meters away, running up the slope toward the elevator.

"WHAT?"

"We have a problem down here." He gulped and looked at the damaged satellite. "Louis and one of the Chinese were wrestling and the other taikonaut smashed his visor with a hammer. He's unconscious and dying right now. There's nothing I can do."

"Damn it!" Anne wailed. "Get out of there RIGHT NOW!"

"I can't. The Chinese have a big head start toward the elevator, and they are armed."

"Then I'll come down. Miles has the code for the gun cabinet."

"Negative." Charlie turned and stared at the rocket. "I might have another way to get to you guys. Then you can shut down the elevator and they'll be trapped down here."

"Charlie, no. We're coming ..."

"That's far too dangerous" he interrupted her. "Put me through to Houston. I need to speak to Harry."

He stared at his oxygen supply. 30 percent. He quickly searched for the bag with the spare cartridges, but couldn't find it before his gaze wandered to the distant cones of light further up. "They've taken the oxygen with them."

"I'm not leaving you alone!" Anne sniffled. "Not a chance!"

"Connect me to Harry!" he said emphatically. "Now!"

It took a few seconds. Then he heard the CAPCOM's voice. "Charlie? What's going on? Louis is ..."

"Dead," he interrupted his superior. "He was murdered. Listen to me. I need to be switched to *speaker*. For the whole Mission Control."

"What? That's not possible. According to the protocol ..."

"Harry. Trust me. There's only one way I can get out of

here alive and we can stop all of us from slaughtering each other up here and starting a war with the Chinese. Just do it."

"Speak now, but I don't know how long they'll let me ..."

"This is Charles Reid from the moon. We have discovered the artifact. It is *not*, I repeat, *NOT* of alien technology, but a crashed Space Force military satellite. It was armed. I'm transmitting my helmet-camera image now."

Charlie pointed the camera at the rocket, moving closer so that it filled his entire field of vision.

"The Chinese took a picture of it. Louis tried to take the camera away from one of them and was killed during the scuffle. The taikonauts are on their way to the elevator and I can't catch up with them. There's only one way for me to get out of here before my oxygen runs out, but I need help. Help from you *and* the Space Force."

There was silence for a few seconds. At first he thought it was the latency between the moon and the Earth, but then the seconds stretched to a minute, then two. He could hear Anne and Miles talking excitedly on their local radio channel, but he concentrated on the rocket and his crazy plan. The taikonauts were now so far away that their outlines looked distorted.

Harry finally returned. "Charlie, we'll get you out of there. There was a little commotion here, but we managed to come to an agreement. Mission Control is now in lockdown, but whether you're a soldier or a civilian, we only have one priority now and that is getting you out of there. Everything else can wait.

"The specifications of the missile are just coming in. It's a new development called the *Zephyr-X*. What you're contemplating is absolute madness, but there are a few engineers at *Flight* who think you could actually do it. We'll send the specs to your forearm display in a moment.

"Until then, we want you to put all the items and materials you have in front of you in the Regolith. Once your data is transferred to the *Liberty*, we want you to set up a direct stream to us."

"Roger that." Charlie licked his lips and calmed his breathing. "Okay, all right."

"We're a long ways away, Charlie, but we're with you. *Everyone* in Mission Control is looking after you now. You're not alone. Do you understand?"

"Yes, thank you. Got it."

He began smoothing out an area in front of the rocket with his gloves and emptying his pockets. Adhesive patches for the suit and visor, too small for the hole in Louis's visor. A small roll of duct tape, a 20-meter safety line, a small spectrometer, a small spirit level, a handheld flashlight and a lithium hydroxide-based CO_2 filter cartridge. It was a fist-sized canister that he could replace in his life support unit. Reluctantly, he went to Louis's frozen corpse and took his friend's gear, too, essentially doubling what he had with him, plus a small cutter to cut lines and cables in an emergency. And all the debris from the satellite, of course.

When he was done, he interrupted the video recording link from his helmet system to *Liberty's* memory and switched over to a direct stream to Houston. The radio bandwidth was terrible, but at least the signal wasn't jammed, and he hoped they recognized the most important information.

"Harry? I'm ready." Eight minutes had passed. That left him perhaps 30 before he suffocated.

"Okay, Charlie, we've got something here. You'll have to fly up with the rocket. Now listen carefully."

CHAPTER 42

The closer they got to Cincinnati, the more Rebecca had to acknowledge that she was getting nervous. She took pride in her rational abilities and her talent for reading people and contexts, although she had to admit that she wasn't particularly empathetic. But she understood what made rational people tick – and that was tremendously helpful. She saw patterns where others only recognized chaos.

The only problem was that even now she recognized a pattern, a trap set by her supposed ally, an *enemy*. Yes, an enemy who wanted her dead because she had kicked a hornet's nest.

Luring Feinman out was a good idea. Doing it the general's way, conversely, was an extremely stupid one. The colonel would know it was just a stopover and that she would be transferred to another aircraft. An abandoned airfield meant open terrain. With the help of the flight data filed at the Pentagon and enough black ops resources or even private mercenaries, he could clear and prepare the entire area.

And if the general got wind of such actions, what was he supposed to do? Turn them around? The Chinook would be at the end of its range when it landed and would need to be refueled. So even if they could escape, they wouldn't get far. A Pentagon Learjet wouldn't help them either. And Eversman? He certainly wouldn't send in a whole regiment. Not with such a sensitive story. It had to happen under the radar, because if he openly cut off a secret funding stream from the White House, he'd be out of a job in no time.

It was a tricky situation from which she saw no escape. So she had to go straight in. Once again.

"Thirty minutes to landing," she heard Hines say over the radio.

Their flight had calmed down considerably a while ago. They had left the storm clouds and the accompanying rain behind them. Below them stretched nighttime Indiana to the north and Kentucky to the south. On the horizon ahead, she could make out the ominous glow of Cincinnati, a dark red in the nighttime humidity that lay over the city as a glowing haze.

Hines steered the Chinook into a gentle right turn and began reducing altitude. Soon she could make out the abandoned airfield. It was an old concrete runway with two vehicles on it, which she recognized by their headlights.

Is that Feinman?

"I see cars," she said into her headset.

"Yes, they're employees of a private company who are going to refuel us."

"Where's the jet?"

"In the background. He's probably switched off the lights, just to be on the safe side. We can call them if you like," the major suggested.

"No, not necessary." She didn't want to make things too easy for Feinman in case his people were indeed lying in wait.

Hines steered them into a wide turn and then lowered the Chinook over a large patch of tarmac with slightly fewer weeds sprouting from it than the rest of the runway. She wondered how safe it was to take off from here in a Learjet. At best, she would find out soon enough.

To the right she saw the waters of the Ohio River, a dark stream in the night, its gentle ripples shining in the moonlight. As they touched down, a jolt went through the cabin.

"Do you have instructions for the arrival?" asked Hines as he shifted into neutral and the rotor noise subsided considerably. His co-pilot got out and talked to the private contractors dressed in high-visibility vests to instruct them on refueling.

Rebecca unbuckled her seatbelt and looked out of the porthole at the tanker and the pickup next to it. The employees were busy unrolling the thick hose from the tanker trunk and towing it to the helicopter.

"No. I thought you knew?"

She picked up her cellphone and dialed Eversman's number.

He answered immediately. "Major. I have just been informed that you have landed," said the general. "The jet is waiting for you at the end of the runway. The two men are experienced pilots from my former command at Edwards. Don't waste any time."

She heard a roar in the background. At first she thought it was coming from the tarmac and a shiver went down her spine. Then she realized it was coming from the telephone receiver.

"All right. Sir ..."

"Yes?"

Rebecca bit her tongue. She didn't want to appear weak, so she swallowed her question. It didn't make any difference now, no matter what he said.

"That's all right. I'll be on my way." She stood up and called into the cockpit: "Thanks for the ride, Major."

"You're welcome. Good luck with whatever," Hines replied. "Tell the general we're even now."

She simply nodded and left the military transport helicopter. Outside, she raised a hand in the direction of the captain, who nodded to her as she passed and then continued with the refueling instructions. The hose's nozzle was inserted into the flank of the helicopter.

She got her bearings briefly, saw that they were at one end of the former tarmac, and jogged in the other direction at a gentle run. After a short time, once her eyes had adjusted to the darkness, she could make out the outline of the Learjet. It stood a few hundred meters away on the concrete like a sleeping bird of prey.

After she had covered half the distance the pilot switched on the nose lights, which blinded her for a moment before her eyes adjusted and she continued to run with her gaze lowered. She kept looking left and right, scanning the sky for helicopters, the embankment by the river for soldiers in ghillie suits or the roaring engines of emergency vehicles from a private security company.

But nothing of the sort happened. As far as she could see, she was all alone as she finally arrived at the lowered stairs of the Learjet, breathing a little more heavily but safe and sound. A man in a black one-piece suit, his hair in a crew cut and a button mic in his ear, beckoned to her and pointed inside.

"Good to see you, Major," he called out just as the turbines were switched on. "Take a seat and we'll be ready for take-off in a moment."

"Thank you," she said as she climbed the ladder. The cabin was flooded with light and had several heavy armchairs. On two of them sat the bodies of the pilots – at least they were dressed in flight uniforms. Colonel Feinman, sitting with his hands spread over his knees, was in a third.

"At last," he said. There was nothing triumphant about his expression, he was too much of a professional. But he looked satisfied.

Rebecca's hands grew clammy, but she wasn't as surprised as she might have anticipated. Maybe this was the trap the general had wanted. The only question left was, which of the two was the better trapper? Who had more resources and contacts, and how expendable was she to Eversman? The two pilots had obviously been.

"I tried not to waste any time," she replied laconically.

"Sit down," he told her and pointed to the empty seat next to her. The man who'd been outside was currently locking the cabin door from the inside and then he knocked on the cockpit door.

"Take-off in two minutes," came from the speakers.

"I didn't want it to come to this," Feinman said when she had taken her seat. The gorilla came back, made her stand, and frisked her roughly and thoroughly. When he had made sure she was unarmed, he walked back toward the cockpit door.

"That sounds like every Bond villain's cliché line," she remarked. He wasn't holding a gun, but she had no illusions about what the guy who had now taken a seat next to the pilot's door would do to her if she did something stupid. She might be an excellent shot, but she'd never had any real experience with hand-to-hand combat. The few weeks' exposure during basic training were as good as forgotten. Apart from that, she was what was widely known as a desk jockey.

"All you had to do was to return to the Pentagon," the colonel continued, as if she hadn't said anything.

"The general? Is he involved?"

"Eversman?" He snorted contemptuously. "If he'd been part of this mission, it would never have succeeded. He's about as secretive as a trumpet and as subtle as a chainsaw."

"Maybe you underestimate him," she returned, although he certainly had a point from an intelligence perspective. "You don't become part of the Joint Chiefs of Staff because you're stupid."

"No, it's because you have connections and wanted to be a politician rather than a soldier." Feinman waved her off and gave her a piercing look. "The file, please. Now."

Rebecca acted surprised. "I don't have the file."

"Don't play games with me, Major." He pointed to the two corpses on the seats in front of them. "I don't like that sort of thing. Not a bit. They were my countrymen. But I know there's something bigger at stake here, and I'm preventing many more people from dying. You may think you're doing the right thing, but you only think that because you can't see even a tiny sliver of the big picture. Do you think I'm a traitor? Then you haven't been thinking properly. I'm a patriot and only do what others are too embarrassed to do, even though they know what ought to be done."

"Sure, the misjudged do-gooder. How could I have missed that?" she replied sarcastically. "I don't have the file. Your gorilla over there can frisk me again if you don't believe me."

Feinman scrutinized her with a stony expression and seemed to assess her closely. Finally, he said in a low voice, "I'm warning you, Major. You'd better tell me right away where it is or this little excursion we're going on won't be a pleasant one for you."

"I didn't expect to get out of this alive anyhow." She pointed to the bodies of Eversman's pilots. "That's not a good advertisement for your credibility if you thought to promise me a way out."

"There are worse things than death."

The turbines suddenly became louder and the jet began to taxi away.

"But I'll make you an offer. You tell me where the file is and I'll make sure you get a place on the project. You know how the game is played. Emotions must not get in the way. I see it quite rationally. You've done a good job, but unfortunately in the wrong direction. So you could also use your skills for the right thing."

"In a secret satellite program for which black budgets are diverted and our own soldiers are killed?" she asked, shaking her head. "I don't think so."

"This isn't just *any* satellite program. And without your intervention, no one would have died."

"No one *else?*"

The colonel's face remained unmoved.

"They knew about the extraterrestrial signal. Even before the alleged discovery," she continued. "Is that why you brought *Sentinel II* up there? To do *what*, exactly?"

"You have no idea what you're talking about, Major, so spare me your fishing in the dark. Either you become part of the program, or we'll keep tightening the thumbscrews until you tell us where the file is. It's your decision. But I'm only giving you until we take off. That should be in about ten seconds."

"I don't think so," she replied as the jet suddenly slowed down and braked after they had gained considerable speed, racing across the relatively uneven concrete runway.

Colonel Feinman looked out the window. His expression remained blank as he pressed a button on his armrest.

"What's going on?"

"There are vehicles coming toward us, sir," a voice – the pilot's, she assumed – replied from the speakers. "We can't take off."

Rebecca watched Feinman, but he didn't let any emotions show. Only the right corner of his mouth twitched a few times.

The jet came to a halt.

"Open," the colonel ordered, and the gorilla unbuckled his seatbelt, unlocked the door, and pushed it outward, whereupon it opened with the steps turning upward. He drew a gun and moved forward. Feinman also stood up and grabbed her roughly by the arm to pull her out of her seat.

Wonderful, now I've gone from bait to hostage. This just keeps getting better, she thought, forcing herself to follow him out into the early Ohio morning. The sun was barely rising in the east, not yet visible above the treetops, but sending a deep red into the midnight blue and blending with it to form an infernal glow.

Rebecca looked to the west and recognized the tanker and pickup truck from the refueling company, which were parked about 50 meters in front of the aircraft with their yellow warning lights on. The employees with their high-visibility vests had gotten out and were holding assault rifles that were angled but made it very clear what their bearers were trying to say: No further. In the background, she saw the Chinook fly off into the night.

Eversman, she thought. Apparently he hadn't been so stupid after all. Almost at the same time, she heard the roar of rotors, but it sounded different from the loud rattling. More muffled, more subtle.

Shortly afterward, two Black Hawk helicopters came swooping over the treetops on the Ohio River embankment, describing two narrow arcs, like the claws of a crab trying to cut them from both sides.

The choppers looked strange, and it took her a few breaths to realize that they were the top-secret stealth variants of the MH-60 Black Hawk, which only became public knowledge through Operation Neptune Spear in the wake of the killing of Osama bin Laden. She had never seen one herself, as they were reserved for top-secret missions by special units like the Navy SEALs.

One of them, more angular, but at the same time also

smoother and utterly black, descended directly in front of them. The door was pushed aside, revealing two hooded soldiers with assault rifles pointing at them. In their midst stood General Eversman in simple camouflage clothing. He held on to a tether and waited for them to touch down before running toward them through the turbulence of the rotor with his head down. The second helicopter remained in the air, also with its door open, and a soldier at the machine gun providing cover.

Rebecca's heart leapt, half from relief, half from a sense of triumph that she couldn't suppress.

"It's over, Feinman," Eversman yelled over the noise and turned to her. "Good work, Major."

She nodded and tore herself away from the colonel.

The general turned to Feinman again. "Give up and don't make a scene. It's over."

"For you," the colonel replied to her horror. He snapped his finger and his goon drew a pistol, with which he shot Eversman in the leg. The general cried out and sank to one knee. His soldiers did not react. Apparently they weren't *his* soldiers. "But I'm glad you could make it."

Feinman signaled to the people from the 'refueling company,' whereupon they withdrew.

"You shouldn't have interfered, sir. You should have just stayed at the Pentagon." The colonel shook his head and beckoned his goon over, who slammed the handle of the gun into Eversman's face and dragged the dazed man into the jet with him. Shortly afterward, while Rebecca stood frozen with shock, he returned with the two dead pilots.

"Is the autopilot set as we discussed?" he asked one of the uniformed officers.

"Yes, sir, it will crash over uninhabited territory two hundred miles to the east."

"Good." Feinman grabbed Rebecca's arm again and pulled her with him to the landed Black Hawk. "You've had your chance, Major. Now let's go for a little ride and then I'll find out everything you know."

CHAPTER 43

"**O**kay, the first thing you have to do is prop up the rocket. It's best if you build a simple tripod from the rubble," Harry said. He sounded very calm and controlled over the radio, which paradoxically made Charlie more nervous, because the CAPCOM usually talked like his mouth was full.

I'm in really deep shit.

"Got it." He picked out one of the 'shovel' pieces – he had no idea what its true purpose was – and stuck it into the regolith. The top had an almost semi-circular indentation where the piece of metal had probably crashed onto a stone. Then he heaved the front third of the rocket into the impro-vised holder so that the engine was half in the dust and the tip was pointing upward.

"Good, that looks good. It's important that it's reasonably stable and that the support doesn't fall over too quickly," Harry continued, whereupon Charlie pulled up two more rockets, which he found behind the shattered solar panels. He cut off two meters of the safety line and connected the rockets to the top of the support. Since it had many holes, it was easy to thread the thin carbon fiber through and knot it before pulling it tight.

"It should be relatively solid," he said. *Never tight enough for a rocket!*

"Good, very good. Now you have to align them near the base station of the elevator. Anne will give you a light signal. Can you see it?"

Charlie looked up at the edge of the crater. It looked so far away that his heart threatened to sink. A light flashed, once, twice, three times.

"I see it." He bent down and picked up the end of the rocket to reposition it.

"According to Anne's distance meter, you are exactly 8.121 kilometers in a straight line from her. Now align the *Zephyr* so that your distance meter is 8.121 meters in a straight line to the upper edge of the crater, right by the light signal," Harry instructed him.

"All right." Charlie did so. It took a few minutes, then he believed that the rocket was correctly aligned. "That should do it. Now it's all about the angle, I suppose."

If I set it even half a degree too low, I'll smash into the crater wall, he thought. *Half a degree too much and I'll shoot too high above it and eventually fall to my death.*

"Right. Now choose a point on the ground to use as a starting point."

Charlie looked at the smooth area under the upper third of the rocket and placed his bubble level there. He made a few adjustments until it was perfectly level and stood back up. "Done."

"Now use the distance meter to measure a known distance from this base point along the ground," said Harry. Charlie lay on his side, marking the base point with his finger. Aligning the laser was not so easy because it was invisible in a vacuum, so he used a finger on the ground in front of his face and measured the distance – one meter – to a stone that he had placed on an imaginary line to the front of the rocket.

"Okay."

"Now you need a long object for the vertical part."

Charlie had already obtained a rod from the destroyed sensor array, and he inserted it at his measuring point.

"And now ..."

" ... make a protractor, of course." Charlie looked for three pencil-like pieces of metal and measured them. One was exactly 30 centimeters long, which he communicated over the radio.

" ... construct a protractor." Due to the signal delay, he hadn't interrupted Harry, he'd simply talked over him, which Houston would only now realize.

"Yes, exactly." The CAPCOM paused for a moment. "The height h of side a is equal to the square root of 3 divided by 2 times 30 centimeters in this case. That makes 25.98 for the length h. Two h is therefore 51.96. If you round both figures up, the angle will be just over 30 degrees and you should get over the edge of the crater. So build a triangle that is 30 by 26 by 52."

Charlie took the metal rods. He used them and his laser cutter to construct a large triangle with the specified dimensions. He attached the corners snugly with duct tape. He then used a plumb line made of rope and a stone to mark half of the side opposite a corner. He then halved the triangle and tied the rope tightly.

"Good, I now have the protractor at a minimum of just greater than 30 degrees." He held the result of his hasty, improvised work in front of his helmet and the camera.

"Good work, Charlie, you're doing very well," said Harry. "Now let's build a safety harness from the rest of the safety line."

"Uhh, my oxygen supply ..."

"This part will be quick. We'll talk you through four knots, all of which you know. Then put the net you've created over the pointed front section. The warhead has been deactivated. Put your arms and legs through the loops," Harry instructed him. "Tie the bottom two in a knot and then push your boots through them. This will give you enough grip because the soles will be pushed against the direction of acceleration. Shortly before the edge of the crater, the rocket will stop firing and the g-forces will disappear. That's the moment when you can get out of the loops. It will be relatively easy."

If I don't get tangled up, turn, crash …

"We expect a maximum acceleration of 2.6 g."

Charlie swallowed, but did not stop weaving the complex knots, which he was fortunate enough to be able to tie in his sleep thanks to his training, even with his clumsy gloved fingers. By the time he had prepared the rocket, he had ten minutes of oxygen left. He went to his equipment, put it in his pockets, and pulled the oxygen cartridge from Louis's life support unit. Using the duct tape, he fastened it to the side of his torso and made sure the narrow valve was facing outward. It was extremely fragile and the tank was still pressurized. Normally it was only intended to be used, not to shoot through space.

"One last thing," said the CAPCOM. "There is a retaining ring on the head of the rocket. You have to remove it. It's a device that blocks any signal after a certain amount of time without contact, so the missile can't be hacked."

That's why the bastards up here haven't blown everything up yet, thought Charlie and, with the help of the step-by-step instructions, set about removing the ring and went back to the rubble.

"Okay, my friend," Harry said, and Charlie almost went crazy with anxiety. *My friend?* "You have to lie down on the rocket now. Make sure you're at least 50 centimeters above the propulsion nacelle. Otherwise it'll burn your feet off when the makeshift harness is pulled backward. Shit, this is the craziest mess I've ever been in, Charlie. If you can do this, you're a fucking hero. And we can use a hero right now, you hear?"

"I'll do my best," he muttered, and climbed onto the rocket. He crossed his hands on the underside and gripped the improvised loops. It took him two minutes to pull his boots through the openings and push them down. The forearm-sized oxygen cartridge pressed against his chest. "Ready. Bloody hell, I'm ready."

"The Space Force guys communicate directly with the rocket's control software. You don't have to do anything. Just don't miss the jump point, which we'll tell you exactly 2.2 seconds in advance. So when you hear us, you immediately detach yourself from the rocket, right?"

"Sure."

"The rocket has modern stability control. So don't worry about anything except holding on tight."

"And to say my prayers."

"We all will, Charlie. God be with you. Count off ... to ten *now*."

"Anne, I'm coming," Charlie said hoarsely.

"You can do it. Don't you dare ..."

Suddenly he shot forward. As if hit by a hammer blow, all his organs sank downward – or at least that's how it felt. His blood supply seemed to suddenly sink into his legs and there was only darkness in front of his visor. He wanted to scream, cry, and plead at the same time. But as always in situations of mortal danger, he withdrew into himself.

Okay, 2.6 g is 9.81 meters per second squared, he thought. *8.121 kilometers distance.* He wispily calculated the equation of motion without initial velocity and converted it to t so that he could determine the flight time. *Root two s by a. 25.66 seconds. Two seconds earlier than this is switched off.*

322

He could still feel his feet. That was a good sign. He even thought he could see lights. Was that the elevator's ground station? The one in the crater? Where were the Chinese? Everything looked blurry. Was it the speed? Or was it the tears of fear in his eyes?

A light appeared in front of him. No, *above* him. The edge of the crater? He turned his head, which was terribly tiring, and could see a huge shadow falling out of the sky. Charlie thought he was losing his mind, but then he saw a gigantic fountain of regolith spurting up and filling the entire horizon. Myriads of fine dust particles were hurled upward as if a meteor had fallen in the desert sands, except that someone had slowed time down sixfold.

The meteor, he thought.

"HARRY?" he shouted, but it only rang in his ear.

The regolith is blocking the signal! The dust was already everywhere, settling over the crater like a cloud of glitter. Slowly, almost weightlessly. An infinite number of statically charged crystal structures – the only thing that could interfere with the ultra-shortwave radio equipment.

But without a radio, they couldn't send a signal as to when he should jump off.

A short jolt went through the rocket. Were these the engines that had switched off according to the programmed burn time? He became almost weightless. The pressure eased. It was a release.

Two seconds! Harry said two seconds! Was it already two seconds?

"FUCK!" Charlie pulled his feet out of the loops, tore at them when they wouldn't release, and freed his hands. He got stuck, then spun uncontrollably. The rocket with him.

Then all of a sudden the horizon turned, becoming alternately pitch black with glitter, then bright white – or gray?

"Anne, Houston? Can anyone hear me? I'm ... I'm crashing."

He groped desperately for the oxygen cartridge on his chest. Was it gone? The ground was rapidly approaching. He knew that the rocket had shot over the edge of the crater at more than 500 meters per second. Its descent had probably been at an angle of less than one degree. The gravitational acceleration was only 1.625 meters per second squared, but that meant that his fall speed increased by this value with every second that passed.

He had been falling for more than three seconds when he finally managed to loosen the cartridge and turn the valve downward. Like a madman, he punched the valve and, like a lucky man, managed to knock it off. The cartridge shot from below against his helmet and almost knocked him unconscious.

Miraculously, he retained hold of the cartridge and clung to it, hoping that it was pointing downward and would break his fall as planned.

Now it seemed like a very stupid plan to him. As the ground came closer at breakneck speed, spinning as if he were on an out-of-control merry-go-round, he began to scream.

Then came the crash. He hit the ground and immediately blacked out.

CHAPTER 44

When Charlie came to, he was in terrible pain. His left shoulder felt as if it had been hit with a sledgehammer, his chest ached, and his forehead was wet. His right leg seemed to be on fire, and every breath sent a wave of tiny pinpricks from his throat to his guts.

"Charlie? Charlie!" He knew that voice. His pain eased a little.

"Anne?" He cautiously opened his eyes and saw the face of his friend and comrade in front of him, separated by two visors. There was a large smudge on his own. "What ... What happened?"

"You're a fucking lunatic!" she admonished him, but he could hear that she was laughing, even though tears were falling from her eyes to her visor and bursting on the glass. She sniffed and shook her head. "A goddamned lunatic!"

She pulled him up a little, causing him to let out an agonized groan.

"You fell out of the sky and somehow slowed yourself down, but you crashed the last fifteen meters. You're lucky I followed your flight with my eyes the whole time and ran in your direction after radio contact was lost," she explained, interrupting herself several times with sniffles and short sobs. "How are you feeling?"

"Like a yeast dough kneaded for three hours without gluten. I think I've broken something."

"I hope not. Your fall looked bad."

Charlie raised his right hand, which intensified the pain in his shoulder, even if it was dull rather than sharp. He tried to wipe the smudge off his visor with his gloved hand.

"Don't!" She took his hand away. "You hit a rock with your visor and the glass cracked. I sealed it with a patch – along with three other spots that leaked little fountains of oxygen. All sealed, I hope."

"Thank you. That explains why my windpipe feels like I've inhaled sandpaper."

"You had hardly any air left, and a lot escaped before I could mend your suit and insert a new cartridge," Anne explained as she helped him to his feet.

He almost fell, but caught himself. It was probably only due to the low lunar gravity that he was able to stay on his feet. He was dizzy and so tired that he would have preferred to fall asleep straight away – not that it would have been possible given the pain he was in.

Suddenly, a thought flashed through his mind like a lightning bolt.

"The taikonauts!"

Anne nodded somberly and pointed to the edge of the crater. Only now did he see that the Rover was standing next to them. "They must have entered the elevator by now."

Charlie gulped and looked around consciously for the first time. They were a few hundred meters from the crater on a regolith field littered with rubble. The surrounding area was full of regolith, but the glittering dust had settled enough that it wouldn't be long before the impact residue covered the ground.

"How long was I unconscious?"

"Not for long. Thirty seconds, maybe. It's hard to say." She scowled at him. "Long enough for my heart to drop down to my ass, anyway."

"You heard ... Louis ..." He stopped, unable to go on.

She nodded. "I know." Anne shook her head sadly. "We got clearance for the weapons."

Charlie frowned, but did not protest. The image of the shorter man ramming the pointed part of the hammer into his friend's face was too fresh.

"Where's the rocket?"

"I don't know." She tapped her helmet. "I don't have a connection to Houston or the *Liberty* anymore. The regolith ..."

He nodded.

"But it ignited again, I think. In any case, the engine lit up after it had flown very far away. Presumably in orbit."

Charlie was about to nod again and ask another question when he paused. He looked at the regolith veil that lay over the entire scene like a kind of crystalline mist. In the west, he saw the *Celestial Dragon*, the Chinese spaceship. The outline of a figure was very close by. That had to be the third taikonaut. Then he looked toward the crater and finally up into the dark starry sky, in which he could see the great crescent of the Earth despite the milky veil.

"Anne ...?"

"Yes?"

"If we have no contact with Houston, the Chinese also have no contact with their ground station in Beijing. But the Space Force has contact with their *Zephyr-X* over here," he said.

At the same moment he saw a shadow chasing across the glitter. His gaze slid to the *Celestial Dragon*. At almost the same time there was a violent explosion. The flames vanished almost immediately, as if they were being sucked away by an invisible force. Regolith sprayed in all directions. The tiny figure of the astronaut crashed in the wave of dust, and the remains of the Chinese spacecraft broke apart. Some areas glowed, but the luminosity quickly disappeared, as there was no oxygen to keep it alive.

"Oh, my God!" Anne gasped. "Did they really just do that?!"

He nodded. Sheer horror seeped into his limbs. "They've seized the moment and taken out the ship. Beijing won't notice a thing."

"On the far side of the moon, they programmed in a final command and accelerated to the required trajectory. The rocket then shot into the target without a propulsion signature. This means that it was not visible on any infrared telescopes."

"The Chinese won't know what happened." Charlie looked to the edge of the crater, then back to *Liberty,* which loomed far away from the lunar landscape like a silver tower with a conical top.

"Charlie, what's going on?"

"The Space Force sent us up here to cover up an armed military satellite before the Chinese discovered it. *That*'s what's going on," he replied grimly, almost forgetting the pain all over his body because of his anger. "When the two taikonauts get here and see what's happened here, they'll ..."

"The two taikonauts," she repeated, "We have to shut down the elevator!"

Before he could reply, she was running to the Rover parked next to them, which was covered in a thin layer of regolith. "Wait!"

"Come here and sit down!"

Groaning, he limped over to her and sat down in the

passenger seat. Bending his right leg sent a sharp pain from his knee all the way to his shoulder. "Fuck."

Anne started the electric motor and drove off. In the all-encompassing silence of the moon, they chased toward the base station of the elevator on the crater rim.

"Where's Miles?"

"He received weapons clearance shortly before the impact. I was supposed to pick him up with the Rover," she replied. Her breathing quickened audibly and she whispered a few of the final syllables.

The weapons, he thought, turning his head to catch a glimpse of the wrecked CNSA spaceship. The debris passed just to the left of his visor.

"Anne," he said, looking to her. "Anne!"

"What?" She sat hunched over the steering wheel and was driving at full speed. The crater and base station were rapidly approaching. They drove over a small bulge in the ground and lifted off, seeming to hover for a moment before gently touching back down.

"What are we going to do when we get there?"

"We'll stop the elevator! I'll switch off the engine. I wanted to do that before, but I didn't know if the plan with the rocket would work. I wanted to keep the only way back open that long," she explained curtly.

"Do we *really* want to lock the taikonauts in the cabin and let them suffocate?" he asked.

"Yes! Yes, damn it! They killed Louis."

"And we have killed at least one of them, and in fact all of them, because they no longer have the option of returning."

"Just as little as we do."

"Louis and the big guy – I think that's their commander – were wrestling with each other because Louis wanted to take the camera away from him. He was trying to prevent the Chinese from taking evidence of the crashed military satellite.

During the scuffle, the other intervened and punctured his visor. Would we have done it any differently?"

"Yes ... I don't know. I don't know." She stopped the Rover when they arrived next to the base station with the aluminum superstructure and the safety structure with the Chinese cable. Charlie felt a mixture of sadness and frustration when he saw it. For a short time they had been sensible, had worked together, had rejoiced at the discovery of water ice in the crater. Now everything had been thrown into chaos. Murder and destruction. He could have screamed.

He had an idea.

"What if we stop the elevator a few meters before they get up here. Then we can give them oxygen and keep them trapped."

"How long will that last?" she asked, walking with him to the edge of the base station. They each held onto one of the aluminum frames and stared down into the darkness. The elevator was in motion, as could be seen from the cones of light from both taikonauts' helmet lamps, which were lost in the void. Below them, the four battery lights that he had set up after their arrival were still shining.

"I don't know. But we can't just murder them, either. At least *I* can't, and I don't want to."

"They're still in a signal hole down there." She pointed to the regolith veil that covered the entire crater, as if fog were rising from the depths. "But if they get out and make contact with the CNSA, they'll tell Beijing what they've found here. How far away is a third world war then, huh? What do you think?"

Charlie bit his lower lip. She was right and yet there had to be a better solution than murder or manslaughter to prevent more murder and manslaughter. He hated this dilemma of the human condition.

"Can you speed up the crank?" he asked.

"It is already running at the permitted maximum speed."

"Can you override that?"

"Yes, but ..."

"If we bring them up faster, we can make them understand their situation and use the oxygen to negotiate. Miles can bring us one of the electric fans that we can use to constantly shoot regolith over them so they don't get a signal. We'll figure something out in that time."

"If the motor operates outside its safety tolerances, it could break or the cable could snap, or ..."

"Those are risks the taikonauts will have to take if we do this my way. I don't want to murder them, but after what they did to Louis, I can live with it if we don't wrap them in cotton batting," he interrupted her. Anne looked him in the eye and then nodded before walking over to the engine and starting to work on the controls.

Meanwhile, Charlie sat down at the edge of the base station and grimaced in pain. He urgently needed medical care, and more than he could provide for himself in his role as on-board paramedic.

The minutes seemed to drag on endlessly while Anne worked, and he tried not to lose his mind, because everything hurt and he wanted nothing more than painkillers.

After what felt like an eternity, she said, "I think I can see Miles."

Charlie turned his head and sure enough, between the large shadow stone and the plain to the east, a small figure came toward them, clearly silhouetted against the huge *Liberty*. But it was still several hundred meters away.

"Miles?" he called over the radio. Enough time must have passed by now for the regolith interference to have subsided. "Can you hear me?"

"Yes, I can hear you ... finally." His friend was breathing very fast. "I'll hurry, I'll be right with you."

"Good, are you armed?"

"Yes. I have two M16s with me and ..."

"Please try not to rush things. We'll keep the two taikonauts in the elevator and then ..." Charlie didn't get any further, as a movement on the winch above him caught his attention. He wheeled around and almost buckled as he had to hop on the spot to make the turn. He watched in sheer horror as the two taikonauts climbed over the edge of the base.

"ANNE!" he shouted. "Cut the cable! Quick!"

It was too late. They had misjudged the speed of the winch. The two Chinese rushed at him. One of them – he thought it was the shorter one – crashed into his chest with his shoulder and sent him onto his back in a wide arc.

Charlie fell into the moon dust and gasped in pain. Stars danced in his field of vision and mingled with the real stars twinkling in the pitch-black sky. The shorter taikonaut was almost back to him as he struggled to his feet. The taller one held the hammer in his hand and leapt toward Anne, who grabbed a stone as if in slow motion and threw it at the taikonaut. She missed him but he briefly lost his footing and didn't manage to hit her as she threw herself at him with a strangled scream.

Charlie reached out with his healthy leg and kicked the smaller taikonaut in the knee when he landed a little too close to him, and he lost his own balance. As the other guy stumbled, Charlie got back to his feet and let out a pained yelp.

They began to tussle. With the sun visors down, he felt as if he were fighting a faceless robot. Fighting in the moon's gravity was strange, as every movement seemed powerless and slowed down like running in deep water. It was more of a wrestling match than an exchange of blows, which brought them dangerously close to the abyss of the crater. They landed on the hard slabs of rock and rolled over each other before separating and getting to their knees. To Charlie's left, the slabs descended steeply into the darkness for two kilometers.

The shorter man fell forward and grabbed him by the shoulders, trying to pull him over, but Charlie saw it coming and shifted his weight, saving himself from a long fall into nothingness.

Then, all at once, the crater lit up. They both paused at the same time and looked to the north, where in the middle of the Shackleton Crater, in the midst of the eternal darkness, a flower of fire blossomed, flickered, and was followed at short intervals by four more. The flames suffocated within a matter of seconds.

Charlie knew what had happened, that the Space Force was back in contact with the *Zephyr-X*, whose security ring he had removed so that they could cover up the evidence of their crime.

And he exploited this knowledge to his advantage. The shorter Chinese man was caught up in the sudden sight for a fraction of a second longer and Charlie grabbed him by the shoulder and pushed him forward.

The taikonaut lost his footing and plunged into the depths, his arms flailing. As horror and disgust mingled within himself, Charlie turned away from the shrinking silhouette being swallowed by the darkness and turned to Anne and the taller Chinese. They were still wrestling with each other.

Anne had grabbed a stone and hit the taikonaut's helmet with it, causing him to stagger backward. He raised his hammer again.

Charlie jumped toward her to help when something happened. The lack of any sound made it seem unreal, like a silent movie presentation. The taikonaut froze as a hole gaped in his suit just above where his sternum would be. His sunshade was not down and Charlie was horrified to see flames behind the glass.

"I got him!" Miles shouted over the radio.

The bullet must have had so much residual heat – or generated enough frictional heat when it penetrated the life support unit on the taikonaut's back – that it had ignited the pure oxygen with which the suit was filled. He and Anne stared helplessly at the Chinese man, who was burning in his own breathing air before their eyes. The man fell to the ground shortly afterward.

"Anne, Charlie? Are you two OK?" Miles called out. Charlie could see him standing less than 100 meters away, possibly considerably less.

"Yes." He swallowed hard. "I think so."

Anne said nothing.

"Anne?" Charlie bridged the few meters that still separated them with two hops and grabbed her by the shoulder, where-upon she sank to her knees. At first he didn't understand, but then he saw how red blood seemed to be sucked out of her body from a hole above her hip. He knew that this was not true, but on the contrary, the high pressure of her vessels and arteries was forcing her lifeblood out of the wound and into the surrounding, unpressurized space.

"No, no, no," he stammered, and pressed his hand to the bullet hole. The flow of blood subsided, but within seconds the next red globules were emerging from between his fingers.

"Ch-Charlie," he heard her whisper. He flipped her sun visor open and looked into her bloodless face. Her lips were blue, her cheeks chalky white.

"Anne ..."

"No lies," she said weakly. "Just stay ... with me."

Charlie sniffed and forced back the tears to be strong for her. In his mind he went through his options, but he had none. He could look for one of his sticky patches, but he didn't know where he'd stashed them because he'd been too stressed before the stunt with the rocket. By the time he found one, her blood loss would have gotten even more severe and killed her, anyway. So, he kept pressure on the wound and looked her in the eye with all the bravery he could muster.

"I'm here. I'm not going anywhere."

"Thank you." She looked past him out into the starry sky. "W ... If they ... Could ... How beautiful ..."

She went limp in his arms.

"*Liberty,* Houston," Harry transmitted.

"*Now* you're coming back?" growled Charlie.

"We've just seen that Anne's vital signs ..."

"She's dead! DEAD!"

" ... have broken off. What happened up there?" There was a pause. "Oh, my God. Charlie, listen, we've got some problems here with the ..."

The CAPCOM's voice broke off. It didn't take much imagination to figure out that Space Force personnel had quite likely just taken over the Mission Control Center. Charlie suspected that, after his revelation, the civilian NASA employees had rebelled and refused to continue doing the Pentagon's dirty work after realizing they'd been forced to participate in this perfidious game by the military liars.

A beeping shook him awake from his stupor. An oxygen warning. He only had 20 percent breathable air left and his CO_2 filter had already reached the limit of its capacity. He had to get back to the *Liberty* as quickly as possible.

He reluctantly let go of Anne's body and was heading for the Rover when Miles reached him. His comrade – his sun visor in the down position – turned to the two corpses in the dust and then to Charlie. He held one rifle in his hands like a soldier on the ground. The other hung over his shoulder. He took it down and handed it to him.

"No," snarled Charlie.

"One of them could still be alive," Miles stated without inflection.

"I did *not* come here to kill." He wanted to cry, but there was a rage inside him that could hardly be contained. And he had to get back to the oxygen of the *Liberty*. "I have to go back."

"How much?"

"Twenty percent."

"You can do that on foot."

"What?"

"I'll need the Rover." Miles, who had put the spare rifle back across his shoulder, pointed in the direction of the Chinese wreck on the horizon. His voice sounded toneless, like that of a robot. "I'm going to see that we're out of danger."

"The bastards blew them sky high. Nobody's alive."

"But I have orders ..."

"*Orders?*" Charlie repeated, staring at his crewmate even though he couldn't see his face through the sunshield visor. "Are you saying that you've been ..."

"No. That means I just got orders to make sure, as quickly as possible, that none of them survive."

"I don't even want to think about what that means." He was practically spitting out the words when Miles abruptly pushed past him and sat down on the Rover. Charlie considered stopping him, but another fight – especially with his friend and crewmate – was the last thing he wanted right now.

So he turned around and started bouncing toward the *Liberty*. Every time he pushed off and every time he came down, sharp pains ran through his entire body. He had endured a lot in the Marines, which was the only reason he was staying on his feet. With every breath, he wanted to give up and just let himself fall. It was so unbearable and getting worse. But he gritted his teeth, refusing to give up because giving up had never been an option.

It felt like it took an eternity. The upright Starship didn't seem to get any bigger on the horizon, and the sound of his breathing became like the background music to his slow decay.

"Charlie, one is still alive. He ..." Miles's radio message, which came in so loudly it startled him out of his trance-like flight to the lifesaving oxygen, broke off.

"Sergeant, this is Colonel Hauser."

Hauser, he thought, remembering the man. A former Air Force engineer who had marched into Houston with the Space Force delegation and had taken over the entire supervision and management of the engineering teams on behalf of the Pentagon. Was he now the new CAPCOM? Had all of his colleagues been instantly stripped of their authority, or even arrested, so that the Department of Defense could protect its secret project?

"I want to talk to Harry."

"That's not possible right now," said Hauser. "We've lost contact with Miles, but we can see that the Rover is still moving."

"What?" Charlie looked at the *Liberty*. According to the distance meter, he had 80 meters to go. He turned around and howled in distress. On the horizon, he saw the vehicle in front of a regolith cloud. It was heading in his direction.

"It is probable that he has been overpowered and that a taikonaut is on his way to you," Hauser continued.

Charlie gasped and turned back to the *Liberty*. He dug into his last reserves of energy and accelerated his jumps, borne by the surging waves of adrenaline pumping through his veins like battery acid. His entire skin began to tingle and his hair stood on end. He thought of the taller man who had been burned to death in his own suit thanks to the bullet. He knew from the war that burns caused the worst pain a person could experience in their lifetime. Burning alive was the most terrible fate he could imagine.

And now there was a taikonaut who wanted to do exactly that to him. He had probably got hold of Miles's weapons.

The meters melted away while his pain increased immeasurably. When he reached the crates standing in the dust in front of the elevator, he saw that there was suddenly a gaping hole in the front one. Then a second one.

Shit! I'm being shot at!

Charlie wasted no time. instead of turning to look, he hopped to the elevator in two long leaps. Once there, he crouched down and pressed the manual emergency switch to raise the platform. Crouching behind the open railing provided virtually no cover, but it felt better than making himself an even bigger target standing up. He even put up with the fact that his right leg felt like it was filled with glowing coals.

The Rover was very close. He could see the figure in the driver's seat – and a muzzle flash. Unlike on Earth, it wasn't a large flower of fire, but a short-lived flare, no bigger than a coin, for a fraction of a second.

Charlie hoped that the bullets would not be able to penetrate *Liberty's* steel hull.

I'm being shot at, Houston, he wanted to say into the radio, but instead he remained silent. The cabin had almost reached the top when the taikonaut stopped by the solar panels and aimed the rifle at him. There was a brief glow in the barrel of the M16 and Charlie's visual field suddenly had a hole in the right side.

He exhaled reflexively, so much so that his lungs seemed to squeeze together. His face suddenly turned cold and seemed to swell up at the same time, as if he had a bad cold. Panic threatened to flare up inside him, but he ignored it and let himself fall into the open airlock. He caught one hand on the elevator control panel as it moved downward and almost fell. Fortunately, he was able to grab hold of a handle in the airlock with his right hand and pull himself in. As his body only weighed around 14 kilograms on the moon, he managed it relatively effortlessly.

With the last of his strength, he hit the button for the atmosphere control and the outer hatch retracted into its socket and locked. He heard a soft hissing sound that grew louder and louder and he fiddled with the fastener of the neck ring between the suit and helmet. However, the lack of oxygen made his fingers weak and he lost his ability to grip anything. Black spots approached from the edges of his field of vision, growing larger and larger as if they wanted to merge with the adhesive patch on his visor.

Charlie didn't know whether it was safe to open his mouth and inhale. The airlock procedure took a while, but he was running out of time.

The desire to take a breath became overwhelming until his body finally took control and forced him to open his mouth to greedily suck oxygen into his lungs.

It was as if he was breathing into a bag, and the blackness at the edge of his field of vision shrank into total darkness.

CHAPTER 45

The flight with the stealth helicopter didn't take long. Apparently they stayed in Cincinnati, because as far as Rebecca could tell, they landed very close to the city on a wide lawn, from where they went into an old ruin that they reached via a cellar accessway. There, one of the black ops soldiers detached an old piece of wood from the wall, revealing a modern control panel with a code device behind it. He stepped back and had Feinman enter six numbers, whereupon an electronic buzzer sounded.

"A black site," she said, "Why am I not surprised."

"I've always been in favor of keeping in touch with the CIA," the colonel replied. She was escorted into the large basement room. Between the concrete pillars she saw a kitchen, a room-sized glass box with a chair in it, a wall of computers and displays, a seating area, and a weapons cabinet.

She was still handcuffed, so she was considered low-threat and was directed to one of the armchairs in the seating area. The goon from the private jet, who had accompanied them inside along with two hooded male soldiers, began to frisk her again at Feinman's suggestion. This time, however, he took a more ruthless approach and pulled all her clothes off after opening them up.

Rebecca refused to let them see her embarrassment, not wanting to give them the satisfaction of seeing how she felt at that moment.

The gorilla searched everything, then pulled her underpants and trousers back up, followed by the rest of her overalls, which had been hanging by the sleeves because of her handcuffs. And finally the jacket, which hung from her hands like a dead second skin.

"She's clean," Feinman's lackey said. "A lot of injuries. Minor cuts on her hip, shoulder, and upper arm and four bruises: neck, shoulder, back, and lower ribcage."

"Car accident," she declared, giving the colonel a dark look. "Very original, by the way."

He just shrugged his shoulders and sat down opposite her. "The file. Where is it?"

"I don't have it," she insisted once again. In the background, she saw the two soldiers sit down at the computers and turn them on. Six displays came to life and a server cabinet further back, which she hadn't noticed before, began to hum loudly.

"You said that already." Feinman sighed and pointed at the glass box. "You know what that is."

Rebecca swallowed as discreetly as she could. She knew. 'Black sites' were called that for a reason, as they were used by various secret services – especially the CIA – as unregistered retreats where they could operate outside the U.S. Constitution if they felt they had to. Only a few functionaries within the Agency knew their coordinates and had access to them. That Feinman was one of them worried her. Apparently his spiderweb was even more extensive than she had assumed.

"So I'll ask you one last time before I leave you here with Fred," he said, pointing to the gorilla. "Alone. You know as well as I do that you'll tell me everything in the end. So spare yourself that. You're a clever woman, Major."

"I have a deal with one of the detectives in Enid."

"Name?"

Rebecca bit her tongue.

"Name!" Feinman demanded in a harsh voice.

"Lucas Darwi."

"What's the deal?"

"If I don't get back to him by twenty hundred hours and confirm that everything went well, he gives a copy to Fox News, CNN, the NY Times, Washington Post ... every outlet he can think of. The whole lot. And the original goes to the FBI," she explained with an indifferent expression.

The colonel nodded, apparently unsurprised. Then he looked down at his wristwatch. "It's nineteen twenty now, so you should make that call."

He gave the gorilla – Fred – a wave, who then grabbed her roughly by the upper arm and pulled her to her feet. Together the three of them went to the two soldiers at the computers.

"We need to make a phone call," Feinman said, whereupon a keyboard rattled. One of the hooded men turned his head slightly.

"Phone number?"

The colonel looked at her challengingly.

Rebecca hesitated, whereupon the gorilla's grip became painful, as if he were tightening a screw clamp that threatened to crush her humerus.

"All right already!" she snapped before reciting the telephone number she had arranged with Darwi.

"Wait!"

"You don't want me to make the call?" she asked in surprise.

"Do you think I'm stupid?" Feinman replied, laughing mirthlessly. "We still have almost forty minutes. That's enough time to get my people in place in Enid. Once my people are in place, we can make the call."

"And, when you've located the signal, grab the detective," she replied with a grim expression.

"Well, yeah, it's not that difficult." He turned to his men. "Get Team Bravo into position in front of the police station and behind it. I don't want them to miss anyone leaving the building."

"Understood, sir."

Rebecca remained calm, just stood there and waited while Feinman spun his web to get his hands on Darwi and the file.

After half an hour, during which time she had to watch helplessly as the colonel positioned his men – who probably didn't even know what it was all about but were paid from the Pentagon's black budget and didn't ask any questions – it was her turn.

One of the hooded soldiers handed her a cellphone that was connected to one of the computers via a cable. On the lower left display was a telephone dialing program, along with an audio graph that showed no line.

"Make the call," Feinman ordered her. "No games unless you want to see more deaths on *your watch.*"

Rebecca was surprised to see the colonel seriously angry. Apparently he was fully convinced that the many people killed by his own men were her fault and not his. From his crazy worldview, that was probably true. If she hadn't disrupted his conspiracy – or rather the one of which he was an important part – everyone involved would still be alive. At the cost of treason and endangering international peace, and apart from the fact that such secret projects required the oversight of the congressional intelligence committees.

Rebecca had the gorilla hold the cellphone to her ear.

"Major!" Darwi answered immediately. He sounded

stressed. "I thought you weren't going to get back to me in time."

"Yes, things took a little longer." She looked at Feinman, who fixed her with a cold stare.

"Is everything all right?"

"Yes, everything's fine. We've arrived. The general is well and the traitor has been overpowered," she said. The colonel signaled for her to end the call. "Don't involve the FBI, that's no longer necessary. I can take care of everything else on my own."

"Good. Understood. Then I'll probably hear from you on the news next time," said Darwi.

The gorilla took the cellphone from her and disconnected.

"That wasn't so difficult now, was it?" Feinman said.

"Cellphone located," said one of the soldiers.

"Where?"

The soldier called up a map program that filled the large screen at the top. A red dot appeared in the middle of a large city.

"In Cincinnati, sir."

"Are you sure?" The colonel looked uncertain for a split second.

"Positive. The signal was detected in the center of Cincinnati. It's accurate to within 20 meters," the soldier confirmed.

Feinman gave her a withering look. "What are you playing at?"

"Darwi flew here with me," she lied, snorting contemptuously. "You don't think I'm stupid enough to leave the file with him at the police station, where he can wait for you to burst in and get it, and then kill him as soon as you have it in hand?"

"Send the tank team," Feinman ordered. "Right away."

"Maybe we'd better change locations," Fred suggested.

"We will do that. But first we have to clean this place up.

Even if half the FBI are looking for us, they won't find us here for a few days." The colonel waved him off. "Take her into the glass case and find out what else she's not telling us."

Feinman looked at her and shook his head. "You made your choices. You shouldn't have lied to me."

"You didn't ask where Darwi was."

He flicked a hand dismissively, whereupon the gorilla pulled her along toward the lonely chair in the glass box.

What followed was the worst half hour of Rebecca's life.

CHAPTER 46

C harlie jolted awake to a scream. The harsh sound echoed through his head and rang in his ears. He opened his eyes so wide that it hurt.

It had been his own scream, a cry for air. In front of him was a cracked visor, and part of his field of vision was black. It took him several greedy breaths, burning in his lungs, to realize that it was the adhesive patch on his visor that lay like a shadow across his field of vision. To the right of it was a coin-sized hole with white cracks running off its edges like the threads of a spider's complex web or an Italian mosaic artwork.

Not dead, he thought. *I am not dead.*

But he felt like he ought to be. *Everything* hurt. His right leg felt as if it had been impaled by thousands of needles, his right shoulder as if someone had injected the whole structure with cramps while he had been unconscious – not to mention he had a roaring headache.

That part is the temporary oxygen deprivation.

Charlie got to his feet by turning onto his stomach on the floor of the airlock, first pushing up on his hands and then onto his knees. Then, when the initial dizziness had subsided, he crawled to the inner hatch and tried to raise his hand to press the control button.

"Help," he groaned. Then he remembered. He wasn't going to get any. They were dead. They were *all* dead. Louis, Miles ... *Anne.*

Charlie slumped back onto the floor and began to cry. He wrapped his arms around his body, causing another wave of pain that spread from the top of his head to the tips of his toes. He just lay there for a while until the tears stopped.

Then he heard a noise that startled him out of his lethargy and depression: a muffled *clonk!*

He sniffled and turned onto his side, which triggered an attack of nausea. Only with great difficulty could he stop himself from throwing up all over the airlock.

"What the heck?" he mumbled, and it sounded like the complaint of a drunk.

Clonk, clonk.

There it was again. Twice. What was that?

He spun around once and heard it again.

Clonk!

The sound echoed in his damaged helmet. Disoriented and confused, he groped for the ring fastener on his neck and fiddled with the safety catch. It took a lot of strength to release it. When he finally managed it, the metallic noise had become a constant companion. It sounded again, and again, and yet again.

Clonk, clonk, clonk.

With a groan, he slipped off the helmet, which fell to the ground far too slowly. Then he unfastened his gloves, screamed twice in pain, and struggled out of the leg section. Now only the torso remained, the heaviest piece, which weighed on his shoulder like a yoke, even though it hardly weighed anything in the moon's low gravity.

He leaned back against the wall while it went *clonk, clonk,*

clonk. Before he began, he took a deep breath. As he exhaled, he raised both arms and screamed without restraint. A hissing pain raced through his shoulder and into his stomach. He threw up several times. The vomit seemed to float to the floor, forming an irregular pool.

It wasn't until a few minutes later that he realized he was lying motionless on his side. Trembling. Time had simply passed by and he again acknowledged he urgently needed medical attention.

Clonk, clonk, clonk.

He squatted carefully and then got to his feet, staggering to the side as a violent dizziness threatened to overwhelm him. He had to brace himself against one of the open lockers.

When he could see clearly again, he looked straight out through the porthole and recoiled. He bumped his head on the locker door with Miles's name on it.

Outside the small window, he saw a Chinese face behind the glass of a helmet. It was sweaty and the taikonaut formed his lips into words he couldn't understand or read.

How did he make it up here? Charlie thought, as he remembered that the stranger had been armed and had just tried to kill him. *Now he wants to finish the job.*

He turned to the inner airlock door and, with minimal movement, hopped on his left leg toward the control button with which he could open it. He pressed it with his fist and heard hissing in the wall before the hatch moved aside and opened the way to the central corridor with its ladders. On the other side, he clamped onto the small ledge with the handholds and held on tight. Then he closed the airlock again and stared through his porthole and the one on the other side at the Chinese man. He tried to read the taikonaut's face.

It looked desperate. Charlie raised one hand in front of the window and formed a pistol with it. Then he shook his head.

The taikonaut also shook his head, then raised both hands in front of his visor so that Charlie could see them.

"If I let you in and you have a gun, you'll kill me," he said out loud.

But can I let you die out there?

"He shot at me!"

We shot his friends, for all he knows.

"I'm safe in here. But if he starts shooting around in the airlock, we'll both get killed."

He could also sabotage the Liberty *from outside!*

Charlie made up his mind. No matter what had happened, he couldn't just leave another spaceman to die. And he could change his mind again in the airlock and not pressurize it. All he had to do was deactivate the internal controls, which he did in a few simple steps on the display next to the hatch.

He opened the outer airlock. It moved to the side, revealing an unarmed taikonaut who hurriedly hopped forward and slipped into the only safe space for miles around.

Charlie hesitated. The Chinese man grabbed his neck and screamed inside his helmet. His eyes bulged out.

Finally, Charlie pressed the button for the closing mechanism of the outer hatch and ordered the atmosphere control system to build up pressure. He then locked both openings and ordered the on-board computer to disconnect the airlock from the system controls.

His mind's eye still saw the taikonaut fumbling in panic for his helmet fastener.

Charlie made his way to the common room, where the small infirmary was located. It included a treatment bed, the medicine cabinet, first aid supplies, and emergency surgical equipment.

With the last of his strength, he placed an indwelling intravenous cannula into his right hand and clamped a bag of saline solution to the hook above him, which he flipped out of its wall socket. Next, he drew up a syringe of ketamine and squeezed the contents into the designated port in the tube. He placed the syringe and the ketamine on the shelf next to him and lay down on the bed.

A relieved sigh escaped his lips as, after a short time, the effect set in and a cloud of comfort settled over his multiple pains. Ranging from stinging to fiery, they became a dull background sensation. He took a few deep breaths and waited a few more minutes before carefully moving his right arm. He was aware that something was wrong and it was not pleasant, but he was now able to act.

Next, he injected himself with an antiemetic to quell the nausea, and modafinil with its amphetamine-like effect. He wanted nothing more than to sleep, but he had to be able to think clearly and take care of himself.

Besides, I have the enemy in my airlock, he thought.

He waited another ten minutes, then carefully began to sit up. His stomach was queasy and he felt a little weak, but otherwise reasonably well, despite the background of pain he was keeping at bay. It was as though he were swimming in the middle of a small pond that was surrounded by the house-sized flames of the Nether Hells, licking toward him and promising him a grisly fate once the pond's water had evaporated.

Charlie undressed and looked at himself. Half his body was covered in bruises. He expertly felt his right leg and almost hit the ceiling when he touched an indent below his knee. His lower leg was broken, that much was certain. He entered his data into the medical 3D printer, which went quickly as his profile was saved. All he had to do was enter the location of the fracture and the machine set about printing him a splint. He then felt his shoulder – the joint was dislocated, probably broken or the trapezius muscle torn. Perhaps both.

He drew up a syringe of muscle relaxant and injected himself in several places in the shoulder muscles.

"That's something I'd hoped I'd never have to use," he muttered and lay down on his side. It didn't work as shown on television, but the pain was portrayed quite realistically in the movies. He let his right arm dangle from the cot. Moving it was still painful, but bearable. Above all, the purely physical mobility remained difficult. It seemed like a miracle that he had managed to get his suit off. Unlike his functional under-wear, he hadn't been able to cut it open.

From below, he reached for the small doctor's case in its holder next to the bed and lifted it so that it acted as a weight pulling lightly on his arm. He began to make gentle rocking movements. Spontaneous repositioning was difficult to achieve, but not impossible with the required patience.

He had bought tolerance with the low-dose ketamine, which wasn't without risks, but he didn't see that he had much choice. The pressure in his shoulder increased until it suddenly disappeared. What remained was the dull feeling of pain kept at bay pharmacologically, reminding him that plenty else was broken inside him.

Charlie rested and crossed his arms in front of his chest so that it took the pressure off his right shoulder. When the 3D printer gave a gentle triad tone, he took out the splint and placed it around his broken lower leg. He then wrapped it, using half of all the gauze bandage rolls he could find, just to be on the safe side, so that everything between his knee and foot was padded. When he rolled his hip to look at his knee, he noticed that an area next to the kneecap was clearly swollen. Along with everything else, he'd probably torn a meniscus.

Could anything go right?

A loud *clonk* echoed through the central corridor.

The taikonaut! He had forgotten all about his Chinese prisoner. A lump formed in his throat and constricted his breathing. He absolutely had to ask Houston what he should do now.

Then he realized that he hadn't had a single radio contact with Mission Control. Not that he was particularly keen to talk to Colonel Hauser or any other military personnel. But he didn't know what to do, and he felt miserable. If there were good reasons to talk to Houston and get help, he had found all of them now.

As if someone 380,000 kilometers away had heard his thoughts, a voice rang out from the speakers. Harry?

"Sergeant Reid? Can you hear me?" It was Hauser.

Charlie sighed.

CHAPTER 47

Rebecca's head throbbed as if someone had administered electric shocks directly into her temples.

Which had, in fact, occurred.

Her head hung limply forward, her chin pressed lightly against her breastbone. A thread of saliva hung from her lips down to her bare chest, to which a wet sponge was held with heavy duty tape. There was a car battery on the floor, connected to the sponge by two clamps.

The gorilla stood in front of her and gripped a fistful of her sweaty hair.

"Last chance, Major."

"I've said everything I know," she mumbled, exhausted. The headache was so bad that she felt like she was in a trance. She just wanted it to stop, but more than that, she wanted Feinman and this neanderthal in front of her to pay for it.

"Fred!" she heard the colonel shout. "Get her out of there. The computers are clean. We can leave."

He obeyed and unlocked her handcuffs from the back of the hard wooden chair on which she was half-slumped. Then he roughly pulled her to her feet and had to half carry her.

She didn't know how much time had passed, but it

seemed like an eternity. At the same time, maybe it hadn't been enough. The ignorance made her almost crazier than the pain.

"I hope," she said, gasping before she could continue, "that you are proud of yourself."

The colonel seemed to understand that she meant him but said nothing and just looked at her from the side.

"It's nothing personal. You could have cooperated. Hell, I would have even offered you a job. I can always use someone like you on my team."

"I ... don't think you need law-abiding officers," she replied, letting herself continue to be half-carried by the gorilla. She didn't want to make it any easier for the pig.

"It's a real shame," said Feinman. "If only you had understood. *Sentinel II* would have secured our dominion over the moon indefinitely. The *Zephyr-Xs* could have flown kinetically and hit any point at the south pole without being detected."

"*Could have?* So it didn't work." Slowly, she began to understand. One of the hooded men went to the control panel next to the door and prepared to enter the code. The colonel stepped up to the panel and turned to her.

"No, it crashed. But we'll send up another one. The moon is the future of our energy supply, Major. Helium-3 in vast quantities for nuclear fusion. We will not and cannot share that with a strategic enemy."

"So, you'll shoot them with missiles."

"No, it will be a random meteorite impact, of which there are countless every month at the lunar south pole. Once they've lost a base, it will set them back far enough for us to create facts up there," he explained.

"You made up this whole *aliens* story to have an excuse to send our astronauts to the moon as quickly as possible and cover the tracks of *Sentinel II*," she concluded. Her pain faded into the background of her racing thoughts. "But you didn't expect the Chinese to jump on it so quickly, and then you couldn't get out of it."

"It should have been kept secret and then we would have been there all alone." Feinman almost growled the words.

"But that didn't work. And the civilian astronauts were a thorn in your side because they don't obey orders like former military personnel," she continued, her heart sinking. "Tell me the truth. Did you and your co-conspirators sabotage *Starship 6* so that the replacement crew of former veterans could launch?"

The colonel avoided her gaze and waved her off. "I don't have to tell you anything."

He opened the door and then nodded to the gorilla. "I've changed my mind. She's not flying with us. Make sure they don't find her body."

"Uhh, sir?" Fred pointed forward. Suddenly everything happened at once.

"FBI! ON THE FLOOR!" several guttural voices shouted simultaneously. Flashlights came on and blinded them. A shot rang out, then more shouting and confusion, moving shadows, lights and figures. From everywhere she heard shouts of "FBI! Down! DOWN! DOWN!"

Then the grip on her upper arm loosened and she fell forward powerlessly. Someone caught her before she landed on her knees. The grasp was solid and powerful. Effortlessly, the figure in front of her lifted her to her feet and supported her entire body weight.

She looked up through her wet eyes at Darwi, who stood before her like a mountain of muscle, looking down at her.

"I'm sorry we're so late, Major," he said, and she began to cry. For the first time in her adult life, Rebecca cried like a bereft child as everything poured out of her: the stress, the fear of death, the loss of Rogers, the pain, the shame and embarrassment, the humiliation of torture. She didn't know how long it took, but eventually she regained self-awareness and found herself outside in the wild meadow in front of the black site, her utility uniform rezipped over her chest. There were FBI emergency-response vehicles everywhere, and two helicopters. But no sign of the stealth Black Hawk.

FBI agents in blue jackets with yellow lettering were walking around together with heavily armored SWAT police officers. She saw an ambulance with its blue lights on, carrying two stretchers.

"Wait," she told Darwi when she saw the colonel being led in that direction by two agents. "I want to talk to him."

The detective accompanied her to the emergency vehicle to which Feinman was being taken. The FBI people, a woman and a man, had just pushed him roughly into the back of an SUV and attached his handcuffs to a device on the passenger seat.

The colonel didn't change expression when he saw her coming. She stopped in front of him and motioned to the agent at the door to wait.

"This won't take long," she said, and the FBI woman eyed her sympathetically before nodding and backing away.

"How?" Feinman asked, seeming to reassess her.

"Geronimo," Rebecca replied, feeling like she was in a James Bond movie. The rescued heroine explaining to the villain how she had put a stop to him, but not until he had confessed everything to her before the grand finale, including his evil plan. If she hadn't been so bruised, she might have laughed at the irony.

"The FBI action against the former commander of Vandenberg?"

"Yes. Back then, I had a chip implanted so that I could be located. I never removed it, but I had it switched off. Thanks to a call to the Inspector General, it was reactivated before I got here."

"You bypassed the general before they got on his helicopter." Feinman ground his jaws.

"Yes. I knew he was going to use me as bait for you. Detective Darwi got in touch with the FBI and gave them the documents from your raid on Walker, along with a copy of the file the Inspector General already had. All they had to do was track my location until the signal cut out, and get to the last known position," she explained with some satisfaction. "And as for my call to Darwi: did you think I was that stupid? Really? Of course I told him beforehand that I would not contact him myself. But if something happened, he should believe the opposite of what I said. *I'm fine, you don't need to do anything, the general is fine, I'll take care of everything.*"

"By the way, we will be able to get you tried in a district court," the detective interjected. "No military prison for you."

The colonel pressed his lips together and averted his eyes. Rebecca saw a man who had been soundly defeated and that was enough for her. She had freed herself from the web and hobbled the spider. But the greatest danger was not yet out of the way.

Darwi led her away from the car to one of the helicopters, where a team of paramedics was waiting for her. "The Inspector General is waiting for you in Washington."

"In Washington?"

"Yes. I assume you are scheduled to testify before a congressional intelligence committee. The Inspector General has announced that he will represent you under the Whistleblower Act."

"Good," she said with relief. "Make sure the colonel gets to the county jail and ends up in the maximum security wing."

"I will," Darwi promised. "But I don't think he'll stay there for long. As soon as Congress is informed, he'll be public enemy number one."

"And, from *witness* number one," she added, "my thanks to you, Detective Darwi."

The mountain of a man merely nodded.

When he helped her into the helicopter, she realized that it was an FBI Medivac. She was placed on a prepared plinth and they began treatment. One of the paramedics buckled the safety straps and then prepared an IV. Another closed the door as a doctor leaned over her.

"Hello. I'm Doctor Feldstein, and we'll be taking you to Washington Central if it's possible. However, if intensive medical care is required, we will have to transfer you to Cincinnati," the doctor explained.

"No, I have to go to Congress," she said. "They need to see me like this."

CHAPTER 48

"I want to talk to the CAPCOM," Charlie said after activating the ship-wide intercom system. He had switched the on-board computer to voice control so that he was connected to the AI from anywhere.

"You are talking to me, *Sergeant*," Colonel Hauser's voice rang out from the speakers.

"I haven't been on duty for a long time. So you don't need to bother with my rank." He just managed to swallow the reflexive *sir*. A stone seemed to form in his stomach for contradicting a high-ranking officer, especially as he was obligated to obey any orders from Houston. "I want to talk to Harry."

"That's not possible at this time." Hauser's voice sounded harsher than before. Charlie didn't care. Let him come and get him.

"Then I'm afraid I won't be able to take orders from you."

"You should reconsider that, Sergeant. Now that this has become a military operation and you are a master sergeant in the reserves, we can hold you accountable in a military court."

"You'll have to bring me back to Earth first," Charlie shot back. "Feel free to come here and arrest me. No, let me rephrase that: I *challenge* you to arrest me. I'll be ready at any time. While you're trying to explain to the public why they can no longer contact us, I'll think about what I'm going to say the next time the cameras and microphones are pointed at me. If I have my way, you and all those involved in this action are traitors to the American people. Not to mention the fact that you have broken international treaties."

He remained silent for a few seconds until he heard the *clonk* again. He waited a while longer for an answer from Houston, but it didn't come. So he carefully shimmied his way up to the airlock using his left foot and left hand, stood on the small platform, and looked through the window.

In the meantime, the taikonaut had freed himself from his spacesuit, which lay next to him like the cast-off shell of a crustacean. Just like the remains of Charlie's, the originally white parts were now grayed due to the moon dust that had settled in its cracks. Not as bad as the Apollo astronauts' suits, which had not been engineered with an electrostatically repellent layer, but collecting some of the razor-sharp microcrystals was impossible to prevent.

Charlie took a closer look at the Chinese man sitting on the other side, his back leaning against the outside hatch. He held his helmet in one hand and occasionally banged it against the wall.

Clonk.

He was slightly smaller than Charlie, but similarly well-trained, as he could see through the tight-fitting white functional underwear. It was soaked with sweat under his arms and on his chest. His short black hair was plastered to his forehead. From his face, he assumed that the taikonaut couldn't be more than 40 years old – about his age. His eyes were closed. The man reminded Charlie of the actor Chow Yun-fat.

He was startled when the taikonaut opened his eyelids and looked at him. His lips moved, but nothing could be heard.

Charlie's finger moved to the intercom button on the control display next to the airlock. But he hesitated.

"*Liberty?* Deactivate the automatic recording and transmission function for the ship's internal audio. Store everything in the memory clusters, but don't allow any data transfers to Houston," he ordered.

"I am happy to do that for you, Charlie," replied the androgynous voice of the on-board AI over the speaker system.

Only now did he press the button for the intercom.

"Hello," he said, feeling rather stupid. But he couldn't think of anything better to say.

"Hello," the Chinese man replied in English and slowly got to his feet. He looked weakened – or perhaps he just wanted Charlie to believe that he was weakened. The taikonaut also appeared unsure of what to say. The situation was equally strange and unpleasant. They were enemies and at the same time the only two living people on the moon, not to mention the many corpses laying around outside their spaceship.

A wave of anger and emotional pain surged through his body as he thought of his dead friends whose remains he had left behind lonely and exposed to the vacuum.

"Identify yourself," he said at last, after regaining control and clearing his throat several times.

"I am Colonel Xiao Zhan." The Chinese man took two slow steps forward so as not to lose his balance and stopped in the middle of the airlock, surrounded by the intermingled remains of their two spacesuits.

"You tried to kill me." It sounded like a simple statement, but Charlie was furious. When he looked at the taikonaut's face, he saw a murderer. Someone who had tried to take his life not so long ago. Someone who ... "My friend Miles. Did you find him ...?"

The Chinese man swallowed and straightened up before replying with an audible accent, but clearly understandable. "I'm not familiar with that name. But there was an astronaut who tried to shoot me after the *Celestial Dragon* exploded. I was able to overpower him."

You killed Miles.

"And then you tried to kill me," said Charlie.

"Yes," Xiao Zhan admitted bluntly. He looked down at his hands and seemed to slump a little before he seemed to remember where he was and pulled his shoulders back, raising his eyes. "My comrades are all dead. They were shot and beaten to death."

"My friends are dead, too. All because your comrade killed my commander with a hammer."

"I don't know anything about that because we had no radio contact. But I did receive information that rockets had been found in the Shackleton Crater."

Charlie didn't answer immediately. They continued to look at each other through the window with somber expressions.

"You're my prisoner now," he eventually said.

"I know. There's nowhere I can go," the Chinese man said, and something about the way he said it gave Charlie a twinge. It was sadness and dejection. He heard it in his voice, saw it behind the painstakingly maintained façade of control and pride that kept this man upright, even though he looked deeply exhausted and traumatized. His skin was pale, his eyes bloodshot and moist, the corners of his mouth slightly downturned, as if he had images of a terrible incident in his head that would not let go of him.

He is a reflection of me and how I feel, he thought. But for all his empathy, Charlie did not forget that he had barely survived after the taikonaut had shot him.

Xiao Zhan, he corrected himself. *The enemy has a name.*

But I mustn't go soft, I mustn't let myself get carried away with anything stupid. One mistake and he'll take over the ship. If he makes contact with Beijing, there may be no Earth for us to return to.

"I'm thirsty," said Xiao Zhan after a while.

"Good," Charlie replied and took his finger off the intercom button. Then he rechecked that the airlock was isolated and disconnected from the rest of the systems. The hatches were both locked and the controls inside were switched off.

Only then did he climb to the crew module next to the common room and lie down in his bunk. The little bit of modafinil he had administered was slowly wearing off and he felt so tired that he could barely stay on his feet. The ketamine was becoming dominant and it wouldn't be long before his body simply shut down thanks to stress and injuries. So he pulled his sleeping bag over himself, closed his eyes, and tried not to think about Anne, and Louis, and Miles.

He did not succeed. Tears trickled from the corners of his eyes as the dark cloak of sleep descended over him. He dreamed of large hammers hitting the bed next to him, making a metallic *clonk, clonk, clonk,* even though somehow he was aware that the mattress was soft. In time, however, the noise subsided because he began to float and sat in heaven with Anne, Louis, and Miles to have breakfast. They were in a good mood and sat at a beautifully set large table. When they asked him if he wanted to help bake bread, they kneaded the dough together and put it in a stone oven on a cloud. Afterward, they wanted to eat, but realized that he'd forgotten the salt. They then turned into skeletons and stared at him reproachfully.

Charlie woke up without knowing whether he had just dozed off for a few minutes or had slept for days. He felt exhausted, but that didn't necessarily mean anything. Half his body was shattered, or at least that was how he felt. His eyelids were swollen and his shoulder ached so badly that he felt nauseous again.

This was not the nausea of the mild concussion that plagued him, it was caused by the overpowering pain. With a groan, he rolled out of his sleeping bag without using his right arm. As he did so, he was once again hit by a violent spinning dizziness that almost sent him back to his bunk. He looked at his watch and frowned.

Apparently – thanks to the ketamine – he had slept for 18 hours..

Ketamine, he thought longingly, and carefully walked to the central corridor, which hollowed out the *Liberty* like an elevator shaft. The best way to get around, he realized, was to take small, gliding steps, as though he were using invisible inline skates in slow motion. It might look strange, but it turned out to be a reliable way to avoid moving too fast or too slow, or bouncing – which was not an acceptable option in his condition.

He had probably made the fracture in his lower leg much worse during his adrenaline-fueled escape on the surface of the moon. *Whatever.*

Charlie climbed to the infirmary in the lounge and started another infusion of ketamine and modafinil. After about an hour the infusion was finished. He removed the cannula and disposed of everything before going to the fridge and grabbing a packet of 'breakfast cereal' which he put in the microwave. After he had eaten, he took one of the water tubes he had prepared yesterday and gradually squeezed half a liter into his mouth.

At their first and only moon breakfast, he and Anne had played with pouring water from the tube into glasses. Due to the low gravity, they had been able to pour the water in a high arc, which had looked extremely fascinating.

The thought of Anne made his heart sink.

He recalled his dream and froze at the thought of the hammer blows.

Xiao Zhan! He had completely forgotten about the Chinese man in the airlock. His prisoner hadn't knocked on the wall since Charlie had awakened.

He quickly attached the water tube to the adhesive pad on his thigh and climbed up to the airlock. Through the window, he saw the taikonaut lying in a corner, appearing to be dead.

Did I kill him? The thought caused Charlie neither satisfaction nor relief, but guilt.

He pressed the intercom button, but then waited.

"*Liberty?*"

"Yes, Charlie? What can I do for you?"

"Has Houston made contact?"

"Yes, two hundred and seventy-eight times. You switched off the ship's internal speakers for external access nineteen hours and twenty-two minutes ago."

He froze. Under normal circumstances, that would have put him in hot water. But now Houston had become the devil's kitchen. The Space Force had taken over, probably to keep their satellite a secret. That could only mean that his friends and colleagues had been banned from the consoles. Until that changed, he had nothing to say to Houston.

"Xiao," he said over the intercom.

"Zhan," the Chinese man replied quietly. He didn't even raise his head.

"Excuse me?"

"My first name is *Zhan*, not *Xiao*."

"You introduced yourself as Xiao Zhan," replied Charlie.

"In China, we designate the family name first. I'm very thirsty."

If I don't want him to die, I have to give him drinking water, he thought. *And eventually, something to eat.*

He saw the yellow liquid in the upturned helmet next to the taikonaut and grimaced.

If I open the hatch, he might attack me.

"It's very amazing," Zhan said, looking up at him. His eyes were bloodshot and half closed. "You try everything to beat us in the race to the moon and you don't learn the simplest things about us."

"We focused on being here first."

"For *freedom.*" He could clearly hear the sarcasm in the Chinese man's tone.

"Certainly not for the communist dictatorship and the oppression of minorities," Charlie shot back.

"I see. Your nation didn't kill the indigenous people and put them on reservations? Nor did you enslave black people and oppress and discriminate against them as second-class human beings until a few decades ago?"

"I'm not saying that our history is perfect. But we have common values and respect human rights. We have worked for democracy and don't censor what everyone is allowed to see and hear."

"Is that so?" asked Xiao Zhan with a tired but combative look. "Your media filter everything through their political glasses. CNN or Fox News are the same thing, just on different sides of the opinion spectrum. They argue about everything and everyone hates each other for it. At your schools, kids are shooting each other."

"Nothing is perfect and we have problems, but at least ..." Charlie faltered. *Let's not fight ideological wars and buy our way into countries around the world in order to put them under pressure,* he had wanted to say. But the words stuck in his throat. China wanted to annex Taiwan and was expanding its influence worldwide through investments and loans. But he already knew the taikonaut's retort before they talked about it. The U.S. had overthrown entire governments in the last one hundred years and replaced them with quasi-puppets. Iran and Peru were just two examples. They had annexed Panama and exerted pressure on entire continents through investments, and the military, and via diplomacy.

"You Americans always see everything through your own glasses," said Xiao Zhan, shaking his head almost imperceptibly. He spoke sluggishly, and his accent had become stronger, but his vocabulary was clear and to the point.

Charlie said nothing in reply. That his country considered itself the center of the universe and was generally more than a little ignorant of the rest of the world was no secret, and something he himself had always criticized.

"China has four times as many people as you do. Our economy is strong, our women, men and children are well educated and the technology is innovative," continued Xiao Zhan. "After a civil war, the fascists moved to Taiwan. Now you are accusing us of imperialism. Yet your military bases are all around us. Japan, South Korea, the Philippines, Southeast Asia. And in the rest of the world. Your military is present all over the world and secures your influence. Far fewer people who hold all the power in their hands and exert it on everyone else."

"That's true," Charlie admitted, "but we respect basic human rights and the equality of all before the law."

"Has that made the world a better place?"

"Yes, I think so."

"I don't believe that. China is not perfect and we have our own problems that we have to solve and will solve," said Xiao Zhan quietly. "But all power in the hands of one person has never been good. No. The world must become multipolar. That can bring peace. And in our recent history, we have never used the army to enforce our will. Unlike the United States."

"Political debates won't get us anywhere now," said Charlie. He had to admit to himself that his prisoner was the first

Chinese person he had talked to about politics and the East-West conflict. He found that strangely depressing. He was part of this conflict, on the front line, even, but had never listened to the other side or even felt the desire to do so. His opinions and beliefs were almost natural states, but that was of course a fallacy. In truth, he merely saw a point of view and had made it his own without questioning it. "To be honest, I hate politics."

"Everyone hates politics," replied the taikonaut, and it didn't sound cynical, but simply like an observation.

Charlie sighed and muttered: "I wish it hadn't come to all this."

Xiao Zhan nodded faintly. "What does *China* mean in your language?"

"Excuse me?"

"The name of my country. What is the meaning?"

"I don't know," Charlie had to admit. "It's just a name."

"In Chinese, nothing is just a name. Every character has a meaning. In Mandarin, your country is called *Měiguó*."

"What does that mean?"

"The beautiful country," said Xiao Zhan.

Charlie swallowed and the jumble of sadness and frustration in his guts became heavier. He couldn't remember the last time he had heard something so sad.

Without hesitation, he pressed the release for the hatch and opened it. The bare steel moved aside. Suddenly the airlock lay open in front of him. At the other end, three meters away, sat the Chinese man, looking up at him with a mixture of surprise and disbelief.

"My shoulder is broken, at least one muscle is torn, my knee is fucked up, and my lower leg is finished. I have a concussion and am only able to stay on my feet thanks to ketamine and an amphetamine-like drug," Charlie said truthfully. "If you want to overpower me, the odds are on your side."

Xiao Zhan stood up slowly. At first he feared that the taikonaut might have tricked him, that he still had his strength, but every little movement showed that he could barely stand on his feet. Even his gaze was lethargic.

"I almost suffocated and am severely dehydrated. I'm sweating and my hands are shaking." Xiao Zhan shook his head slightly, swaying. "If there has to be a fight, I would like to ... postpone it."

"Good." Charlie detached the water tube from the adhesive strip on his thigh and threw it to his counterpart. Despite the tube's sluggish flight, his reaction was too slow and he missed, but then picked it up from the floor and began to drink greedily.

Meanwhile, Charlie withdrew and closed the hatch. He then climbed into the common room and warmed up another breakfast packet, which he placed in Xiao Zhan's airlock. The taikonaut made no move to attack him or anything.

"Xièxiè," said the Chinese man.

"Uhh."

"Thank you," came from the speakers. Xiao Zhan began to eat very slowly and in a controlled manner, although he looked half-starved. "I speak your language, but you don't speak mine."

"That's right."

The taikonaut nodded. "Every Chinese child learns English at school. I don't think American children learn Mandarin?"

"Not many, I'm afraid. That's rather rare."

"Three hundred and fifty million Americans, one point four billion Chinese."

"I understand," sighed Charlie. "To be fair, you have to admit that English is probably much easier than Chinese."

"Yes, very simple language. That shouldn't be considered an insult."

"That's all right. I guess that's true. You said you were a colonel."

"Yes. I was a fighter pilot in the People's Liberation Army Air Force. In fact, that's still the case."

"Do you have a family?" Charlie asked.

Xiao Zhan looked up, scrutinizing him through the glass as if trying to understand the background to the question. "Two daughters, Mi-Lai and Yang-Fen." An enraptured expression came into the Chinese man's dark eyes.

"Yet you signed up for this mission? Even though it's a mission of no return?"

"Of course."

"Why?"

"Because my country chose me for this. I serve my country," Xiao Zhan explained, as if he didn't understand the point of the question. When Charlie didn't answer, he chewed on his breakfast porridge and gazed into space before looking back at him. "There's a lot of competition in China. Nearly one and a half billion people, and just like every American, we are trying to live a better life than the generation before. Parents like my wife and myself want to give our children a better life. Becoming a fighter pilot was a great honor for me. For five years, I only got to see my family for a weekend every other month."

"Didn't that break your heart?" Charlie asked in surprise.

"Yes, but I went on *for them*. Many families have to have their children raised by their parents in their home province so that they can earn enough money to send them to the best schools," continued Xiao Zhan. "With my contribution to this mission, I am ensuring that my wife and my two girls have the best prospects for the future. I am giving them a better tomorrow. For them and for China. What about you, American?"

"I ..." Charlie thought about it. "I always wanted to see

space and do something after the military that would help humanity. To push the boundaries, to make the impossible possible. I think I also wanted to prove to myself that I could do it."

"I see."

"Do you have a family?"

"A sister. I used to be married, but that didn't work out."

"I see."

"Sometimes I wish I'd had children. To leave something behind, you know?" Charlie leaned his head against the window, exhausted, and stared at his feet. His lower right leg looked as if a giant spider had wrapped it in silk.

"Children are the greatest gift in life," said Xiao Zhan. "Creating something you love more than yourself."

"Incoming connection from Houston," *Liberty* said over the speaker.

CHAPTER 49

Rebecca squared her shoulders and walked past the two columns of FBI agents who were dressed in civilian clothes. The infiltration of the JSC in Houston had taken almost 20 hours. A total of 200 police officers had been infiltrated – in plain clothes with fake IDs and authorization cards that an engineer named Marty had helped them create. Luckily, she'd gotten along well with the cheerful nerdy fellow during her short time here in Houston.

When she felt ready, she nodded to the head of operations. Special Agent Samioni stood at the door, waiting for her. The agents were armed and ready, holding the Glocks of the disarmed Space Force soldiers who were being held in the foyer until it was all over. Two of them were standing against the wall next to the door, their submachine guns having been taken from them.

"Ready, Major?" Samioni asked kindly. Normally, she hated receiving special treatment out of pity, especially being handled with 'kid gloves.'

This time, however, she was prepared to make an exception. He let her go first and she thanked him with a brief bow of her head before pushing down the handle and going inside.

Her chin held high, she straightened her pantsuit in the small entry corridor, and then entered the Mission Control Center. She saw the lined-up monitors, their workstations all facing the huge display wall, and at the very back was the glass wall of the visitors' room, which was guarded on both sides by soldiers.

At first no one paid any attention to her because it was so busy. Half of the seats were occupied by soldiers in uniform who looked overwhelmed, the other half by civilian NASA employees.

A colonel stood at the very back. He only noticed her when someone pointed at her, even though she was standing at the very front as if she were interrupting a movie.

The officer frowned and reached for his radio and spoke into it, but then seemed to realize that no one was answering him.

"I am Major Rebecca Hinrichs. On behalf of the President, I order everyone in uniform to stop working immediately, stand up, and put your hands on your heads," she shouted loudly, effortlessly drowning out the murmured conversations and the humming of the computers.

"What?" barked the colonel. "Disregard that order! Nobody moves!"

While soldiers and NASA employees were still trying to determine whether this was a bad joke or whether they were dreaming, the FBI agents approached from both sides through entrances to the right and left of the console stands. They weren't wearing blue jackets because of the camouflage, but they had lanyards bearing badges around their necks and pistols in their hands.

There was movement in the control center. Everyone present stood up from their workstations and raised their hands, the NASA civilians like startled children caught in a prank, the soldiers a little more disciplined, complying with the original order, standing up and folding their hands over their heads.

That is, except the colonel, who came down the steps via the central corridor and toward her. When he saw her battered face with its stitched wounds and bloodshot eyes, he stopped short. Before he could say anything, she held the Presidential order in front of his face. In the background, the FBI agents proceeded to handcuff the soldiers.

The colonel scratched his gray temples and seemed about to say something else, but then nodded and handed the paper back to her.

"What happens now?" he asked impersonally.

"You and your people are in for a few weeks of intensive questioning to find out who all had knowledge of *Sentinel II* and in what form," Rebecca said.

Samioni came up behind the colonel – his name was Hauser according to his chest patch – and forced his hands behind his back to handcuff him as well. "So we'll be talking a lot more in the near future."

She nodded gratefully to the Special Agent, whereupon he winked – in typical Texan fashion – and led the colonel away. Meanwhile, she walked up the side aisle toward the visitors' room, where the specialists on duty were forced to hand over their weapons. They put up no resistance, looking more as if they had suddenly ended up in the wrong movie.

"All civilian staff stay in your places," she shouted over the murmuring in the room. "There are four astronauts up there who still need our help."

When she reached the visitors' room door she ordered one of the specialists to open it. The young man quickly complied and she entered. Several rows of upholstered, inter-connected seats led a few meters upward, rising like in a theater. About a dozen men and women stood there staring at her. She recognized one of them, the head of the Astronaut

Office and true CAPCOM of the moon mission, Harry Johnson.

"Dr. Johnson," she said, "I'm here on the President's orders. All military personnel are being withdrawn from JSC as we speak and taken to a designated location for questioning. You must ensure that the mission continues and that our astronauts up there are brought to safety."

When she got no reaction other than a grim nod and long faces all around, she frowned.

"What's wrong?"

"There's only one astronaut left. Charlie Reid," Harry Johnson replied. "The others are dead."

"What?" she asked, blinking in surprise. It wasn't often that she was caught on the wrong foot, and if the man hadn't been so pale, she would have thought his words were a bad joke.

"There was a conflict with the Chinese. They killed each other and things aren't looking good for Reid either. His condition is critical." Johnson ran his fingers through his thinning hair. "It's clear you already know about the damn satellite. The bastards locked us in here when we refused to give them control."

Rebecca nodded. "That's over now. Who's the mission director?"

"I am." A man with a distinct Indian descent came forward. With his rumpled flannel shirt and disheveled hair, he looked more like a transient than one of NASA's most important employees.

"Good. You are back in charge here. Administrator Miller will be here in a few hours to brief you all. Until then, take care of Charlie Reid as best you can. Do your best to avoid an international conflict."

"I'm afraid there's not that much we can do, ma'am. The damage is already done."

"The Chinese don't know about this satellite business yet. At your end, make sure it stays that way. I'll take care of everything else," she replied, fervently hoping that she was right.

"Okay," Ramaswami said and seemed to want to add something else.

"Out with it." She motioned for him to speak.

"Ma'am. We can't get Reid back."

"What? Why not?" Rebecca narrowed her eyes and eyed him like a hawk eyeing its prey.

"Because we don't have a suitable starship. There is no other back-up starship."

"I thought that we could simply refuel the *Liberty*."

"There's nothing simple about it," explained Harry Johnson. "SpaceX is in the planning phase for a tanker version of the Starship. It's well advanced, but not expected to be functional before the end of the decade."

"How long would it take if we did everything we could to develop a modified basic version *now*?" she asked, but she could see from their expressions that this could not be the solution.

"A year, if everything were to go perfectly. Designs would have to be worked out and prototypes built."

"A few of them will fly into the air before there is a successful orbital flight," Ramaswami interjected.

"That's on top of everything else."

"What if we send food and oxygen to Reid? We have starships that can land there unmanned," she suggested.

"Yes, that could work, but if we send a spaceship there, it will ..."

" ... then China will send one too." Rebecca thought feverishly.

"Besides, it doesn't solve the problem of Reid dying if he doesn't return as soon as possible," Harry Johnson said, and it was clear to Rebecca this was not a mission result he would accept.

"Charlie Reid is returning home," she said firmly. She remembered the brief conversation with President Hernandez, who had made it very clear that he intended to do everything he could to make the mission a success for the public, while rooting out the Space Force covert operation, and factions within the Pentagon, and bringing those responsible to justice. Rebecca had expected nothing less. Such top-secret operations were readily used and encouraged by the knowledgeable few, people or agencies, as long as they produced results. If they failed or became exposed, all the heads that could fit under the guillotine would roll.

"Then there's only one possible solution," said Ramaswami, exchanging a tense look with Johnson before looking back at Rebecca. "We need help from the Chinese."

"Excuse me?"

"We're pretty sure they also had a spare spaceship up their sleeve, but they didn't need it because the first one worked."

"Even if that's true, I was informed that the *Celestial Dragon* is a one-time-use spaceship," she replied.

"For a mission involving a landing, yes. But, without a landing maneuver, the ship might make it back to Earth on the same fuel. We would just have to catch it in orbit if it's not optimized for re-entry," Johnson explained. "But that could certainly be solved with a Dragon or Orion capsule that we shoot up with a Falcon 9. We just need a solution for a suitable airlock and for getting Reid into orbit."

"Okay, I have no idea. But even if it were technically possible, why should the Chinese help us?"

"Because Charlie Reid is not the only survivor. One of the CNSA taikonauts also survived," said Ramaswami.

Rebecca let out a heavy sigh. "That makes diplomacy a little more difficult ..."

CHAPTER 50

"I don't want to talk to the colonel."

"It's Harry Johnson."

"Harry?" Charlie was shocked and took his finger off the intercom button for the airlock. "I want to hear him."

"Charlie? Charlie! This is CAPCOM speaking."

"Harry!" he replied after pressing the button again. "Thank goodness! What's going on with you? Where's Hauser?"

"There have been a few changes here in Houston," Harry said. But he didn't sound as happy as he should have.

"Good ones, I hope."

"Yes, I think so. But there's a lot to do."

"That's right," said Charlie, peering through the window at Xiao Zhan, who was looking at him attentively.

"We want to get you home, but we can't do it without the Chinese. But you'll have to convince your ... uhh ... *guest* to convince the CNSA to work with us."

"Okay ... I don't know if I can do that."

"That's not all. You'll need more food and oxygen if you want to survive until then."

"The Chinese ship is destroyed, Harry. The Space Force made sure of that."

"But there's *Starship 5*," replied the CAPCOM.

"We have no more suits. They're all destroyed."

"We pretty much figured on that. You have to fly there."

"Excuse me? I'm not a pilot." Charlie swallowed.

"No, but you've done the emergency training and you have some time to practice."

"And how are we supposed to get the supplies without suits?"

"We're currently working on a solution, but you won't like it."

When they had finished their conversation, Charlie opened the hatch. Xiao Zhan, who was sitting in the middle of the airlock and had just finished his breakfast, looked up in surprise. For a few heartbeats, they just stared at each other. Each seemed to be waiting for the other to do something.

"My name is Charlie," he began. "I don't know whether to be sad, or desperate, or angry. I think I'm all of the above. I hate you for killing Miles, but I also understand your hatred of me for pushing one of your friends into the crater. We have no comrades left up here. We're two competitors in a predicament. All of that is true.

"But I also know that underneath the anger and hatred, a more level-headed part of me knows that every death is horrible, and these deaths should have been prevented. My government says you're my enemy, and everything I've experienced out there tells me so too. But I don't want to be your enemy. I want you and me to be *people*. People who can manage to look past these things, despite the pain we've caused each other. I want us to get out of here and go back to Earth..

"There is a way, but I can't do it alone. We can only do it together. I'm badly hurt and you could probably overpower me now. If that's your plan, now's your chance."

He waited while Xiao Zhan scrutinized him. When the taikonaut took a step toward him, Charlie didn't even flinch. He had meant every word.

"If you make mistakes and don't correct them, you make new mistakes," the Chinese man said slowly, and held out his hand. "I told you my name, American, but you didn't tell me your full name."

"Charlie Reid," he replied.

The taikonaut found a smile, even if it didn't touch his eyes. "So, let's get started. What's the plan?" Xiao Zhan inquired in his soft accent.

"First, a shower."

The Chinese man frowned.

"You stink." He tried a smile and it soothed his deep-seated pain a little, which had nothing to do with his battered body.

After the taikonaut had showered and was wearing new functional underwear and overalls with Louis's patch, which made Charlie shudder briefly, he explained the plan to Zhan.

"You want me to talk to the CNSA and suggest that they work with NASA? They should send a possible second *Celestial Dragon* spacecraft that we need to intercept and board in lunar orbit," summarized Xiao Zhan.

"Yes."

"If there *is* a second spaceship."

Charlie tilted his head.

"I'll talk to my superiors."

"With the ambassador. He was asked to go to Houston. A direct call to the CNSA was rejected by Beijing."

"I see." The taikonaut seemed to be waiting for something.

"Do you have any questions?"

"I assumed that I would be given a text to recite. To protect your secret."

"No." Charlie shook his head. "We realize that we can't force you to do anything, and without Chinese help, there's no way to rescue us. But not without American help, too, because otherwise we won't get into orbit."

Xiao Zhan nodded in understanding. "I'll do it."

"Harry? We're ready. Is the ambassador there?"

"Yes, he's in the visitors' room," the CAPCOM replied. He sounded excited. "He's being fetched right now."

There was silence for a few minutes, then a Chinese voice rang out. Xiao Zhan spoke in Mandarin and there was a brief exchange of words, followed by a slightly longer monologue from the taikonaut before he nodded to Charlie.

"What did you tell him?"

"That we are the only survivors and that we are working together," said his counterpart. His face looked pale in the blue light of the cockpit displays. "And that we've made a discovery."

Charlie swallowed. "Did you ...?"

"No. Only that we've made a discovery, and I can't say anything more about it for the time being."

The taikonaut had unmistakably emphasized the words *for the time being*.

"I see."

"Well, uhh, umm," stuttered Harry over the radio, "we're going to start planning the repair of one of the spacesuits. One of you will have to go over to *Starship 5*. We'll take as long as we need. You've got a week at least, and that should be enough. If you have the supplies and oxygen, you can survive for up to four weeks. Our job will be to get a spaceship to you by then."

"Are there any plans for the suit repair yet?" asked Charlie.

"Yes. For that you have to ... remove the dust from one of

the suits and spread it out in the airlock so that we can see it clearly."

He exchanged a glance with Xiao Zhan.

"I will go," the Chinese man answered the unspoken question that stood between them like the proverbial elephant in the room. "You are in no physical condition for a field mission."

Charlie wanted to object out of a sense of honor and duty, but he just nodded.

They spent the next few days in a routine that quickly became familiar and yet seemed strange whenever he thought about it. His friends were dead and the hole in his heart could not be filled. In the morning he felt as if someone had beaten him to death – and the same every evening. But in between, he worked like a madman with Xiao Zhan to find a solution to their supply problem.

Life support and supplies on the *Liberty* were planned for a week's stay plus four days on arrival and four days for the departure phase. Two days had been added as a safety buffer. That brought them to a total of 17 days, four of which they had 'used up' with the journey there and three on the moon. However, there were now only two people instead of four, which would have effectively increased the 10 days to 20 if there wasn't a problem: Louis had loaded the Rover with over 30 oxygen cartridges for their crater mission. They were now outside on the vehicle, which was about 50 meters away from them. What's more, Miles hadn't locked the airlock properly, so the on-board computer had intervened after the safety margin had been exceeded and closed the outer hatch. As a result, another portion of the oxygen supply had been lost.

That left them with 13 days of breathable air – not enough, even if Washington and Beijing were to agree on a joint rescue operation. So they had a choice, presuming they could patch up Zhan's suit for a short mission outside: Rover or *Starship 5*. However, as the latter had plenty more than just oxygen supplies, they preferred to take the risk of the short flight. According to the projections of the teams in Houston, the remaining fuel would be enough to reach both the unmanned sister ship and into orbit. Their choice fell on *Liberty's* sister ship.

Their 'preparation phase' began something like this: Charlie slept badly because he dreamed that Zhan was strangling him in his sleep. After two rough nights, he learned that his involuntary comrade had experienced the same dreams, and they even laughed about it somewhat cautiously. Then Charlie started the day with a ketamine and modafinil infusion so that he was able to think clearly while they worked. First they checked the taikonaut's suit for damage, which took an entire day. They spent the next day trying to seal ten tiny perforations with adhesive patches. They were in contact with Houston and the CNSA, which had apparently sent its own scientists to Texas and had now been assigned its own area in the Mission Control Center.

However, they didn't have time to celebrate this miracle of cooperation, as they had to test the suit. In the evening, they ate together and talked about their respective homelands. Charlie found it exciting to hear about a life so different from the one he knew in the United States.

The Chinese perspective was enriching. For example, he learned that the Middle Kingdom had known rudimentary book printing centuries before Guttenberg, and had probably produced the first continuous written language with a clear grammar. Nor did he know that China had known how to use black powder long before the Europeans, but unlike the Westerners, did not come up with the idea of using it to make murder weapons, but rather fireworks to entertain people.

With each passing day he became more able to put himself in the shoes of this astonishingly bright fighter pilot, who in return listened to him just as attentively during the hour they spent together every evening. He found it fascinating to learn that Chinese parents generally did not dictate what their children should become – they were in principle free to choose. He also learned that attaining higher education in China worked in a manner very similar to in the United States, with an elite university system and horrendous tuition fees that sometimes had to be paid off over a whole generation or two if the children wanted to become something that required a specialized degree.

After the successful patching, however, the 16-hour days were not yet over. Following another dose of ketamine, Charlie had to get into the cockpit and practice his flying skills in simulation mode, which SpaceX had fortunately programmed in by default. This took an average of three hours, during which he went through the flight simulation on the display with the two tiny flight sticks on Louis's seat, again and yet again, until his dreams at night were haunted by the short distance of 1.6 kilometers ... after Zhan stopped trying to throttle him.

On the third day, after hanging Zhan's suit in the airlock and filling it with air, they depressurized the airlock and waited five minutes. It remained inflated as if someone was stuck inside it. After this success, they dared to do a dress rehearsal. The taikonaut slipped in and Charlie let the air out of the room. They waited 15 minutes, at Houston's direction, to be on the safe side.

"Everything's fine," Zhan radioed. Charlie had spent hours working with the Chinese and American engineering teams to make the radios compatible, which had only worked after to updates from Earth. "The oxygen levels are stable. I don't see any escaping air."

"Me neither. Wait." Charlie checked all the cameras in the

airlock very carefully, then nodded. "I think we did it! Houston, it looks good."

"That's good to hear, Charlie," said Harry. Since the forced cooperation with the Chinese, the CAPCOM had conspicuously avoided pronouncing the name *Liberty*. "Then you should initiate the flight after the next sleep phase. We'll send you a final confirmation of the trajectory and burn time of the Raptor engines two hours beforehand."

"Understood."

"Charlie."

"Yes?" He waited for the two-second latency.

"You can do this."

"That's very reassuring. Really."

CHAPTER 51

Afer many days in Washington, from the Capitol to the White House, over to the Pentagon in Arlington and back again, Rebecca was glad to be back in Houston. Despite the crazy full-speed pace at which they were working to rescue astronaut Charles Reid and taikonaut Xiao Zhan, everything seemed to be going quietly. Quiet and focused, which she appreciated.

The security check at the gate took almost 15 minutes, but she patiently endured it and then headed straight for the Mission Control Center. Once there, she looked for Mission Director Ramaswami, who was standing upstairs talking quietly with a Chinese CNSA colleague.

"Oh, Colonel," he said when he noticed her. "Nice to see you again, ma'am. Congratulations on your promotion."

"Thank you. I'd like to talk to you in private." She nodded politely to the older Chinese man with the full head of gray hair. He smiled kindly and bowed before going to his colleagues, who occupied two entire rows of work consoles with 'CNSA' signs over them.

"Come on, let's go to the visitors' room," Ramaswami indicated. She nodded and greeted Harry Johnson with a thumbs up when he noticed her and waved while he continued speaking into his headset.

Grainy camera images of Charles Reid in the pilot's seat of the *Liberty* and Xiao Zhan in his suit in the airlock could be seen on the big screen. Below them was a countdown currently sitting at half an hour.

"We're about to start," said the Mission Director with barely concealed excitement, running his fingers through his tangled hair.

"I know. I'm here to get an update for the President."

"For the President? We report to his Chief of Staff every hour." Ramaswami frowned in irritation.

"He wants me to make sure personally that the collaboration is working as it should," she explained.

"Ah, I see. Yes, it's all going smoothly. But our Chinese partners have no knowledge of what happened on the moon. All they know is that three of our astronauts are dead, as are two of theirs, leaving each group with a single survivor." The Mission Director paused and looked at her. "What you really want to ask is, have the Chinese discovered the truth, or haven't they?"

"Correct. And I hope they haven't?"

"So far, there's no sign of that, no. Or else they're the best actors on the planet."

"Good. What are the chances that the planned maneuver will work?"

"Eighty-twenty."

"That's not bad," she said, nodding. "How far along are we with the replacement ship?"

"I thought you already knew that."

She raised both palms, signaling him to answer.

"Well, CNSA has a ship and they are making it available. At the moment, our team is on its way to Beijing to check the integration possibilities of a retrofittable airlock," explained

Ramaswami. "And of course they are looking to see if we can improve the efficiency of the spacecraft with our knowledge."

He looked at her questioningly.

"The President will agree to a *controlled* technology transfer. But he will do it personally."

"In person?"

"Yes. He's flying to Beijing."

"Wait a minute. That means he's going to ..." The mission director turned pale.

"Yes, he will tell the Chinese President the truth. In private."

"But ..."

"It's the only option. At some point, taikonaut Xiao is going to announce it, one way or another, and President Hernandez wants to stay ahead of the game, so to speak. From now on, the only option is to flee forward. Air Force One takes off in two days," Rebecca explained, pointing to his chest with an outstretched index finger. "Until then, *you* must make sure that the truth stays under wraps, because I'm going to accompany the President to China."

"How am I supposed to do that? I ..."

"Be creative," she suggested. "The main thing is that you're successful. On another subject, how long will it take for the new spaceship to arrive in lunar orbit and collect the two astronauts?"

"Four weeks. Five at most."

"Will Charles Reid survive that long?"

Ramaswami looked disheartened. "We don't know. He can't do blood tests, and there's no X-ray machine. It doesn't look like he's had any internal bleeding, but there will be long-term consequences even if he even makes it through the ordeal of re-entry."

"He *has to* survive."

"Colonel, I'm not a magician. I'm a physicist and ..."

"Get them *both* home, at all costs." Rebecca considered putting a hand on his shoulder, but she didn't want to stretch that far outside her comfort zone. She just hoped that he understood the urgency of the situation.

After she left Mission Control, she called her contact at NewsNation. "You have clearance for broadcast in 24 hours, assuming you've received verbal confirmation from my secretary that the maneuver on the moon was successful."

CHAPTER 52

"*Liberty,* Houston. You have a Go for launch," Harry said, followed by a short speech in Mandarin from the Chinese CAPCOM equivalent. Charlie had agreed with Zhan that the announcements should be made in two languages – for both of them to hear, and without separate contact with Earth.

"Understood. Cockpit ready," Charlie said.

"Kōngqì suǒ yǐjīng zhǔnbèi hǎo," said Zhan in a voice slightly distorted by the radio. Charlie could see him on one of his displays, holding a thumb up toward the camera. "Airlock ready."

"Then hold on tight. Initiating flight sequence." Charlie pressed the appropriate button on the display, which initiated the programmed sequence. His control inputs would only be needed shortly before landing, as the terrain could not be scanned well enough by *Sentinel I* and the meteorite impact very close to *Starship 5* had changed the topography slightly.

The *Liberty* came to life with the loud roar of the turbopumps, which pressed liquid methane and liquid oxygen into the combustion chambers. The engines announced themselves almost simultaneously, which, inside the ship, sounded like the hissing of a cat.

He watched the fuel and attitude control data on the display and saw out of the corner of his eye how Zhan's figure in the airlock began to shake slightly. One of the external cameras showed them slowly moving away from a perfect circle of swirling regolith that shot hundreds of meters in all directions. If this south pole of the moon had not become a place of horror and death for him forever, he would have found it beautiful.

"Fifty meters," he stated. "Horizontal phase initiated."

"Confirm, Charlie. Everything looks good from down here."

The *Liberty* hovered over the surface with a glowing plasma tail before the Draco maneuver jets turned on and began firing according to their programming from Houston. A total of 16 of them ejected cold nitrogen to send the huge spaceship floating across the lunar surface toward the relative northwest like an upside-down candle in a space séance.

Everything wobbled and vibrated. A piece of loose paneling rattled somewhere.

From the edge of the crater, the sight would have been sublime. A 50-meter-high spaceship with a shiny silver steel hull, from which more than a dozen gas fountains kept shooting to keep it upright. It flew sideways on the flames of three powerful engines, whirling up vast quantities of moon dust and creating a storm of dust that settled like time-defying, glittering rain.

But the only witnesses to this sight were the five dead people they had to leave behind, colleagues, comrades, crewmates, friends who had long since frozen into blocks of ice.

"Approaching *Starship 5*," he said and switched on all the external cameras. He then saw *Liberty's* identical clone getting bigger and bigger. The test ship stood between two house-sized boulders or rocks; it was difficult to see due to the lighting conditions, as most of the ship was in shadow. Only the tip protruded into the low-angled sun and shone like polished sheet metal.

Charlie narrowed his eyes and searched for his target.

"There!" he exclaimed when he saw the square section of the cargo hatch, which was in the same place as *Liberty's* external airlock. *Starship 5* didn't have an airlock because it hadn't needed one for the test flight with only cargo inside.

"Forty meters to the target. Landing surface looks level," he said, licking his dry lips. "Taking direct helm control."

He placed the thumbs and index fingers of his hands on the flight sticks at the forward end of the armrests. Fortunately, the sophisticated control software provided correction impulses, so he didn't have to worry about the *Liberty* staying upright.

Not colliding with their target was enough of a challenge. He had to get within three meters and land with pinpoint accuracy. If he accidentally hit *Starship 5*, it was over for them. Obviously.

With careful, tiny inputs, he brought the largest spaceship ever built by humans closer to its target point, which the flight computer projected onto the image reduced to a scheme in false colors, that the sensors put together.

The vibrations increased, as did his heart rate. A jolt went through the *Liberty,* then they touched down and he exhaled sharply.

"Target point ... *optimal!"* came the relieved and relieving words from Houston. The regolith between the two space-ships slowly settled in the camera views. Charlie looked at the section of *Starship 5*'s cargo hatch and compared the expected distance value: 2.5 meters. He had managed the alignment perfectly.

"Shit!" a rare profanity escaped him and he ruffled his hair. "I did it!"

For a few seconds, he forgot his grief and the pain in his shoulder and leg.

"Zhan! We're in position!"

"Understood, Charlie, I'm ready."

"Are you all right?" he asked, looking at the camera image of the airlock. The taikonaut was standing in his patchwork-repaired suit and had turned toward the outer hatch.

"A bit wobbly. But the view was very nice."

"I'm delighted. In the future we should set up our own business and offer round trips to the moon," said Charlie jokingly, with undisguised relief in his voice, which ran through his body like a wave.

"That's a nice idea," Zhan replied, sounding a little sad.

What could have been, Charlie thought.

"Good work, Charlie," Harry interjected. "We'll be ready as soon as you are."

"Zhan is ready."

After two seconds, the answer came. "Opening cargo hatch now."

Houston had direct access to *Starship 5*'s on-board computer, unlike Charlie. On the external cameras, he saw the square-cornered, slightly curved hatch on the unmanned spaceship clone open silently – precisely opposite the outer hatch of their airlock.

"Zhan, I'm releasing the pressure now."

The taikonaut raised a hand and gave a thumbs-up. The atmosphere escaped within a few seconds. Then Zhan opened the door to the outside with one hand, which folded down and became the elevator platform, just like when Charlie first arrived on the moon.

With slow movements, the Chinese man assembled the elevator cabin with astonishing precision and concentration, although he had only practiced it in theory with procedure booklets and on the simulations in the cockpit.

He set the side railings, but not the front ones, and attached the retaining cables to the connector of the main cable on the winch, which was extended above him like a telescopic arm. After 20 minutes he returned. Charlie triggered the closure of the spare hatch and then climbed to the airlock. As soon as the pressure was restored he went to Zhan and took the cable from the oxygen compressor to refill his suit. Since the Chinese man's survival unit wasn't compatible with the American ones, they couldn't use oxygen cartridges or refill anything. So they had improvised a valve through which they simply injected air into the suit's interior, which lasted about 25 minutes according to their tests.

They had also briefly considered using the EMUs for emergency EVAs, but they were designed for microgravity and were far too heavy for the moon. In addition, they could not repel dust and would therefore probably break down quickly.

"How do you feel?" Charlie asked as he pulled the oxygen cable off.

"Everything's fine," Zhan replied with a focused expression.

"Good." He withdrew into the corridor and quickly sealed the airlock before releasing the pressure. Time was precious now.

Back in the cockpit, he watched as the taikonaut stepped out onto the platform, which was open at the front. Beyond the edge, 30 centimeters away and above the abyss, was *Starship 5's* open cargo hatch, like the maw of a yawning monster. The elevator cabin now formed a kind of bridge to their only means of supply.

Charlie hated not being able to do anything at this point, but he knew that he would have been an error risk even if they'd had another suit available. It was miracle enough that he had managed the flight with all the medication in his system.

So he watched as Zhan disappeared inside *Starship 5*. From time to time, he saw the beams of the taikonaut's helmet lights move back and forth and caught a glimpse of the shadows cast by wall mounts and magnetically attached crates.

The taikonaut then began to bring over the first pieces of cargo. First were the oxygen cartridges in large containers, which he had to pull despite the low gravity.

After each of Zhan's trips, Charlie returned to the airlock, replaced his oxygen, and released Zhan back outside. To protect his damaged body, he stayed in front of the inner airlock door, as the walking back and forth was already taking its toll in the form of increased pain.

After three hours, the necessary oxygen was available.

"Should I bring more oxygen or more breakfast food?" asked Zhan by radio as he stood in the square hatch of the sister ship. "My spare CO2 filter shows twenty-five minutes left. So I can manage two more crates."

"Oxygen," Charlie replied immediately. "We have enough food. Water, too. The recycling plant is working fine."

"Good."

"Houston, we have the target. Xiao Zhan is doing one last walk around."

"Understood, Charlie," said Harry. Cheers could be heard in the background from the Mission Control Center. "That's good news. Very good news."

Charlie sighed with relief and watched through the window as the light from Zhan's helmet moved back and forth. The safety line connected him to the *Liberty* like a long umbilical cord.

The taikonaut was holding a slightly smaller crate when he returned.

Disaster struck when he caught one hand on the edge of

the open hatch and stumbled. Charlie was about to shout a warning when Zhan lost his balance. The weight of the crate sent him tumbling forward. The edge of the lid fell against the edge of the platform and bounced open. Oxygen cartridges slowly rolled out over the cabin and down into the abyss.

One of the cartridges apparently crashed with its valve striking the metal of the railing and it became a projectile. Like a rocket with a bright gas tail, it hurtled toward Zhan and hit him in the chest. The Chinese man was thrown back and disappeared into the darkness.

"Zhan!" Charlie shouted in horror. "Zhan!"

No answer. He pulled out his tablet and called up the taikonaut's vital signs. He had a pulse, but it was low.

"Houston, Zhan is injured. He's not answering." The two seconds until the answer felt like an eternity.

"We see it, Charlie. Stand by."

"I have to help him. He only has twenty minutes of air left," he shouted helplessly, thinking feverishly. There was no suit left, apart from the EVA suit, which he would never be able to put on quickly enough.

Then he had an idea. One that he didn't like the least little bit, but it could perhaps work.

You're going to die, he thought. *I'll die without him anyway. And I have to try.*

"Houston, I have an idea." Without waiting for an answer, he began to explain it. The fact that Harry didn't contradict him showed once again how important it was to everyone involved that Charlie *and* Xiao Zhan survived. They were no longer just two people fighting for survival, but political figures who ensured peace on Earth. At least for the time being.

He quickly climbed into the storage compartment and fetched three rolls of extra-reinforced duct tape, an emergency oxygen kit with face mask, a belt bottle with a tube, then a pair of long compression stockings, which they had to wear during the long periods of sitting during take-off and re-entry. He also took a pair of Anne's. Then he secured the airlock, went inside, and hurriedly pulled on the compression stockings. He pulled Anne's over his arms, which weren't as thick as her legs, but at least they gave a little pressure.

He then began to wrap himself in the duct tape. He started with his feet, making sure the material was firmly in place and building up so much pressure that it was uncomfortable. Each layer stayed close to the previous one so that after ten minutes he looked like a dark gray mummy.

His plan was crazy but not impossible. The primary problem with a moonwalk was the vacuum. Due to the lack of atmospheric pressure literally holding his body together, without manmade protection, his entire vascular system would expand due to the pressure inside his body. The vessels would simply burst and his lungs would collapse. The next problem was oxygen. Like the situation on Earth, where people cannot breathe at an altitude of ten kilometers because the oxygen content in the air is too low and they can only remain conscious for a minute or two. This is due to the lower barometric pressure.

His breathing mask would provide him with positive pressure ventilation, which meant that the air from the bottle on his belt would be forced into his lungs to prevent them from collapsing. However, there was a potentially fatal pitfall here, too. If the pressure became too great, forcing the pure oxygen into his chest while the vessels in the lung tissue expanded without the external oxygen, there was a risk that they would rupture even faster and his blood would begin to 'boil' – without being hot. Similar to the situation on Earth, where water at higher altitudes begins to reach boiling point at 70 or even 60 degrees Celsius due to the lower barometric pressure, this happens even faster in a vacuum. Put simply, there was no counter-pressure. Gas bubbles would then pass directly into his blood and trigger embolisms.

Fortunately, he was able to set the breathing apparatus on the bottle to seven percent atmospheric pressure, which was above the Armstrong limit, i.e. the point below which gas bubbles would form in his blood. However, it was only possible to maintain this condition if the tape generated sufficient counterpressure.

Almost 20 minutes had passed by the time he had finished. His body felt squashed together.

"Houston, I'm ready," he said, taking a quick breath in and out before hitting the depressurize button.

Through his plugged ears, he heard the hissing of the escaping air, which quickly quieted. A breath later it was dead silent and the lamp above him glowed red. It felt as though he were dying. His chest seemed to be on the verge of bursting. His eyes swelled. The outer hatch opened and he was enveloped in the silence of the vacuum. His skin felt as if he had been in a freezer for hours. A horrible beeping sound rose in his ears.

The worst thing, however, was the pain in his shoulder and knee, which had suddenly increased.

Charlie ignored all of this as he hopped onto the platform. His body seemed to have swollen to twice its normal size, and not even two seconds had passed. He forced himself to keep breathing and bridged the few meters to the opening in the sister ship.

Once in the storeroom he saw the source of light on Zhan's helmet, a beacon in the darkness. Everything was blurry and it was getting worse. Whether it was his breathing mask fogging up or his eyes expanding, he didn't know. But it didn't matter.

Charlie bent down and grabbed the taikonaut. He paid no attention to where he was holding him, but pulled on him with all his strength and dragged him back toward the *Liberty*. He had reached 8 seconds in his head.

Arrived on the platform at 15.

Although he knew he was outside on the moon, he blocked everything out, screaming into his mask again and again to drown out the horrible beeping in his ears and remind himself that he was still alive. He felt like a balloon that had been overinflated and was about to burst.

So he pulled Zhan farther and farther with him, back into the airlock. Everything seemed to go infinitely slowly because every step was agony. His every breath felt like the last.

When he had managed to pull the taikonaut behind the outer hatch, he turned to the button for the locking mechanism and swayed. Plagued by dizziness, he had to blink several times to get his bearings. Everything was blurred before his eyes, as if someone had dripped a foamy liquid onto his eyeballs.

Charlie struck with his fist and the hatch snapped into its socket. He sank to his knees and clutched his head as if he could prevent it from bursting with sheer muscle power.

He was cold and hot at the same time.

Suddenly he heard a scream and realized that it had been his own. The pressure had built up. Oxygen had returned.

A total of 22 seconds.

He tore off his breathing mask and felt for Zhan's helmet, which he only vaguely recognized. But his hands were glued together to form tape mittens, which reduced his motor skills to those of a Lego man. So he began to peel off the tape – starting on his fingers. Then he opened the ring fastener of the helmet.

"Zhan? Can you hear me?"

"Yes," groaned the Chinese man. "What happened?"

"I think an oxygen cartridge knocked you out." Charlie let himself fall onto his back and breathed in and out. The feeling of bursting had subsided, but he was still terribly cold and everything felt ... *wrong*. As if his organs were not in the right places. He was disoriented and everything was spinning.

"Charlie? What did you do?"

CHAPTER 53

"That's the craziest thing I've ever seen," Zhan said, looking at the wall screen on which the camera images of the duct-tape 'field operation' were playing. The Chinese man shook his head and pushed Charlie back onto the treatment bed. He began to dress the seven places where Charlie's skin had burst open because the arterial pressure had caused bleeding by taking advantage of tiny openings in the tape.

"It's also the craziest thing I'll ever do," he replied wearily. Thanks to a new ketamine infusion, he was beginning to feel better, but he knew that his body was just a wreck that he would have to drag back to Earth in a few more weeks if possible. If he could manage to do that. "But it worked."

"You saved me." Zhan dabbed the last wound and bandaged it. "Thank you."

"Oh, I was just saving myself." He waved it off, which hurt his shoulder. "Ouch."

"Seriously, thank you."

Charlie just nodded. "I'm sure you would have done the same."

"Not on your life," Zhan replied, grinning for the first time since they had initially seen each other in the airlock.

Charlie was confused at first. Then they laughed for a few minutes. It was a sound of release and letting go that filled the *Liberty* as all the weight of their traumas and stresses of the last few days fell away from them in one fell swoop.

Eventually they ate together and reported in detail to their respective space agencies in Houston, going over everything that had happened. They sent the camera footage and sensor data and then went to sleep.

The mission was saved. For the time being.

Charlie slept for 14 hours straight and didn't dream this time.

Zhan had been awake for a long time and greeted him in the common room with a ready-made breakfast. "Good morning," he said in his Chinese accent, which had become familiar to Charlie. "Are you ready for the next problem?"

"No," he replied sleepily and lay down on the hospital bed to have his daily infusion. He was already dreading the time when the saline solution would run out. According to his calculations, that would be the case in a week's time.

"The safety line is jammed in the airlock."

"What?" Charlie closed his eyes. "Of course. I didn't separate them. I didn't even think about that."

"It is a problem, but it's not fatal."

"We can forget about the airlock."

"Yes. We have to blow off the outer hatch before launching into orbit," Zhan replied.

"Even if the cable pulls your suit out and we don't get into trouble because something gets snagged, we'll be pulling an object with us, which is something you don't want with any rocket," Charlie said.

"The suit will hit the hull, but it shouldn't cause any damage. At least that's what Houston says."

"And we can no longer open the airlock. Although we have to in order to get to *Celestial Dragon 2.*"

"*Green Star Dragon*," the taikonaut corrected him.

"Excuse me?"

"The ship has been given its own official name: *Green Star Dragon*. Green is the color of hope and new beginnings in China."

Charlie thought about it. "That's a nice name. So our governments have come to an agreement?"

Zhan nodded. "It looks like it, yes."

They spent the next two days carefully evaluating their situation, going over all supplies and ship systems in detail with Houston to get a clean bill of health. They then received word that there had been government consultations between their countries and the program had been given a timetable. The *Green Star Dragon* had been fitted with an American airlock and would launch in three weeks and then arrive in lunar orbit four days later.

This meant that they had almost four weeks to go through the moon's launch maneuver into orbit. There was also a lot of boredom, which Charlie used to lie down as much as possible to heal his injuries. His shoulder had become terribly misaligned as a result of constant resting posture tensions, even though Zhan had made him an arm sling with 3D-printed elements.

There were also endless drills in case Charlie had to take over manual control, which was most unlikely. For one thing, the on-board computer's control software was capable of doing this even without input from Houston – much more precisely than a human – and for another, the software engineers were improving the code all the time to take into account the open airlock and the safety cable that would be hanging out with the attached spacesuit.

They had to fly with an open flank for the interception

maneuver of their cab to Earth, as blowing off the outer airlock hatch in zero gravity would have caused an uncontrolled tumbling motion that would have cost too much in cold gas, the only means they had for the ship's attitude control. This also meant that they had to open the inner door beforehand and let all the atmosphere escape – for the same reason. So, they would have to spend the entire flight into orbit in the two EVA suits, which meant they wouldn't fit in the cockpit seats. Houston made the decision that they would take the suits inside and seal the bridge until it was time to leave the *Liberty*.

Daily, they practiced putting on the EVA suits. Charlie explained every detail to Zhan, as the taikonaut had never worked with this system. They developed an almost boring routine of doing the same essential things. They ate, drank, worked, slept, ate, drank, worked, and slept. Soon they knew each other almost inside and out because they talked, morning and night, about God and the world, and they even dared to talk about their deceased friends and crewmates.

They told each other stories about their training, about the peculiarities of their dead comrades, and mourned together when they were overcome with emotional pain. It was a strange time when Charlie had the feeling that his head no longer understood how to categorize and process his emotions.

Perhaps it was simply too, too much for a single human to handle.

"There are American TV programs about the two of us, did you know that?" Charlie asked Zhan when their launch day had finally arrived. The *Green Star Dragon* had taken off perfectly and there had been no incidents. Amazingly, every detail seemed to fit and it would enter lunar orbit on schedule, at the precise planned time. For two weeks, two different teams had been working on their rescue: Flight Control at the

CNSA in Beijing with NASA employees as guests, and Mission Control in Houston had a mirrored arrangement.

"No, I didn't know that. What kind of programs?"

"Mainly documentaries. The material was probably released by NASA in consultation with our two governments. Perhaps China has its own programs."

"Perhaps," Zhan echoed with a shrug.

They sat strapped into the cockpit, wearing no suits, just their functional underwear so that they could slip into their EVA suits as quickly as possible when the time came.

"We'd better make sure all the stories have a happy ending, eh?" Charlie forced himself to smile. The pain had lessened even though he no longer had the supplies to inject himself with ketamine. It was not so close to the surface anymore. But he could no longer ignore the pervasive feeling that something was wrong. His body was permanently damaged, and he was afraid to find out how badly.

And this was without the effect of Earth's gravity. Any problems with his bones and muscles on the moon felt one-sixth as bad as they would feel on their home planet. That meant that saving him would also mean that his injuries would worsen sixfold – a prospect that didn't exactly make him optimistic.

"Charlie, Zhan," radioed Mission Director Ramaswami. "Countdown at one minute."

"Understood, Houston. We're ready," Charlie replied and held out his hand to Zhan. He looked at it briefly and then took it. "In case all this was just a crazy dream, it was an honor."

"An honor for me, too," the taikonaut replied.

Charlie saw the same turmoil in the eyes of his unwilling comrade on this mission. It was pure necessity that had brought them together, and some of the pain of having killed each other's friends would always stand between them. But there was also something else, something new, that had come along, and it felt like a friendship that could only have been formed through unimaginable sacrifice and hardship.

"Ten, nine, eight, seven, six, five, four, three, two, one, ignition!" he counted off from the display and once again *Liberty* began *to* shake and vibrate as the three Raptor engines fired and pushed it upward in a seemingly sedate manner. Charlie immediately felt the increasing acceleration forces in his bones and grimaced.

The *Liberty* rose from the lunar surface, sending the now-familiar regolith glow in all directions. The life support warnings about the ship being exposed to vacuum – except for the cockpit – had long since been switched off, but the flashing red symbol for the open airlock continued to fight for his attention.

The moon moved farther and farther away from them as they shot vertically upward.

"Trajectory stable," said Ramaswami.

"Confirm," replied Charlie.

The vertical thrust phase lasted less than 30 seconds before the Draco maneuvering thrusters tilted their trajectory to build up a horizontal velocity component. The *Liberty* tilted relatively abruptly into the new trajectory because, unlike on Earth, they did not have to change their inclination slowly to efficiently counter air resistance.

The horizontal speed would ultimately enable it to reach the necessary orbital speed of around 1.68 kilometers per second.

"Goodbye, moon," Zhan murmured, and looked out the window.

Charlie followed his gaze and looked at the receding reliefs of the south pole below them, which looked like a marble slab of black and gray fields disfigured by deep holes.

They sped toward their target altitude of 110 kilometers,

causing the moon to shrink further. On the night side, it looked as if they were orbiting a black hole. The onset of weightlessness was a relief for him, taking the pressure off his bones and the pain from his head.

Charlie looked at the navigation screen and saw the dotted line that represented their flight. It turned away from the moon and became longer. A second, solid line came from further out, faster than *Liberty*, and approached their vector toward a point where they would be perfectly parallel.

"Three minutes," he read off. "All systems are working to standard."

"Confirmed, *Liberty*," Ramaswami said. "You should suit up now."

"Understood."

They unbuckled themselves and floated to their prepared suits, which were tied to the back of the cockpit like empty shells. They left the tethers in place and slipped into the assembled torso, arms, and helmets from below. They had practiced this for a long time and were accordingly skillful, and the microgravity helped rather than hindered them.

Attaching the leg sections was a little more difficult without help, but they managed that, too. A few minutes later Houston confirmed that the *Green Star Dragon* was 20 meters away and parallel to them, and that the maneuver had gone perfectly.

"Radio check," Charlie said.

"Loud and clear," Zhan replied.

"Houston, we're ready to open the hatch."

"Got it. Five seconds," said Ramaswami over their radio.

As it happened, the hatch flew open and tore halfway off its hinges. The air escaped like a hurricane, with a brief rush before it was suddenly dead quiet. Small pieces floated through the cockpit, things that had escaped the terrible suction.

"Cutting loose now." Charlie applied the cutting knife to the tether cables and cut himself free. When he was finished, he let the taikonaut go first. "Your spaceship."

Zhan smiled and tilted his head behind his huge glass bell visor. Then he shimmied out of the open hatch into the central corridor, from handhold to handhold through the eerie silence.

As only the airlock was illuminated, Charlie felt as if he was floating through a black liquid toward a light-filled tunnel.

They proceeded cautiously, avoiding risks, as they had ten minutes for the maneuver before the orbitals would separate because *Liberty's* was not stable. Its tanks for the Dracos were empty.

Zhan stood in the square cutout of the airlock, beyond which the *Green Star Dragon* could be seen, a tiny capsule compared to the *Liberty,* but the most welcome sight in a long time. The infinite canopy of stars glittered in the background.

"On my way now," Zhan said in English and then in Chinese. He fired the thrusters of his EMU unit, which ejected tiny clouds of cold gas and sent him in the direction of the Chinese space capsule. Slowly and under control, he glided toward their salvation, the clunky airlock on the side looking like a squeezed-out pimple with its hatch open.

Charlie held his breath until the taikonaut had reached his target, precise and controlled. Traveling without tethers almost made him nauseous with nervousness. In space, any mistake was potentially fatal, and if he missed the ship and couldn't correct his course quickly enough, he would be lost forever.

"Ready, Charlie?" Zhan asked, raising a hand from the airlock 20 meters away.

"All right, I'm on my way." He ignited his own thrusters and flew slowly toward the Chinese man, the white figure on the other side of the abyss of infinity.

But suddenly Zhan was no longer directly in front of him. He slid off to the left.

"Charlie, correct to the right!"

"I ... I can't." His right arm cramped, no longer obeying him and making the wrong steering inputs. Everything began to spin. *Liberty,* space capsule, stars, Zhan, space capsule, *Liberty.*

"Charlie!"

He felt nauseous, and vomited into his helmet. The stinking liquid splashed into his face as he rolled over.

"SWITCH OFF!" Zhan shouted over the radio. But how was he supposed to switch off? He didn't even know where he was relative to the ships. His whole world was spinning and the shoulder pain was driving him crazy. All at once, he collided with something hard and groaned.

But he stabilized and his staggering movements decreased. As he moved to the right and left, darkness turned to white and then he bumped his back against something even harder.

"Charlie." The voice belonged to Zhan. "Can you hear me?"

"Y-Yes."

"I've got you."

"What? How?"

"We're stuck on the *Liberty's* hull. I've switched off your EMU unit and am now disconnecting it."

"But then all I have left is the air in my ..."

"That will be enough." The taikonaut spoke so calmly that panic threatened to spread through Charlie. He was breathing far too fast and forced himself to take more control. After narrowing his eyes, he looked past the vomit and saw the *Green Star Dragon,* just as far away as he had seen it from the airlock.

"My thrusters are empty," Zhan explained.

"You shouldn't have saved me!"

"Just stay calm and don't move. I'll push us off so that we can make it into the airlock."

That's far too dangerous, he wanted to say. But what choice did they have now? If the taikonaut didn't make it back because of him ...

Suddenly a jolt went through his body and he slid toward the space capsule. The airlock grew larger as he watched. His breath echoed through the helmet and the sound became a real rush. There was nothing they could do now. Nothing more to correct.

Charlie plunged through the opening, lightly touching the edge with his shoulder and instinctively grabbing a support on the white inner wall with his left hand. As he did so, he spun around and held out his right hand to Zhan, who had hit the top edge with his helmet and was in danger of drifting off.

Miraculously, their hands found each other and embraced. It was a magical moment, as if the universe itself had intervened, because the Chinese man could not even see him. Charlie pulled the taikonaut inside, even though his shoulder protested painfully.

When they had locked the hatch, Charlie took the Chinese man in his arms and didn't let go. He sobbed, and then they started laughing like two crazy people.

EPILOGUE: TWO MONTHS LATER

Looking at Charles Reid, Rebecca asked, "Are you sure you've memorized everything?"

The astronaut looked much better than he had after his landing in the Atlantic, but still badly marked by his injuries. His shoulder was pulled forward and hung down, making him look like a hunchback. According to the doctors, this would improve with subsequent surgeries. His lung damage caused his breathing to wheeze slightly, and the stiffened leg would remain stiff. But despite everything he'd endured, she saw in him a deeply felt serenity. Something shone from his eyes that she wished for herself, without understanding what it was.

"Of course," the astronaut said with a wink. "I've got it all memorized."

"That's a lie, isn't it?"

"Yes."

She sighed. "Make sure there's no scandal, will you? This whole thing is exquisitely fragile until we get down to the real work."

"I know."

"One more thing. Thank you for your testimony before

the Select Committee. I appreciate it very much. So does the President, by the way."

"He seems to like us both, Colonel. Assistant to the Inspector General? I heard you were the youngest in American history to hold that post."

"I'm just doing my job," she said seriously, patting him on the shoulder without thinking about it. "Now go out there and make eight billion people happy."

"There's nothing better than that," he replied and winked again. Leaning on his walking stick, he hobbled toward the curtain next to the stage. Two Chinese government employees cleared the way for him.

Rebecca caught a glimpse of the stage at the China National Congress Center in Beijing. The presenter stood in front of the table with the two chairs and name tags and spoke in Chinese and English to the thousands of spectators in the audience. When he said, "Xiao Zhan and Charles Reid," thunderous applause rang out, augmented by a swelling of deeper thunder produced by the stamping of shoes.

We really are superstars, thought Charlie as he stepped onto the stage and waved his free hand a little sheepishly. Zhan came toward him from the other side, waving and smiling too.

So many faces and they were just a carbon copy of those who had watched the livestreams they hadn't even known about during their time together on the *Liberty*. They had made history. He just hoped it was for a good, long-term cause.

When he met Zhan, they bowed briefly to each other in the Chinese style and then embraced before sitting down on their designated chairs.

They talked a little about their mission, but it seemed like a dream, as they had given so many interviews by now, it was nothing new. Then the questions from the audience began.

"How's your Chinese, Mr. Reid," someone asked.

"Wǒ měitiān nǔlì xuéxí," he replied sheepishly. "I study every day. And I really hope my inflection was correct and that I didn't say that I'm the son of a sheep and a sperm whale or something. Zhan?"

"No. A penguin and a chamois."

The audience laughed uproariously.

"You see? He's already learning American humor. What have I done?"

This went on for an hour. He was congratulated on his new position as head of the Astronaut Office in Houston, and many questions were asked about his recovery. Everything would be fine, at least he wasn't expected to die anytime soon, which he considered a pretty big win. So far, all routine. But then came the question they had always been shielded from. It came from a spectator who had certainly been instructed to ask this specifically, it having been banned previously in China.

"What did you discover out there?"

Charlie swallowed, his mouth dry.

"The question goes to Xiao Zhan," the questioner clarified.

Zhan looked at him and rubbed his chin. The taikonaut was acting surprised. Hadn't the party office told him what to say? Was this the breaking point that would destroy all the peace they had laboriously maintained? Had they turned him into a pawn? Had he not even told them what they had found?

"We were looking into the abyss," Zhan said at last, and turned to Charlie. Their eyes met and the room fell dead silent. "And even if we couldn't find any signs of extraterrestrial life, we did discover something. Yes, we may have made humanity's most important discovery when we found our shared humanity."

Charlie sighed softly with relief and smiled. Tears ran down his cheeks, but he didn't care.

"Also," said Zhan, "we have something new to announce. Later this year, the CNSA and NASA will begin planning a joint lunar program."

The audience cheered. The spectators stood and clapped wildly.

"As equal partners," Charlie added. "Together, we will build a base and people will stay on the moon. With Xiao Zhan as commander of the first binational mission."

"But that will only be the first step," Zhan added when the cheers had died down a little after a few minutes. "Because we also want to penetrate further into our solar system. To Mars and the moons of the outer planets. Together and in peace. In the name of humanity."

AFTERWORD

Dear reader,

I hope you enjoyed *The Shackleton Signal*. Endless research and conversations with astrophysicists and engineers went into this book, and for the first time in a long while I had to do a lot of math. Some details had to give way to creative license for drama, but that will always have to be the case with a good book. If you notice any scientific errors, please feel free to report them to me at the e-mail address below, which almost always leads to nice conversations. This book is self-contained and there will be no sequels.

If you enjoyed this book, I would be delighted to receive a 5-star rating at the end of this e-book, or a short review on Amazon. It's the best way to help authors continue to write exciting books in the future. If you want to get in touch with me directly, you can do so at joshua@joshuatcalvert.com – I answer every email!

If you subscribe to my newsletter, I'll regularly share a little bit about myself, writing, and the big issues in science fiction. As a thank you, you'll also receive my e-book *Rift: The Transition* exclusively for free: www.joshuatcalvert.com

Best regards,
  Joshua T. Calvert